FAIRY TALES TRANSFORMED?

SERIES IN FAIRY-TALE STUDIES

General Editor
Donald Haase, Wayne State University

Advisory Editors
Cristina Bacchilega, University of Hawai'i, Mānoa
Stephen Benson, University of East Anglia
Nancy L. Canepa, Dartmouth College
Anne E. Duggan, Wayne State University
Pauline Greenhill, University of Winnipeg
Christine A. Jones, University of Utah
Janet Langlois, Wayne State University
Ulrich Marzolph, University of Göttingen
Carolina Fernández Rodríguez, University of Oviedo
Maria Tatar, Harvard University
Jack Zipes, University of Minnesota

A complete listing of the books in this series
can be found online at wsupress.wayne.edu

FAIRY TALES TRANSFORMED?

Twenty-First-Century Adaptations
and the Politics of Wonder

CRISTINA BACCHILEGA

Wayne State University Press   Detroit

17 16 15 14 13   5 4 3 2 1

ISBN: 978-0-8143-3487-4 (pbk.: alk paper)
ISBN: 978-0-8143-3928-2 (ebook)

Library of Congress Control Number: 2013941168

Published with the assistance of a fund established by
Thelma Gray James of Wayne State University
for the publication of folklore and English studies.

Designed by Ashley Muehlbauer
Typeset by E. T. Lowe
Composed in Scala and ScalaSansPro

To the many from whom I continue to learn
and to John Rieder, compagno della mia vita

CONTENTS

PREFACE

How and to what uses are fairy tales being adapted in the twenty-first century?

What are the stakes, and for whom, of adapting fairy tales in the twenty-first century?

These are the questions. To highlight widely divergent yet interwoven social projects that fairy-tale adaptations circulating in early twenty-first century globalized popular culture envision and instigate, this book takes an intertextual and geopolitical fairy-tale web of reading and writing practices as its methodological field. I argue that we should consider the gender politics of fairy-tale adaptations in relation to other dynamics of power and experiences of disjunction. I also argue that we should reexamine the relationship of the fairy tale with other genres, including the folktale, as constitutive of its hybridity, in order to become better attuned to *competing* uses of magic, enchantment, and wonder across cultures and media platforms. Today's fairy-tale transformations activate multiple—and not so predictable—intertextual and generic links that both expand and decenter the narrow conception of the genre fixed in Disneyfied pre-1970s popular cultural memory. In responding to this multivocality, I suggest we are experiencing the emergence of a renewed poetics and politics of wonder that, although hardly cohesive, are situated responses to the hegemony of a colonizing, Orientalizing, and commercialized poetics of magic. I contend that when we connect the fairy tale's story power with the twin structures of power of capitalism and colonialism, the need to "provincialize" the Euro-American literary fairy tale emerges as an important critical task for fairy-tale studies to pursue.

The introduction maps out major changes in the cultural deployment of fairy tales since the 1980s, my approach to the twin questions with which the book engages, and my use of the fairy-tale web as a methodology. The project is further articulated through four chapters that focus on selected but varied ways in which activist adaptations of folk and fairy tales relocate the genre from counterhegemonic perspectives on orality (chapter 1); the act of reading fairy tales is staged cinematographically as a critical performance (chapter 2); generic remixes hybridize and creolize folk and fairy tales on the screen (chapter 3); and adaptations of the *Arabian Nights* contest (or not) the vilification of Arabs and the subordination of exoticized "wonder" to fairy-tale hegemony (chapter 4). Each chapter explores what is at stake and for whom in the relationships these adaptations seek to mold with their audiences as well as in the activation of specific historical, cultural, and generic links these adaptations pursue. Exploring these questions does not lead me to a comprehensive explanation of what fairy tales do in the early twenty-first century; rather, I seek to underscore how activist adaptations are wielding the powers of wonder to contest the hegemony of Euro-American fairy-tale magic, and I call for remapping the fairy-tale genre onto a worldly, not worldwide, web.

The Fairy-Tale Web

Intertextual and Multimedial Practices in Globalized Culture, a Geopolitics of Inequality, and (Un)Predictable Links

ADAPTING FAIRY TALES, TO WHAT ENDS?

In 2005 the Bloomingdale's holiday window display in New York City featured eight popular fairy-tale scenes, ranging from "Cinderella" to "Aladdin." Highlights of what in that context was a mixed bag of traditions—narrative, festive, commercial, and touristic—remain viewable on About.com Travel to New York City Guide as a series of ten images. The "Cinderella" scene is tagged "Imagine being invited to the ball," and the "Aladdin" one "Imagine the ride of your life." In these windows, the magic helper who makes such wishes come true—respectively, the fairy godmother and the genie—has a large presence. Each chosen scene of the ensemble projects a sense of anticipation and attainable gratification. In the "Frog Prince" display, the frog is handing the young woman a translucent ball. Both characters wear crowns, signaling that their common royal status will eventually bring them together. How? No matter what the Brothers Grimm wrote, and as the very red lips of the frog in the window signal, the answer in popular cultural memory is "with a kiss."

Not only are the frog's lips larger and redder than the princess's, but also his hard and sparkling "body" is more like a gigantic conglomerate of costume jewelry than a slippery force of nature. In contrast, the fairy-tale heroine is bland, a well-dressed life-size mannequin with no expression or light of her own. The

PLATE 1. The Frog Prince window display, Bloomingdale's 2005, by Heather Cross. *New York City Travel* (December 13, 2005), http://gonyc.about.com/od/christmassights/ss/2005_bloomies_9.htm.

precious ball between them looks like an oversized pearl or perhaps a magic ball in which to read one's future; also strategically placed between the frog suitor and the princess but more in the background, a golden reindeer conflates the magic of fairy tales with the gift-giving rituals of the season. The scene anticipates romance and fulfillment in a preset fantasy world for both characters, and the presence of the reindeer further suggests this is a "free" exchange that is part of a gift economy. Of course, the association of fairy tales with the holiday season is hardly new, as seen in British pantomime and Christmas editions of tales of magic for children. But in its fantastic showcasing of artificiality, this display is decidedly hyperreal, simulating an original that never existed and presenting it as not only desirable but also attainable. With the swipe of a credit card. In this fairy-tale scene the princess-like mannequin stands in for the consumer of a happily-ever-after fantasy that the amphibian rep for capitalism offers her.

To cash in on the genre's worldwide appeal is common in globalized consumer capitalism, where plots, metaphors, and expectations associated with fairy tales pervade popular culture, from jokes and publicity to TV shows and songs. This confirms that fairy tales continue to exercise their powers on adults as well as children. *Powers*, I stress, not power, because, historically as in the present, fairy tales come in many versions and are in turn interpreted in varied ways that speak to specific social concerns, struggles, and dreams. Even the Bloomingdale's "Frog Prince" scene tells more than the "shopping will buy you romance and happiness" story. In the online picture, we see the potential consumer reflected in the soft glow of the fake "pearl" in the window, but s/he need not be taken in by the glamour. After all, we are not passive consumers, and this is but one scene in the tale; we can imagine different choices and endings, and we do.

In Jack Zipes's words, "Fairy tales are informed by a human disposition to action—to transform the world and make it more adaptable to human needs, while we try to change and make ourselves fit for the world" (Zipes 2012, 2). This statement is not, given Zipes's project in *The Irresistible Fairy Tale* (2012), to be understood as a definition that encompasses the genre of the fairy tale, but it identifies transformation as central to what most fairy tales do or anticipate. Like Zipes, I am interested in exploring how fairy tales affect the making of who we are and of the world we are in, and I agree that thinking about transformation— within the tales' storyworlds; in the genre's ongoing process of production, reception, reproduction, adaptation, and translation; in the fairy-tale's relation to other genres; and more generally as action in the social world—offers a spacious and productive way into that exploration.

Fairy tales interpellate us as consumers *and* producers of transformation. For instance, in 2009, the same year in which Tiana of *The Princess and the Frog* entered the ranks of Disney princesses, Canadian photographer Dina Goldstein put on the World Wide Web her *Fallen Princesses* series, in which she imagines fairy-tale heroines in "modern day scenarios" and replaces the "happily ever after" with a hyper "realistic outcome" of a different kind: "Cinderella sits in a dive bar in Vancouver's infamous Hastings Street. Snow White is trapped in a domestic nightmare, surrounded by unkempt children, with a lazy out of work prince in the background" ("About the Series" on www.fallenprincesses.com/). Just as striking as the transformative work of "critical disenchantment"—noted by Catriona McAra and David Calvin in their introduction to *Anti-Tales: The Uses of Disenchantment* (2011, 1–15)—that Goldstein's photographs do, is the public response that they have in turn produced, ranging from a *Marie Claire* article (published in November 2009) to innumerable blogs and fan letters.[1] And even more striking perhaps is the online debate that Goldstein's project sparked, not only in defense of the positive role Disney magic has played in real-life individual experience but also in presenting a range of critical takes on the tales as well as on the photographs. Goldstein's photographs make visible the contradiction between what Angela Carter critically called "mythic women" and the problems we face in everyday life, including loneliness, aging, and illness, and in doing so she clearly touched a nerve with the public. But the controversy also suggests that to change women's images or more generally to disenchant the genre is not the only fairy-tale transformation in which the thousands of individuals who were touched enough to respond are invested.[2]

"Fairy tales are ideologically variable desire machines," I wrote a few years ago in *Postmodern Fairy Tales*, and I stand by this statement, which I realize could be said of all stories really, but perhaps holds higher stakes when applied to a genre that so overtly puts a desire for transformation in motion and one that is too often reduced to the narrative articulation of purportedly universal wish fulfillment. Just as Salman Rushdie's child protagonist in *Haroun and the Sea of Stories* confronts the question, "What is the use of stories that aren't even true?" (1990, 22), scholars have asked: what does the fairy tale do? Providing a neat definition of the genre within a framework that recognizes its multiple social valence is difficult, then, and necessarily self-contradictory. Fairy tales have been central to reproducing ingrained or second-nature habits, what Pierre Bourdieu calls *habitus* and Edward Said "structures of feeling"—*and* to destabilizing them. Characterized in Marina Warner's words by "pleasure in the fantastic" and "curiosity about the real" (1994, xx), fairy tales have historically scripted a wide range of desires while maintaining a strong grip on ordinary social life. With an eye to solving problems, at least some versions are also produced and/or received as inspirations to undo privilege and prejudice.

To develop the idea that fairy tales "are informed by a human disposition to action" (Zipes 2012, 2), we need to ask what do they do to inspire us to seek change, in ourselves, in order to fit in the social world and/or in the social world in order for it to accommodate us. For some, fairy tales instigate compensatory escapism, while for others they offer wisdom; alternatively, fairy tales are seen to project social delusions that hold us captive under their spell; or else they promote a sense of justice by narrating the success of unpromisingly small, poor, or otherwise oppressed protagonists. Maria Tatar's recent "quilting" of published writers' and public figures' commentary on fairy tales, "passages that move us to think about the deeper meaning of fairy tales and how they have affected our lives and those of others" (2010, 305), significantly has a patchwork effect. Our ideas about the genre's poetics depend on whether we associate the fairy tale as symbolic act with wish fulfillment, role-playing, idealization, survival, or something else; in other words, on how we use the genre. In the last two hundred years—the Grimms' *Kinder- und Hausmärchen*'s volumes were first published in 1812–15—the fairy tale has served multiple sociocultural functions.

But I believe it is also safe to say that since the popularizing of the Grimms' collection, as a genre the fairy tale's dominant or hegemonic association has been with magic and enchantment, as a result of several convergences: the segregation of fairy tales to the nursery where "magic" is normalized as the mysterious ways in which the world works to produce immediate gratification and where "enchantment" is at the service of a spellbinding discipline that has the "child exactly where we want her or him" (Haase 1999, 363),[3] the universalizing of "happily ever after" as the signature mark of the fairy tale, the repurposing in mass culture of fairy tales for advertising products that fulfill our every wish (Dégh 1994), and the spectacle of the fairy tale as an American capitalist utopia (Zipes 1999) and as "consumer romance" (Haase 1999, 354) in Disney's films and other fairy-tale commodities.

If generally the desired effect of this poetics of enchantment is the consumer's buying into magic, the contemporary call for disenchanting the fairy tale is directly related to a now-public dissatisfaction with its magic as trick or (ultimately disempowering) deception, a disillusionment with the reality of the social conditions that canonized tales of magic idealize. However, magic and pacifying enchantment are not the only poetics of the fairy tale, historically or in the present. As medievalist Jan Ziolkowski reminds us, "Wonder is the effect [fairy] tales seek to achieve, while magic is the means that they employ to attain this goal" (2006, 64).[4] It is no accident that fairy tales are also known as "wonder tales."[5] As an effect, wonder involves both awe and curiosity. In Marina Warner's eloquent words, "Wonder has no opposite; it springs already doubled in itself, compounded of dread and desire at once, attraction and recoil, producing a thrill, the shudder of pleasure and of fear. It names the marvel, the prodigy, the surprise as well as the responses they excite, of fascination and inquiry; it conveys the active motion towards experience and the passive stance of enrapturement" (2004, 3).

Fairy tales can invite us to dwell in astonishment and explore new possibilities, to engage in *wondering* and *wandering*.[6] It is in this symbolic enactment of possibilities, "announcing what might be"—and taking us *ex-cursus*, off course, or off socially sanctioned paths to "unlock social and public possibilities," to explore alternatives we hope for—that the fairy tale's "mood is optative" (Warner 1994, xx) and wonder producing.[7] Furthermore, wonder has been recognized as a significantly complex effect of fairy tales, but the genre's links with wonder have a complicated history, including the secularization of religious legends and miracle tales in medieval Europe (Ziolkowski 2006, 232–34; Zipes 2001, 847);

the transformation of ancient pagan tales; and, with *Arabian Nights* being the most well-known case, the appropriative translation of what Donald Haase calls other cultures' "wonder genres" (e-mail communication with the author).

I contend that actively contesting an impoverished poetics of magic, a renewed, though hardly cohesive, poetics and politics of wonder are at work in the contemporary cultural production and reception of fairy tales. And while remaining within the purview of primarily North American and European fairy-tale production, I explore this hypothesis within a larger framework that remaps today's fairy-tale adaptations and their potential for transformation.

How and to what uses are fairy tales being adapted in and to the twenty-first century? This is the umbrella question I engage with in this book while keeping in the foreground its corollary, why should we care? For Arthur W. Frank in *Letting Stories Breathe: A Socio-Narratology* (2010), "not all stories engage all people" (4), an important point suggesting how stories do not just connect human beings but reflect and generate differences among us; however, stories of all kinds do animate, instigate, conduct, and emplot human lives. Two of Frank's socionarratological insights about stories in general resonate with and in my project. The first is that of the making and unmaking of narrative emplotment in both fiction and life: "Stories project possible futures, and those projections affect what comes to be, although this will rarely be the future projected in the story. Stories work to *emplot* lives: they offer a plot that makes some particular future not only plausible but also compelling. . . . We humans spend our lives . . . adapting stories we were once told. . . . Not least among human freedoms is the ability to tell the story differently and to begin living according to that different story" (Frank 2010, 10). The dynamics of emplotment seem to me particularly relevant to reflecting on fairy tales in social practice because this genre is so basically tied up in plot, has been hegemonically utilized to emplot or frame our lives within a heteronormative capitalist economy, and yet has such a history of and potential for adaptability as well as subversion because it operates in the optative mode.

The second of Frank's insights is a set of questions that, adapting Bakhtinian dialogism, informs his critical analysis of storytelling, which he sees as the symbiotic and dynamic work that people and stories do with, for, and on one another. Frank asks, "*what is at stake* for whom, including storyteller and protagonist in the story, listeners who are present at the storytelling, and others who may not be present but are implicated in the story? How does the story, and the particular way it is told, define or redefine those stakes, raising or lowering them? How does the story change people's sense of what is possible, what is permitted, and what is responsible or irresponsible?" (Frank 2010, 74–75, italics in the original).

Readers familiar with fairy-tale studies will recognize these as the issues that Jack Zipes's critical oeuvre, from *Breaking the Magic Spell* (1979) on to *The Irresistible Fairy Tale* (2012), has taken on to trace the cultural and social history of the fairy-tale genre. Within this larger framework I ask more specific questions about the here and now: What are the stakes of adapting the fairy tale in the early twenty-first century? For whom? And how do today's fairy-tale adaptations affect "people's sense of what is possible," or of what transformations to anticipate/fear/desire? Because the genre's popularity is both persistent and pervasive and because questions of individual agency and social transformation are central to the tales' narrative permutations, reflecting on today's fairy-tale adaptations—both their production and reception—illuminates and affects how we construct human relations in the present and how we map out our options for the future. This broadly intellectual concern motivates my continued inquiry into the genre and its varied poetics and politics of magic, enchantment, and wonder.

FAIRY TALES TRANSFORMED? MULTIVOCAL AND MULTIMEDIAL PRACTICES IN GLOBALIZED CULTURE

This book begins by asking how and to what effects contemporary understandings and social uses of the fairy tale have changed since the 1970s, a significant conjuncture in the Euro-American history of the genre and its adaptations, and it is from within a North American context and history that I pursue these questions. At that time, North American feminists were arguing vehemently in the public sphere about the value of fairy tales in the shaping of gendered attitudes about self, romance, marriage, family, and social power. Anne Sexton's publication of *Transformations* was a wake-up call in 1971 for women to read the Grimms' collection of fairy tales in a different key, "As if an enlarged paper clip / could be a sculpture. / (And it could)" (Sexton 1971, 2).[8] While psychologist Bruno Bettelheim's popular book, *The Uses of Enchantment* (1976), claimed that the fairy tale's symbolism and healing enchantment trumped any gender considerations, some educators and scholars blamed classic and Disney fairy tales for reinforcing female passivity, whereas others pointed approvingly to strong heroines in less known tales of magic as role models for girls. Illustrated books such as Jane Yolen's *Sleeping Ugly* (1981) and anthologies like *Tatterhood and Other Tales* edited by Ethel Johnston Phelps (1978) sought to address these issues in English-language children's literature. In addition to Anne Sexton's *Transformations*, Angela Carter's *The Bloody Chamber* (1979) and Margaret Atwood's *Bluebeard's Egg* (1983) boldly proceeded from woman-centered perspectives to rewrite the genre for adults.[9] And other writers also looked to the fairy tale as a genre to renew "exhausted" fiction-making conventions or to explore new permutations of narrative and cognitive mappings. Robert Coover, A. S. Byatt, Jeanette Winterson, and Salman Rushdie are the best-known representatives. Together with Atwood and Carter, John Barth, and the widely translated Italo Calvino, they constitute what Stephen Benson called "the fairy-tale generation in the sense that their fictional projects are intimately and variously tied to tales and tale-telling" (2008, 2).[10] Quite sensibly, Vanessa Joosen links "this fairy-tale renaissance" not only to the 1968 social uprisings and the second-wave feminist movement but also to "developments in literature and literary criticism" (2011, 4), including the heightened attention paid in both fields to parody, metafiction, and most importantly intertextuality.

Simultaneously and for similar reasons, fairy-tale studies emerged as a field where sociohistorical analysis has been challenging romanticized and nation-centered views of the genre.[11] Noting that Angela Carter's *The Bloody Chamber* and Jack Zipes's *Breaking the Magic Spell* both came out in 1979, Stephen Benson reminds us in his introduction to *Contemporary Fiction and the Fairy Tale* of "the extraordinary synchronicity, in the final decades of the twentieth century, of [fairy-tale] fiction and fairy-tale scholarship" (2008, 5). For example, the early 1990s saw Carter's edited collections of *The Virago Book of Fairy Tales* (1990 and 1993) alongside Marina Warner's *From the Beast to the Blonde* (1994), each making a singular and lasting intervention in the ongoing feminist debate over fairy tales. One could say that if today, as Donald Haase's introduction to the 2008 *Greenwood Encyclopedia of Folktales and Fairy Tales* authoritatively attests, the international and interdisciplinary institutionalization of fairy-tale studies is a fait accompli, this has a lot to do with the extraordinary literary production by writers of "the fairy-tale generation" as well as with leftist and second-wave feminist interrogations of the value of fairy tales. Vanessa Joosen's important book, *Critical and Creative Perspectives on Fairy Tales: An Intertextual Dialogue between Fairy-Tale Scholarship and Postmodern Retellings* (2011), develops our understanding of this dialogue by centering her analysis on three key critical texts from the 1970s—Marcia K. Lieberman's "Some Day My Prince Will Come," Bruno Bettelheim's *The Uses of Enchantment*, and Sandra M. Gilbert and Susan Gubar's *The Madwoman in the Attic*—that she links thematically with an impressively "large number of retellings and illustrated versions" (Joosen 2011, 7) of six well-known fairy tales. Basic to her tracing of this dynamic dialogue is Joosen's starting point that "any intertextual analysis of contemporary fairy-tale retellings has to take into account that the best-known fairy tales have been reproduced in innumerable variants and that fairy-tale material has generated countless verbal and nonverbal manifestations" (10).

I agree that this image of the fairy-tale genre as "a shape shifter and medium breaker" (Pauline Greenhill's and Sidney Eve Matrix's felicitous phrase in "Envisioning Ambiguity," 2010, 3) has a contemporaneity that makes it a "period performance" (Benson 2008, 13). And I believe it is so due to the conjuncture not only of social and literary movements but also of technological and economic developments; namely, the Internet *and* globalization, within what Henry Jenkins calls convergence culture (2008). In the aftermath of the 1970s, the recognition that "fairy tales provide intertexts par excellence" (Greenhill and Matrix 2010, 2), and are thus a multimedial or transmedial phenomenon,[12] has not only informed scholarly perspectives but also taken hold in public discourses and popular consciousness, thanks to the electronic accessibility of a wide range of fairy tales, the filtering of feminist and other social critiques into children's education and globalized popular culture, and the greater possibilities for reader response to become production and be shared in new media.

As Theo Meder documented, folktale collections on the Internet have provided an impressive array of texts to researchers: "One of the earliest (1994) and still one of the finest folktale collections is the German Gutenberg Project, which as of 2006 contained some 1,600 fairy tales," and its English-language version includes not only Charles Perrault's and the Brothers Grimm's canonical texts, but also Giambattista Basile's, Marie-Catherine d'Aulnoy, and *The Arabian Nights* (Meder 2008, 490). And D. L. Ashliman's extensive online research tools Folklore and Mythology: Electronic Texts, and Folklinks: Folk and Fairy Tale Sites, both of which originated in 1996, provide folktale and fairy-tale texts and links to other collections and critical resources on the Internet, some of encyclopedic nature (most prominently the *Enzyklopädie des Märchens*, the leading German-language reference on folk and fairy tales in an international research context), others devoted to specific tales (for example, Kay E. Vandergrift's Snow White site, created in 1997), still others consisting of scholarly journals (for example, *Marvels & Tales: Journal of Fairy-Tale Studies*, a print publication also available through Project MUSE and JSTOR).[13] During the 1996–2006 period, Folklinks alone had over one million visits, while the Folklore and Mythology: Electronic Texts had more than three million visitors by June 2011.[14] Two other well-respected fairy-tale sites, Endicott Studio and SurLaLune Fairy Tales, are also quite popular, and as such it is instructive to take a look at their profiles and trajectories.

Founded in 1987 and directed by writer-artist-scholars Terri Windling and Midori Snyder, the Endicott Studio website and its *Journal of Mythic Arts* are "dedicated to literary, visual, performance, and environmental arts rooted in myth, folklore, fairy tales, and the traditional stories of people the world over."[15]

Created in 1999 by librarian and researcher Heidi Anne Heiner, SurLaLune Fairy Tales "features 49 annotated fairy tales, including their histories, similar tales across cultures, modern interpretations and over 1,500 illustrations"; it also includes over 1,600 folktales and fairy tales from around the world in electronic books and a discussion forum.[16] Both Endicott Studio and SurLaLune were envisioned and are run by indefatigable and creative women who have put their visionary expertise at the service of scholars, writers, teachers, students, and the public at large, and both sites have strong women-centered and feminist profiles, as seen in the essays of the *Journal of the Mythic Arts* and judging from the discussion board on SurLaLune. While "mythic projects" and healing in literary and visual arts are more of a focus in Windling's and Snyder's nonprofit project,[17] Heiner states she "created [hers] strictly for educational and entertainment purposes."[18] Informed by folklore and fairy-tale studies scholarship, both sites are configured to make their visitors' experience of the many wonder tales into a transformative journey, whether mythic or educational. Over time the two websites have also transformed. A small nonprofit, Endicott Studio has since 2008 reduced its activities but maintains its archives and a blog with news about Endicott-Studio-associated artists' publications and awards, and currently has a presence on YouTube and Facebook. Strengthened somewhat by its association with Amazon.com, SurLaLune continues to expand its reach. The blog, which Heiner started in June 2009, is dizzyingly filled with news about fairy-tale books, films, illustrations, and more.[19] Furthermore, Heiner has also started to publish print volumes in the SurLaLune Fairy-Tale series, including *Rapunzel and Other Maiden in the Tower Tales from Around the World* (2010), *The Frog Prince and Other Frog Tales from Around the World* (2010), *Bluebeard: Tales from Around the World* (2011), and *Cinderella: Tales from Around the World* (2012).

The fact that websites are doing more than providing a wealth of folktale and fairy-tale primary texts to those who can access the Internet is further brought home by the multiplying of online publications, like the English-language *Cabinet de Fées* and *Fairy Tale Review* (both of which have issues also available in print); discussion forums, such as SurLaLune's, which in the October 2000–June 2011 period had 3,761 average visits per day and 23,391 total posts on over six hundred different topics[20]; blogs, including Breezes from Wonderland by Harvard-based fairy-tale scholar Maria Tatar and the one Michael Lundell has maintained since 2007, The Journal of 1001 Nights; and Facebook groups like Fairy Tale Films Research.[21] In addition to providing resources and opportunities for publication, exchanging ideas, and sharing news about fairy-tale related events (publications, performances, bits of news that make a fairy-tale association), the Internet is a significant site for the circulation of fairy-tale parodies and jokes.

PLATE 2. "Disney's Desperate Housewives." MOTHER GOOSE & GRIMM © 2006 Grimmy, Inc. Distributed by King Features Inc.

I refer here to two examples. The cartoon, "Disney's Desperate Housewives," in the *Mother Goose and Grimm* series by Mike Peters, was originally published in syndicated newspapers on January 1, 2006, and since then has made its way into numerous websites and blogs. The humorous digital image "What Disney Princes Teach Men about Attracting Women," a companion piece to the "What Disney Princesses Teach Women," has been circulating at least since 2009 in a number of blogs. The message, no matter which Disney film is visually referenced, is "Be rich, charming, famous, and good looking."[22] To my knowledge, the source of "What Disney Princes Teach Men" remains unknown so far, but the cartoon has elicited a great number of comments responding to its bonus question—"What are these guys' names? (Aladdin doesn't count.)"—as well as attesting to the success of its irony.[23]

These parodies point to how Disney is key to the image of the fairy tale in popular cultural memory, and also to how people are questioning the authority (on their lives) of the Disneyfied fairy tales that sugarcoated the Brothers Grimm's and Charles Perrault's tales to produce a romantically enchanting happily ever after. What "popular cultural memory" identifies, after all, is "a repository of conventions and imagery that are continually reconstructed" (Kukkonen 2008, 261) in living culture. To make this very argument, Cathy Lynn Preston began her 2004 groundbreaking essay, "Disrupting the Boundaries of Genre and Gender: Postmodernism and the Fairy Tale," by reproducing a 1999 e-mail joke, "Once upon a time . . . (offensive to frogs)" (Preston 2004, 198). This joke—which continues to circulate on the Internet, where it is sometimes labeled "the feminist version"—parodies the idea of the happily ever after in "The Frog Prince," first by repeating some of its formulas and then by "breaking the fairy-tale frame" when, in the end, the princess enjoys her "repast of lightly sautéed frog legs seasoned in a white wine and onion sauce" and comments sarcastically on the frog's request for a kiss (Preston 2004, 199 and 198). In drawing an analysis of how this joke and other popular-culture texts blur genre boundaries to break away, or not, from fairy-tale gender expectations,[24] Preston suggests:

> In this time and place, for many people the accumulated web of feminist critique (created through academic discourse, folk performance, and popular media) may function as an emergent and authoritative—though fragmented and still under negotiation—multivocality that cumulatively is competitive with the surface monovocality of the mainstream older fairy-tale tradition, particularly that tradition as it was mainstreamed into American culture by means of Perrault's and the Grimm brothers' editions of fairy tales, Disney movie adaptations, senior proms, romance novels, television shows like *The Dating Game*, and so on. (2004, 199–200)

I agree with her that in twenty-first-century North America, the popularization of feminist critiques and ideals is making a difference in people's investment in and relation to the fairy-tale genre. The outcomes of this popularizing are mixed, and at times conservative or "faux" in popular culture; and I will be focusing on some of these investments in chapter 2 and when I discuss genre mixing in chapter 3. For now, the relevant observation is that whether individuals identify with feminism or not, there is a widespread sensibility to issues of gender in fairy tales, and we see this on and off the Internet.

Children in the early decades of the twenty-first century may very well be exposed to *Shrek* films, DreamWorks' parodies of Disney, before viewing what baby boomers would consider fairy-tale "classics." For some, this raises the question of whether the magic of fairy tales is over: "There's something a little sad about kids growing up in a culture where fairy tales come pre-satirized, the skepticism, critique and revision having been done for them by the mama birds of Hollywood" (Poniewozik 2009, 396). But the multivocality of the fairy tale also means that it's not just large entertainment businesses like Hollywood "puncturing" Disney and, perhaps more significantly, that a simple poking fun at or denigrating of Disney is not the only way in which people—producers and consumers, educators and parents, adults and children—are seeking to experience and transform the fairy tale. *The Girl Who Circumnavigated Fairyland in a Ship of Her Own Making* by Catherynne M. Valente, an illustrated book for young adults (YA), begins, "Once upon a time, a girl named September grew very tired indeed of her father's house, where she washed the same pink and yellow teacups and matching gravy boats every day, slept on the same embroidered pillow, and played with the same small and amiable dog" (Valente 2011, 1). The book features the adventures of a clever and bold heroine, and, while funny, it is also filled with wonder. In May 2011, the book made the New York Times Best-seller List.[25] What the somewhat surprising popularity of this YA novel shows is not clear as far as what children want or expect in a fairy tale, especially since several reviews foreground how this is also a good read for adults, but it does suggest once more that adults today are quite receptive to the changing fairy tale and that we are not done with fairy tales as narratives of emplotment, and especially not with transforming them.

Some of this new creative and critical consciousness is also evident in new-media texts adapting the fairy tale. For instance, Donna Leishman's digital fairy tales, *Red Riding Hood* (2000), *The Bloody Chamber V1* (April 2002), and *The Bloody Chamber* (2003) require interactivity on the part of readers in order for the sequence of events to develop, though an ending or outcome is not guaranteed to occur; unlike games, this interactivity is not goal oriented and can be seen as "a commercially weak experimental art form" (Leishman 2000). In the credits for *Red Riding Hood*, Leishman thanks Angela Carter "for starting it all." These new-media fairy tales incorporate music, a few words, and prime-color images that will yield different spatial and narrative movement depending on the user's activity and focus; through the play of structure, the narratives become a coproduction of sorts involving Leishman, older fairy-tale texts, and individual performances of her digitized structures. Leishman, who has a PhD from the Glasgow School of Art and is interested in "the particular resonance found when teaming . . . folkloric content with contemporary technologies," uses her platform "to show and test visual interactive and hybrid narratives structures" (www.6amhoover.com/index_flash.html); having experienced the narrative through "participatory re-action," the interactive reader is invited to comment to the author via e-mail.

Similarly incorporating scholarly interests with the production of digitized fairy tales, but not with an avant-garde aesthetics, is the 2011 website and documentary project written and directed by Sarah Gibson, Re-Enchantment: Not All Fairy Tales Are for Children. Launched as a multiplatform experience via the Australian ABC online, television and radio programs in March 2011 and available internationally online a few months later, Re-Enchantment explores six popular fairy tales in an interactive enchanted forest to provide, in the words of its creators, "an immersive journey into the hidden meanings of fairy tales," a journey that includes "animated objects and pathway, images, video, graphics, music and sound effects"; it is visually compelling, highly informative, psychologically enriching, and even "community building." At the website's gateway, visitors are also informed: "there will be many ways for you to add your own stories, images, ideas and interpretations through using the CREATE and DIS-CUSS buttons. Visit the GALLERY at the heart of the forest to view artist exhibitions, contribute your own re-imaginings and meet other members of the Re-enchantment community" (www.abc.net.au/tv/re-enchantment/, accessed June 29, 2011). The gallery includes powerful reimaginings of fairy-tale heroines, for instance, by visual artists Paula Rego, Jazmina Chininas, and Yanagi Miwa. New-media and multimedial artistic and intellectual projects like the ones by Leishman and Gibson respond to a twenty-first-century understanding of the genre and have the *potential*—partly because of their built-in interactivity and discussion—for further transforming the (adult) public's experience not only of fairy tales on the Internet but also of fairy tales more generally, their significance in narrative and social life.

One may think I have been looking at electronic cultural (re)production and reception through rosy fairy-tale glasses, but I did say "the Internet *and* globalization." I realize the circulation of the fairy-tale texts I have discussed is bound to and structured by the circulation of multinational capital in ways that are "not democratically controlled and organized, even though consumers are highly dispersed" (Harvey 1989, 347). But based on such an understanding, I wanted first to foreground how these consumers "have more than a little to say in what is produced and what aesthetic values shall be conveyed" (Harvey 1989, 347) and how this has impacted public perception of and interaction with the genre of the fairy tale, in particular. In other words, this explosion of fairy-tale information *and* (critical) creativity in what Manuel Castells calls a "network so-ciety" operates within the logic and interests of capitalism and globalization but is not "reducible to the expression of such interests" (Castells 1996, 13), which moves me to reflect on twenty-first-century fairy-tale production and ask about the counterhegemonic projects it may be participating in.

I believe the twenty-first-century production and reception of fairy tales (or any other cultural texts) cannot be approached soundly without consider-ing how they are conditioned by and respond to the promises and pressures of globalization. I realize the "world-altering transformations" that information technology brings about affect the economies of surveillance and knowledge in ways that privilege information over intellectual reflection and threaten to turn education into training of labor across nations, as well as the economy of labor across nations (Zuern 2010). In particular, the examples I provided above are, regardless of artists' and editors' individual intentions, to be understood as operating within the logic of hypercommodification and deregulation of capi-tal flows since fairy-tale T-shirts, books, knowledge, and art are advertised and sold online. Aiming at the flexible accumulation of capital, globalization works through multinational corporations, centralized banking, outsourcing, media conglomerates that dominate global markets, information and entertainment on demand, short-lived commodities, and the sale of services—all of which are naturalized on the Internet as the electronic age's *habitus*.

Furthermore, within globalization, electronic culture (not the technology as such but its hegemonic business) enhances a type of space-time compression that is grounded in and reinforces social inequality on a global scale: "we can be everywhere faster and faster" is the fantasy that supports our sense of reality if we have access to the technology; in the proliferation of images, stories, and communication we experience, the distance from those who cannot materially move across borders or become producers on the Internet appears to shrink, while the reality of an economic and social gap is actually growing.[26] Cultural production and distribution within this system are dominated by American conglomerates, like the Disney Corporation, which recently absorbed Pixar; has worldwide rights to distribute Studio Ghibli films by Hayao Miyazaki;[27] has books, toys, videogames, and "worlds" franchises; and now owns Lucasfilm. This domination contributes to the social divide and the "global designs," in Walter Mignolo's (2002b) terms, that sustain it.

Jack Zipes offered a provocative and important critique in *Relentless Progress* of how the interests of globalization are reconfiguring not only children's litera-ture, fairy tales, and storytelling within the culture industry, but also the child as consumer and, more generally, human or social relations: "Globalization con-tinues to terrorize and minimize the lives of most people on this globe while providing excessive forms of movement and consumption for privileged groups of people who set ever-changing norms that rationalize their choices and life styles" (Zipes 2009b, 147). My own analysis takes Zipes's warnings seriously by (a) attending closely to specific *struggles* that are at work within fairy-tale cultural production and reception in the electronic age of consumer capitalism and glob-alization; (b) by asking what are the stakes of the fairy tale's varied transforma-tions today, for whom, and looking to what kind of social possibilities; (c) and by considering these texts' conditions of production and reception within both socioeconomic and geopolitical frames of reference. However, as I have argued before (Bacchilega 2011), I do not apply the binary logic that Zipes has power-fully wielded to neatly separate out conservative fairy-tale "duplications" from progressive "revisions."

Within a critical and historicizing framework, my analytical focus is on the multivocality of millennial and early twenty-first-century transformations of fairy tales, and because fairy tales have not always been for children only, and quite visibly are not so nowadays, my focus is not on the fairy tale as children's literature but on fairy-tale adaptations for adults and young adults. My aim is to reflect on the linked and yet divergent social projects that fairy-tale adaptations imagine, the multiple worlds they construct, the ideological moorings of their appeal and permutations, their putting into play ideas about the fairy-tale genre, the import of their generic mingling, their participation and competition in multiple genre and media systems, their translations of wonder. Questions of gender, genre, performance, coloniality, decolonization, and translation (or transcoding across cultures, epistemologies, media, genre systems, and languages) intersect in my analytical practice, which draws on fairy-tale studies, folklore and literature approaches, coloniality studies, and cultural studies.

While I devote some attention to television, comics, visual art, and drama, most of the fairy-tale adaptations I analyze in this book are literary and cinematic. My goal in adopting this selective scope of analysis is dual. One, these are the media platforms that have the broadest distribution and visibility within the fairy-tale web as well as the most power within the articulation of what the critical field of fairy-tale studies is and does. Two, I believe that conceptualizing a twenty-first-century "fairy-tale web" as a field of reading and writing practices has instigated me to ask new or at least different questions about fairy-tale literature and film.

THE FAIRY-TALE WEB: INTERTEXTUAL PRACTICES, THE GEOPOLITICS OF INEQUALITY, AND (UN)PREDICTABLE LINKS

In the previous section I outlined, from within a North-American-centered position, some changes in fairy-tale cultural production from the 1970s into the early twenty-first century; the following two sketches loosely adapt Pierre Bourdieu's figuration of the nineteenth-century French literary field of production (1993, 49) in order to visualize this "transformation." They are necessarily sketches, simplified and localized. For instance, the name "Angela Carter" stands in for "the Angela Carter generation" (Benson 2008, 2) of writers, Robert Coover, Salman Rushdie, A. S. Byatt, Margaret Atwood, who innovatively engaged with the fairy-tale genre in a sustained way; there is no mention of fairy-tale theater, television, or art, and neither is oral storytelling taken into account. The field of production outlined is clearly centered in an English-language environment, specifically American.

I venture sharing these sketches not as realistic images, but to highlight the multimedial or transmedial proliferation of fairy-tale transformations in recent

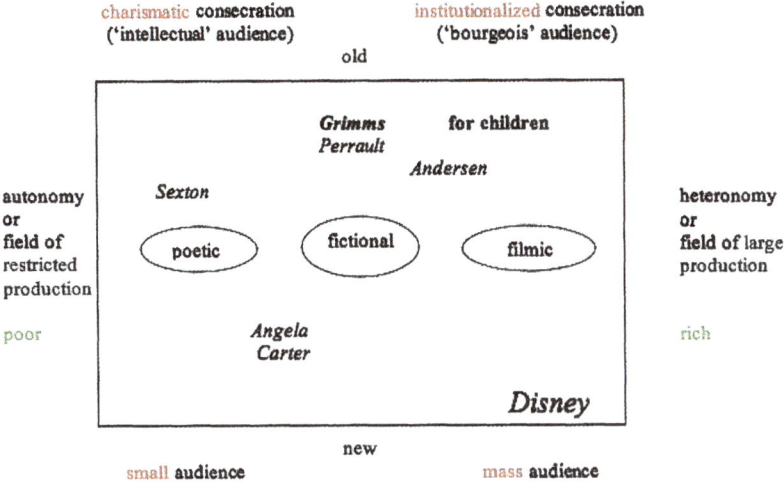

PLATE 3. Field of Fairy-Tale Cultural Production (1970s).

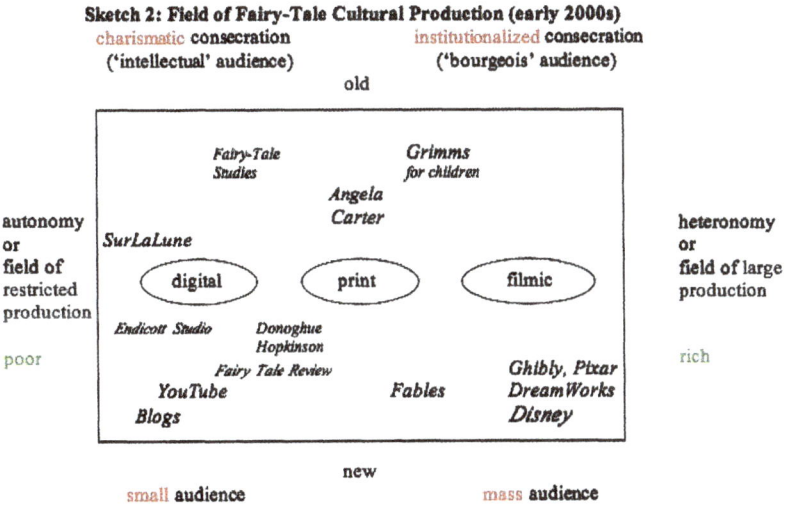

PLATE 4. Field of Fairy-Tale Cultural Production (early 2000s).

years and to show how the *position* of a text or producer can and does change, and so do audience dispositions to the genre. The contemporary production and reception of fairy-tale texts plays out a plurality of "dispositions" and "position takings," in Pierre Bourdieu's terms, that compete with one another in the larger field of globalized cultural production, within and against the culture industry and its enchanting spectacles. But as much as Bourdieu sought to understand practices and histories, his figure outlines structures of power and does not convey the messiness of stories in actions. To respond critically to the *multivalent currency* of the fairy tale, we need to approach the genre's social uses and effects in ways that account for how this multiplicity of position takings produces not ideological binaries, but complex alignments and alliances. Even more specifically, to ask who is reactivating a fairy-tale poetics of wonder and for whom, I find it helpful to think *with* a contemporary fairy-tale web.

The fairy-tale web as I conceptualize it is necessarily a twenty-first-century construct that accounts for, even depends to some extent on, the World Wide Web's impact. As such, the "fairy-tale web" seemingly builds on fashionable terminology and is an easily graspable concept, but I do not mean it at all to be coterminous with the circulation of fairy tales on the Internet. The twenty-first-century fairy-tale web I envision is more a methodological field than a state of affairs. Analytically, it has a history, or better, histories—both as metaphor and reading practice—and, I hope to show, it has critical potential. Proposing the fairy-tale web as a general site for critical inquiry into the genre's activity has a twofold purpose: to further the construction of a history and remapping of the genre that are not insulated from the power structures and struggles of capitalism, colonialism, coloniality, and disciplinarity; and to envision current fairy-tale cultural practices in an intertextual dialogue with one another that is informed not only by the interests of the entertainment or culture industry and the dynamics of globalization in a "postfeminist" climate but also by more multivocal and unpredictable uses of the genre.

The association of storytelling with the practice and metaphor of weaving, and spinning of course, has a long tradition in literature. Examples are Ovid's classic stories of Arachne's weaving contest with Athena and of Philomela's woven tapestry denouncing her rapist brother-in-law as well as Native American creation stories featuring Spider Grandmother and her singing. In language this metaphor appears in English when we "spin tales," which have "threads," and when we "weave a spell." The weaving metaphor in modern books' representation of fairy tales as children's literature is exemplified through the image of old women, iconically Mother Goose, spinning flax and tales. The metaphor shows up in narrative studies, since Roland Barthes reminded us that "etymologically, the text is a tissue, a woven fabric" and that "the plural of the Text depends, that is, not on the ambiguity of its contents but on what might be called the stereographic plurality of its weave of signifiers" (Barthes 1989, 168); and in fairy-tale studies, most prominently with Karen Rowe proposing that "strand by strand weaving, like the craft practiced on Philomela's loom or in the hand-spinning of Mother Goose, is the true art of the fairy tale" in her landmark essay "To Spin a Yarn" (1999 [1986]). With varying emphases, the metaphor connects storytelling with women, intertextuality, and action or response in the face of unequal power relations of weavers, fabrication of meanings, and media or crafts. I aim to keep these links active in my exploration of the fairy-tale web, along with some ideas about what a spider's web does in nature. The spider's web catches prey, just as we get caught up in stories; it sparkles, the way fairy-tale magic or wonder does in successful performances. But it has a dilatory pattern and center because it emanates from one spinner, *unlike* the fairy-tale or any other intertextual web that depends on the activity, memories, locations, and responses of many individuals and institutions.[28]

When it comes to storytelling in practice, we are now very familiar with the idea that all texts—oral, written, visual, and social—participate in a web of intertextual relations. While intertextuality has been central to both oral poetics and textual criticism "since the latter part of the seventeenth century, when oral tradition became a key element in marking the juncture between premodern and modern epochs in the evolution of language and culture" (Bauman 2004, 1), thinking about intertextuality as a web implies a critical conception of it that originated with Julia Kristeva and was informed by Mikhail Bakhtin's multivocality. Verbal intertextuality, to gloss Kristeva, is not the dialogue of fixed meanings or texts with one another; it is an intersection of several speech acts and discourses (the writer's, the speaker's, the addressee, earlier writers' and speakers'), whereby meanings emerge in the process of how something is told and valued, where, to whom, and in relation to which other utterances. "Stories echo with other stories, with those echoes adding force to the present story. Stories are also told to be echoed in future stories. Stories summon up whole cultures" (Frank 2010, 37). To put it differently, and as I will further develop in chapter 1, "each act of textual production presupposes antecedent texts and anticipates prospective ones" (Bauman 2004, 4), and how that works is somewhat out of the control of any one individual or group.[29] We cannot fully predict or control which stories mingle with, influence, anticipate, interrupt, take over, or support one another because every teller and recipient of a tale brings to it her or his own texts; we also cannot fully anticipate how a story, no matter how the teller or writer intends it, will act on its listeners/readers/viewers. Thus the readings of fairy-tale adaptations I will propose in the following chapters are necessarily subjective, located, and provisional; they are not intended to finalize the adaptations' meanings, but to pose questions and comment on specific links—historical, cultural, generic, figurative, ideological—activated by necessarily selective texts within the extended web.

As a reading practice, the twenty-first-century fairy-tale web reaches back in history and across space to intersect with multiple story-weaving traditions. Several scholars have shown how French, German, and British women's fairy tales assumed a subaltern position within literary histories of the genre that revolve around the canonical figures of Charles Perrault, the Brothers Grimm, and Oscar Wilde. Tracing the history of the genre has meant highlighting the pioneering role of Giovan Francesco Straparola and Giambattista Basile in establishing the fairy tale as a print genre in sixteenth-century Venice and seventeenth-century Naples, respectively, or showing how fairy tales circulated *ante nominem* in ancient world and medieval Latin texts. Other researchers have contributed to our understanding of how tales in the oral tradition from the nineteenth century into the present popularize, talk back at, or diverge from the literary ones. And transnational research on *The Arabian Nights* has reconfigured it as a "huge narrative wheel" whereby stories "flowed with the traffic across the frontier of Islam and Christendom, a frontier that was more porous, commercially and culturally, than military and ideological history will admit" (Warner 2012, 9, 12).[30] Today, the kind of multilayered and multiperspectival reading of the fairy tale that Angela Carter's *The Bloody Chamber* inaugurated has become part of increasingly knowing adult readers' expectations. A greater awareness of multiple traditions and voices, I will continue to emphasize, is not limited to academic circles but also informs varied contemporary fairy-tale practices in popular culture.

However, while the twenty-first-century fairy-tale web is complex, not all its links are equal since, as mentioned earlier, maintaining a socioeconomic and cultural divide is built into a for-profit globalizing economy of cultural production. The reach of small-press authors, independent filmmakers and artists as well as the cultural capital of genre fiction—with which the fairy tale is increasingly merged—are small compared to those of the multinational corporate media circuits. This inequality, I want to underscore here, extends to the construction of the fairy-tale web's history and its geopolitics of knowledge. If "fairy tales are fiction's natural migrants" (Teverson 2008, 54), historically their traffic has been regulated by commerce, religion, and prejudice—which is not always recognized and results in an unequal flow of tales and an unequal valorization of different tellers' located knowledges. As a methodological field—whereby the web is "experienced in the activity of production" (Barthes 1989, 167), that is, of *reading*, rather than as a received or preexisting object—it matters how through the construction and reconstruction of a web of intertextuality we make multiple (hi)stories of the genre visible/narratable, or not; for instance, how we link fairy tales with folktales.

In the introduction to *The Virago Book of Fairy Tales*, Angela Carter provocatively insisted on weaving them into a "great mass of infinitely various narrative" (1990, ix): "Ours is a highly individualized culture, with a great faith in the work of art as a unique one-off, and the artist as an original, a godlike and inspired creator of unique one-offs. But fairy tales are not like that, nor are their makers. Who first invented meatballs? In what country? Is there a definitive recipe for potato soup? Think in terms of the domestic arts. 'This is how *I* make potato soup'" (1990, x). But in actuality, the fairy tale comes to us today manufactured and branded differently from the folktale. As Jan M. Ziolkowski writes, "fairy tales have acquired their current niche in Western and even in world culture thanks to the imprimatur of having been subsumed in collections that are not at all anonymous or collective (as would be expected with folk literature) but that are instead attached indissolubly to particular writers" (2006, 236). The published tales associated with Charles Perrault, Jacob and Wilhelm Grimm, and Hans Christian Andersen have epitomized what is commonly understood to be the fairy-tale genre and its "universal" appeal, as opposed to the outmoded and simple "folktales," which are instead associated with a specific kind of group identity (ethnic, national, gendered). As this generally accepted narrative goes, fairy tales develop out of folktales by turning a staple of narrative sustenance into a chef's signature dish, and the chef—no matter where the staple came from—could only be in the literate classes and, more specifically, the literate classes of Europe.

This popular construction of the fairy tale as a modern genre, then, reproduces what Dipesh Chakrabarty identifies as the stagist historicism of European modernity that "came to non-European peoples in the nineteenth century as somebody's way of saying 'not yet' to somebody else" (2007, 8). The genre of the "fairy tale" is still generally understood as European and North American; the Middle East constructed as the Orient has produced *The Thousand and One Nights*, wonder tales that have become identified with exotic magic and fantasy; most of the rest of the world has or had "folktales" that can become "fairy tales," but are not yet. It is from the vantage point of those who have "progressed" from listening to folktales to reading fairy tales (to children) that storytelling and story power in general are measured. Within this ethnocentric construction of magic, wonder, and enchantment, some peoples and some groups have imaginations that make art and reach for symbolic truth, and others have limited inventiveness that is hopelessly fantastic or obsolete and ultimately untrue.[31] Furthermore, historically, the translation of oral stories from "exotic" places and cultures into European languages has meant that radically different narrative forms—including nonfiction—were reduced to and marketed as "fairy" stories. The fairy tale's cultural capital today continues to accrue interest on the commodification and appropriation of both oral and non-European storytelling traditions.

I am pointing out that privileging the fairy tale over folktales or other wonder genres is a common conception that unself-consciously reproduces a logic in which modernity is coupled not only with colonialism and Orientalism but also with coloniality as a necessary component of capitalism. A critical concept Peruvian sociologist Anibal Quijano introduced in the 1980s, and Walter Mignolo (Argentine professor of literature and cultural anthropology) developed, "coloniality" refers to the conceptual and ideological "matrix of power" that "emerged in the Atlantic world in the sixteenth century and brought imperialism and capitalism together" (Mignolo and Tlostanova 2007, 109). Capitalism emerged from the massive appropriation of land and labor in the Americas, Asia, Africa, and later Oceania, thanks to and for the sake of capital accumulation. This understanding of colonialism as girding capitalism and modernity exposes how "a capitalist economy as we know it today could not have existed without the discovery of America" (Mignolo and Tlostanova 2007, 111). Coloniality is the ideological engine that in the fifteenth- and sixteenth-century colonization of South America crystallized the orality versus writing opposition into a hierarchy where the colonized and so-called illiterate people are defined as inferior.[32] The racism that informs this coloniality of power is less about skin color, according to this argument, than about a "standard of humanity" and a "teleological framework of progress," the framework that Jack Zipes also denounces in his book *Relentless Progress* (2009b), one that denies history and value to the social organizations, literacies, and knowledge of "the other."

This has consequences, I believe, for how we approach the fairy-tale genre today. At the same time that it anticipated emancipatory social transformations for European aristocratic women and the middle classes, the emergence in seventeenth-century Europe of the fairy tale as a newly named print genre (*conte de fées*) depended not only on the fictionalization of so-called outmoded belief systems and ways of life—the transformation of "wonder" into modern "magic" within a more scientifically oriented Europe—but also on a politics of inequality that (in and out of Europe both) devalued orality as illiteracy, the quintessential sign of the premodern, at the very same time that it appropriated or simulated storytelling on the page and through translation.[33] Constructing a rigidly *literary* history of the fairy tale, as Ruth B. Bottigheimer's 2009 book, *Fairy Tales: A*

New History, does to the extreme, and assuming that "folktales are a universal and indigenous narrative form" that guarantees "cultural diversity" even when collected in English-language nineteenth-century books (Gottschall 2008, 177), are two sides of a discourse that ignores the material, ideological, and symbolic interdependence of these two genres (and their relations to more than one genre system as well). And this discursive regime unwittingly replicates and reinforces an ideological framing of language, narrative, and expressive culture that champions the modern in opposition to and at the expense of what and who is identified as the premodern: the illiterate peasant classes within Europe (see Bauman and Briggs 2003), and also the non-Europeans encountered through commerce, war, human trade, Orientalism, and colonialism. This is why I believe that the need to "provincialize" the Euro-American literary fairy tale has emerged as an important critical task for fairy-tale studies to pursue.

Critical reading and writing practices in the fairy-tale web can work to activate, rather than obliterate, these structures of power and geopolitical relations in our approach to fairy tales; thus I refuse to de-link the cultural production of European "fairy tales," *Arabian Nights* fantasies, and "folktales" in print from a larger intertextuality of multiple genre systems and from the global dynamics of Orientalism and coloniality, both conjunctures of capitalism and colonialism. In this project, I link up with other scholars. Folklorist Sadhana Naithani's research, for instance, has eloquently shown how colonialism and coloniality further impacted the construction of "folktale" collections from the colonies published in Europe during the nineteenth century. Examining in *The Story-Time of the British Empire* a number of South Asian and African colonial collections, Naithani concludes: "The oral narratives of the colonized were subject to complete change of identity in their international *avatar* in the English language" (2010, 96) as a result of the European collectors' motives, methods, and theories, which overall deracinated tales from living cultures, ignored existing genre systems and social uses, and unequivocally made the orality/writing difference into a hierarchy. These structures of power impacted the circulation of folktales and fairy tales from and in the Caribbean and the Pacific (Seifert 2002; Bacchilega and Arista 2007; Teverson 2010; Do Rozario 2011). Collections of international fairy tales like Andrew Lang's Fairy Books (1889–1910), Sara Hines suggests, "rather than simply corroborating nineteenth-century discourse on colonialism . . . embody the same possibilities for collection, possession, and exhibition prevalent throughout the period" (Hines 2010, 51) and were developed in the British colonies.

Just as Naithani forcefully shifts the attention of folklorists to understanding the production and reception of folktales in print within a transnational and global framework, Donald Haase emphasizes how "decolonizing fairy-tale studies" requires resisting "the twin urges to universalize traditional narratives at the expense of their specific historical and sociocultural contexts and to generalize the European fairy tale as an ahistorical global genre" (2010, 29). Haase continues, and I agree, "The challenge, it seems to me, is . . . to understand [folktale and] fairy-tale production and reception precisely as acts of translation, transformation, and transcultural communication" (30). While this approach has been productive in transnational discussions of *The Arabian Nights* (Marzolph 2007; Warner 2012), there is much more to be done, especially to historicize these processes of transformation in relation to social structures of change, taking into account that if "British colonialism created a global cultural network that . . . is at the crux of current hybrid cultures [and] transformed the oral expressive of different people," it was not for their sake or benefit (Naithani 2010, 7). Today, some storytellers in a range of media are reinterpreting this network from postcolonial and anticolonial perspectives, linking with one another in decolonizing and creolizing projects, working to unlearn Orientalism, and bringing new knowledges and critiques *to and about* the fairy-tale web.

In January 2010, *The New Yorker's* online piece "Nalo Hopkinson's Other World" featured images from five fabric designs Nalo Hopkinson created, introducing her as a writer of "science-fiction histories and science-fiction fairy tales." About the making of her artwork for one of the designs, *Still Rather Fond of Red*, Nalo Hopkinson included the following information: "I incorporated elements of two historical images into a mixed-media collage that also includes paint, ink, a chunk of old costume jewellery, a snippet from a hand-crocheted lace doily, and my own drawing and writing." More generally, in answering Nick Liptak's questions about the relationship between her writing and her fabric designs, Hopkinson stated, "they are fuelled by the same passions and obsessions of mine," and then proceeded to describe a project that she was in the process of working out:

> It's a digital collage that so far incorporates old, whimsical family photos of black people and old drawings of Indigenous peoples from the South Pacific and the Caribbean done by white visitors to those regions. Not sure where I'm going with it: something about the Caribbean (I'm Jamaican by birth and background, Canadian by naturalization); something about the globalizing conjunction of cultures that brought African bodies and South Pacific produce to Taino-Arawak-Carib lands; something about the representation of the Indigenous peoples who were already there; something about how rarely one sees historical images of black people made by us for ourselves in which we're relaxing and cutting up for the camera. (Hopkinson and Liptak 2010)

PLATE 5. Nalo Hopkinson, *Still Rather Fond of Red* (2007). Reproduced with permission of the artist.

As a storyteller in various media and genres, Nalo Hopkinson is one artist re-interpreting and subverting the colonial network and structures of power from an epistemological and enunciative location of "colonial difference" (Mignolo 2002b). This project is clearly at work, as I will develop in chapter 1, in her adaptations of "Little Red Riding Hood" and other folk and fairy tales.

What does *Still Rather Fond of Red* do? For me, it visually makes an in-your-face point: the association of wolves and a woman in red clothing may be universal, but this Red Riding Hood is black, and her encounters with "wolfie" are shaped by the politics of colonialism and also class. *Still Rather Fond of Red* further works to creolize "Red Riding Hood" in various ways: the plural provenance of the text's materials contributes to making this point without reaching for authenticity, or establishing a history/story divide; and *Still Rather Fond of Red* has a history within Hopkinson's work that is interwoven with the story of "Red Riding Hood" in the fairy-tale web.

The words in *Still Rather Fond of Red* are excerpted from "Riding the Red," the opening story in Hopkinson's collection *Skin Folk*: "I forgot wolfie. I forgot that riding the red was more than a thing of soiled rags and squalling newborns and . . ." (2001, 3). This short story, which first appeared in *Black Swan, White Raven* edited by Ellen Datlow and Terri Windling (1997), did not update "Little Red Riding Hood" but powerfully relocated it in a contemporary sexual politics that highlights the materiality—rather than the fabled morality—of bodies, desires, and work. Hopkinson wrote "Riding the Red" at a Clarion Writing Workshop in 1995 and claims that it adapts "Red Riding Hood" to redeem "poor wolfie, so maligned" and to repower the metaphor and materiality of "riding the red" as menstruation. "I often get readers assuming that the grandmother in 'Riding the Red' is black, Caribbean, and speaking Jamaican English. She isn't. Whatever her race, I imagine her as an English farming woman, somewhere circa 17th or 18th century" (Hopkinson's blog, December 31, 2006). Later on, Hopkinson did write "Red Rider," another first-person narrative, this time in Jamaican vernacular and set in the bush, as a monologue for black actors in Canada. In "Red Rider," Granny is "an old farm woman in plain clothing, [who] sits in her home in a rocking chair, darning by the light of a kerosene lamp on a table beside her"; there is no wolf, but Brer Tiger; and her words are, "tell you true; I really forget Master Puss. I forget that riding the red is more than blood between your thighs and pickney a-bawl and . . ." (2000, 13).

When we consider how *Still Rather Fond of Red* visually reiterates aspects of both "Riding the Red" and "Red Rider," we can see that it does not replicate or replace either one in different media. I see these three Hopkinson adaptations of "Red Riding Hood" as intertexts that work to cross conceptual and geopolitical horizons rather than to simply overturn a binary hierarchy. And yet Hopkinson ironically asserts that "having made the woman in this collage a black woman, I figure I'll never be able to convince some people now that 'Riding the Red' isn't written in Jamaican English" (Nalo Hopkinson's blog, July 21, 2007). A lot will depend not only on where cultural production is located but also on where and from which knowledge systems, cultural *habitus*, and critical agendas the reader or interpreter accesses the fairy-tale web. This resonates with the multivocality of this web and also cautions that my readings in this book are necessarily limited by my positionality in accessing the fairy-tale web.

READING ADAPTATIONS IN THE FAIRY-TALE WEB: A VARIED POLITICS OF WONDER

Within the globalized economy of the early twenty-first century, fairy tales are produced and experienced as intertextual, multivocal, and transmedial cultural practices that individually and in relation to one another seem to put into action, not necessarily the complexities of feminist or other social critiques but a complex sense of what fairy tales do, a more generalized awareness that the fairy tale as a genre is not simple or one. By sketching the historical transformation of the fairy tale since the 1970s as complex and contradictory, and by insisting on the importance of weaving the genre's polymorphic intertextuality and history with narratives of a global economy, my aim has been to make a critical intervention in the field of fairy-tale studies that immerses, as thoroughly as I can, the practice of reading intertextually in social changes. Within this framework, the rest of the book seeks to develop the following interrelated propositions and critical questions about the twenty-first-century fairy-tale web as a network of reading and writing practices.

1. In the twenty-first-century fairy-tale web, links are "hypertextual," as Donald Haase put it, that is, not referring back to *one* center (2006). The authority of the canonized Perrault-Grimms-Disney triad is still at stake in the re-creation of fairy tales, but it is no longer *the* central pretext for their adaptations in literature, film, or other media. The existence of competitive authorities and the awareness of multiple traditions—in terms of genre and gender—that feminist and other critiques have brought into popular culture since the 1970s *has*, I argue, affected power dynamics within and among fairy-tale texts.

2. This proliferation of adaptations of and twists on the fairy tale, however, does *not* guarantee the articulation of new social possibilities for the genre. Neither does recognizing the genre's ideologically nuanced variability and

multiplicity of traditions in today's fairy-tale web exonerate cultural critics and fairy-tale scholars from reflecting on its hegemonic uses. How has feminism impacted the production and reception of fairy tales in a globalized "culture of spectacle"? When does parody serve consumerism? In the culture industry, the signature mark of the fairy-tale genre continues to be its "happily-ever-after" ending. Getting there, to the HEA (as we tag it in my classes), involves magic, and ritually marking the HEA are the wedding and the beautiful bride. For the fairy-tale alliance of fantasy and romance to "sell," it is however increasingly camouflaged in "faux feminism" (Pershing and Gablehouse 2010, 151) or dressed up in generic remix.

3. The contemporary proliferation of fairy-tale transformations in convergence culture does mean that the genre has *multivalent currency*, and we need to think of the fairy tale's social uses and effects in increasingly nuanced ways while asking who is reactivating a fairy-tale poetics of wonder and for whom. Even in mainstream fairy-tale cinema today, there is no such thing as *the* fairy tale or one main use of it. This multiplicity of position-takings does not polarize ideological differences, but rather produces complex alignments and alliances in the contemporary fairy-tale web.

4. Within this web of fairy-tale practices, the authority of the genre and its gender representations has become more multivocal, especially in the production of small-press literature and in alliance with genre fiction. English-language women writers like Emma Donoghue, Francesca Lia Block, Terri Windling, Aimee Bender, Kelly Link, Margo Lanagan, Theodora Goss, and Nalo Hopkinson share the fairy tale as part of their storied or "invisible" luggage, but they carry it differently from the Angela Carter generation (Bacchilega 2008; Orme 2010a; Carney 2012). This historical transformation is key to enabling some fairy-tale fiction writers, regardless of gender, to articulate desires and imagine possibilities that were marginalized in or excluded from the genre's predominantly heteronormative and Western canon.

5. One of the more prevalent transformations of the fairy tale today, in the culture industry as well as in counterhegemonic practices, has to do with genre mixing, placing the fairy tale in new dynamics of competition and alliance with other genres. I pay attention to this in every chapter. From the understanding that "instead of being 'in' a genre, texts are transformative instantiations of genres" (Frow 2007, 1633) and that different genre systems compete as sites of knowledge production, I am interested in what kind of trouble mixing genres makes and for whom. I ask three complementary sets of questions.

- What are the stakes of mixing fairy tales with other—realistic and supernatural—genres within a Euro-American economy of genres? I will suggest that in some cases, the mix seeks to bolster the fantasy of globalized capital in which we live; in other genre-bending cases, the fairy tale may be reinterpreted as traumatic emplotment of individual lives as well as social life, or wonder-producing opportunity for survival (chapters 2 and 3).

- What are the stakes of mixing fairy tales with non-Western poetics of wonder in a global economy where fairy-tale magic is the norm? In remixes that are enabled by specific historical circumstances, postcolonial concerns and transnational dynamics are both hybridizing and creolizing the fairy tale in popular culture. Unlike *hybridity*, the generalized grafting process that characterizes creativity where cultures clash, *creolization* brings about the rearticulation of the fairy tale's rhetorical world mapping from the perspective of local histories and oppressed traditions, whereby the "other" is positioned as the producer of decolonizing knowledges (chapters 1 and 3).

- And what are the stakes of mixing *Arabian Nights* magic within an economy of genres where the Euro-American fairy tale is the norm? To what uses are Orientalizing and de-Orientalizing practices of translation and adaptation put in today's popular culture? The pressure on these questions is particularly strong in a post-9/11 world where the violent rhetoric of an us/them binary has gone viral. I am interested in considering whether and how *Arabian Nights* remixes and remediations, which tend to cluster around visually powerful tropes, may reinforce or destabilize stereotypes (chapter 4).

6. While for some the fairy tale functions as a form of escape from reality, others see it as a form of enchantment that epitomizes, to borrow from Slavoj Žižek and refer back to the Bloomingdale's window display, some of the fantasies that are at work in producing our shared sense of reality. The varied poetics of fairy-tale transformation, genre bending, remix, and creolization that are emerging into the twenty-first century from specific, historically situated, intertextual and intercultural dynamics should not be folded into a narrative of genre continuity that privileges formal strategies. What is the transformative social potential of the varied poetics of wonder that is emerging from different sites in the fairy-tale web? How are readers as consumers and interpreters contributing to this social transformation of the fairy tale? And what are our responsibilities

as fairy-tale scholars and cultural critics in this globalized electronic culture that continues to thrive on social inequality?

7. In considering these dynamics and questions, I do not aim to classify adaptations or to authorize a single contemporary fairy-tale poetics and politics of wonder;[34] rather, I hope to explore the transformative possibilities and limitations that fairy tales as one wonder genre among others hold for the human imagination today, in a world that has been characterized as disenchanted.

1

Activist Responses

Adaptation, Remediation, and Relocation

Any text is an intertext; other texts are present in it, at varying
levels, in more or less recognizable forms: the texts of the previous
and surrounding culture; any text is a new tissue of past citations.

ROLAND BARTHES, "Theory of the Text"

Reading is just as creative an activity as writing and most intellectual development depends upon new readings of old texts.

ANGELA CARTER, "Notes from the Front Line"

Intrinsic in story telling is a focus on dialogue and conversations
among ourselves as indigenous peoples, to ourselves and for
ourselves.

LINDA TUHIWAI SMITH, *Decolonizing Methodologies*

What is "adaptation"? And what does conceptualizing it to approach a fairy-tale
web of reading and writing practices enable?

Experientially, we know we are dealing with an adaptation when in reading,
listening to, or viewing a narrative text we recognize its close resemblance with,
or immediately connect it with, another text, at the same time that we acknowledge they are differently located texts, whether the change has to do with genre,
medium, space, or discourse. In order to call this déjà vu or *déjà lu* an adaptation, some scholars require that the text's double exposure be announced or
sustained, or both.[1] The title of Angela Carter's short story, "Ashputtle *or* The

Mother's Ghost: Three Versions in One Story" (in Carter 1993), for instance, announces to readers who are familiar with the Grimms that this is a "Cinderella" adaptation, and Carter's readers more generally will recognize characters, plot elements, and images from the tale as it persists in popular cultural memory; at the same time though, there is no mistaking that Carter's narrative triptych sets up an ironic, postmodern, and feminist relationship with the "Cinderella" folktale or fairy tale.

Once we have recognized a text to be an adaptation, how do we respond to it? How do we read it as an adaptation? Linda Hutcheon's *A Theory of Adaptation* presents complementary arguments about this reading process that synthesize responses from both lay and scholarly audiences. On the one hand, to underscore the appeal of adaptations, she shows how it comes from the pleasure *and* the risk taking of "repetition with variation, from the comfort of ritual combined with the piquancy of surprise" (2006, 4). On the other hand, to debunk the critical cliché that adaptations are mostly derivative or inferior, she reads them within the framework of intertextuality, whereby to engage with Roland Barthes's point that "any text is an intertext"[2] means, first of all, approaching adaptation as one of the many forms of rewriting we encounter in a text—quotation, collage, palimpsest, parody, translation, and so on. In support of her two-pronged proposition, Hutcheon analyzes adaptation as both product and process, focusing on "what" is adapted in various media, what motivates adapters and audiences ("why" and "who"), and how the "where" and "when" of adaptation matter.

This approach suggests thinking of adaptation not as a practice that involves the exclusive connection between two texts at a time (the "original" and its "imitation," or the hypotext and hypertext for Gérard Genette), but as a practice that weaves multiple texts with one another, translating them across media and audiences, connecting them not only intertextually but also hypertextually (Haase 2006). There is no "original" or single hypotext in Carter's "Ashputtle *or* The Mother's Ghost: Three Versions in One Story" because the fairy tale circulates as a text that is already plural (Carter revived not only the Grimms' "Ashputtel" but also Giambattista Basile's "La Gatta Cenerentola" and some closely related oral traditions featuring a traveling heroine), and also because Carter's adaptation works to question the "innocent heroine" portrayal of Cinderella and the fantasy of an upward heterosexual marriage that Charles Perrault as well as the 1950 Disney movie popularized. Because her fiction weaves other "Cinderella" intertexts together, whether Carter's readers have read Basile or the Grimms is not essential to perceiving it as an adaptation. Akin to "mutual and reciprocal inverse translation" (Elliott 2003, 229), adaptations are not simply influenced by their pre-texts, but reflect back on them, coloring our view of them, whether we are familiar or not with every specific pre-text, and intervening on our earlier readings of them—and of other related texts.

Hutcheon and others theorizing adaptation have canonical literature in mind as pre-texts, which explains the persistence of fidelity debates in the field. When we consider folk and fairy tales as pre-texts, the dynamics of cultural capital are quite different, given the privileging of authored and canonical Literature, with a capital L, over oral traditions or children's literature. As we move from story-telling to the Grimms on to Carter and other literary adapters, value increases on the scale. Thus centering the discussion of fairy tales, intertextuality, and adaptations exclusively in the literary domain is a common approach.

At the intersection of literary studies, linguistics, and fairy-tale studies, Ute Heidmann and Jean-Michel Adam have shown how Perrault's and other French tales of his time participate in this kind of dialogue. Heidmann and Adam em-phasize the European-wide and multilingual scope of this dialogue with an-cient and modern texts, and how it further participates in genericity (*genericité*), a continuous process of redeployment of genres that is "inseparable from the genre system of a period or a social group" ("inseparable du système de genres d'une époque ou d'un groupe social") (Heidmann and Adam 2010, 19). Their table (160), which I translate below, offers a complex representation of how in the production and reception of any literary text, fairy tales included, centripetal and centrifugal dialogic tensions are at work, and these are intertextual (among texts), metatextual (about texts), paratextual (with variations in its paratext, for example, illustrations, prefaces, title), cotextual (with its own textual variations), and discursive (involving various languages and genres). Relevant to the pro-duction and reception of "Ashputtle" within this framework are the intertexts I mentioned and Carter's and others' metanarrative comments about the genre or the "Cinderella" tale;[3] the different paratexts that frame her short story in the 1987, 1993, and subsequent publications; the various published versions of the story and its relation to Carter's other works; and the fairy-tale genre and its multilingual history in Europe, extending back in time to literature in Latin as well as transnationally to German, French, and other literatures.[4]

Heidmann and Adam's approach to intertextuality (which draws on Bakhtin and Tzvetan Todorov) significantly amplifies methodological and analytical pos-sibilities for showing how any (fairy-tale) text, and especially an adaptation, in-tervenes in dialogues that are not restricted to how tale X varies from tale Y and instead intrinsically speaks to the tensions that motivate adaptations—which, as readers and scholars of the fairy-tale genre know well, range from seeking to reproduce the power of pre-texts to calling it into question—as well as to the textual history of literary genres.[5] Whether they have read Carter or not, writers

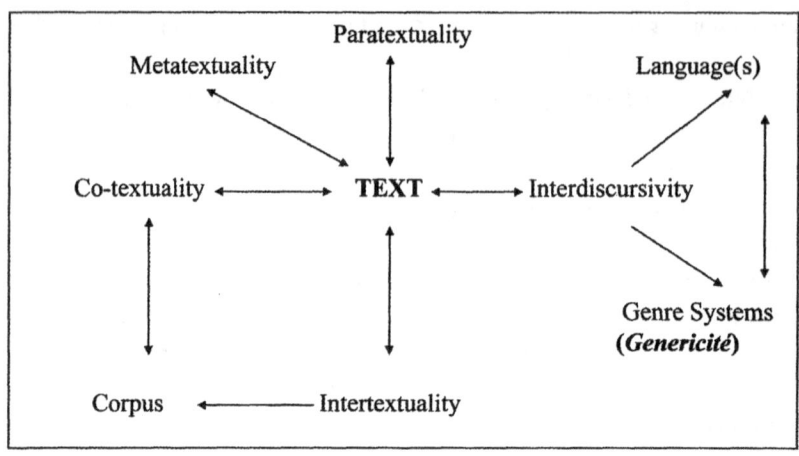

FIGURE 1. From Ute Heidmann and Jean-Michel Adam's *Textualité et intertextualité des contes* (original in French, 2010). Reproduced with permission of the authors.

(re)turning to the fairy tale in the 1990s and into the twenty-first century have her fairy-tale adaptations as one of their potential pre-texts: the possibility for writers and readers of making this link is one of the ways in which the "Angela Carter generation" changed fairy-tale fiction and its potential for magic and wonder.

Inter/hypertextual dialogue is operative both in the production, as rereading and rewriting, of adaptations and in their reception when texts resonate with one another in new contexts or in surprising ways. Also building on Barthes, Bakhtin, and Kristeva, but questioning the scope of textuality as literary and even linguistic, film critic Robert Stam emphasized in 2000 that since adaptations "can take an activist stance towards their source[s]," we can insert them "into a much broader intertextual dialogism," that is, "the infinite and open-ended possibilities generated by all the discursive practices of a culture, the entire matrix of communicative utterances within which the artistic text is situated, which reach the text not only through recognizable influences, but also through a subtle process of dissemination" (Stam 2000, 64). I see the cultural turn in adaptation studies that Stam initiated as key to further opening up possibilities for intertextual readings of fairy tales to reach into a range of discourses and link to social activism. After all, dialogues are not between texts as such and, as I put it in my introduction, stories and people work with, for, and on one another. Angela Carter's "Ashputtle" is in critical dialogue not only with multiple versions and remediations of "Cinderella," but also with nineteenth- and twentieth-century ideas of womanhood, marriage, nuclear family, mourning, and mother-daughter relations in a range of discourses, including psychoanalysis, sociology, marxism, and feminism, as well as everyday practices.[6] Her intervention in the genre of the fairy tale is literary, but not insulated from materiality or power dynamics; in fact, as many have shown, her work offers a prime example of the worldliness of literary and nonliterary genres.

That an adaptation is potentially both activist in its motivations and unpredictable in its effects places it in closer affinity with other forms of rewriting and intertextual dialogue, such as parody, retelling, or re-vision. And all of these terms and more—including "transformation, anti-fairy tale, postmodern fairy tale, fractured fairy tale, and re-cycled fairy tale" (Joosen 2011, 9) and "remake" (Zipes 2012 passim)—have been deployed to discuss contemporary adaptations of fairy tales.[7] In my earlier work, for instance, I have read Carter's short story as a postmodern fairy tale, a re-vision (in Adrienne Rich's words, "the act of looking back, of seeing with fresh eyes, of entering an old text from a new critical direction" [1972, 18]), and a phantasmagoria (Bacchilega 2008). Far from disavowing the usefulness of these concepts, I choose "adaptation" as my operative construct here in order to emphasize that the fairy-tale web is not only an inter/hypertextual, but also an intermedial and multimedial, symptomatic, and possibly transformative reading practice.

Centrally productive to my approach to adaptations is Hutcheon's attention to how they engage audiences in medium-specific ways that for instance may translate *telling* into *showing* and vice versa, make use of the aural or not, dramatize via different conventions, or induce interactivity. Adaptation often involves remediation (Bolter and Grusin 2000) or better, in a process of translation that is less focused on the limitations of individual media, "intermedial transposition" (Wolf 2005). Especially since the fairy tale has such a long history of circulating as multimedial storytelling, that is, in multiple media, I believe that attending to adaptations' intermedial processes and effects can bolster our reading of what fairy-tale adaptations do as narratives. Reading texts as adaptations focuses our attention on how they are, as narratives, shaped by "the protocols of a distinct medium" and "mediated by a series of filters" that in film, for example, include "studio style, ideological fashion, political and economic constraints, *auteurist* predilections, charismatic stars, cultural values, and so forth" (Stam 2005, 45). To consider fairy-tale adaptations in print, film, comics, theater, television, and photographs demands some attention to how their narrative power draws upon their "mediality": the semiotics of each media, the senses they address, their "spatio-temporal extension," their signs' materiality, and their "cultural role and methods of production/

distribution" (Ryan 2004, 18–19). It will also matter to the adaptations' narrative power whether or not a medium affords "plurimediality" (Wolf 2011), meaning it communicates through multiple sensory tracks that can produce heterogeneous (for example, music and script in a film) or hybrid (graphic novel) effects.[8]

In approaching the fairy-tale web, I find it productive to emphasize another aspect of adaptation: its symptomatic value in the larger field of cultural production. This results in foregrounding how a fairy-tale adaptation functions in the cultural "system that produces [it] and generates a series of norms of selection and transposition observable in other adaptations" (García 2005, 239). An adaptation is influenced by previous adaptations of the same text and also by contemporary adaptations of other texts and genres that share similar approaches. Taking this into account helps to place the analysis of a specific adaptation's interplay with its pre-texts within the adaptation's new cultural and social location, bringing into view its activation of specific fairy-tale links as strategies of hegemonic and counterhegemonic translation.

Finally, "because adaptation is a form of repetition without replication" (Hutcheon 2006, xvi), key to the production and the reception of adaptations are the impulse, the pleasure, and the risk-taking not only to revisit but also to transform. Just as with the fairy tale, which is "informed by a human disposition to action—to transform the world and make it more adaptable to human needs while we try to change and make ourselves fit for the world" (Zipes 2012, 2), the promise adaptations hold is twofold. To adapt is to "adjust to," or fit in, *and* to "alter," even offer an alternative. As a student asked in my 21st-Century Fairy-Tale Adaptations class (Birkeland 2009), what are contemporary fairy-tale adapters dissatisfied with? What kinds of changes do they want to bring about? There can be no single satisfactory answer. But if some transformative poetics and politics of the fairy tale are emerging today, the frame of adaptation as activist responses can help us focus on how to read hegemonic and counterhegemonic practices that are changing the twenty-first-century fairy-tale web. "Activist" here refers to an adaptation's responses to pre-texts as well as to the response it instigates in listeners/readers/viewers: the two do not necessarily go together, nor does the latter necessarily mark a progressive position. "Adaptations redistribute energies and intensities, provoke flows and displacements" (Stam 2005, 46) as they keep their pre-texts in play but also reaccentuate or destabilize them, and some relocate them.[9]

RELOCATING THE FAIRY TALE

In a narrow sense, relocation is one of many possible adaptive strategies: it moves a pre-text to a different setting, as the film *Enchanted* does by transporting its

Disney fairy-tale characters and plot to New York City. But what I am referring to as *relocation* is a politicized kind of response by which texts, genres, and knowledges that have been naturalized as normative or central are remapped from within the perspectives and frames of specifically located knowledges and histories. In these emergent spaces of articulation and reorientation, adaptation provides a relational, rather than oppositional, framework for transformation.

My focus in the rest of this chapter is on reading three such adaptations intertextually: Nalo Hopkinson's *Skin Folk* (2001), Emma Donoghue's *Kissing the Witch* (1997, 1999), and Dan Taulapapa McMullin's intermedial *Sinalela* narratives (2001, 2003, 2004). While intertextual possibilities are unlimited, and reading these texts through other interpretive lenses and networks can be just as productive, here—and in the rest of the book—I focus on tracing and, more importantly, contextualizing announced fairy-tale pre-texts as well as intertextual and hypertextual links that emerge in the process of reading these texts as "fairy-tale adaptations." Reading intertextually even when the focus is on fairy-tale links can take varied paths and shapes, and methodologically my three readings are not the same. What they have in common is my privileging of links that—in approaching the questions, "How and to what uses are fairy tales being adapted in the twenty-first century? And what are the stakes, and for whom?"—expand and decenter the narrow conception of the genre fixed in Disneyfied pre-1970s popular cultural memory.

Specifically, I argue that each of these differently located fairy-tale adaptations takes an activist stance not only in response to its pre-texts but also to the hegemonic uses we make of fairy tales in the world today. If "happily ever after" (HEA) is the signature mark of this hegemony, it is so by scripting transformation as entrepreneurial or colonizing-capitalist progress and its happy end(ing) as heteronormative. Rather than mocking this HEA or making room for new heroes and brides in it, *Skin Folk*, *Kissing the Witch*, and "Sinalela and the One-Eyed Fish" rethink the fairy tale starting from located knowledges, struggles, and desires the genre conspires, in its hegemony, to disavow or bypass. Given the three adaptations' different contexts of production and reception, their activist responses to the fairy tale result in different acts of relocation.

Metacritically, my discussion seeks to highlight how Hopkinson's, Donoghue's, and McMullin's adaptations activate alternative links in the folk and fairy-tale web of writing and reading practices, links that at the production end enact, and at the reception end suggest, a reorientation to the genre and its uses. I will focus on three aspects of this relocation. One, for these artists, creolizing and indigenizing, both of which are imbricated with queering, are the grounds— the materiality of emplaced and embodied experiences—for a decolonizing transformation of both storyworld and world. As subjects and ways of being in the world that have been devalued are placed center stage, these texts open up their target audiences and readers more generally to imagining alternative (hi)stories and futures the HEA forecloses. Two, the deployment of remediation in these three texts is key to the genre's relocation, as their different representations of orality claim space and value on the page. Three, Hopkinson, Donoghue, and McMullin resituate the fairy tale in relation to other narratives (wonder genres and everyday *habitus*) that also emplot human lives.

Reading *Skin Folk* Intertextually: Relocation, Take #1

Nalo Hopkinson is an award-winning author most commonly associated with fantasy and science fiction who, in addition to the short-story collection *Skin Folk* (2001), has published four novels (*Brown Girl in the Ring* [1998], *Midnight Robber* [2000], *The Salt Roads* [2003], *The New Moon's Arms* [2007]), edited four anthologies (*Whispers from the Cotton Tree: Caribbean Fabulist Fiction* [2000], *Mojo: Conjure Stories* [2003], *So Long Been Dreaming: Postcolonial Science Fiction and Fantasy* [2004], *Tesseracts Nine* [2005]), and made her debut as a young adult (YA) writer with *The Chaos* in 2012. An excerpt from her *Midnight Robber* is included in the 2012 landmark anthology of indigenous science fiction, *Walking the Clouds* (Dillon 2012). Of Taino/Arawak and Afro-Caribbean descent, Hopkinson consciously draws on worldwide folklore, Taino narratives, and Afro-Caribbean culture to produce speculative fiction (spec-fic) where traditional tales, indigenous beliefs, memory, and near-future urban adventures mix at the boundaries of science fiction and fantasy.[10]

A voracious reader from childhood, Hopkinson tells the following story in several interviews: "[as a child] I was already reading a lot of fantasy. And a lot of folktales—Caribbean, Chinese, European. . . . I was reading anything that had some element of fantasy in it—C. S. Lewis's children's stories or *Gulliver's Travels* or Homer's *Iliad*, which I was reading when I was quite young" (Hopkinson and Magnus 2005). For an interview that appeared in *Social Text* shortly after the publication of *Skin Folk*, she articulated one of the ways in which folktales relate to the literature she writes, and I quote from it at some length:

> [Spec-fic] is a set of literatures that examine the effects on humans and human societies of the fact that we are toolmakers. We are always trying to control or improve our environments. Those tools may be tangible (such as machines) or intangible (such as laws, mores, belief systems). Spec-fic tells us stories about our lives with our creations. . . . [To me] as a young

reader . . . folktales and fables and the old epics (Homer's *Iliad*, for instance) felt as though they lived in a different dimension. . . . Call it escapism, because at some level it is, but I think that goes back to human beings being tool-users. We imagine what we want from the world, then we try to find a way to make it happen. Escapism can be the first step to creating a new reality, whether it's a personal change or a larger change in the world. For me, spec-fic is a contemporary literature that is performing that act of the imagination—as opposed to the old traditional folk, fairy, and epic allegorical tales, which I think of as a historical literature of the imagination. And here I need to qualify, because all fiction is imaginative and much of it transcends the quotidian. I'm just trying to identify science fiction/fantasy/horror/magical realism as fiction that starts from the principle of making the impossible possible. (Hopkinson and Nelson 2002, 98)

I take it that for Hopkinson the tie between "historical" and present-day speculative fictions, between fairy tales and her tales is that they all start "from the principle of making the impossible possible," thus activating transformations that can be individual and/or social in their effects. I also get how she is interested in intervening in the relationship among genres rather than in reasserting their set boundaries. The fairy tale is not privileged among the many forms of what she calls "historical literature of the imagination," and in her own crafting of fiction she interweaves narratives to test their utility, to reflect on how humans—especially unprivileged ones in the places she has inhabited and written about, the Caribbean and postcolonial Toronto in Canada—live with them.

An epigraph introduces *Skin Folk*: "Throughout the Caribbean, under different names, you'll find stories about people who aren't what they seem. Skin gives these skin folk their human shape. When the skin comes off, their true selves emerge. They may be owls. They may be vampiric balls of fire. And always, whatever the burden their skins bear, once they remove them—once they get under their own skins—they can fly. It seemed an apt metaphor to use for these stories collectively" (Hopkinson 2001, 1). Three of her fifteen stories can be easily identified as adapting folktales that, in the long-established Aarne-Thompson-Uther system of folkloristics, are specifically classified as tales of magic or fairy tales: "Riding the Red" of "Little Red Riding Hood" (ATU 333); "The Glass Bottle Trick" of "Maiden-Killer" or "Bluebeard" (ATU 312); "Precious" of "The Kind and Unkind Girls" (ATU 480).[11] Another, "Under Glass," is a postapocalyptic re-vision of Hans Christian Andersen's literary fairy tale, "The Snow Queen." While each adaptation deserves critical attention, I focus here on how more generally Hopkinson's adaptive strategies can instigate, especially for those of us who are at home in her fairy-tale intertexts, a reorientation to the genre.[12]

To start with, the epigraph immediately alerts readers to the genre's relocation in the world of Caribbean folklore and Hopkinson's spec-fic imagination, where transformation is just as common as it is in fairy tales, but transbiology is more belief than fiction, and flying as a result of it is the metaphor of choice.[13] Whether Hopkinson's protagonists "can fly" literally or figuratively, their potential is announced as different from that of the traditional European fairy tales, which Marina Warner notes "avoid scenes of flying, perhaps through anxiety of contamination by sorcery" (2012, 333).[14] Never simply narratives that colonize minds (though that is their history of contact in the Caribbean), fairy tales and their transformations are negotiated in *Skin Folk* within Hopkinson's gendered and creolized storyworlds and poetics.

"Riding the Red" and "Precious," as the initial and final stories respectively in the collection, offer some insight into which aspects of this "historical literature of the imagination" Hopkinson finds her storytelling scripted into and/or she wants to tap. Certainly, *transformation*. The tales—and actually the whole collection—hinge on it, proposing a character's inner transformation, but not delivering the skin folk into flight. To transform, the protagonist must struggle with "supernatural" beings or forces that are, in the fairy-tale style, externalized. But the ending is not the HEA of canonical fairy tales. "At the end of an Anancy story, unlike at the end of the European folk fairy tale, the hero's great triumph usually consists in staying alive" (D'Costa 1990, 258), and this contrast comes alive also in Hopkinson's texts. In her adaptations, magic is no mere "labor-saving device" (Hopkinson 2010, 347), as characters striving to make it remove the skin that burdens them—the fiction that tells them who they are.[15] Each story ends on the verge of resolution, taking the protagonist and us as readers to the threshold of transformation, or just beyond it, into the liminal moment when the ending is the beginning of another story.

"Riding the Red" is Grandma's monologue as she waits for her red-riding or coming-of-age granddaughter. In her mind, Grandma is telling the girl "the facts of life before it's too late. . . . Pretty soon now, you're going to be riding the red, and if you don't look smart, next stop is wolfie's house, and wolfie, doesn't he just love the smell of that blood, oh yes" (Hopkinson 2001, 1). But along with the warning comes the memory of Grandma's own dance as a young girl with wolfie, her tongue-in-cheek comment that "there is much plucking to be done in the dance of riding the red" (2), her fantasizing about one last exciting measure with wolfie (4). The final line of the tale anticipates a transformative possibility, but we do not know the nature of Grandma's "last sweet dance. Listen: is that a knock at the door?" (5). Even if I am accustomed to thinking that sexual initiation, violence, and intergenerational knowledge are core thematic elements of "Little Red Riding Hood," the first-person assertion of Grandma's desire for and memory of sexual pleasure in Hopkinson's text makes for new permutations of the granny/wolf/girl triangulations as they slide in and out of each other's skins. For this reader, intertextual links are activated not only with the "Little Red Riding Hood" tale in several of its versions (Perrault's and the Grimms', and also the unsanitized "Story of Grandmother"), but also with its critical interpretations (for example, Röhrich 2011; Verdier 1978; Zipes 1993) as well as with contemporary intertexts, including Robert Coover's "The Door: A Prologue of Sorts" (1969) and Angela Carter's wolf-girl trilogy in *The Bloody Chamber* (1979); and also filmic adaptations that do not cloak the sexual subtexts of the tale, from Tex Avery's cartoon *Red Hot Riding Hood* (1943) to Neil Jordan's 1984 *The Company of Wolves* (written by Neil Jordan and Angela Carter; starring Angela Lansbury and Sarah Patterson) and Matthew Bright's 1996 *Freeway* (with Reese Witherspoon and Kiefer Sutherland).

Experiencing the tale anew can "turn the key" for the writer as well as her readers, opening "into a hidden room . . . the center of the labyrinth of desire" (Warner 2001, 250).[16] *Sexuality and sexual politics.* By conjuring "Little Red Riding Hood," "Riding the Red" takes on menstrual blood—as well as the blood of sex, birth, and violent death—as the symbolic tie that connects women with fairy tales (Cardigos 1996), giving us a taste of how Hopkinson, in her engagement with the fairy tale, is cognizant of feminist questions and uses of the genre. "Precious," at the end of the collection, explodes into a self-affirming narrative in which the woman from whose lips fall jewels when she speaks, in a modern-day sequel to "The Kind and Unkind Girls," finds that voicing her anger at being exploited frees her from the spell that oppresses her. *Voice.* Increasingly in adaptations, fairy-tale villains and side characters tell their stories (for example, Sara Maitland's 1987 "The Wicked Stepmother's Lament"; Gregory Maguire's 1995 *Wicked*), and the underbelly of the heroine's story is revealed (Neil Gaiman's "Snow, Glass, Apples"). Both "Riding the Red" and "Precious" break with the conventional morality that punishes women for expressing active sexual desire or anger, the regulatory moral of the tales where the submissive "good" girl is rewarded. It is not surprising that "Riding the Red" and "Precious" were first published by Ellen Datlow and Terri Windling in *Black Swan, White Raven* (1997) and *Silver Birch, Blood Moon* (1999) respectively.

Hopkinson's thematic inquiries (into the process of transformation, regulation of desire, abuse, injustice, and more) and narrative strategies (first-person narrator, contemporary or historical setting, characters' psychological development, plot extended into a prequel or sequel) have a lot in common with other fairy-tale adaptations in those popular millennial anthologies. And yet, as I wrote in 2008, reading her collection was a turning point for me as a feminist scholar of folklore and literature and fairy-tale studies because Hopkinson's writing overall engages with fairy tales, folktales, and spec-fic from a racialized position and a creolizing poetics.[17] This kind of activist adaptation emerges from a history and a project that even when the genre's multiple and gendered Western traditions are considered have not been central to the fairy tale's canon.[18]

Those of us who have already paid some critical attention specifically to Hopkinson's fairy-tale adaptations have done so within the framework of creolization, but not necessarily striking the same key.[19] In her 2009 essay, "Rattling Perrault's Dry Bones: Nalo Hopkinson's Literary Voodoo in *Skin Folk*," Martine Hennard Dutheil de la Rochère (2009b) develops the following thesis: "Hopkinson's tropicalised tales thus convey a complex heritage through hybrid, creolized literary strategies that reflect the multicultural makeup of Caribbean society and uncover the 'dark secrets' that still haunt its present. The author's appropriation of the European fairy tale tradition thus becomes a deeply ambivalent, creative and critical gesture which serves to conjure up the colonial heritage the better to exorcise it" (213). In weaving together her analysis of literary strategies and (post)colonial histories, Hennard Dutheil de la Rochère aptly foregrounds salient aspects of *créolité*, creolization or creoleness, which is identified with the abrupt mixing of peoples and traditions in an unequal-power relation (such as colonialism) that creates in a specific location (such as islands) new and unpredictable social formations, languages, and traditions (Bernabé, Chamoiseau, and Confiant 1993; Seifert 2002; Haring 2004). Within this framework, Hennard Dutheil de la Rochère's insightful and elegant analysis of "Riding the Red," "The Glass Bottle Trick," and "Precious" points to the clash between colonizing authorities and "Obeah religion practiced by black slaves in the British West Indies (usually referred to as voodoo in North America and the West)" (2009b, 214) and elucidates Hopkinson's transformative craft, whereby Charles Perrault's tales become "(counter-)discursive practices with retributive but also healing properties, just like voodoo itself" (215). While agreeing with much of her analysis, I take issue with Hennard Dutheil de la Rochère's focus on the European *literary* tradition of the fairy tale as an essential place from which Hopkinson's adaptation draws its empowering and counterhegemonic force.

Like Hennard Dutheil de la Rochère, I highlight creoleness in Hopkinson's stories as symptomatic of a "convergence of traditions, oppression of a subordinated group, and an unpredictable novelty" (Haring 2004, 23). Hopkinson's self-presentation as a writer invites this framing, as she writes in the essay "Dark

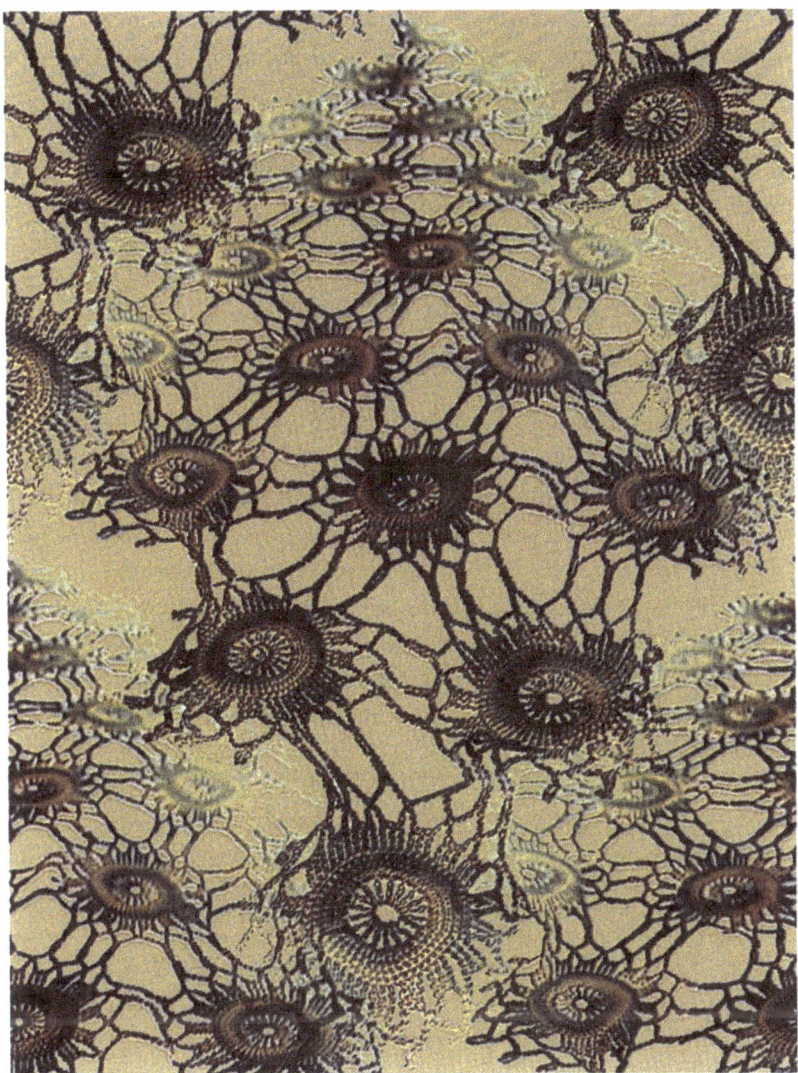

Ink: Science Fiction Writers in Colour" (n.d.): "My history and background combine Canadian, Trinidadian, Jamaican, and Guyanese cultures. 'Culture' is no one monolithic thing for me, and I draw on that varied heritage when I write." For Hopkinson, raised on islands that share experiences of colonization and of creolization as "political consciousness" (Seifert 2002, 216), mixing and grafting in Caribbean cultures are understood as "a strategy for survival and resistance"; as she affirms in another essay, "Code Sliding" (n.d.), her characters' use of Caribbean Creoles reflects this.[20]

Such a located and politicized understanding of creolization means that "code sliding" is at work on all levels to articulate and locate difference or power dynamics. For instance, in "The Glass Bottle Trick," the plot of "Bluebeard" is creolized not so much because curried eggs and duppies are in it, but because issues of race and sexual power are thematized together. The murderous husband wants to "whiten" his wife by keeping her out of the sun and in his "air-tight" air-conditioned house: "When the sun touched her, it brought out the sepia and cinnamon in her blood, overpowered the milk and honey, and he could no longer pretend she was white" (Hopkinson 2001, 93–94). Once Beatrice realizes he despises his own blackness, racial politics come to inform the traditional Bluebeard abhorrence of pregnancy and reproduction.[21] Still unaware of what her husband had done to his previous pregnant wives, Beatrice "remembered him joking that no woman should have to give birth to his ugly black babies, but she would show him how beautiful their children would be, little brown bodies new as the earth after the rain. She would show him how to love himself in them" (96). By the end, she must turn away from such a benevolent fiction in order to defend herself and their brown baby from her husband's self-hatred and her earlier compliance to it.

Similarly, Hopkinson's use of Caribbean Creoles in *Skin Folk* as a collection is not for "color," nostalgia, or the picturesque. "To speak in the hacked languages is not just to speak in an accent or a creole; to say the words aloud is an act of referencing history and claiming space" ("Code Sliding," n.d.).[22] Linguistically, Creoles as spoken by several of Hopkinson's characters inform and transform the Euro-American scripts. Her characters speak in a mix of Caribbean Creoles—Trinidadian and Jamaican especially—which (as she states in "Code Sliding") she uses, the former to signal "emphasis/irony," and the latter to signal "opposition." As Hopkinson likes to remind interviewers, the epigraph for *Midnight Robber* is, "I stole the torturer's tongue," from a poem by David Findlay (Hopkinson and Jarvey 2011).

But, significantly, the protagonists of "The Glass Bottle Trick" and "Precious" speak Standard English. This sign of their acculturation through schooling, metanarratively points to how the fairy tale is of a different order, in the transformative mix of creolized literature, from the Anansi tales or Taino tales that reference histories and beliefs of Afro and First Peoples of the Caribbean. In the twentieth-century Caribbean islands where Hopkinson grew up, classic fairy tales may be not so much what people tell themselves, but what they are made to fit into—what they read in school, or are exposed to in mainstream culture.[23] Not to say that fairy tales are useless to Hopkinson or her characters—we see them draw on the tales' transformative powers—but that the vital connection is not to their literary versions. In "Riding the Red," the first tale in the collection, Grandma's vernacular has an old-world lilt to it. Her voice introduces us to the storyworlds of *Skin Folk* in the mode of the "historical literature of the imagination," linking Hopkinson's writing to oral traditions as "the most vital connection we have," in Angela Carter's words, "with the imaginations of the ordinary men and women whose labour created our worlds" (Carter 1990, ix). Although not in *Skin Folk*, Hopkinson does linguistically creolize "Riding the Red" in her "Red Riding" monologue for stage production (2000) and later in the visual collage I discussed in my introduction. Hopkinson's intervention is not focused exclusively on the fairy-tale's literary tradition, but on its inter- and multimediality in history and living cultures.

As Hopkinson is well aware, creolization will impact audiences differently depending on their cultural knowledge, competences, and expectations. Encountering in one of her stories a "soucouyant" (and not a "succubus" or a "vampire") or "duppy" rather than a ghost produces a metonymic gap: it jars a reader such as myself out of the familiar into new territory and makes me cognizant of its distinctiveness without it being explained.[24] At the same time, this referencing of a located history opens up possibilities of intimacy for eastern Caribbean readers, claiming a space for their realities and beliefs. And for diasporic Afro-Caribbean readers, who like her characters in the cold of Toronto gain strength from reencountering their forgotten "skin folk," the hacked language holds potential for a positive transformation that is also collective. These readers, on the islands and in the diaspora, as well as other fans of spec-fic who have "craved non-White voices, characters, and perspectives" (Rutledge 2002, 3) are hardly the only ones Hopkinson wants to reach, but they are the ones for whom she is saving "the best seats in the house" (Sullivan 2003),[25] the ones who are most invested in being attuned to her poetics.

Hopkinson's creolizing strategies crack the delusion of universality often associated with the cultural landscape of the fairy tale, a move that Hennard Dutheil de la Rochère and Natalie Robinson both recognize. But I want to underscore how Hopkinson's strategies also provincialize the Perrault and Grimm printed tales that for readers such as myself are the home texts. The Euro-American folk and fairy tale is after all only one of many possible genres—among the ones that have impacted the history of storytelling and literature in the Caribbean—on which Hopkinson's indigenous/postcolonial creolized spec-fic can draw, and the European tradition of the literary fairy tale Perrault exemplifies is hardly central to its intertextual web. As seen in Walter Jekyll's 1907 collection, *Jamaican Song and Story: Anancy Stories, Digging Sings, Ring Tunes, and Dancing Tunes*, "Bluebeard" has long been part of the Jamaican story-telling tradition (Jekyll 1907, 35–37). This tale bears some jumbled resemblance to Perrault's text, with, for instance, its reference to Sister Ann. And this points both to its literary European provenance and to the possible circumstances of its circulation in colonial Jamaica: the telling of fairy tales to slaves and servants by the children of their European masters (Jekyll 1907, xxvii). Already in this version, music and song are radically transforming the fairy tale's form and uses, moving it from the white nursery into a Creole world of survival.

Hopkinson's relocation of "Bluebeard" in "The Glass Bottle Trick" does not involve a jumbled plot. Rather, she weaves *around* it the sung words "from an old-time story" also collected by Jekyll: "Yung-Kyung-Pyung, what a pretty basket! / Mary Powell Alone, what a pretty basket! / Eggie-law, what a pretty basket!" (2001, 88–89). The verse is associated with an Anansi story, as Natalie Robinson remarks (2011, 259), in which the trickster, having learned the secret names of the king's three daughters ("Yung-kyum-pyung, Eggie-Law, Marg'ret-Powell-Alone" in this order in Jekyll), wins one in marriage and becomes king. The "pretty basket" is Anansi's tool for tricking the three sisters into his power,[26] and the name of one of the girls, Powell, is Beatrice's married name. The story of "Yung Kyum Pyung" is not recounted in Hopkinson's text; instead, the song is evoked as Beatrice's "one cherished memory" of her father, who would swing her as a child through the air and chant the words.[27] Significantly, this memory comes to Beatrice just after she has by chance liberated the spirits of Samuel's two dead wives from the blue bottles in which he had contained them. "Two little dust devils danced briefly around Beatrice" (Hopkinson 2001, 88). Beatrice is at this point unaware of her husband's crimes and the danger she is in. By the time he returns and angrily summons her, Beatrice has been in the forbidden and bloody chamber, and the wives' ghosts are feeding on their own blood, strengthening themselves to get their revenge. As she moves to greet her murderous husband in the final scene of "The Glass Bottle Trick," Beatrice wonders if, "when they had fed," the "duppy wives" would "come and save her, or would they take revenge on her, their usurper, as well as on Samuel?" (101). Hopkinson again offers no resolution, but the final words are those of the song, "Eggie-Law, what a pretty basket!" (101). Now that she knows the trickster for who he is, she has a chance; maybe he does not know her secret name after all, and she is not just "Mistress Powell," but a survivor.[28]

The two duppies may elicit horror, as the Furies in ancient Greek stories did, but they are Beatrice's potential helpers and sisters. To me their revitalization, like the return of Beatrice's "cherished memory" of song and like the irruption of warmth into the air-conditioned "closed-up home" (Hopkinson 2001, 97), is key to how Beatrice "gets under [her] own skin" possibly enough to transform or fly. While for Hennard Dutheil de la Rochère the crucial conversation is between Hopkinson and Perrault,[29] my reading of intertextuality in Hopkinson's work seeks to emphasize the relatively minor place that the Perrault and Grimm print tradition play in the transformation of Beatrice into a survivor. As Hopkinson writes in the introduction to the collection *So Long Been Dreaming: Postcolonial Science Fiction and Fantasy* (Hopkinson and Mehan 2004): "In my hands, massa's tools don't dismantle massa's house—and in fact, I don't want to destroy it so much as I want to undertake massive renovations—they build me a house of my own" (8). The model for this house is hardly Perrault's palace or the Grimms' cottages; though their mirrors and twigs respectively are there to be seen, they don't hold the house up. And duppies, selkies, female river deities, and Anansi stories along with Red Riding Hood's Grandma inhabit *Skin Folk.*

Moving to this house is a constructive critique that also potentially enacts an epistemic relocation. If Hopkinson writes spec-fic that "explores what we believe" (Hopkinson and Magnus 2005), her adaptation of the folk and fairy-tale genre is part of the process to overcome the "technoscientism" of a human-centered ideology of progress that relegates magical thinking, "old wives' tales," and ways of relating to the world as animate (indigenous knowledge systems and practices) to the premodern. Grace Dillon's essay, "Indigenous Scientific Literacies in Nalo Hopkinson's Ceremonial Worlds," develops how in three of Hopkinson's novels "this overcoming [of 'technoscientism'] occurs by going back, way back, to tradition through the telling of story/ceremony, and by going forward, by mining the imagination to construct an ameliorated technology informed by indigenous tradition and practice" (Dillon 2007, 24–25). The skin in "when the skin comes off" applies to fruit, trees, animals, humans, computerized images, stories, creation, and more. A reading of *Skin Folk* in this vein would yield further insights into what and how Hopkinson seeks to change the fictions we live with and what we believe.[30] My view is that her creolization of the European literary fairy tale recognizes the potential for wonder that marks the folk and fairy-tale genre, well beyond the narrow uses that capitalism and coloniality have made of its magic, *and* at the same time provincializes it within a new arrangement of wonder genres or spec-fic.

In adapting the folk and fairy tale, Hopkinson revitalizes the genre's link with oral tradition, both historically and in the present, through performance and on the page. "Red Rider," linguistically in Creole, was written for actors as an African Canadian monologue in 2000; and in 2001 CBC Radio broadcast a

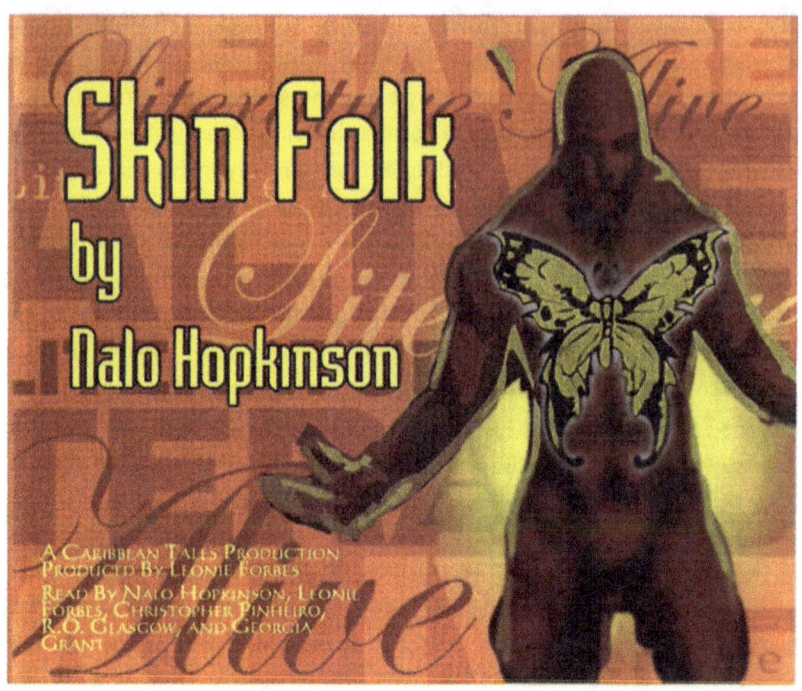

PLATE 7. Nalo Hopkinson, *Skin Folk* audio book cover (2003). Reproduced by permission of Caribbean Tales Worldwide Distribution.

version of "Riding the Red" performed by Nalo Hopkinson along with an original score by jazz artist William Sperandel (http://nalohopkinson.com/writing/fiction/shortfiction/riding_the_red_rider). In 2003 the audio book *Skin Folk* was made available by Caribbean Tales Production as part of its Literature Alive joint initiative with Leda Serene Films that "celebrates the rich tradition of Caribbean heritage storytelling."[31] These oral performances do not replace but multiply the intermediality of the printed *Skin Folk*, in which Hopkinson works to recode the power of storytelling in various ways. I have mentioned how in the collection, through her characters' speech, Hopkinson invites us not only to think or "see hybrid" but also to "hear creole." We know that vernacular voices have often come to represent "orality" in literature, and that at the same time such representations of orality have implicitly primitivized colonized languages and confined them to the past. Other adaptive strategies seek to disable such a reading of Creole as "residual" in Hopkinson's work, and one of them is her innovative permutation of a device that printed fairy-tale collections are well known for, one that mimics the "performative nature" of storytelling on the page (Benson 2003): the cycle of stories.[32]

In collections such as *The Arabian Nights* or Basile's *The Tale of Tales*, this staged orality is achieved through framing. A dramatic situation generates strings of embedded narratives told by characters turned narrators, each speaking in some way or another to the drama of Shahrazad and Shahriyar, and eventually contributing to restoring life to them and their kingdom. The same is true of Basile's collection in which the fifty tales told by ten different narrators at the Prince's court play to the dramatic competition of his false bride and the heroine Zoza for him. And as Elizabeth Wanning Harries has documented, the French *conteuses* in the late seventeenth and early eighteenth centuries adopted similar strategies of embedding tales to approximate storytelling and conversational practices (2001).[33] In Hopkinson's collection, there is no apparent external dramatic situation framing the fifteen stories, but the "skin folk" metaphor in the epigraph encapsulates multiple dramas that are enacted in the tales. Some of the stories are told in the first person, but others are not. Rather, stringing the stories together is a set of authorial statements, an epigraph—often in the first person— preceding each story. Some are about the making of the story that follows; others are explanations. Hopkinson "speaks" to readers, mimicking the ways in which writers transition from story to story when giving a reading, the most common context in which a writer's voice can now be heard and s/he also turns "narrator." Even when the story is a monologue, Hopkinson's "I-statements" frame it, struggle against the usually disembodied narrative transaction occurring between writer and reader, thus staging an opening for conversation.

What's more, some of the statements refer to the "I" being moved to tell the story as a result of hearing another voice—a published poem by her father Slade Hopkinson, "a response a student once wrote on a test, if one can believe any of the endless e-mail spam one gets" (Hopkinson 2001, 23), a song, a saying, a folktale, a warning. So these stories are explicitly connected to a larger web of multimedia storytelling. And within this web, the "I" makes explicit references to a very specific and "real" storytelling context that precedes the one on the page: "In 1995, I was accepted into the Clarion Science Fiction and Fantasy Writers' Workshop at Michigan State University" (Hopkinson 2001, 45). Workshops where professional writers and creative-writing students write, read, and *hear* one another's stories are perhaps today's equivalent in North America of the *Decameron*'s secluded Tuscan villa. While the workshop as "storytelling community" is rarely mentioned in publications, it is perhaps one of the most real, though staged and temporary, "communities" for North American writers today. And for one of Hopkinson's fairy-tale adaptations, "Riding the Red," the Clarion

Writing Workshop was a central site of production and conversation (see http://nalohopkinson.com/writing/fiction/shortfiction/riding_the_red_rider). This is another significant way in which *Skin Folk* relocates the older, generative force of the fairy-tale story cycle in print and at the same time refashions contemporary technologies in a refusal to disembody her storytelling web.

Reading *Kissing the Witch* Intertextually: Relocation, Take #2

Published in 1997 in the United Kingdom as a Hamish Hamilton illustrated edition for adults (that is now out of print) and in the USA as a young adult (YA) imprint within HarperCollins (with no illustrations, but the added subtitle *Old Tales in New Skins*), *Kissing the Witch* was short-listed for a James Tiptree Award that same year and named an American Library Association Popular Paperback for Young Adults in 2000. It has been translated into Dutch, Spanish, and Italian. Born in 1969 in Dublin and currently living in Ontario, Canada, Emma Donoghue is an award-winning Irish and Irish Canadian author whose novel *Room*, with over a million copies sold since August 2010, is an international best seller. While *Kissing the Witch* is somewhat unique as a YA text within her literary production,[34] this collection of short stories has established Donoghue as one of the most innovative fairy-tale voices of the post–Angela Carter generation.

Readers and scholars of fairy tales are likely to have picked up *Kissing the Witch* for themselves or for teen readers partly because it announces itself as "fairy-tale" material. The kiss and the witch in the title are popular fairy-tale icons, though hardly associated with each other. The expectations the subtitle raises are reinforced in the blurb on the American edition's back cover: "Thirteen tales are unspun from the deeply familiar, and woven anew into a collection of fairy tales that wind back through time." On the author's website, not only are the fairy-tale pre-texts of *Kissing the Witch* spelled out, but also her stories in the collection are themselves referred to as "fairy tales" (www.emmadonoghue.com/writings/short-story-listing.htm#FairyTales). Well reviewed from the start in the mainstream press in the United Kingdom and North America, *Kissing the Witch* has also increasingly received sustained attention in the fields of English-language women's literature, children's literature, and fairy-tale studies (Harries 2001; Coppola 2001; Sellers 2001; Palmer 2004; Zipes 2006b; Bacchilega 2008; Hennard Dutheil de la Rochère 2009a; Orme 2010a; Crowley and Pennington, 2010; Martin 2010; Joosen 2011). My analysis, thus, will draw on this critical discussion as well as on my own experience responding to and teaching the text in order to foreground how, in reading *Kissing the Witch*, hypertextual links do not refer back to *one* center or tradition (Haase 2006). In the process, I argue,

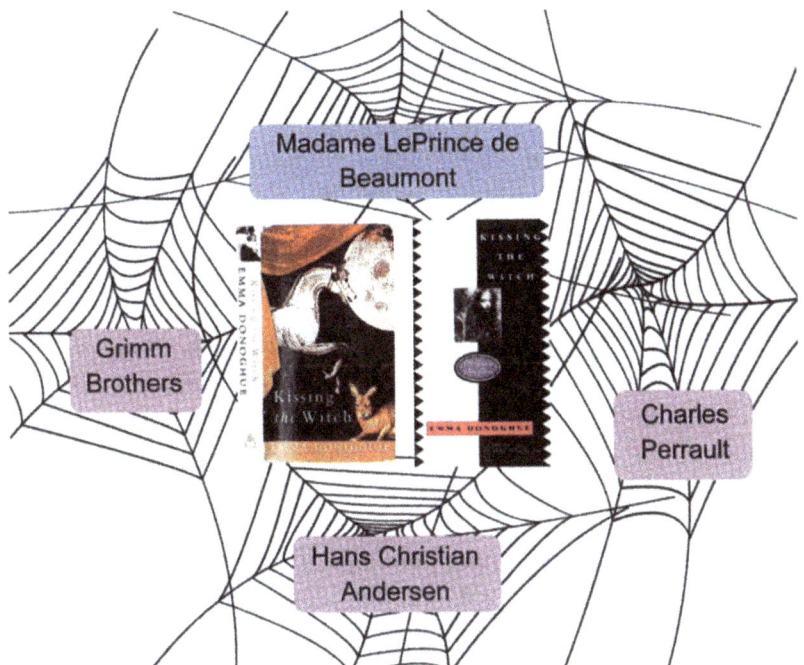

PLATE 8. Steven Gin, "Reading *Kissing the Witch* Intertextually" (1). Courtesy of Steven Gin, adapted from his Flash presentation (2011). *Kissing the Witch* by Emma Donoghue (Hamish Hamilton, 1998). Copyright © Emma Donoghue, 1997. Cover reproduced by permission of Penguin Books Ltd. Illustrator unknown. *Kissing the Witch* 1999 cover. © Eric Dinyer/Illustration Source

Donoghue's adaptation performs the work of relocation, specifically by decentering the heteronormativity and HEA of the hegemonic fairy tale, insisting on the performative potential of orality in its textual remediation, and connecting folk and fairy tales with personal narratives and "witching" culture.

Let me state my three main points. One, the authority of the canonized fairy tale is still at stake in the re-creation of Donoghue's tales, but it is no longer *the* central pre-text. While as acknowledged on her website, seven of Donoghue's thirteen stories draw on tales by the Brothers Grimm and five on Charles Perrault, Madame LePrince de Beaumont, and Hans Christian Andersen,[35] I see Donoghue's fairy tales as activist responses to these authoritative pre-texts, which end up playing minor roles in the reading process as intertextual links proliferate in response to her new storytelling scenarios. Accompanying my verbal reading, still images adapted from Steven Gin's computer-animated Flash text, "Reading *Kissing the Witch* Intertextually," visualize—and approximate in another medium—this process.[36]

Two, whether it is because they were written explicitly for younger readers or not, sex and desire in Emma Donoghue's tales, just as in "classic" fairy tales, are powerfully conjured only via indirection or metaphor. Taking off from queer (odd and in excess of regulatory sexual and gender norms) moments in the classic tales, *Kissing the Witch* is not so much a collection of lesbian fairy tales but "tales of nonnormative subjects and desires actively resisting heteropatriarchal ideologies" (Orme 2010a, 121).

Three, *Kissing the Witch* calls for an antistereotyping act of healing, countering the demonization—what I am calling witchification—of girls and women who are seen as "deviant" in the popular imagination; it is also a contemporary reclamation of the witch and her knowledge in the everyday, a reading of the Grimms' and other fairy tales for alternative desires and enchantments, a reaching for a longer history of folk and fairy tales in Europe rooted in pagan belief systems.[37] In fairy-tale studies, this reading goes hand in hand with Kay Stone's *Some Day Your Witch Will Come* (2008) and Kay Turner's and Pauline Greenhill's critical project in *Transgressive Tales: Queering the Grimms* (2012);[38] and it resonates in folklore studies with Sabina Magliocco's analysis in *Witching Culture* (2004) of how contemporary Pagans use folktales to reenchant our commodified world.

Adaptations, Linda Hutcheon reminds us, engage in an ongoing dialogue with the past that creates "the double pleasure of the palimpsest: more than one text is experienced—and knowingly so" (2006, 116). The fourth story in Donoghue's collection, "The Tale of the Apple," extensively engages with the well-known fairy tale of "Snow White" (ATU 709). To knowing readers, the first scene in her adaptation announces Donoghue's revisitation of the Grimms' version in particular: "As the story went, my mother sat one day beside an open window looking out over the snow" (43).[39] The image (which is also in Walt Disney's ever-popular movie based on the Grimms and is often pictured in illustrated children's versions, such as Trina Schart Hyman's 1974 beautiful book) is familiar enough that we expect the three drops of blood and the queen's formulaic wish to follow—and they do. However, in this case "as the story went" refers not to the authoritative version of "Snow White" or to popular cultural memory, but to the family story the queen's child will hear over and over again from the maid who raises her. And in this telling, the queen's speech act is not a wish but a prophecy of self-replication that points to her own lack of fulfillment: "The daughter I carry will have hair as black as ebony, lips as red as blood, skin as white as snow. What will she have that will save her from my fate?" (44).

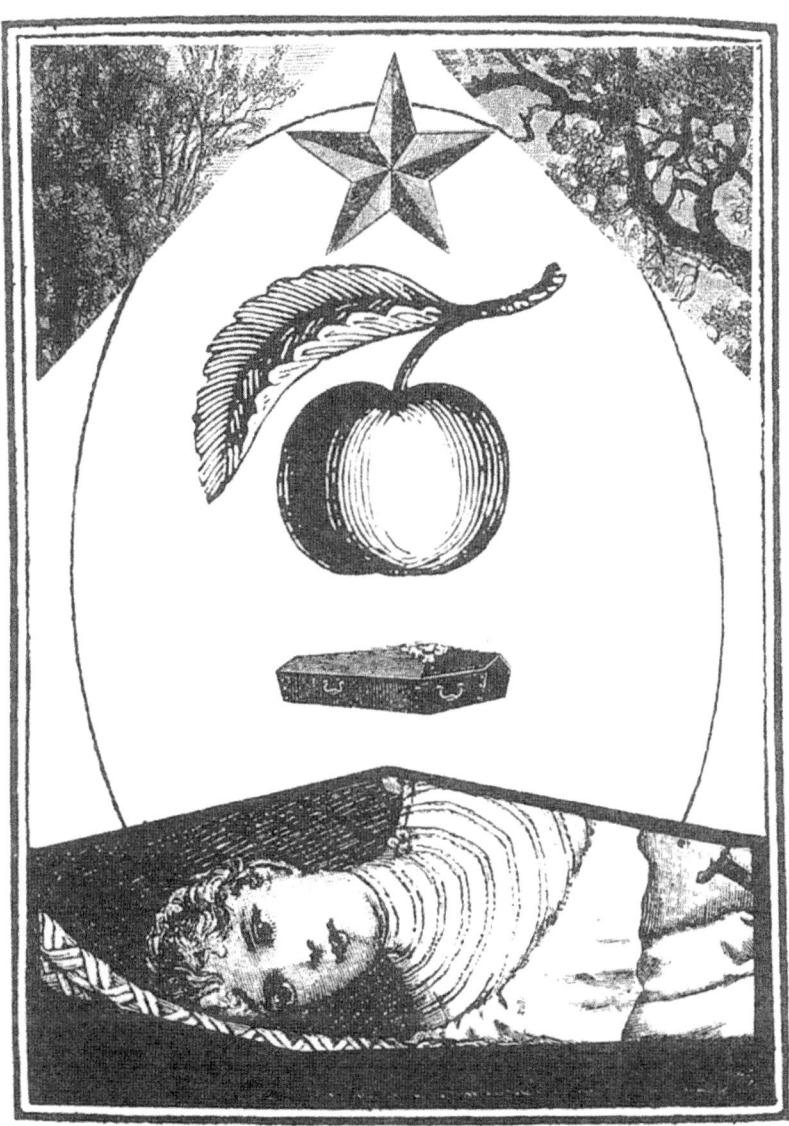

FIGURE 2. "The Tale of the Apple" in *Kissing the Witch* (1997). Illustrator anonymous. Image from *Kissing the Witch* by Emma Donoghue (Hamish Hamilton, 1998). Copyright © Emma Donoghue, 1997. Reproduced by permission of Penguin Books Ltd. Illustrator unknown.

PLATE 9. Steven Gin, "Reading *Kissing the Witch* Intertextually" (2). Courtesy of Steven Gin, adapted from his Flash presentation (2011).

The first-person adult narrator of "The Tale of the Apple" recounts the maid's tale and the queen's story to illustrate her own ties with both women. She and Donoghue call attention to this triangulated connection from the very start: "The maid who brought me up told me that my mother was restless" (43). This one sentence already queers the typical (and dysfunctional) nuclear family of fairy tales and points to an alternate economy of caring and "intergenerational collaborations" (Martin 2010). Introducing "Snow White" as a tale told by women also expands its web of relations for the reader as well and regenders the telling.

By choosing to begin her story with and from a female genealogy of tales and tellers, the narrator as a grown woman signifies not her fall into formulaic expectations—the innocent Snow White who inevitably becomes the seductive and then labored-with-children Eve (the one that Dina Goldstein captures in her "Fallen Princesses" photography)—but the start of, and the impetus for, her transformation as the I-character. Her own tale reminds us of the Grimms' but is hardly founded on it.[40]

In her allusion to and departure from the Grimms' versions of "Snow White," Donoghue sets up her readers to recognize how our expectations are based on hegemonic uses of the fairy tale and its gendered scripts in the culture industry today, where—whether we are familiar with the Grimms or not—advertisements and Disney products, from princesses to wedding packages, lead us to expect the fairy-tale alliance of fantasy and romance as well as its specifically gender-marked wish fulfillment, that of wedding and childbearing, the regulated pathways of which are made to appear natural. It is no accident that in Walt Disney's 1937 film, Snow White received "magic" help from birds and bunnies even to accomplish her domestic tasks. In this world, it is "natural" for the queen to persecute Snow White, just as it is for everyone else she encounters in the forest to help her because they conflate her outer beauty with her pure nature and natural purity. In the Grimms' tale of Snow White, the talking mirror explicitly produces such naturalized magic, which there and also in Disney's iconic film traps the queen "in the spectacle of male illusions" (Zipes 2011, 116), setting the rules of the game in which the two beauties must compete.

Perhaps not surprisingly, just as in Angela Carter's "The Snow Child," there is no magic mirror in Donoghue's adaptation of "Snow White." Rather, in "The Story of the Apple," it is the king who asks his daughter and her new stepmother, "which of you is the fairest of them all?" (46). The two young women, who are sitting "cross-legged" on the bed, "trying how each earring looked against the other's ear" (46), stare at each other. Following the king's question, the potential friendship that was beginning to develop between the two young women is shattered, and their eyes are "like mirrors set opposite each other, making a corridor of reflections, infinitely hollow" (47). Vanessa Joosen remarks, "the mirrors in the women's eyes function as an intertextual marker, drawing attention to the object that speaks the father's words in the traditional tale" (2011, 222). In these mirrors, the two women are reduced to competing beauties; the stepmother who is expected to produce a male heir wins this round. Interrogating these mirrors, not for what they reveal but for the hollowness they frame as well as for what they leave out, becomes in Emma Donoghue's tale a critical comment on the violence or regulatory power of heteronormativity in fairy tales. The narrator in "The Tale of the Apple" admits, "I know now that I would have liked her if we could have met as girls, ankle deep in a river. . . . I could have loved her if, if, if. . . . But I knew from the songs that a stepmother's smile is like a snake's" (46).

As the well-known story goes, the snake invites the mythical woman—be it Eve or Snow White—to take a bite of the apple, and as the title of Donoghue's tale announces, the apple is key symbolically to the transformative power of her adaptation. Contesting, from the beginning of "The Tale of the Apple," the association with the Garden of Eden is the fruit the maid would bring the princess, the I-character, when she was little: "It was the maid who cared for me as I grew. Every autumn in her pocket she brought me the first apple from the orchard. This was not the mellow globe they served my father a month later, but the hardly bearable tang of the first ripening, so sharp it made me shudder" (44). When, much later in the tale, the stepmother, like the witch in "Snow White," offers the I-character an apple, she ambiguously remarks: "there was nothing of the mother about her" (57). We expect the princess to choke, and she does. When she bites into it, the I-narrator tells her audience, "fear and excitement locked in struggle in my throat, and blackness seeped across my eyes. I fell to the ground" (57).

But in the end, there is no poisoned apple, only—when coughing it up, she comes to—the girl's refusal to accept the woodsmen's and our own ready-made *misrecognition* of the apple as poison. Rather than spitting the juicy apple out, she bites down, and its sharp tang tells her it is "the first apple of the year from [her] father's orchard" (58). No icon, this apple is more of an indexical sign, pointing to the stepmother's recognition of the protagonist's specific experience of how "the hardly bearable tang of the first ripening" had made her shudder (44). This apple is the stepmother's offer that they should care for each other and share in the excitement of a new relationship. Strengthened by this new knowledge, the protagonist of "The Tale of the Apple" turns away from the woodsmen who want to take her to some other kingdom where "they'll know how to treat a princess" (58) and starts walking toward the woman who has reawakened her desire for first experiences. Learning to decode the script that her own life had started to enact turns her refusal to compete with the other woman into the beginning of a different story, the promise of an alternate set of relations.

Donoghue's "old tales in new skins," as the American edition tags them, deliver neither the magic nor the HEA ending that are commonly perceived as the signature marks of the fairy-tale genre. If the Grimms and Disney, together with Andersen and Perrault, have in popular cultural memory been made to stand for all fairy tales, Donoghue shows how their endlessly self-reproductive images and relations can be interrupted by expanding their "what if?" moments (as Hennard Dutheil de la Rochère elucidates in her reading of "The Tale of the Shoe" [2009a]) and transforming them into a "matrix of possibilities" (Kukkonen 2008, 271).

At the same time, by drawing on de Beaumont's "Beauty and the Beast" (ATU 425C) for "The Tale of the Rose" and on Marina Warner's *From the Beast to the Blonde*'s critical work for "The Tale of the Witch" (the thirteenth tale, for which the author claims no fictional pre-text), Donoghue also shows how that "matrix of possibilities" has been active all along, in women's written fairy tales.[41] It is—and aptly so—in "The Tale of the Rose," after all, that the Beauty-like protagonist realizes the masked "beast" is not an ogre or troll, but a woman, and

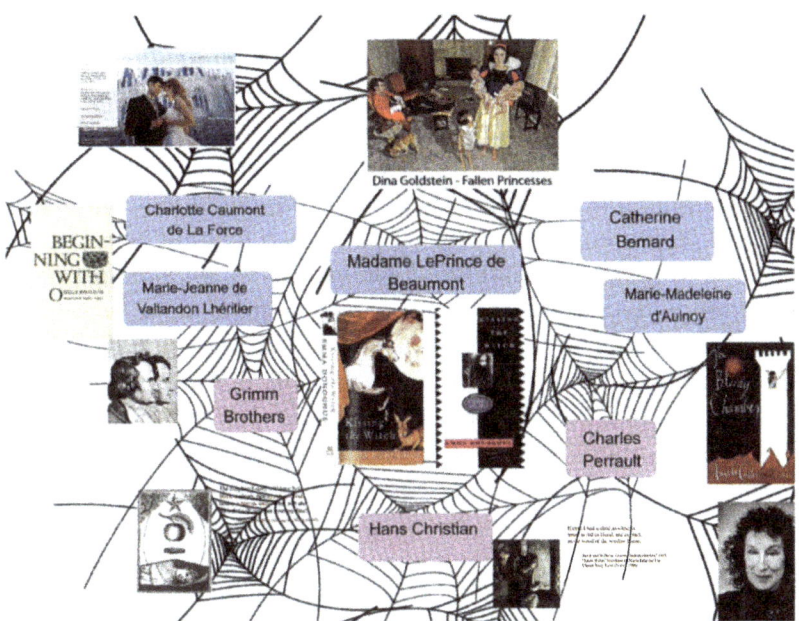

PLATE 10. Steven Gin, "Reading *Kissing the Witch* Intertextually" (3). Courtesy of Steven Gin, adapted from his Flash presentation (2011). Dina Goldstein's photograph reproduced with permission of the artist, www.dinagoldstein.com/fallenprincesses.com.

that theirs "was a strange story, one [she] would have to learn a new language to read, a language [she] could not learn except by trying to read the story" (39).[42] By relocating symbols, desires, and plots "back" to embodied experiences—different but shared in the storytelling—the women narrators learn to read their "strange" life stories, to counter the fated scripts that call them deviant with alternative literacies of desire.

In *Twice Upon a Time: Women Writers and the History of the Fairy Tale*, Elizabeth Wanning Harries reads Donoghue's tales as performing what the poet Olga Broumas (who also rewrote fairy tales and myths in the key of women's same-sex desires in *Beginning with O*, 1977) called "the art of transliteration," the invention "of a language for the experiences that cannot be caught in any language that already exists" (Harries 2001, 135). Harries also writes eloquently and persuasively about the intertextual connections of Donoghue's *Kissing the Witch* with the tradition of "complex" fairy-tale narratives by French aristocratic women in the late seventeenth and early eighteenth centuries.

The complex tales of Marie d'Aulnoy, Marie-Jeanne L'Héritier, Catherine Bernard, and others were embedded in a larger fiction. This framing, we know, characterizes not only the *Panchatantra* and *The Arabian Nights* but also Straparola's *The Pleasant Nights* and Basile's *Tale of Tales* or *Pentamerone*; the *conteuses*, unlike Perrault whose compact or stand-alone tales are now the standard model for fairy tales, continued in this tradition (Harries 2001, 104–7). Explicitly framed within storytelling situations where the fictive narrators have bodies, histories, motives, and philosophies, the tales the *conteuses* wrote are in conversation with one another. Like the conversational framing of the *conteuses*, Donoghue's mise-en-scène of storytelling on the page encourages us to read the tales not as universal truths—a move that many in fairy-tale studies also advocated, which extends Donoghue's fairy-tale web even further—but as performances, "instructions" that in everyday contexts map out varied possibilities, arguments, and perspectives.

Within the tales, this multiplicity is clearest at the level of story or events where Donoghue's individuated protagonists embody different desires and project themselves into a range of future scenarios. "The desires encoded in the stories are as varied as the tellers themselves. They include same-sex sexual desire between women, heterosexual desire of women for men, desires for autonomy and freedom, and desires for individual subjectivity, for belonging, and for knowledge" (Orme 2010a, 117). In "The Tale of the Rose," which precedes "The Tale of the Apple," the protagonist chooses to live with the masked woman whose beauty she has come to appreciate, whether the stories told about them identify them as "a beast and a beauty," "two beauties," or "two beasts" (Donoghue 1999, 40). But romance or sexual desire is not the issue in "The Tale of the Handkerchief," which follows "The Tale of the Apple" and adapts the Grimms' "The Goose Girl" (ATU 533), one of the least well-known pre-texts in the collection. In the Grimms' pre-text, the socially conservative plot naturalizes the princess/maid hierarchy: the maid may dress like the princess, and the princess may work temporarily as a goose girl, but her royal nature will in the end become visible, and the usurper punished. Donoghue's tale, in contrast, is not so much about social order as it is about the two girls' temperaments and their wanting different kinds of freedoms: one from class obligations, the other from hard work. The princess turned goose girl says to the woman who has taken over her privilege: "I have found the fields are wider than any garden. I was always nervous, when I was a princess, in case I would forget what to do. You fit the dresses better; you carry it off" (74).[43] Both young women refuse "to follow the paths mapped out for [them] by their mothers and their mothers before them"

(80); by acting on their different ambitions, they do not necessarily get a happy ending, but they are no longer competing with each other.

While the storytelling in *Kissing the Witch* involves women only, and the narrators, focalizers, and main characters are female, they each resist hetero-patriarchal scripts in different ways (Martin 2010, 19–20). Their choices for independence do not, however, lead to the HEA or to stable identities,[44] but to more challenges and transformations, as they find themselves crossing into and resisting other plots. The final line of "The Tale of the Shoe"—the tale in which the Cinderella-like girl rejects the prince for the older and wondrous woman who showed her "how to waltz without getting dizzy" (6)—intimates an ephem-eral or tentative happiness: "She then took me home, or I took her home, or we were both somehow taken to the closest thing" (8). For YA readers who for vari-ous reasons do not identify with the ubiquitous Disney princesses, Donoghue's tales offer nonnormative possibilities for coming-of-age experiences, including those of coming out, but no set paths or utopias. Recognizing these possibilities for the characters within the text emerges from the "mouth to mouth" exchange to which Jennifer Orme's essay cleverly refers.

The protagonist's savoring of the "first apple" in "The Tale of the Apple" is certainly not the only way in which Donoghue's collection suggests that we revalue orality, whether it be the site of sexual desire, the sense of taste, the act of kissing, or the experience of storytelling. The twelve storytelling vignettes that connect the tales in the collection are both formulaic *and* situated in place and time. Let's take the ones preceding and following "The Tale of the Apple." These conversations link the tales in the collection to one another and further expand our reading of each female figure beyond her "once-upon-a-time" story. As a result of the first conversation, the character who in "The Tale of the Rose" wore the "faceless mask" of "the beast" in order to escape "the things queens are supposed to do" (36) becomes the I-narrator of "The Tale of the Apple." In the next conversation that follows her tale-telling of events that took place ear-lier in her life, she becomes the listener when her stepmother tells the story of how, as a young maid determined to have a crown, she had impersonated the "true" princess bride. All of Donoghue's thirteen characters, to adapt Tzvetan Todorov's insight about *The Arabian Nights*, are "narrative women," but they are also willing and active listeners.

Furthermore, even if each of them tells one story only as her own, that story is filled with other tales, and each woman belongs to more than one story, as others' tales continue to transform her. These narrative women are not weaving or being woven into a single script. She, who could have been Snow White and

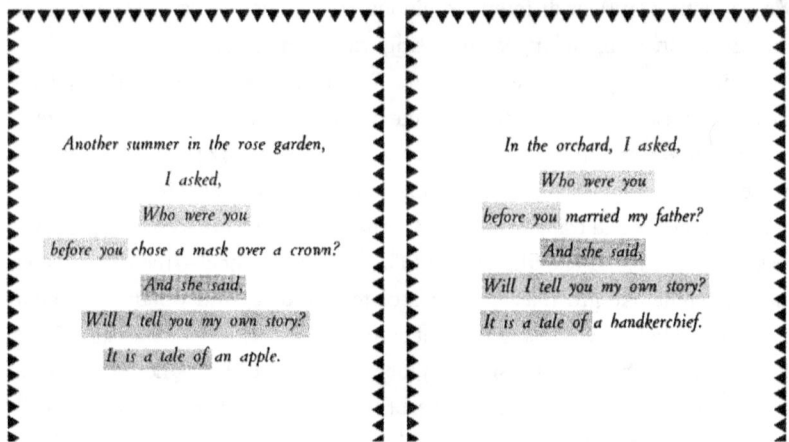

PLATE 11. Steven Gin, "Reading *Kissing the Witch* Intertextually (4). Courtesy of Steven Gin, adapted from his Flash presentation (2011).

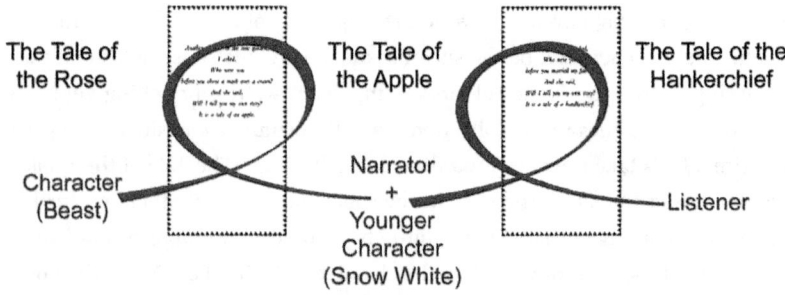

PLATE 12. Steven Gin, "Reading *Kissing the Witch* Intertextually" (5). Courtesy of Steven Gin, adapted from his Flash presentation (2011).

instead asked her stepmother "who were you before you married my father" (Donoghue 1999, 59), sometime later in her life started wearing a mask and was said to be the Beast, and then became Beauty for a while at least in the eyes of another Beauty—who then transformed into a bird ("The Tale of the Bird"). She who as a child had listened to her maid telling her about her mother's restlessness then listened as an adult to her stepmother's story, and partly in response to these stories "chose a mask over a crown" (41). "The narrator in each case is

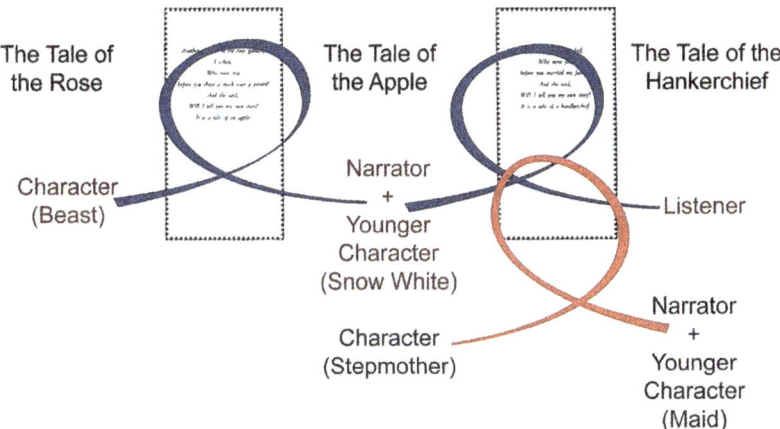

The Tale of the Rose

The Tale of the Apple

The Tale of the Hankerchief

Character (Beast)

Narrator + Younger Character (Snow White)

Listener

Character (Stepmother)

Narrator + Younger Character (Maid)

PLATE 13. Steven Gin, "Reading *Kissing the Witch* Intertextually" (6). Courtesy of Steven Gin, adapted from his Flash presentation (2011).

the character as an older, wiser self" (Orme 2010a, 116), and allowing herself to be touched by the other women's stories enables that transformation. She is clearly not one or the same in any of these tales, which loop back and forth into one another, without coming to closure or happy ending. In turning a character from "The Tale of the Rose" into the I-narrator of "The Tale of the Apple," and that narrator into the listener of "The Tale of the Handkerchief" that is told by a character in "The Tale of the Apple," the storytelling loops take each narrator spiraling back in time to her earlier life experiences and each listener spiraling forward toward another transformation.

Each loop also takes us as readers spiraling forward toward the final and "new" tale, "The Tale of the Kiss," where the "witch" explains how, as a young redhead who refused to become the object of scorn just because she was barren, she went to live alone in a cave. There, instead of the freedom she sought, she found "power" (209). People, who brought her offerings, problems, and secrets, wanted a witch, someone in whom to invest power over their lives and, at the same time, keep separate from themselves and their community. And so she learned to be the witch they wanted, until a bold, restless girl broke her isolation with a kiss. . . . I am not going to retell what happens to the girl and the witch, but one of my responses as a reader of the tale is that kissing the witch can unmake her witchification, which in turn may result in my listening to and retelling fairy tales differently. In Donoghue's hypertextual (un)spinning of the fairy-tale web, what melts in the end is not the "beautiful wickedness" of the witch, but prejudice and the popular coding of spinster = lesbian = witch.

I have intertextually connected with *The Wizard of Oz* film, but I could have just as well made reference to Andrew Lang, whose colorful collection provides another link in the hegemonic history of the fairy tale that Donoghue's collection is an activist response to.

> To Frances,
> My mother and first storyteller,
> Who read me Andrew Lang's
> "Pinkel and the Witch"
> more times than she can bear
> to remember,
> this book is dedicated
> with gratitude and love.

Donoghue's dedication of the book, in fact, bridges Andrew Lang's "Pinkel the Thief" in the *Orange Fairy Book* with *Kissing the Witch* by retitling Lang's story "Pinkel and the Witch."[45] Donoghue's individuation of the witch as one of the tale's protagonists (rather than a simple antagonist not deserving of top billing) enacts a queer reading of the tale that is a necessary step for another witch to become narrator in Donoghue's "The Tale of the Kiss."

In Lang's story, the witch is simply a resource: it is assumed that whatever her power, it can and should be taken from her; the witch's gold is there to be stolen; Pinkel is rewarded for being a "great knave" and seems proud of it even as he calls her "dear mother" (Lang 1968, 159). How did the "witch" come into possession of the golden lantern, goat with golden horns and bells, and her golden cloak? Who is she? Was she always a witch? And what about her daughter, who lives with the witch on a small but wondrously lit island? These questions have no place in the narrative economy of "Pinkel the Thief," but they are the catalyst for Donoghue's storytelling. Stripping the witch figure of her assumed evil, *Kissing the Witch* develops the hypothesis that "perhaps it is the not being kissed that makes her a witch" (209) and seeks to undo social prejudice by investigating her story—"Climbing to the witch's cave, I called out, Who were you before you came to live here?"—and by giving her a voice as narrator of her own story: "And she said, Will I tell you my own story? It is a tale of a kiss" (205). Donoghue's adaptations voice the tales of many witchlike or stepmother figures in the first person, not as vindications but as openings in a call-and-response situation toward transformation and new collaborations. Responding to "Pinkel the Thief," where the exploitation of the witch (a powerful mother figure to take from) is naturalized, Donoghue's stories reconnect us with the luminosity of the witch's gold as love rather than material riches.

Just as significantly, Donoghue's dedication acknowledges "with gratitude and love" her mother's reading of Lang's fairy tale to her when she was a child. Thus this paratextual storytelling loop extends the female genealogy of tellers and tales that Donoghue traces inside the book to her own life experience. Mediating and transforming the iconic and regulatory "once-upon-a-time" stories, the tensile strength of these ♀ storytelling loops proves strong in the whole collection as it does in "The Tale of the Apple." It is ultimately in the storytelling, and not in the single tale, that meaning emerges, and the telling is already plural and populated by various other stories, for the tellers as for the listeners. The final line of "The Tale of the Kiss" and of the book is "This is the story you asked for. I leave it in your mouth" (228). Receiving these stories calls for an embodied response (Orme's "chew on them, swallow them, spit them out, or pass them along with stories and kisses?" [2010a, 129]), coming into new knowledge of oneself in relation to others, and telling another tale or more on the part of each reader from her experience with emplotment and transformation.

This leads me to read Donoghue's collection in critical dialogue also with Basile's seventeenth-century *The Tale of Tales* or *Pentamerone*, where the tellers are (in Nancy Canepa's translation) "ten women, the best of the city, the ones who appeared to be the most expert and quick-tongued. They were: lame Zeza, twisted Cecca, goitered Meneca, big-nosed Tolla, hunchback Popa, drooling Antonella, snout-faced Ciulla, cross-eyed Paola, mangy Ciommetella, and shitty Iacova" (Basile 2007, 41–42). These are expert storytellers, but they are also deformed subalterns, outsiders at the court where they perform. In the book, these witchified women comment on one another's tales, but these brief interludes do not erode the social prejudice that, no matter how wonderful his tales and style are, informs the structure and ideology of Basile's collection. Their stories in the end lead to the restoration of Princess Zoza as Prince Taddeo's wife and the death sentence of Lucia, the dark-skinned slave who had usurped her place, but the ten witchified old women are not even mentioned in the conclusion of the *Pentamerone*. Like them, Donoghue's narrators are raised in a world that— because of their sexuality, class, gender, mental abilities ("The Tale of the Cottage"), inability to reproduce, beliefs, and emotions—subordinates or alienates them from what they know and want; in Basile's and Donoghue's texts, these narrators' tales carry alternate knowledge as well as transformative potential. However, in contrast to Basile's textual storytellers, the powers of the thirteen

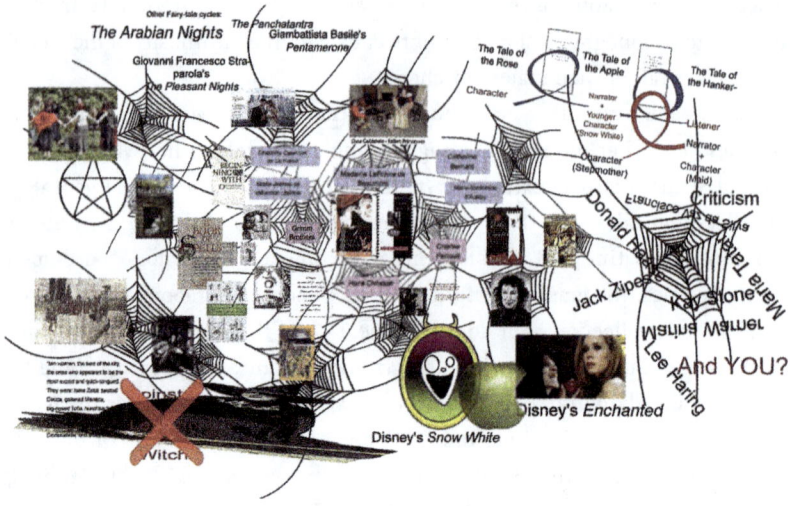

PLATE 14. Steven Gin, "Reading *Kissing the Witch* Intertextually" (7). Courtesy of Steven Gin, adapted from his Flash presentation (2011). Dina Goldstein's photograph reproduced with permission of the artist, www.dinagoldstein.com/fallenprincesses.com.

tellers in Donoghue's collection are not simply instrumental to the transformation of the one chosen heroine.

The narrators-storytellers in *Kissing the Witch* form a different kind of witches' coven, where "witches, crones, and wicked stepmothers are transformed, as are their supposed victims" (Stone 2008, 289). This coven is perhaps inspired by and, in the reading process, strongly linkable with the eclectic beliefs and practices of today's Neo-Paganism. In her 2004 observer-participant study of this movement, Sabina Magliocco focuses on how it freely draws on folk practices and discourses that "preserved elements of the [European] pre-Enlightenment magico-religious worldview and practice" (2004, 9) for transformative rituals. In particular, her research shows how North American Neo-Pagans today turn to folk and fairy tales as rife with "alternative ways of knowing" that have been marginalized as superstition, with symbols to meditate on and transform, with experiences of the world as enchanted and animate. The tales, especially when they are retold in Neo-Pagan rituals, are seen as containing "the instructions for a transformative journey" (143), not based on Jungian abstractions, but on the experience of practitioners.[46] Analogously, we readers of Donoghue's characters' embodied experiences and her wiser narrators' reflections are led to connect anew with the symbols they deploy and to learn from the witching and empowering (as opposed to witchifying) effect these storytellers have on one another.

The process of reading intertextually can only be open ended, but I hope to have suggested how the fairy-tale web that Emma Donoghue's *Kissing the Witch* participates in and transforms is multivocal and multimedial, and its intertextual links do not refer back to the canonized Perrault-Grimms-Disney triad as *central* pre-texts. Donoghue's adaptive practices are not unique but, among contemporary fairy-tale adaptations, *Kissing the Witch* distinguishes itself by relocating coming-of-age transformations in a nonnormative and varied syntax of desire and knowledge. From this imaginative space, *Kissing the Witch* lovingly queries and queers the genre in ways that prime us to learn a new language for reading fairy tale intertextuality, what Turner and Greenhill call "queer(y)ing tales" (2012, 3).

Reading "Sinalela" Intertextually: Relocation, Take #3

"Two analytical issues guaranteed to raise questions, eyebrows, hackles, and other bits and bobs are *sex* and *nationhood*, and both issues elicit a wide range of intellectual and emotional responses" (xiii), write Daniel Heath Justice and James H. Cox to introduce "Queering Native Literature, Indigenizing Queer Theory" as a themed cluster for the fall 2008 issue of *SAIL: Studies in American Indian Literatures*. No matter how much the Disneyfied fairy tale may disavow it, sex and nationalism have long been recognized as significant subtexts in and motivations for the production and reception of folk and fairy tales. In Dan Taulapapa McMullin's *fa'afafine* adaptations of "Cinderella" and other folk/fairy tales, these themes come to the foreground or the surface—just as "while [Sinalela] was washing dishes, / Out of the sink popped a one-eyed fish" (McMullin 2004, 19)—from a queering perspective that rests on both Samoan traditions of gendering and *fāgogo* (night or bedtime informal stories told in the home).[47]

An award-winning Samoan American painter, media artist, and writer, Dan Taulapapa McMullin tells various "Sinalela" tales.[48] They range from *Sinalela* (2001), which he describes as "a video short . . . shot in Samoa in 2001, a version of the Cinderella story but with fa'afafine" (McMullin 2003, 115); to the poem, "The One-Eyed Fish," where "Once upon a time there was a faafafine named Sina. . . . The stepsisters changed Sina's name to Sinalela / Which means / 'That Sina!'" (113); to another poem, "Sinalela and the One-Eyed Fish," in which once again Sinalela asks "One-eyed-fish, one-eyed fish, take me to my Prince!" (McMullin 2004, 19) and is suddenly transformed; to "Auntie Sinavela," a short

PLATE 15. *Sinalela*, directed by Dan Taulapapa McMullin (2001). Production photo courtesy of Dan Taulapapa McMullin.

story based on an English-language translation of the Grimms' "Cinderella" (and to be included in his collection in progress, "Ponopono Girls School Dropout and Other Stories"), which begins: "There was once a fa'afafine named Sinavela and this is her story."[49]

In all iterations, the ending is a happy one, but not the commercialized HEA. In the short film, we see that, thanks to the one-eyed fish or the "aiku spirits," Sinalela is with the "Prince"; Sinalela says: "He lives in San Francisco, but he has nice tattoos." In the poems, Sinalela has become a spider who in the end, seeing "the beauty of Ui" [then Maui] "drifting in the water near the shore" transforms into

The spider tattoo on Maui's hand,	The spider tattoo on Maui's hand,
And there Sinalela lived,	There to dwell
Happily	Happily
Ever	Ever
After.	After.
(2003, 114)	(2004, 20)

This "happily ever after" is a different kind of writing or love-letter writing on the body. In Albert Wendt's words, "tatauing is part of everything else that is the people, the aiga, the village, the community, the environment, the cosmos.

It is a way of life that relates the tufuga ta tatau to the person being tatued and to their community and history and beliefs to do with service, courage, masculinity, femininity, gender, identity, sexuality, beauty, symmetry, balance, aptness and other art forms and the future because a tatau or a malu is for the rest of your life and when you die, your children will inherit its reputation and stories, your stories, stories about you and your relationships" (Wendt 2009, 89).[50] The resolution of Sinalela's story anchors itself to a way of life that has a history and moves into a future that will tell different stories. I am not attempting to explain this, but to highlight how Wendt and McMullin theorize a paradigm shift, a located system of knowledge that McMullin's short movie and poems also enact: "Without relationship there is no identity" (McMullin, 2011a, 82).

In each version, Sinalela is a *fa'afafine*. The movie and "Sinalela and the One-Eyed Fish" do not refer to Sinalela as *fa'afafine*; rather, visually or verbally, they let the protagonist's desires and behaviors suggest it.

"*Sinalela* is a three-minute video about drag queens in Samoa. In Samoa we use the term fa'afafine to mean "the-way-of-a-woman," (fa'a = way; fafine = woman). Lately we also use the term mala, which could mean queer. I prefer fa'afafine because it is intersexual. Fa'afafine refers to gender expression, not necessarily to sexuality. For that reason, straight men who sometimes sleep with fa'afafine consider themselves straight, not bisexual. This is a good thing if you're fa'afafine." From Dan Taulapapa McMullin's exhibit *Coming of Age in Amelika* (fall 2001) at the A/P/A Gallery at NYU.

"The standard practice among fa'afafine (MTF) and fa'afatama (FTM) is that one's sexual partners are 'straight': fa'afafine will sleep with straight men, and fa'afatama with straight women. Most fa'afafine do not see themselves as women, but also do not identify as gay men" (113). From the Artist's Note that accompanies "The One-Eyed Fish" (2003).

"The procedure being a separation of the prefix *fa'a*, meaning to cause or be alike, and *fafine*, meaning woman. The overall being the position fafine and the action fa'a, and the position fa'a and the action fafine." From Dan Taulapapa McMullin's "Fa'afafine Notes: On Tagaloa, Jesus, and Nafanua" (2011).

In "This Bridge of Two Backs: Making the Two-Spirit Erotics of Community," Sophie Mayer comments on how McMullin's "Sinalela and the One-Eyed Fish" challenges readers to understand *fa'afafine*, without explaining it, "except to affirm that this form of two-spiritedness is culturally specific and carries its own mythic, cultural, and social freight" (Mayer 2008, 19).

Thus to move out of the kitchen where Sinalela is confined to washing tin dishes and "asked to perform impossible tasks with the make-up box" on her stepmother (who is an ogre [Mayer 2008, 19]), the protagonist draws for help (the one-eyed fish) and joy (Maui) on the sea. "Moana was the Ocean / The ocean's name was Moana / The whole world was Moana" (McMullin 2004, 5), writes McMullin in another poem, "The Old Way," connecting to Polynesian belief systems, to human relations with a powerfully animated nature that are filled with transformations and interdependence.[51] "The appearance of Sina's lover is presaged by a one-eyed fish, and the fa'afafine's relation with the natural world suggests that fluidity across genders and sexualities is part of a continuum in which not only human but also animal, plant, and mineral bodies are intrinsically related and can thus transform into one another" (Mayer 2008, 19). Another of McMullin's transformative tales, "Monsieur Cochon," shows how this fluidity has been constrained, but persists in "strange" ways. When the widow Fua and Mister Pig "made love under the trees" they became respectively a "lovely young woman" and a strong man, but "one day, after they made love, her husband, Monsieur / Cochon, did not turn back into a pig again. He remained a / man and stood dumbfounded. He was only truly happy / when he was a pig listening to the sea all day. . . . Madame Cochon was not happy either, she missed her love / pig, but a husband at home? She thought she was long / done with that" (McMullin 2011b, 39–40). In this playful reversal of the "Animal Groom" tale, Fua and Monsieur Cochon agree, " 'We must find a taulaitu,' Madame said, 'A witch doctor / can turn you back to a pig.' / But times had changed. The missionaries had burned all / the taulaitu up. There was only Fa'api left. / It was a strange creature Fa'api who showed up at their/ doorway looking like Pearl Bailey with a voice like Louis Armstrong" (40). More transformations follow.

Sinalela's connection with the ocean and a more fluid world can only be a *re*-connection given the colonial history of Samoa. Let's keep in mind: the London Missionary Society started to Christianize Samoans in 1830, and this was a violent process, conducted under the protection of British gunships; British, German, and US governments and businesses have had strong interests in Samoa, resulting in the partition of the islands in 1899 into a German Samoa (turned over to New Zealand—and thus the British Empire—during World War I and independent since 1962) and an American Samoa; the islands in Amerika/ Amelika Samoa, as Samoans call it, are since 1900, the "unincorporated and unorganized territory of the United States."[52]

And so McMullin's relocation of "Cinderella" to a Samoan specificity links also with Epeli Hau'ofa's famous call to decolonize lands, economies, and minds: "We [Pacific Islanders] are the sea, we are the ocean, we must awake to this ancient truth and together use it to overturn all hegemonic views that aim ultimately to confine us again, physically and psychologically, in the tiny spaces that we have resisted accepting as our sole appointed places" (Hau'ofa 2008, 39). Struggling against the internalization of "derogatory and belittling views of indigenous cultures" (Hau'ofa 2008, 28) and fighting for political sovereignty are strongly related to undoing "the sexual Puritanism, capitalism, and heteronormativity that necessarily accompanied colonization and that continue as the dominant cultural form in postcolonial societies" (Mayer 2008, 3). When McMullin's Sinalela goes to the *poula*, it is not the ball that Perrault's and the Grimms' heroines went to, but a "night dance" (as the word translates into English) that in Samoa "has the sense of laughter or joy, echoed in *'ula*, or lei garland, and *'ula*, or crimson, golden, and joyous. But for the monotheists night was heathen, the time of the *pouliuli*, po/night, uli/black, the darkest times before Eurocentric monotheism" (McMullin 2011a, 90).[53]

One of the ways in which McMullin's writing counters the contemporary homophobia of an Americanized Samoa and globalized popular culture is to offer Sinalela a flamboyantly alter-Native joyous ending.[54] Another is the foregrounding—in multiple ways—of orality as McMullin experiments with intermediality and narrative voice in his *fa'agogo* or *fāgogo*-anchored relocation of the fairy tale. These are some of the links I have become aware of.

One, the Samoan name "Sinalela" is an example (and not the only one) of the "specific type of complex visual and *aural* patterning" that Chadwick Allen calls "bilingual punning" (2007, 11, my emphasis) and identifies as a significant indigenizing methodology. The sound patterns remind us of slurred (pun intended) Cinderella, while the letters on the page refer us to Sina, who "in Samoa, has been the heroine of a vast number of stories and songs. As Hina, Sina or Ina, she is as prominent or more prominent than Maui in the stories of Polynesia" (McMullin 2001). Filled with folkloric resonance, the meanings of "Sinalela" are not reducible to what the stepsisters meant as the derogatory "That Sina!"[55] Two, when McMullin refers to "Cinderella" as a pre-text of the short movie *Sinalela* (2001), he is quick to specify that for him "the Cinderella story in Europe goes back to Psyche (Cinderella) and Aphrodite (the Stepmother) with references to the resurrection of Eros from Hades. The roots of the story go back to the Middle East, Egypt and Africa"; that he is thinking of "the Euro-Afro-Asian Cinderella story" (McMullin 2001). Three, referring to Richard Moyle's recordings of *fa'agogo* (the 1981 bilingual edition, but also the larger archive at Auckland University), McMullin wrote to me, "It's an amazing collection, I want to go back and just work with those recordings in future. The world of those stories inspired me more than the Grimm Bros story world. But both worlds are singular, one might say from the blood of the people, or spirit embodied" (e-mail communication, April 21, 2012).[56] Following up on his observation that fairy tales are "the oral tradition of women," he connected *fa'agogo* with storytelling at home: "my mother Lupelele, grandmother Sisipeni, and great grandmother Fa'asapa were all great storytellers, also my father Samuelu" (e-mail communication, April 24, 2012).

Four, like many contemporary adaptors of fairy tales, McMullin plays with narrative voice, in Stam's words, to "redistribute energies and intensities, provoke flows and displacements" (Stam 2005). While an external narrator tells the "One-Eyed Fish" and "Auntie Sinavela" tales, the other two are in the first-person: "My name is Sinalela and this is my movie" (*Sinalela* 2001 and "Sinalela and the One-Eyed Fish" in McMullin 2004, 19). "My movie": this is what the I-narrator says even in the poem (2004), thus evoking film as a powerful site for fantasy and emplotment. I find it significant how the I-narrator does its decolonizing work in the different media. In the poem, the I-narrator asserts a *fa'afafine* way of life to counter the authority of the customarily external narrator and also, as I mentioned earlier, to counter an individual and human-centered worldview. In the short film *Sinalela*, where the first-person narrative is conveyed through voice-over, we see the character, Sinalela, in action, but not speaking the words "My name is Sinalela." On screen, by taking on the authority of the customarily external narrator, Sinalela actually puts into action and performs her statement "and this is my movie."

■ ■ ■

All kinds of fairy-tale adaptations proliferate in today's fairy-tale web. In this chapter, I zoomed in on adaptations that enact a politicized challenge to the hegemonic tropes of the genre, from within the perspectives and frames of located knowledges, subjectivities, and histories that are commonly suppressed or colonized in cultural popular memory. I suggested how these adaptations perform a significant *relocation* of the genre in its normative conception and also how, within the process of reception, the fairy-tale web as a methodological field can further enable the critical decentering or provincializing of *the* European literary fairy-tale tradition. Hopkinson, Donoghue, and McMullin adapt the fairy tale to widely divergent social projects that are, however, interwoven by the reading practices that constitute the fairy-tale web, which encompasses but is not limited to the artists' own responses and experiences as well as those of their readers. I want to emphasize in closing how these adaptations are symptomatic of an emergent politics and poetics of wonder.

Articulating different historical, intercultural, and intertextual dynamics, the adaptations discussed in this chapter each start from the perspectives, geopolitical locations, and poetics that the normative fairy-tale genre and its Disney-fied magic dismiss or colonize. I hear the adaptors, from their distinct enunciative loci of "colonial difference" (Mignolo 2002b), asking: "When the fairy tale interpellates us today, which it does whether we want it to or not, what enables us culturally to respond without being diminished by its emplotment? What does the fairy tale offer us that can be used to decolonize our storyworlds and worlds?" These questions constitute one of the significant differences between these adaptations and others, whether they are part of the culture industry—where the reproduction of hegemonic hierarchies and economies of power continues to be the goal of adaptation—or they exhibit a postmodern poetics—in which case the double movement of the two questions may pull toward queering, but, as I explore this tension in chapter 3, more toward hybridizing rather than indigenizing or creolizing. In this framework, creolization, like indigenization, is not a general condition of postmodernity but rather "a convergence of cultures under forces of dominance and oppression" and a creative resource for subversion with a long history within this context (Haring 2012). In its broad sense, Hopkinson's, Donoghue's, and McMullin's reimaginings affect a form of queering, one that troubles sex/gender/sexuality normative categories[57] *and* relocates the genre geopolitically, socially, and generically. This relocation of the fairy tale activates links to contemporary belief systems that counter coloniality and/or heteronormativity, to wonder genres that have been primitivized or relegated to the "ethnographic present" (Fabian 1983), and to multiple storytelling traditions of transformation.

"If the Eurocentric imaginary of modernity has forgotten colonialism and relegated the colonized spaces to the periphery and to the past in its description of universal reality (even if that 'past' paradoxically exists in the 'present'), the task of the colonial difference is to reinscribe simultaneity" (Alcoff 2007, 87). These adaptations urge us to consider that when we say the fairy tale calls for "suspension of disbelief," we are not simply entering a fictional world; rather, this specific form of storyworld-making is always already mingling with and in competition with others that are neither simply confined to the past nor necessarily fictional. Legitimating and advancing suppressed and colonized knowledges and genres is part of the impetus for these activist responses to the fairy tale. I have thus focused on the valorization of orality in these adaptations, not as a nostalgic representation of premodern exchanges, but as an everyday practice for the transmission of knowledges and the envisioning of alternative futures. And I have emphasized how these adaptations relate the fairy tale to other narrative genres in ways that point to multiple genre systems and social systems, a poetics I also further explore in later chapters.

When it comes to narrative strategies and even the double movement of "exposure" (denaturalizing or erasing magic *and* making visible hidden or forgotten wonder), these adaptations are not that different from those by the Angela Carter generation. However, to read them primarily as self-reflexive transformations of the fairy tale as a Euro-American literary genre would be limiting, something of a continuation of our Western practice of understanding ourselves through the Other. If, as I have been arguing, these adaptations decenter the Perrault-Grimms-Disney normative canon to rethink the genre in its optative mood from counterhegemonic locations and in the interest of decolonizing the future, I see them as providing us scholars with opportunities for a critical reorientation toward decolonizing fairy-tale studies.

2

Double Exposures

Reading (in) Fairy-Tale Films

> Each of us constructs our own personal mythology from bits and
> fragments of information extracted from the media flow and
> transformed into resources through which we make sense of our
> everyday lives.
>
> HENRY JENKINS, *Convergence Culture*

In the twenty-first century, we tell, receive, retell, reject, recall, look for stories,
and are touched, surprised, repelled, inspired, and mobilized by them in what
Henry Jenkins has described as convergence culture, "where old and new media
collide, where grassroots and corporate media intersect, where the power of the
media producer and the power of the media consumer interact in unpredictable
ways" (2008, 2). Focusing on *American Idol, The Matrix, Star Wars,* and *Harry
Potter* as cases of transmedia storytelling in which fans are actively engaged
and involved, Jenkins's project discusses the relationship of media convergence
with participatory culture and collective intelligence, stressing the need to learn
and apply "new participatory skills through our relation to commercial entertainment" (257) and advocating a politics of "critical utopianism," which he
contrasts to the "critical pessimism" of media critics whose main thesis is that
media concentration can only disempower consumers.

Convergence culture, of course, does not guarantee democratizing media just
as even the largest media conglomerates do not fully control the affective economics, multiplatform avatars, and user-generated content of their entertainment

products. Story power flows—though not equally—in more than one direction. For instance, as I write this in January 2012, the first season of the ABC television series *Once Upon a Time* is being broadcast internationally, including in Canada, Argentina, the Philippines, Italy, and Estonia; within the United States, the series is not only watchable online thanks to Hulu.com, but ABC also has set up a constellation of "experiences" for its fans, including photos "behind the scenes" taken by Ginnifer Goodwin (who plays Snow White), bios for the various characters and actors, and Twitter and Facebook discussion of questions such as, "Who is the mysterious new stranger?" This transmedia or multiplatform storytelling is not simply ancillary to the show, because each activity can serve as a point of entry into the narrative and also contributes in specific ways to its knowledge and appreciation. Fan blogs have since then multiplied. This transmedia storytelling also encourages fans to "assume the role of hunters and gatherers, chasing down bits of the story across media channels, comparing notes with each other via online discussion groups, and collaborating" (Jenkins 2008, 21) to make meaning together of the *Once Upon a Time* storyworld.

Fans' reactions and responses surely influence writers and producers; at the same time, the series' producers are also setting up the terms or protocols of the "official" conversation. On their web page, Adam Horowitz, cocreator and executive producer, is quoted as stating, "*Snow White* was the first movie I saw as a child—and in many ways it is 'ground zero' for Fairy Tales . . . it was my introduction to storytelling"; interestingly, this is the "blurb" for the book *Once Upon a Time*, illustrated by Kevin Tong, available for purchase to "re-acquaint yourself with the stories and characters you know and love" and "bring your family together to rediscover the magic." Does this language sound familiar? It is no surprise perhaps since the highly diversified and powerful Walt Disney Company owns the ABC Television Group. And yet again, this does not mean that corporate convergence can or will gobble up viewers' and fans' imaginations, especially because—rather than in spite of the fact that—it capitalizes intertextually on allusions to much-loved-and-despised Disney fairy-tale films and princess merchandise as well as to the mythically popular TV show *Lost* (to which Horowitz and Ken Kitsis also contributed). Referring, somewhat sweepingly, to "folk culture" as emerging "in a context where creativity occurs on a grassroots level" (2008, 325), Jenkins asserts the significance of a "grassroots convergence" when he observes optimistically: "the modern mass media builds upon borrowings from folk culture; the new convergence culture will be built on borrowings from various media conglomerates" (141).

This chapter does not focus on fairy tales in social media or on fan culture.[1] Rather, my overall question is, how does thinking of the fairy-tale genre as a web whose hypertextual links participate in convergence culture impact my under-standing as a folklorist and cultural critic of the genre's remediation in today's films? Critics, bloggers, Facebook group discussants, fans, movie reviewers, we continue to wonder about the reasons for the recent proliferation of fairy-tale films.[2] For instance, in her online forum Breezes from Wonderland, scholar Maria Tatar comments on a March 2011 newspaper article:

> The reporter links the resurgence of interest in fairy tales to the success of Tim Burton's *Alice in Wonderland* film and to the fact that producers do not have to pay for the rights to these stories. I wonder if that's all there is to it. I think we may be giving these stories more air-time, letting them breathe as Arthur W. Frank puts it, in part because we need their power surges now more than ever. The mythical always stages a comeback in times of high anxiety about technology and the atrophy of our affective life. (http://blogs.law.harvard.edu/tatar/2011/03/07/grimm-hollywood)

In another blog, some fans responding to the post "Upcoming Fairy Tale Films" (January 20, 2012, www.sarahsawyer.com/2012/01/upcoming-fairy-tale-films/#comments) state they are happy with the trend, whatever its causes; others express concern that the trend increasingly foregrounds the "dark" and "disturb-ing" aspects of fairy tales.[3] As part of the discussion, the blogger comments, "I do think the current increased interest in fairy tales is a natural part of the heightened demand for all things speculative"; and

> I'm not sure what exactly sparked this heightened wave of interest. I know that the *Once Upon a Time* producers spoke of returning to fairy tale inspi-ration because fairy tales are about hope, which people need in troubled times. Perhaps there's also a component of looking for an economic sure thing. People are drawn to fairy tales, so if filmmakers borrow elements from these familiar stories, it is an instant audience hook.

Also focusing on economics, Jack Zipes addressed Emma Mustich's question, are these "dark fairy tales more authentic?" on Salon.com (August 20, 2011), by zooming in on the films' hype as a sales strategy: "They're trying to titillate you, to say that this is going to be *the* film that will expose the deep darkness, the profound darkness of these tales." For him, with the exception of a few films discussed in the final chapter of *The Enchanted Screen*, lamentably, "Hollywood, for the most part, has not really taken fairy tales seriously," no matter how many of them are being produced (Mustich). Comments to the interview ranged widely, passionately defending Disney, denouncing "consumerist garbage," and questioning the critic's authority based on his liking a particular film or not.

Is corporate greed alone responsible for this Hollywood fairy-tale deluge, or are these films responding to a need that young people today have for hope? This kind of polarizing question will yield few results. I agree that the fairy tale continues to be hypercommodified, and not just in the film industry, and that the fairy tale has, together with other fantasy or speculative genres, a renewed appeal today; however, I want to stress once again that the genre's social uses are—as they have been in the past—multiple and somewhat unpredictable, and that in today's convergence culture audiences are more knowledgeable and active participants.

At play in the currency of twenty-first-century fairy-tale adaptations is a (mis) match between the economy of profit, which makes stories that are not protected by copyright and come in (un)familiar versions particularly attractive to cultural conglomerates and writers, and what I have described as a new economy of knowledge, whereby today's young adult and adult public has acquired or has the potential to access a more complex and expansive sense of the "fairy tale" than what was generally available some thirty years ago. Increasingly, the culture industry can depend on and be challenged by adult audiences who want fairy-tale films to incorporate the elements *people know* were part of the pre-Disney genre, or whose immediate recognition of the fairy-tale icons of popular cultural memory gives rise to ambivalence, a double take that is not feeding simply into nostalgia, but moving outward to multiple links in the fairy-tale web. As small and nonunified samples of such knowledge communities, the thirty-one comments to Zipes's online interview I read included unsolicited references to *Undine*, Neil Jordan's *The Company of Wolves*, Aesop, Neil Gaiman, Joseph Campbell, Maria Tatar, Bill Ellis, Richard Dorson, the Motion Picture Production Code, African folktales, George MacDonald, *Star Wars*, Angela Carter, Clive Barker, Stephen Sondheim's *Into the Woods*, and more, as well as specific reactions to Tim Burton's *Alice in Wonderland* (2010), Jan Švankmajer's *Little Otik* (2000) and *Lunacy* (2005), competing fairy-tale versions by the Grimms and Perrault, and Japanese and South Korean filmic uses of "fairy tales and folklore."

Metacritically this chapter seeks to activate links in the transmedial web of folk and fairy tales to three specific points girding Jenkins's analysis of convergence culture: rather than replacing each other, "old and new media will interact in ever more complex ways" (Jenkins 2008, 6); "corporate convergence coexists with grassroots convergence" (18); and "fans envision a world where all of us can participate in the creation and circulation of central cultural myths" (267). To do so, I focus on the ways in which more traditional consumer and participatory protocols—those of "reading" tales—are harnessed in recent films to the production of fairy-tale enchantment, magic, horror, uncanniness, and wonder.

Ordinary people have historically participated in the creation and circulation of folk and fairy tales, and continue to do so, and, whether they want to control or unleash it, film producers and directors, among others, exhibit an awareness of this participatory process. I ask, how does the mise-en-scène of "reading" within fairy-tale films envision and solicit such participation? In other words, as I respond with enthusiasm to the assertion that convergence is at work within individual brains and in social as well as media interaction, my concern here is with the intertextual and multimedial ways in which the fairy tale continues to be narratively constructed as a powerful cultural myth within a single medium (film in this case) and what kinds of uses of the genre are thereby imagined for audiences to engage and participate in.

Take Disney's 2007 movie *Enchanted*.[4] When we first meet Morgan, the six-year-old is in a New York cab with her father, Robert, and she is unwrapping a present. She looks quite disappointed when it turns out to be the book *Important Women of Our Times*. "I know it's not that fairy-tale book you wanted, but this is better," says her father, a New York divorce lawyer played by Patrick Dempsey. Morgan (Rachel Covey) is interpellated here as a young reader who should grow out of fairy tales and find her role models in the likes of Marie Curie and Rosa Parks, not the princesses and fairies that don't belong in the "real" world. In the next scene, however, Morgan is not reading the book and instead jumps out of the cab because, as she tells Robert, she believes she's seen a princess. From then on, the unexpected presence in early twenty-first-century Manhattan of Giselle, the innocent persecuted heroine from the irony-free fairy-tale land of Andalasia (well impersonated by Amy Adams), works to disprove that book's sense of what makes women important.

To these scenes from *Enchanted* I juxtapose an early one in Guillermo del Toro's 2006 film *El laberinto del fauno*, known in English as *Pan's Labyrinth*. Young Ofelia (Ivana Baquero) is in a car with her mother (Ariadna Gil); it is 1944, and the action is set in Spain after the Civil War; they are being driven to a mill in the countryside where Ofelia's new stepfather, the fascist Captain Vidal (Sergi López), exercises his power to squelch local resistance to Franco's regime. Ofelia is reading a book of fairy tales illustrated by Arthur Rackham, but her mother takes the book away, urging the child to abandon such "nonsense."[5] Here Ofelia is interpellated as a reader who is "a bit too old" for fairy tales and should instead accept her mother's experience of poverty, dependence, and submission as governing her own lot in life. When the car stops and Ofelia wanders down the path a bit, she believes she's seen (something like) a fairy, but—in contrast to Morgan's father in *Enchanted* actually meeting Giselle—no one else does. Throughout the movie, no other character in the "real" storyworld sees any of the magical beings she encounters, and while Ofelia ends up heroically saving her baby brother's life, within that storyworld she does not disprove her mother's sense of women's place in a patriarchal world, nor does she keep her own life.

This chapter discusses three interrelated issues these scenes raise—the function of books, especially storybooks, in fairy-tale films; the positioning in relation to us, as spectators, of the child who reads or is being read to within these films; and the production of gendered emplotment within the cinematographic mise-en-scène of reading fairy tales—in order to foreground how superimposing storybook reading and film viewing on each other brings about a kind of double exposure of the fairy-tale genre and its ghostlike relationship to the social world. Both *Enchanted* and *Pan's Labyrinth* suggest that believing in the spirit of fairy tales can change how we live in the world. I ask, what is different about their projection on screen of how and why reading fairy tales matters? And how does the gendered projection of the girl child figure in this double exposure? To answer these questions and to get at what uses we, as film viewers, may be incited to make of the fairy-tale genre, I look to the representations of books and reading in *Enchanted*, *Pan's Labyrinth*, and two more fairy-tale films, *Bluebeard* (2009) and *Hansel and Gretel* (2007). The first pair of films adapts the fairy-tale's genre conventions and affect, and the others adapt and comment on well-known individual tales that do not, however, belong in the "Disney princess" repertoire.

READING TO (DE)COMMODIFY FAIRY-TALE MAGIC: *ENCHANTED* AND *PAN'S LABYRINTH*

The trope of storybooks in fairy-tale films is formulaic and, as Jack Zipes puts it in *The Enchanted Screen*, it is part of a recipe, a proven recipe that Walt Disney inaugurated with *Snow White and the Seven Dwarves* and continued to follow over and over again. The very first ingredient is: "Begin the film in the first frame with a beautiful gilded book that opens elegantly and a master voiceover as authoritative storyteller and make it seem as though the charming images represent a veritable fairy tale" (Zipes 2011, 88). Starting with the 1937 *Snow White*, book and movie opened in unison, and reading the words "ONCE UPON A TIME there was a lovely little Princess named Snow White" was the entry point to the fairy tale's animated storyworld. According to what Donald Haase calls The Law of Replication, this image of an open storybook became key to the success of Disney's technologically new magic on screen (Haase 2006, 223), visually appropriating the authority of classic fairy-tale authors like the Brothers Grimm and Charles Perrault (for *Snow White* and *Cinderella* respectively).

In later films, whether it is a reliable character such as Jiminy Cricket in *Pinocchio* (1940) or the female "once upon a time" narrator in *Cinderella* (1950), the storytelling voice-over aurally presents Disney, the adapter turned auteur, as *the* authorized reader or interpreter of the tale, which is still introduced as a book or something like it (for example, a stained glass paneled window replicating a picture book in *Beauty and the Beast*, 1991).[6] From the start, these formulaic framing devices marked the emergence of Disney as a transmedia brand name and sought to infantilize child and adult spectators, holding us captive to reading fairy tales as romance-with-happy-ending "enchantment" over and over again.[7]

By 2001, DreamWorks, Disney's rival in the animation industry, was openly and successfully parodying this recipe and storybook opening in its technologically innovative computer-generated imagery (CGI). The omniscient or trustworthy narrator gave way to the voice of a somewhat questionable character, with the wry intonations of Shrek (Canadian Mike Myers) in *Shrek* and the elevated inflections of Prince Charming (British-born Rupert Everett) in *Shrek 2* respectively conveying the ogre's reluctance to identify with the knight in shining armor and Charming's desperate eagerness to inhabit the role. In *Shrek the Third*, the storybook opening made way for a stage parody of the maiden-in-the-tower plot where, as long as Charming is cast as the idealized hero of the show, cheap special effects and theatrical props are foregrounded to further deflate him and his Disneyfied fairy-tale scenario. The audience within the film finds Charming's antics ridiculously "boring," the implication being that Disney's charm no longer works its magic even with its own. When they applaud the entrance of the Shrek impersonator on stage, the audience represented on screen—and we as viewers of the film—are invited to identify Shrek as the not-so-handsome but likeable hero of the new fairy-tale film and to recognize DreamWorks as heir to the throne of visual entertainment.

As the adage goes, "The King is dead! Long live the King!" While the image of the book is no longer there, the all-too-common alliance of fairy tale and romance still ends up shaping *Shrek*'s comic plot and emotional power. Rather than discarding the authority of the Disneyfied storybook on screen, these films find their new source of entertainment and authority by offering a carnival-mirror image of it, a magnified and distorted view of it from within. Audiences in our contemporary visual culture no longer need the magic images to lift off the pages of a storybook, but we as spectators are still held captive to their enchantment and are unequivocally positioned to identify with the desire for magic and a happy ending in the fairy tale's storyworld, however humorously they are presented.

That the Walt Disney Company learned from DreamWorks' play of double exposures undoubtedly shows in *Enchanted*, where the "Once Upon a Time" opening features a CGI "classic" Disney pop-up book in which the paper evil queen of "the magical kingdom of Andalasia" is a look-alike of Susan Sarandon, who plays the evil Narissa in the film; then from the forest in the pop-up book the camera zooms into the two-dimensionally animated storyworld of Giselle, the "special maiden" that Narissa will persecute; and the scene quickly bubbles into an affectionately robust self-parody, accentuated by the voice-over, this time Julie Andrews, with Disney cashing in on her association with *Mary Poppins*, *The Sound of Music*, *The Princess Diaries*, and *Shrek* too.[8] The ending of the film takes us back to the CGI pop-up book, with the iconic Cinderella shoe referring to the right fit and ending for all, and finally to parallel scenes or pages: one in Andalasia, the happy wedding of Prince Edward and the Cinderella-wanna-be Nancy from New York City; the other in Manhattan, a glimpse of the cheerful family life of Robert, Giselle, and Morgan.

Significant to achieving this balance between the animated fantasy of Andalasia and the live-action storyworld of Manhattan on screen is Morgan's dismissal of the book *Important Women of Our Time*, the scene with which I started. Morgan looks at some of its black-and-white photographs but clearly resists reading the book. The newly immigrated and culture-shocked Giselle is the one who later in Robert's living room is shown to skim if not read the book, and it clearly does not change her aspirations or, unlike her discovery of dating rituals, help her to achieve them. Her wishful dreams, as she acculturates just enough to New York City to use kitchen appliances and go shopping, continue to be pastel-hued scenes of sing-along domesticity, where she is the make-it-all-magically-better wife and mother. By the end of the film she has extended her dress-designing talents to starting the business of Andalasia Fashions, where her new family and all the girls who enjoy princess outfits can play out their participation in that fantasy world. As Linda Pershing and Lisa Gablehouse point out in their analysis of "Patriarchal Backlash and Nostalgia" in *Enchanted*, this scene of the little girls "dressed in pink and pastel princess and fairy costumes, excitedly exploring Giselle's latest designs and thereby ensuring the perpetuation of princess culture by the next generation of consumers" (Pershing and Gablehouse 2010, 152) spills over into the promotion of and off-screen commercial success of more and more Disney princess merchandise.

Within this context, Morgan is proven right, as the one who—unlike the nostalgic but hardened adult characters—*never* doubts the key role this romance-and-magic formula plays in producing and regulating what counts as "success" for women in a consumer capitalist world. While she is not shown reading fairy tales or any other books, Morgan enjoys dressing up as a little fairy with a wand, and among the toys in her room we can spot Belle, another Disney princess, behind sunglasses.[9] What she wishes to be is ready-made, the path to attain it has been charted over and over again, and she knows that a credit card works like a wand to facilitate the process. If Morgan ultimately comes to represent the moral compass in the film, it is because she is the unquestioning and steadfast consumer of Disneyfied fantasies, fantasies that actually help to produce a shared sense of capitalist reality in the United States and in our globalized world.

I will argue that in contrast to this poster child for the rewards of indulging in consumerism, Ofelia is presented as the moral compass in *Pan's Labyrinth*'s storyworlds because she is an active, critical reader of the relationship between fantasy and her social world, and of what to do with fairy tales, too. There is no storybook framing Guillermo del Toro's fairy-tale film, but, within it, both the book of illustrated fairy tales that Ofelia enjoys reading and the magic book that the Faun gives Ofelia are shown to be part of her resistant negotiations with the oppressively dark social world she inhabits. As I mentioned earlier, when she sees a stick insect that looks like the fairy from her storybook, she tells her mother, "I saw a fairy," but finds herself once again dismissed. Later that evening, when the clucking fairy-like insect reappears in her bedroom, Ofelia shows this small creature her book-bound avatar, and this in the director's commentary is described as del Toro's "favorite magical moment in the film," the moment when the child's "fantasy starts to become material." The camera records the transformation of the insect-like creature (created in turn by del Toro's team to reference a stick insect and interpreted by several viewers as referencing a praying mantis) into the "fairy" in a way that does not call attention to its fantastic quality but simply establishes its camera reality.[10] What I want to underscore about this scene is how Ofelia's desire for her vision to be realized does not shy away from confronting the gaps between ready-made images and her own imaginings. In her wondering about the relationship between the bookish image and the being she feels connected with, Ofelia instigates a transformation that, in del Toro's words, employs "the drawing as a reference," but does not replicate it. Rather than corporealizing the Victorian silhouette in Tinkerbell fashion, the "bug" transforms into a hairless creature modeled on the somewhat sinister fairy we have already seen in del Toro's superhero film, *Hellboy*. This is a complex process of cross-references that somewhat parallels the material and composite transformation, in the making of the film, of del Toro's own drawings and notebooks into magical creatures on screen, whether computer generated like the fairies or grotesquely costumed like the Pale Man (played, as the Faun is

PLATE 16. Transformation in *Pan's Labyrinth*.

too, by Doug Jones).[11] Like del Toro and his team, within the film Ofelia employs multiple codes of reference to confront the challenges of "real" and fairy-tale beings, objects, and tests at the crossroads of her own insights, desires, and fears.

The Book of Crossroads that the Faun in the labyrinth gives Ofelia functions as an objective correlative of sorts to show the movie's audience this conflicted interplay of imaginations at work in Ofelia's experience. The Faun has told her "[the book] will show you your future, show you what must be done." And Ofelia does look to the magic book for guidance. But she also disobeys the script she is supposed to live out—rejecting the illocutionary force of the book's, the fairies', and eventually the Faun's pronouncements, just as much as she has resisted her mother's and stepfather's will to control her actions and the future. In her discussion of "Narrative Desire and Disobedience in *Pan's Labyrinth*," Jennifer Orme persuasively shows how Ofelia's transgressions are part and parcel with the "multiple forms of disobedience" (2010b, 232), generic, moral, and political, that the film enacts.[12] My own humbler point here is that adhering to the identification with Ofelia that the film's narration promotes for its viewers means first

"Use the chalk to trace a door

PLATE 17. From the Book of the Crossroads in *Pan's Labyrinth*.

and foremost to recognize Ofelia's rescripting agency as an active reader and questioning adaptor and disruptor of totalizing scripts, whether they are fairy tales, destiny, or ruling histories and truths.

While not as iconic as the Disney storybook, representing the act of reading as significant is hardly unique to *Pan's Labyrinth* among fairy-tale films. Think back to the frame of *The Princess Bride* (directed by Carl Reiner and written by William Goldman) in 1987, which plays out the interaction between the grandfather (Peter Falk) reading from a fairy-tale book and his grandson, a rather reluctant listener. Or to Belle's characterization as a reader in Disney's *Beauty and the Beast* in 1991, possibly riding the wave of the "Lifelong Reader" campaign and other US nationwide efforts to promote reading. Learning to read is presented symbolically as empowerment for the Red Riding Hood character, Vanessa, in Matthew Bright's *Freeway* (1996); and in *MirrorMask* (2005), books turn into magic-carpet-like vehicles when properly cajoled by the teenage heroine, Helena (Stephanie Leonidas). What is unusually powerful in today's popular culture is the approach to reading fairy tales that *Pan's Labyrinth* takes and models.

If the double exposure to which *Enchanted* subjects the fairy tale is at one end of spectrum, actively selling the idea that in our hypermodern citified lives, girls and women wish to be consumed by fairy tales that buy us a pink and glittery happiness, then *Pan's Labyrinth*'s is at the other end, activating the transformative potential of reading fairy tales as "instructions" of variable use that, however, kindle a sense of opportunity. As Arthur W. Frank reminds us, "stories work to *emplot* lives," projecting possible futures for humans, but we can exercise the freedom not to be "conducted" by these stories, to change received stories as well as our lives (2010, 10). Similarly, the writer Neil Gaiman notes in his poem about fairy tales titled "Instructions," "the road between dreams and reality is one that must be negotiated, not walked" (1998, 61). Just as del Toro references multiple paintings and films without compromising his creative style,[13] Ofelia fearlessly negotiates her way among multiple nightmares in both the magic and the "real" storyworlds by actively decoding but also recoding, interrupting, and intervening in the scripts she finds herself written into: the pliable and grateful daughter, the *Alice in Wonderland* Disney heroine she is dressed up as, the girl who ought to know her place, the princess who must pass three magical tests.[14]

While Ofelia's resistant reading and bold rewriting of her roles do not guarantee her a happy ending, they have the potential to activate something in us as viewers: not necessarily the belief in her fantasy world,[15] but our responseability to the powers of fantasy in social life. What really places *Pan's Labyrinth* at the other end of the double-exposure spectrum from Disney's *Enchanted* is del Toro's refusal to patronize Ofelia, refusal to infantilize the genre of the fairy tale, and refusal to insulate her and the fantasy world from the horrors of history and totalitarianism in family as well as state politics. This is how *Pan's Labyrinth* connects to how, historically, even as in Germany "educational and cultural institutions of the National Socialists appropriated the fairy tale . . . adults and children victimized by the Nazis reclaimed the genre" (Haase 1998, 99) as psychological defense and "device to represent and interpret the landscape of a violent childhood" (Haase 2000, 373).[16] It is also how *Pan's Labyrinth inspires* more responsible and counterhegemonic uses of fairy tales (and more generally fantasy) in today's world, uses that are not reducible to a magic formula or a commodity.

Ofelia, as a girl child character in a violent world, is particularly susceptible to fantasy; however, she is neither prey to it nor is its storyworld her refuge.[17] The director and visual storyteller del Toro shrinks the storyworld of her first two magic tests to Ofelia's size, allowing her to confront one monster at a time, one-on-one, following the two-to-a-scene "law" of folk narrative. Within the enclosed spaces of the ancient fig tree and the uterine dining room, she sizes each of her opponents up, the Toad and the Pale Man respectively; she makes her own decisions, succeeds and survives, thus learning by taking risks to trust herself. In his "Power of Myth" commentary, del Toro states that she is "giving birth to herself," which enables her to exercise her agency in the equally "brutal" parallel world of Captain Vidal and the Spanish civil war. When, in the final labyrinth showdown, she faces two opponents in close succession, Ofelia steadfastly refuses to give up her brother, whether it is to the Faun's promises or Vidal's threats. Does she fail or does she succeed in her final test? Thanks to her innocence, in the third of four endings to the film, after Vidal shoots her, Ofelia is reborn to her storyworld, family, and status of origin. Regardless of which ending we find believable, she has found enough confidence and resourcefulness in confronting the first two magic tests to resist dehumanizing choices. And, I would argue, regardless of whether we as viewers grant "reality" status to the underground labyrinthine fairy-tale world or not, del Toro's cinematography encourages us to consider the fairy-tale active reading and disobedient reenacting that Ofelia engages in her "one-on-one" scenes as different from the fairy-tale mythology world from which Princess Moanna escaped and ultimately returns to. The made-to-size and uncanny fairy-tale world in which Ofelia confronts the horror and learns to take responsibility for her choices, one by one, is not necessarily the same as the one in which she achieves the all too hieratic returning-home happy ending.

And then, again, whichever ending we find believable or satisfying, as viewers we recognize Ofelia as the film's moral compass because the film's dialogue and camera work diegetically valorize her being curious, bold, and willful. When she tells her unborn brother a story, the camera takes us effortlessly into the storyworld she is creating and also makes visible Ofelia's nurturing relation with her in-utero narratee. Her power of both storytelling and rescripting make her the hero, and the film's color palette and visual architecture associate her power with a warm and feminine life force.

However, it is Ofelia's innocence as a prepubescent child rather than her sex/gender as a girl that mark her potential as a hero in the various worlds she inhabits as a character. This is particularly evident, I think, in the film's multiple endings, especially the final one, when the male voice-over tells us that Ofelia "left behind small traces of her time on earth visible only to those who know where to look," and the camera points to a small, white flower—which references, but does not replicate, the rose of immortality that was the focus of the only tale *she* tells in the film—and to a praying mantis, both implicitly waiting to be transformed by discerning viewers. To put it plainly, the film *Pan's Labyrinth* leaves the girl's mark symbolically on the world, but regrettably she is not of this world. In del Toro's vision, redeeming the world from social oppression depends on human beings, regardless of gender, who take responsibility and become responsive to what Judith Butler (2004) calls the critical promise of fantasy, its challenge of "the contingent limits of what will/will not be called reality."

READING FAIRY TALES TO (DE)COMMODIFY
THE GENDERED CHILD: *BLUEBEARD*
AND *HANSEL AND GRETEL*

French director Catherine Breillat brings an avowed feminist investment to the project of activating this critical promise of fantasy with her 2009 film, *La Barbe bleue*, marketed as *Bluebeard* in North America. I will be looking at how within her film Breillat represents the *scene* of reading the gruesome tale of "Bluebeard" and how this reflects on what is at stake in feminist rereadings of fairy tales today, especially for young girls in a society that continues to sexualize violence against women and blame its victims. Because Breillat's *Bluebeard* is likely to be less familiar to non-French readers than the more widely distributed *Enchanted* and *Pan's Labyrinth*, I will start with some general information.

Catherine Breillat (b. 1948) is a rather controversial filmmaker and one of still relatively few women in the profession; furthermore, her unruly feminism and provocative filmic takes on sexuality are somewhat reminiscent of Angela Carter's demythologizing strategies that were hotly debated in the 1980s. Unlike her other works and possibly because it was originally made for French television and so many of its actors are minors, *Bluebeard* does not feature any explicit sex scenes; rather, in fairy-tale style, it employs symbolism to explore sex-gender politics. *Bluebeard* was produced by Flach Film as the first in a series of adaptations of popular tales by well-known artists for the ARTE television channel, a French and German coproduction.[18] Breillat, who then directed *Sleeping Beauty* (2010) also for ARTE, is apparently working on the third film in her fairy-tale trilogy, adapting "Beauty and the Beast." *Bluebeard* was fairly low budget and shot in HD digital video; following its TV showings and at art film festivals, it was released in UK and US theaters in 2010 and then in DVD format. An art film whose circuit and audiences differ greatly from *Enchanted* and *Pan's Labyrinth*, *Bluebeard* shares with *Pan's Labyrinth* the status of film d'auteur and the promise, as seen in a few blogs, of acquiring specific groups of greatly devoted fans.

Bluebeard declares itself to be an adaptation, specifically of a tale that Breillat says to have read over and over again as a child. While the "Bluebeard" tale (ATU 312) does not figure in the North American children's literature canon of fairy tales, it is referenced often enough in popular culture as featuring a bloody chamber, a curious wife, a magic key, a serial killer, and elements of horror and suspense rather than magic and wonder. Like the other films discussed in this chapter, Breillat's *Bluebeard* has a double plot, but this one hinges not so much on travel to a different space as on the reading out loud of a specific tale, Charles Perrault's "La Barbe bleue," originally published in 1697; I am particularly interested in how and to what effects the ghostly figure of Perrault's tale makes itself felt as script in one storyworld and as performance in the other.[19]

The very first scenes introduce two sisters, young teenagers, in a storyworld that could be seventeenth-century France—the time when Perrault was writing—and on the day the death of their father radically changed their lives. The two girls, Anne and Marie-Catherine (played respectively by Daphné Blaiwir and Lola Créton), are obliged to leave the private convent in which they were being educated and go back home, facing the poverty to which their father's death and debts have condemned them; their mother worries about the girls' future, which she predicts will involve their becoming nuns or ladies in waiting in order to survive. The dialogue shows that both girls are aware of social injustice in their world, but they show their resentment in different ways: Anne, the older, by presenting herself as well mannered and docile in public, while lashing out with her mother; the younger Marie-Catherine by articulating in private and public settings her outrage, loss, *and* determination to become rich. Even before we meet Marie-Catherine, the mother superior in the convent has labeled her as a "bad seed," and that is when the scene shifts to the 1950s with two little girls climbing the stairs to an attic and the younger one, a six- or seven-year-old, saying "Mom didn't say it was forbidden." Marie-Catherine, who in the historical plot will marry *and* survive Bluebeard, is thus immediately linked with Catherine (played by Marilou Lopes-Bennites), the curious and clever little girl in the attic who in the modern plot reads the "Bluebeard" tale to the demure and somewhat reluctant Marie-Anne (played by Lola Giovannetti).

The characterization of the two pairs of sisters in the different plots is similar, and so are the dynamics of rivalry and affection that bond them, dynamics that could also lead us to see the four sisters as multiple versions of one another, externalizing competitive responses to gender acculturation in different historical contexts.[20] The outcome of this rivalry and scapegoating plays out differently in the two storyworlds, in the process also offering different takes on the "Bluebeard" tale.

In the scene when Catherine begins to read to Marie-Anne, clearly, the two little girls already know the story of "Bluebeard" and select it over "The Little Mermaid" (which, by the way, would not be in the Perrault book, but has been a subtext in other films Breillat directed[21]). When shown the book of fairy tales on screen, we spectators see its red cover, the title page—*Contes des Fées par Charles*

Perrault—and next to it the frontispiece illustration from "Le Petit Poucet," or "Little Tom Thumb," which portrays the ogre and his wife in the kitchen, with him saying in the caption, "Je sens la chair fraîche, te dis-je encore une fois" ["I smell fresh meat, I tell you again"], a preview of sorts. We may not notice that this is an "édition révue" or revised edition, probably for children, but the illustration functions somewhat as a preview of the position that Catherine, the young reader, sees these tales initiating young girls into: that of "fresh meat" in a world of heteronormative ogres.[22] As Marina Warner remarks, the fairy-tale cannibalistic ogre "is a subject in a gendered plot," whereby "in tales starring male heroes, the ogre's appetite tests their strength and cunning in survival," and for heroines "annihilation arises from sexual congress" (Warner 1998, 311). At first Catherine reads Perrault's "La Barbe bleue" text verbatim ("Il était une fois un homme qui avait de belles maisons à la ville et à la campagne" ["There was once a man who owned beautifully town and country houses"]), but later she skips a few words—such as the comment that the widows' daughters to whom Bluebeard proposes are both "parfaitement belles," or "perfectly lovely beautiful" (Perrault 2002, 138, 139).

Within this mise-en-scène of reading it is significant that Catherine, the younger sister, has made the book hers to read and takes a leading role in the exploration of the story's meaning, for instance, when she comments to Marie-Anne, "Do you understand? Bluebeard is very ugly, but very rich. You have to be poor to love him." Marie-Anne disagrees: "A distinguished lady can't [really] be poor," she protests (with the French for "distinguished" being "une dame de qualité"); overall, Marie-Anne is ambivalent about the reading, claiming the story makes her cry because she is sensitive, but also urging Catherine on, "Keep reading." Later, when Marie-Anne once again recoils from listening, Catherine calls her a "scaredy cat," and they have an apparently naive conversation that is actually about the body-mind relation and the role of agency in responding to narratives that emplot our lives:

MARIE-ANNE: If I listen, it will break my ears.

CATHERINE: You talk nonsense.

MARIE-ANNE: It is not my fault. I don't do the thinking, my brain does.

CATHERINE: Your brain is yours.

MARIE-ANNE: No, it was given to me.

Agreeing to disagree, as they keep doing throughout the film, Catherine asks, "Can I keep on reading?" She is only halfway through the first paragraph of Perrault's text, with Bluebeard ready to marry either of the two beautiful sisters,

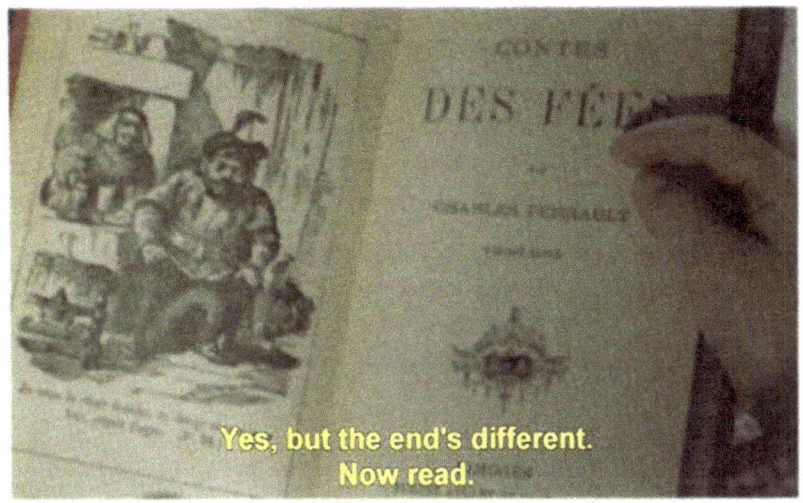

PLATE 18. Charles Perrault's *Contes des fées* in *Bluebeard*.

even as they are both disgusted by him because "no one knew what had become" of the women he'd previously married. Neither do we, as viewers, know what will become of Catherine and Marie-Anne as their act of reading phantasmatically begins to invoke the horror within the tale for them to confront.

While Catherine is unequivocally reading Charles Perrault's text, the story of Marie Catherine, Anne, and Bluebeard (Dominique Thomas) that is dramatized in the film does not replicate that text. Whether we know Perrault's tale or not, once we've heard Catherine read its beginning we realize it bears no resemblance with the start of the film *Bluebeard*. Rather, the scenes in the convent, at the father's funeral, and so on seem to be inferred and developed from Perrault's script, based on historical knowledge of the mores of seventeenth-century France and women's conditions at the time, and inflected by Breillat's feminist sensibilities as writer and director. Her focus is not on Bluebeard as the starting point or on the heroine's brothers in the final rescue scene, but on the two girls throughout, on the fragility of women's material conditions with no man looking after them, the limited options that women had to improve their economic lot, what the two sisters make of their experience of loss. Perrault's storybook stands in a precariously unstable relationship to the "Bluebeard" reenactment in the early-modern storyworld as well as to the reading performance of the tale in the twentieth-century setting. Perrault's tale is cited but not replicated in either storyworld, and there are no bridging shots between them.

Not only is Breillat's adaptation of Perrault's text amplifying it and refocusing it in her early-modern plot, but also Catherine's reading out loud in the attic—like Ofelia's reading of the Book of Crossroads—turns, for a while at least, into her own storytelling that generates new content. In the following dialogue, the different sensibilities of the girls (and their age groups) are brought to bear on their engagement with the fairy-tale genre.

CATHERINE (gesticulating): For Bluebeard, marriage is difficult because he kills the children. He has a large pot where he stews them. He has a trap door where he scoops out the eggs, and with a big ladle, he pulls out the girl and eats her. That's how he gets fat and meets a beautiful green ogress with big teeth.

MARIE-ANNE: You mix up everything, stupid.

CATHERINE: I do? So what's marriage?

MARIE-ANNE: Marriage is when two people love each other and kiss in front of everybody and wear a golden ring. It's so beautiful!

CATHERINE: And then an ogress eats them.

MARIE-ANNE: Stop talking about that ogress. The young woman has a pretty white wedding dress.

CATHERINE: And she becomes an ogress.

MARIE-ANNE: Enough with that ogress. She's very beautiful.

CATHERINE: Bluebeard devours everything.

Fairy tales signal romance to Marie-Anne, but a "devour or be devoured" struggle for Catherine that is perhaps inchoate in the illustration from Perrault's book. When later Catherine returns to reading Perrault's text, viewers who are familiar with it will recognize Perrault's words, but the order and frequency of episodes in the tale's dramatization are performed differently. For instance, Perrault had Bluebeard testing his wife just once, while for Breillat, who dwells on the odd affinity at work in the relationship between the young wife and Bluebeard, it's on his second trip away that Marie-Catherine cannot resist entering the forbidden room and finds the corpses of Bluebeard's previous wives.

This is when the film's two storyworlds suddenly collide, and we see not the young bride, but Catherine the child reader entering the bloody chamber, confronting its horror, but refusing even in her shock to be scared (as she repeats "j'ais pas peur, j'ais pas peur" "I'm not afraid, I'm not afraid" as a charm). Focusing on the film's production as a whole, Catherine's irruption into the bloody chamber, like a mise en abyme, exemplifies Breillat's intervention as a director to advocate for "a symbolic reappropriation of a feminine realm that for centuries has been dissected by the imaginary of men" (Gillain 2003, 204, qtd. in Ince 2006, 157). At the same time, this scene visualizes a practice that "perverse" spectators (Staiger 2000, 53) and readers engage in to produce new materials out of any given narrative. By inserting herself into the "Bluebeard" storyworld, Catherine asserts her own boldness and transgressive desire to be alive in the "bloody chamber," to be marked not by fear of death but by the "eternally fresh blood" of women.[23] In a genre-specific way, the scene also makes visible the empowering potential that fairy tales as fantastic encounters with death, violence, and injustice may have for the young, the small, the ones who read them not wanting to turn into "fresh meat." Because she is not simply imitating or becoming Marie-Catherine, Catherine's exploration of the bloody chamber, like her disobedient reading of Perrault's fairy tales as stories of initiation into the "ogritude" of adulthood and marriage, can be seen as a form of disidentification, a productive survival strategy.[24]

When we see Marie-Catherine in the "Bluebeard" storyworld again, we realize that facing the truth about her serial-killer husband made her stronger too; this enables her to manipulate him into delaying her death at his hand, and that plot takes its well-known course, with Marie-Catherine proving she is not a victim, but "the final girl" we recognize from horror movies. As in Perrault's tale, sister Anne is the key liaison with family and the outer world helping Marie-Catherine survive.[25] The sisters in the Bluebeard adaptation within the film manage to remain connected even when marriage separates them; this bond, along with Marie-Catherine's cleverness and boldness, ensures that she is not an isolated prey falling into Bluebeard's trap. Jack Zipes writes in his analysis that, as the first European woman filmmaker to adapt "Bluebeard," Breillat "has managed to transform Perrault's 'Bluebeard' into a film that explores a young woman's rebellion rather than her victimization" (2012, 51).

By emphasizing the coded communication between women in the face of violence and by developing throughout the film the heroine's singular personality and desire for knowledge, Breillat's *Bluebeard* is clearly aligned with the many feminist readings that have in the last forty years, both in fiction and scholarship, revisited the deadly and gendered power game of the "Bluebeard" script to offer an empowering—rather than disparaging—view of "female curiosity."[26] Especially crucial to this feminist reading was the decoupling of this curiosity from sexual infidelity or voracity, making Breillat's representation of Marie-Catherine's and Bluebeard's relationship as asexual particularly significant. The consequences of female curiosity in the film, as Breillat suggests in an interview, are "dire" (Breillat and Anderson 2010) not for the heroine but for

the Bluebeard figure, whose absolute power—signaled by his splendid attire and colossal physique—comes undone when, way before the arrival of the muske-teers, he is clearly unable to follow through with his death sentence. Unlike the expression of shame we see in popular illustrations, such as Edmund Dulac's, of a "Bluebeard" heroine after her transgression, there is no shame about her curi-osity in Marie-Catherine's comportment when Bluebeard wants to punish her.

However, to Marie-Catherine's vindication in the "Bluebeard" storyworld, Breillat juxtaposes another horror, this time in the twentieth-century attic, the scene of Catherine's reading. Like Bluebeard's former wives, Marie-Anne is filled by uncontrollable fear when, in the story that Catherine keeps reading to her, Bluebeard's wife is threatened with death: "il faut mourir" / "you must die." For Marie-Anne, as a listener or narratee, the horror of Bluebeard's violence against women is that she, like Marie-Catherine, could be his next victim. And to Catherine's and the viewers' shock, Marie-Anne indeed meets with death, as she backs away from her sister's reading—which so drastically threatens her belief in the magic of fairy-tale marriage—and (accidentally?) falls through the attic's hatch. Marie-Anne, the dreamy-eyed and not-as-clever older sister in the attic cannot keep up with Catherine (or with Marie-Catherine and Anne who joined forces to survive): alone in her fear, identifying herself as a victim, Marie-Anne falls through the "Bluebeard" trapdoor to join symbolically his other dead wives. If, in the tradition of fairy-tale externalization, we think of Marie-Anne and Catherine as two split sides of one being, we could also say that Catherine has eliminated her own fear, has refused to be turned into a victim herself. Either way, this scene of reading acts as an important reminder of how different identifications as well as disidentifications are possible in response to a tale in each and every performance of it, and that we should not generalize about what fairy tales do or how they apply to individual lives.

As a cinematic auteur, Catherine Breillat makes no mystery of her personal interest in making not only a film about "Bluebeard" but also a fairy-tale trilogy: "Fairy tales are the origins of our childhood. At the same time, they are projections into the unknown. As children, they allow us to voyage to the unknown. That's what they were for me when I was growing up" (Breillat and Garcia 2011). Clearly, fairy tales are narratives of initiation for Breillat into a future that is not already set or predictable; they are tales where she claims to have formed her imagination in the 1950s and also to have figured herself as the younger or youngest girl, and the boldest.[27] However, rather than simply leading to an autobiographical reading of her fairy-tale films, the multiple (dis)identifications of the girls in *Bluebeard* with fairy-tale heroines dramatize Breillat's desire—as a film auteur—to redirect and intervene in her spectators' reception and reading of this violent tale. In an interview published in *Cineaste* (Breillat and Garcia 2011), she stated, "The reason I am obsessed by young girls is that they are individuals who exist but also do not yet exist. They are afraid, and they're strong

PLATE 20. Marie-Anne in *Bluebeard*

and weak at the same time. They confront life violently. They are weak because they do not know who they are going to become."

What are you and I as adult viewers to learn from the violent outcome of two young French girls' reading "Bluebeard" in this *Bluebeard* film? Clearly, the fairy-tale film's "instructions" will vary as we negotiate not only the road between dreams and reality but also the road between dream and nightmare in varied realities. From my situated knowledge of and experience with fairy tales, feminisms, and Breillat's poetics, this is what I am emboldened to take away. Looking *with* Catherine down to the doll-like broken body of Marie-Anne—as the sequence of low-angle and high-angle shots invites viewers to do just after Marie-Anne's fall—draws me to think not only of sex-gender politics within the tale of "Bluebeard," or of the ways in which the tale has been used to keep women "in their place," but also to reflect on the reach and impact in the twenty-first century of the second-wave feminist reading of "Bluebeard" as an empowering fairy tale. Not all women are on board, and the "Bluebeard" plot continues insidiously to captivate women in today's so-called postfeminist world. Bluebeard's killings are not over, and the final girl's success may depend not on her solidarity with other women as much as on her complicity with Bluebeard, a theme director Breillat develops as the uneasy bond between two misfits, but the character of young Catherine labels as the heroine's becoming "an ogress," and Marie-Catherine's caressing Bluebeard's head ambiguously embodies in the film's final tableau vivant.

In the costume drama, Marie-Catherine survives as a result of Bluebeard's decapitation; not only that, she fulfills her desire, expressed early in the film when she was outraged at the unjust impact of poverty on her young life, to live in his great castle and be powerful.[28] Has Marie-Catherine become an ogress, inhabiting Bluebeard's castle and taking over his riches? Breillat's composition superimposes Marie-Catherine onto the biblical Salome, slayer of John the Baptiste, and/or the biblical Judith, slayer of Holofernes.[29] The female protagonist of "Bluebeard" tales has been associated with these sexualized murderers before, most visibly as part of an antifeminist backlash in the early twentieth century.[30] What is different about Breillat's intertextual links? Her positive portrayal throughout the film of Marie-Catherine's defiance of the status quo, the forceful desexualizing of Marie-Catherine's and Bluebeard's relationship, and the uncompromisingly material economy framing their interactions as well as their bonding together as social misfits all work against a reading that simply blames Marie-Catherine for her appetites and the symbolic castration. Marie-Catherine is not one and the same as Perrault's heroine. Breillat's tableau remarks on the ongoing competition of feminist and antifeminist reading codes

PLATE 21. Fede Galizia, Italian, 1578–1630. *Judith with the Head of Holofernes*, 1596. Oil on canvas, 47 1/2 x 37 inches. SN684. Gift of Mr. and Mrs. Jacob Polak, 1969. Collection of The John and Mable Ringling Museum of Art, the State Art Museum of Florida.

PLATE 22. Marie-Catherine in *Bluebeard*.

for making sense of "Bluebeard" and on the violence that the tale's narrative economy demands. Not quite still, but wondering (perhaps about her future), Marie-Catherine goes back and forth lightly caressing Bluebeard's head and moving her hand away from it, tilting ever so slightly her head this way and that in her troubled and troubling "triumph." A choir of off-screen young voices intones what Anne and other young girls in the convent were singing at the start of the movie, the "Kyrié Eleïsson" (Lord Have Mercy).[31]

And has the child Catherine in the 1950s scenario unwittingly become "an ogress"? When her mother comes looking for her and seems not to miss Marie-Anne or be aware of her demise, Catherine appears pleased and basks in the maternal embrace. There is something mischievous about Catherine's expression, a relief to be rid of her goodie-goodie sister, at least in this over-the-top performance in the attic. Breillat, whose first name you will recall is Catherine, offers no answer, but she has stated in several interviews how she would read "Bluebeard," her favorite tale, as a very young child together with her sister, Marie-Hélène: "And I was very proud of the fact that even though I was younger than her, she would be the one who would start to cry before me in reading that tale. And at the same time I actually find it so surprising that young girls of no more than six or seven read this tale in which they are taught to love the man who is going to kill them" (Breillat and Kenny 2009). Like Catherine in her film, Breillat takes pride in being strong and bold; however, in Breillat's recounting

PLATE 23. Bernardino Luini, Italian (Milanese), active 1512–died in 1532. *Salome with the Head of Saint John the Baptist.* Oil on panel, 62.23 x 51.43 cm (24 1/2 x 20 1/4 inches). Museum of Fine Arts, Boston. Gift of Mrs. W. Scott Fitz. 21.2287.

of the scene of reading in her own life, both she and her sister end up crying. The interaction between the two sisters in her film brings to our attention how these tears are, in the film director's later and somewhat ironic view, in response to violent social scripts.

Unlike del Toro's, Breillat's film does not seek to renew human beings' experience of wonder in the world, but rather to replay the scene of "Bluebeard" reading in childhood as a traumatic site for girls specifically, one that may work to empower them to be bold in the face of psychic and social challenges, but also continues to reproduce and naturalize an "eat or be eaten" violence at work in patriarchal nuclear family power dynamics. Whether the young girls in the film identify with Bluebeard's survivors or victims, to me Breillat's refusal to deliver a moral compass in either storyworld stages this gruesome fairy tale for her spectators as putting into relief what feminist therapists have called "insidious trauma," the "traumatogenic effects of oppression that are not necessarily overtly violent or threatening to bodily well-being at a given moment but that do violence to the soul and spirit" (Maria Root, qtd. in Brown 1995). At the same time, the disidentification that Breillat's character, Catherine, creatively produces in her reading of "Bluebeard" is a call for self-reflection, the uneasy recognition that empowerment and integration of self often take place at the expense of others in a culture that normalizes and eroticizes violence.

While siding with the transgressively curious Catherine and the feminist readings from the 1990s that had rehabilitated the tale for us, Breillat's re-vision of "Bluebeard" projects a sense of discomfort, if not horror, a call for recognizing that the nightmare in the twenty-first century differs from the seventeenth-century and 1950s scenarios, but is not over. The ways in which sexual desires play out as "devouring" one another in some fairy tales cannot be separated from the desire for upward social mobility that Marie-Catherine exhibits, or the complicitous way in which the ogress in "Tom Thumb" appeases her husband, or the violence the "Bluebeard" scenario necessarily entails. Young girls' surviving the commodification of their bodies and desires continues to be a part of their "confronting life violently," even as material circumstances and the allures and dangers of the "happily-ever-after" script change. The film thus offers no closure, no therapeutic "remembering to forget" the horror, that is, the dead women in Bluebeard's cellar, the violence the "final girl" scenario uncannily perpetuates, and the various ways in which this tale emplots our lives. Rather, Breillat's film artfully rearranges emotions of loss, fear, surprise, and horror within the two storyworlds and through their contrast in order to reawaken us to reading the "Bluebeard" fairy tale not only for its positive outcome but also for its multiple and unsettling warnings to women and girls today.

If we are cautioned of the unpredictable and ongoing horror of the eat-or-be-eaten logic of "Bluebeard" through the varied readings that hopeful/bold/fearful/reflective young girls in Breillat's film provide of it, the Korean director Pil-Sung Yim takes on that horror in his 2007 film 헨젤과 그레텔, or *Hansel and Gretel*, to explore the dangers of turning children's needs into consumer fantasies. *Hansel and Gretel* is only the second movie directed by Pil-Sung Yim, who also collaborated on the screenplay. Produced by a large South Korean conglomerate, Barunson Film Division, and distributed internationally by CJ Entertainment, which has had strong ties with DreamWorks,[32] the film has been better received in Germany, France, Belgium, and Canada, than in Korea.[33] It won the 2009 International Fantasy Film Special Jury Award, but it has also been praised within the Korean horror film tradition. Several reviewers point to parallels between this "dark" fairy tale and del Toro's *Pan's Labyrinth*.[34] Like Breillat's *Bluebeard*, Pil-Sung Yim's *Hansel and Gretel* is a relatively low-budget filmic adaptation that gains much from excellent child actors and high production values.[35]

The film opens with a dreamlike sequence: black-and-white shots of a young man running in a forest toward the camera, jumbled color images of a large house and small toys. The character-bound voice-over muses: "In this world . . . In an unimaginably strange place . . . A deep forest that one could suddenly fall into exists somewhere out there. Every thing started in this deep, dense forest." Close-ups of several pen and ink drawings follow: a forest, a boy and a girl wandering alone in the forest, their hope when they see shelter, a child imprisoned in a cage, a human leg clad in a witchlike shoe sticking out of the oven of an old-fashioned stove, a man welcoming two children back home, once more a somewhat surreal forest. The iris shots visually suggest a parallel between the journey of the man and that of the children in the drawings. Superimposed on the last of these still images is the title of the film, which confirms that in sequence they have plotted the basic ingredients of the "Hansel and Gretel" (ATU 327A) tale.[36] Without representing a book the way Disney animated movies do to frame their "once upon a time" narrative, these still images remediate an earlier use of the frontispiece illustration as a "rhetorical memory device" (Hermansson 2009, 85) in fairy-tale books, announcing that Pil-Sung Yim's *Hansel and Gretel* focuses in on the visual, more than the verbal, power of fairy tales.

Hansel and Gretel, which is classified generically as both fantasy and horror, tells the story of Eun-Soo (played by Jeong-Myeong Cheon), a young man who, following a car accident, is lost in a forest, confronts his childhood trauma of abandonment, and emerges transformed into a responsible and loving family man. Told in a *Twilight Zone* style, the tale of Eun-Soo is intertwined with that of

PLATE 24. Iris shot of the "deep, dense forest" in *Hansel and Gretel*.

three children who live in the labyrinthine forest. In the warm yet eerie "House of Happy Children," the three siblings have surrounded themselves with Christmas decorations and endless toys, cakes, sweets, teddy bears, bunnies; an unplugged 1950s-like black-and-white TV runs the same violent cartoon sequence over and over again; on the same TV we see some Christmas hype, with an excited reporter announcing how Santa Claus grants children all their wishes. In the course of the movie, each of the children exhibits special powers: telepathy for Young-Hee (Eun-Kyung Sim), the older prepubescent sister; telekinetic abilities for the brother, Man-Bok (Eun Won-Jae); and the temporary animation of objects for younger doll-like sister, Jung-Soon (Jin Ji-Hee or Ji-Hee Jin). As Eun-Soo soon discovers, their unrequited wish, however, is to be cared for by loving parents. Following disappointing and violent attempts to form a family unit with other adults (also lost in the forest), the children—who call Eun-Soo "Uncle"—want him to take care of them and "live happily ever after" in their toy land.

The plot, like the forest, has many twists and turns, as the topoi of horror mix with those of morality tale and thriller, all greatly enhanced by Lee Byung-Woo's musical score. Not only are the children not what they seem, but also a serial killer threatens to take over the household and to kill Eun-Soo. In a climactic scene, it is the children who, deploying their rage and special powers, rescue Eun-Soo and themselves. In the end, once the mystery of the three children's unhappiness and powers is revealed, Eun-Soo proves himself different from the other adult "false heroes" and, thanks to Young-Hee's help, is able to leave the nightmarish forest. Whether his encounter with the children occurred in Eun-Soo's mind after the car accident or not, the epilogue shows that Young-Hee, Man-Bok, and Jung-Soon also choose to make a fresh start; they have left their artificial haven, perhaps looking for an answer to the question Young-Hee had asked Eun-Soo just before he returned to his world: "can children live happily there?"

As Zipes suggests, the film raises "controversial questions through horror about how children are treated today" (2011, 197). My focus is on how an illustrated *Hansel and Gretel* book plays multiple roles in developing the fantasy aspect of these questions and in bringing about the denouement of *Hansel and Gretel*'s double plot. Eun-Soo first finds the book hidden in a Christmas box in the children's closet. When he leafs through it, we see some of the illustrations from the start of the film again, while he reads out loud what the caption translates as "Once upon a time in the thick, deep forest . . ." The faces of the happy family in the final drawing are torn out; all but the father's—which remains a blank—have been replaced with photos of Jung-Soon, Man-Bok, and Young-Hee. Like young Catherine in Breillat's *Bluebeard*, these children have inserted themselves into the "Hansel and Gretel" story. Upset by Eun-Soo's intrusion, Man-Bok demands the book back. Because he continues to follow the children around and to explore the house and forest in spite of Man-Bok's injunctions not to do so, Eun-Soo eventually realizes how central the fairy-tale book is to the children's story.

It is thanks to the book and, in particular, the illustration of the witch's demise, that Jung-Soon, Man-Bok, and Young-Hee are, so to speak, alive.[37] In a flashback narrated by Young-Hee, we see the horrendous abuse that "a long time ago" the three siblings and other children endured in the "House of Happy Children"—then a dingy and isolated orphanage—at the hands of their keeper who demanded they call him "Father." All the children were starved and beaten, Young-Hee endured sexual abuse to protect her younger sister, and at least one child was beaten to death.[38] Unexpectedly, one Christmas, a man and a woman from a charitable organization brought sweets and gifts to the orphans. We see the three children avidly taking in the illustrations of the *Hansel and Gretel* book they received. Dressed as Santa Claus, the man tells Jung-Soon, Man-Bok, and Young-Hee: "Starting today, if you just imagine it, and want it, all your wishes will be granted." Starved for wish fulfillment, the children believe him. Later that night, in a memorable scene, the three children stand up to their abuser and, releasing their rage and pain, telekinetically back him into the open woodstove. Threatened with annihilation, like Gretel in the tale, they push the witch into the oven.

FIGURE 3. Killing the witch in "Hansel and Gretel," drawing by Sunkyung Cho. Reproduced with permission of the artist.

Clearly, the *Hansel and Gretel* book illustrations have inspired them to envision how to punish and get rid of their prison-keeper. More than its words, this fairy tale's idea that children can defeat the powerful witch or ogre (in the ATU system, "Hansel and Gretel" is part of the larger tale type, "The Children and the Ogre," to which "Tom Thumb" also belongs) offers hope.[39] In the case of the three children in Pil-Sung Yim's movie, the *Hansel and Gretel* book images fuel their imaginations and result in ostensive action (Dégh 1994; Ellis 2001) that frees them of their abuser.

But the role of the fairy-tale book is not represented simply as positive in the film. It is clear that the children become trapped themselves in the "eat-or-be-eaten" / "consume-or-be-consumed" logic of ogritude, whereby they can only punish by killing, and in one case cannibalizing, those adults who do not answer to their expectations. At the same time, what they wish for is also caught in a happily-ever-after fantasy, which, unlike Ofelia and Catherine, they do not question. Rather than reading the fairy-tale book for themselves, they treat it as a fetish or a magical object, something like the wish-granting lamp or ring of many a fairy tale. To wish for something—revenge on an "evil stepmother" type, or happily-ever-after bliss with Uncle Eun-Soo—they draw it in bright-colored crayons, hoping to repeat their first successful move from imag(in)ing

PLATE 25. The "Happy Family" in *Hansel and Gretel*.

to making it happen. Sketching their fears, anger, and desires onto their note-books is a creative act, but their imaginations continue through the drawings to reproduce fairy-tale scenarios of deathly punishment and family happiness.

Their compulsive quest for scripted bliss yields at most an artificially static portrait of a "happy bourgeois family." The adult couple, as Eun-Soo discovers, is held captive by the children, who in turn seem to content themselves with simu-lacra of family life. In excess of this commercial for timeless "happy days," Pil-Sung Yim's camerawork zooms into the diffidence and anger of Man-Bok, the tears of Jung-Soon, and the pleasing ways of Young-Hee. Caught in a punish/reward binary, they keep pleading, "we are not bad children." They are spoiled children to all effects, tyrannical in their construction of a toys-and-treats house-hold, but most of all damaged by the adults' abuses of power—their material and symbolic violence, both of which ignore the children's needs. Conforming to the expectations of their abuser and the commodified image of fairy tales, each child embodies a gendered stereotype: the son at war with the all-powerful father, the innocent and helpless girl-child, the seductive daughter. They are stuck in a loop in which they have access only to unsatisfactory substitutes for a ready-made image of happiness.

As Eun-Soo's words and actions at the end of the film make clear, and Pil-Sung Yim's nuanced cinematographical portraits of the children's misguided hope and trust visualize throughout, Jung-Soon, Man-Bok, and Young-Hee are

FIGURE 4. Rabbits in "Hansel and Gretel," drawing by Sunkyung Cho. Reproduced with permission of the artist.

not to be held responsible for compulsively repeating the cycle of violence they seek to leave behind. Neither are they simply to be indulged in their wish for an impossibly endless and happy childhood. While the many versions of "Hansel and Gretel," regardless of the happy ending, narrate the instability and ambivalence both parents and children associate with home, Santa Claus's packaging of the tale as magic object "promises something durable that it cannot fulfill" (Zipes 2011, 194). The promise concerns unending security and protection for children on the part of adults and also the fulfillment through commodities of every wish the child expresses. That the promise is delivered at Christmas furthers the film's critique of a paternalistic capitalism that turns children and infantilized adults into consumers of endless products and of an unattainable fantasy of childhood.

At the start of *Hansel and Gretel*, Eun-Soo, who quite tellingly works for the toy industry, is a young man who sulks about his own childhood; he too is trapped in that fantasy of childhood—that is why he is in the forest, after all— until he realizes the harm that abusive adults *and* promises of instant gratification do. Rather than offering himself as protector and "Uncle" to make up for the children's pain, Eun-Soo reaffirms his desire to be, however imperfectly, with his own family and encourages the siblings to leave the house and become

FIGURE 5. Rabbits in "Hansel and Gretel," drawing by Sunkyung Cho. Reproduced with permission of the artist.

responsible for their own lives. The key to his deliverance is burning the notebook titled "Being Happy Forever with Uncle," in which the children have imagined him as their hero. By responding emotionally to the children's pain but not letting himself be consumed by them, Eun-Soo undoes the script in which they were all trapped, restoring agency to himself and the children as well as some credibility to the transformative potential of fairy tales. When the credits roll, the film's score, until then dominated by strings, shifts to a choir of haunting young voices.[40]

A powerful visual adapter of the fairy tale, Pil-Sung Yim leaves a trail of images for viewers not to lose hope at the "House of Happy Children," in the clutter of stuffed animals, toys, and pop-culture icons, as well as in the *Hansel and Gretel* illustrations. It is the trail of bunnies, with the rabbit being a significant symbol in globalized children's literature (from the white rabbit in *Alice in Wonderland*, Hazel and others in *Watership Down*, to Peter Rabbit in Beatrix Potter's books, and *The Velveteen Rabbit*), popular culture and folklores (Br'er Rabbit in the *Uncle Remus* tales and the Warner Bros. Bugs Bunny cartoon in the United States, but also the rabbit of the Chinese lunar calendar and the Great Rabbit in Native American traditions), and particularly Korean culture. In Korean tales, not unlike those of other cultures, the rabbit is a trickster figure, a small but witty animal who succeeds in saving his own life (as in the "Rabbit Visits the Dragon's Palace" tale), and a culture hero whose selflessness is rewarded (as in "The Rabbit in the Moon").[41] The children in *Hansel and Gretel* show courage and use their wits when defeating ogreish adults; Young-Hee also exhibits selflessness when she tells Eun-Soo how he needs to burn the notebook in order to leave their "story." In the *Hansel and Gretel* images by Sunkyung Cho,[42] the Seoul picture book illustrator who did the artwork for the film, large rabbits are disguised in the forest landscape, small ones seem to look over the lost children, and the "gingerbread house" resembles a large Totoro from Hayao Miyazaki's film.

I find it significant that the rabbits populate both the book illustrations, which never achieve camera reality in this film, and the fantasy-like "Children's Happy House." In disguise in both settings, they are almost invisible, because they are not expected to be in the "Hansel and Gretel" story, as we know it from the German tradition, and because they are all too expected in the nursery. At the dramatic climax of the film, when the flashback of the children overcoming the brutal father in the orphanage mingles with their overpowering the serial killer, the camera jump-cuts to the colorful painting in the living room of the "happy house," where the anthropomorphized rabbits in the forest suddenly appear to be alive, their eyes taking in the extraordinary event. As the painting suddenly acquires movement and depth, it contrasts with both the pen and ink book illustrations and with the children's densely saturated color drawings. This is the only break in the film from the static representation of two-dimensional images. I see it as an invitation to re-view the uncanny trail of rabbits in the film and to wonder at what the commodified fairy tale absconds.

Like *Pan's Labyrinth, Hansel and Gretel* does shine a positive light on the potential for utilizing fairy-tale wonder, but the bulk of the film shows the dangers of the fairy tale's rote capitalization. The film projects a deep ambivalence toward the "Hansel and Gretel" tale, its inflexible and doomed power games, and its capacity for transformation. When the children in the epilogue leave a notebook under the Christmas tree for Eun-Soo and/or his new child, the pages, except for the hopeful happy-ending illustration, are all blank; this points to the capacity that we have to unwrite set fairy-tale plots while sustaining the genre's smart optimism, but Eun-Soo's tears as he leafs through the notebook also show that he pities Young-Hee, Man-Bok, and Jung-Soon as they continue on their quest. They walk, as Francisco Vaz da Silva notes (2012), past a signpost that reads DREAM, and there is no telling whether that will be another nightmare or not. Eliciting both horror and hope, Pil-Sung Yim's *Hansel and Gretel*, I have been arguing, critiques the use of commodified fairy tales as infantilizing narratives that reproduce consumerist wish fulfillment; while the film shows how the fairy tale may help children and others to envision survival strategies against excesses of power, its denouement suggests that we are only beginning to imagine plots where empowerment does not require complicity in the logic of consumption and greed. Like *Bluebeard*, *Hansel and Gretel* invokes fantasy not so much to open viewers up to new possibilities, but to put into stark relief the fantasies that, as Slavoj Žižek (1989) has it, are at work in producing our shared sense of reality.

■　■　■

As I come to the conclusion of this chapter on the representation of storybooks and reading in *Enchanted*, *Pan's Labyrinth*, *Bluebeard*, and *Hansel and Gretel*, I return to my initial questions: How do their projections on screen of why fairy tales matter diverge? How does the construction of the gendered child figure in this production of genre? And what uses of the fairy-tale genre are we film viewers incited to make in our lives? I hope to have shown that *Pan's Labyrinth*, *Bluebeard*, and *Hansel and Gretel* invoke the fairy-tale genre or a specific fairy tale in order to confront social trauma, thus working at odds with Disney's *Enchanted* and DreamWorks' *Shrek*, which instead reaffirm the romance-and-magic formula as a core ingredient for wish fulfillment and success in our consumer capitalist world. Del Toro, Breillat, and Pil-Sung Yim decommodify this magic by reading the genre for its wonder, horror, and uncanniness respectively and by refiguring the child as active reader and adapter of the genre. In doing so, these fairy-tale films also inscribe and critique different ways in which the genre has scripted gendered power play, without, however, isolating gender from other social issues.

By foregrounding the changes in the storybook/reading convention from the early authoritative Disney formula, to the *Shrek* parody strategy, to the critical negotiation of scripts and readers in *Pan's Labyrinth*, *Bluebeard*, and *Hansel and Gretel*, I have also suggested that hegemonic and counterhegemonic uses of the fairy tale are not in binary opposition to each other, neither are they in simple alignment with the films' gender politics. Rather, these films revisit and produce multiple images of the fairy-tale genre and its phantasmatic relation to our social world, images that do not replace one another in a narrative of progress but are in active competition with one other. "The toys, films, and storybooks of today's children's culture reflect like two-way mirrors our expectations of children and our images of ourselves, *in potentia*" (Warner 1998, 16). Paying attention to how the activity of reading fairy tales works within these films clues us in to whether and how as adult spectators we are encouraged to take responsibility for the uses we make of fairy tales in our lives and in our negotiations with gendered and other social scripts.

Significantly, the popular success of *Pan's Labyrinth* has matched its critical acclaim, and, as my references to blogs and online reviews show, all three films have on different scales and in different communities acquired fans who are intrigued, fascinated, or delighted by these fairy-tale double exposures. Addressing the public's responses to del Toro's, Breillat's, and Pil-Sung Yim's fairy-tale films is beyond the scope of this chapter, but it is a productive avenue of research for furthering our understanding of how the dynamics of convergence culture impact the production and reception of the fairy tale.

3

Fairy-Tale Remix in Film
Genres, Histories, and Economies

Genre is neither a property of (and located "in") texts, nor a
projection of (and located "in") readers; it exists as a part of the
relationships between texts and readers, and it has a systematic
existence. It is a shared convention with a social force.

JOHN FROW, *Genre*

What happens when the [fairy tale as] intertext is reformulated as
more hybrid?

MERJA MAKINEN, "Theorizing Fairy-Tale Fiction"

While folklorists often define the fairy tale as transporting us to a storyworld
where the supernatural is never questioned and the audience's absolute suspension of disbelief is required, recent fairy-tale films seem to thrive on blurring
the boundaries of and raising questions about the relationship between fantasy
and reality. Some fairy-tale films have also relocated fairy tales and their heroines to more realistic storyworlds, be they pseudo-historical as in the horror-
thriller *Red Riding Hood* (Dir. Catherine Hardwicke 2011) or modern as in the
teen comedy *Sydney White* (Dir. Joe Nussbaum 2007). In the trend-setting 1998
film *Ever After* (Dir. Andy Tennant), the heroine's self-proclaimed great-great-
granddaughter states: "While Cinderella and her prince did live happily ever
after, the point, gentlemen, is that she lived." Bringing closure to the tale she
has just told the two men identified as the Brothers Grimm, she reinforces this

assertion by producing material evidence: not only a Leonardo portrait that is possibly of her Cinderella ancestor, but also another precious heirloom, the heroine's ornate and "real" glass shoe.[1]

Charles Perrault's glass slippers lose their magic perhaps in that scene, but their material presence on screen adds to the realism that has inflected the noblewoman's telling of "Cinderella" not as a fairy tale but as family history, or, at the very least, legend. This Cinderella is a larger-than-life figure—an active, educated, willful, *and* flawed woman—with whom the teller proudly associates herself, and one whom, presumably, girls at the end of the twentieth century would not dismiss as an outdated fantasy.[2]

To reach adolescents, its target audience, at the turn of the twenty-first century, this PG-13 film had to be "realistic," which meant using live action and also presenting more rounded characters than Disney's, and not relying on the supernatural to bring about the heroine's success. The film ascribed some degree of historical plausibility or legendary dimension to the Cinderella story by grounding its believability in family history and its cultural significance in humanistic progress. Cathy Lynn Preston persuasively develops such a reading of *Ever After* (2004). Placing her discussion in the broader popular-culture context of contemporary fairy-tale jokes, TV shows, and folk criticism, Preston describes *Ever After* as an "American popular culture production of the Cinderella tale that cleverly blurs the boundaries between folktale and legend in an attempt to retrieve the romantic possibilities of 'true love' for the generation currently raised in the aftermath/afterglow of second-wave feminism and post-Marxist critique" (200). More specifically, Preston suggests that the film's combining of "the shift in genre from fairy tale to legend" with "a shift in gender patterns" is a response to "the last thirty years of feminist critique of gender construction in respect to key Western European popularized versions of the fairy tale (in particular those of Perrault, the Brothers Grimm, and Disney)" (203).[3]

Preston's reading of *Ever After* links genre blurring with social forces, and as such it has implications for how folklorists and cultural critics read the deployment of multiple, competing traditions and performances in the contemporary fairy-tale web as well as, more specifically, the genre's hypercommodification in mainstream films. For instance, in approaching this new or transformed pervasiveness of fairy-tale magic in North American popular culture today, folklorist Jeana Jorgensen builds on Linda Dégh's analysis of fairy tales in advertising (1994), and on Preston's observation that "in postmodernity the stuff of fairy tales exists as fragments" acquired through a number of possible forms of cultural production (Preston 2004, 210), to tackle a crucial question: how to deal with films and other popular-culture texts that "make money on fairy tales while critiquing them" (Jorgensen 2007, 219), and that engage with the fairy tale, but "cannot be reduced to individual fairy-tale plots" (218). "These fragments," Jorgensen declares, "whether fairy-tale motifs, characters, or plots, are the building blocks of new media texts, inspired by fairy tales but not quite fairy tales themselves." She calls them "fairy-tale pastiches . . . to privilege their 'schizophrenic instrumentalization of fairy-tale matter'" (218).[4]

Indeed, many early twenty-first-century films, regardless of their classification as comedy, drama, or fantasy, make use of fairy-tale elements drawn from a range of canonical images and topoi, such as the young girl's red hoodie referencing "Little Red Riding Hood" (ATU 333) in *Hard Candy* (Dir. David Slade 2005), the magic slipper in the happy ending of *Sex and the City* (Dir. Michael Patrick King 2008), or the animal helpers in the various *Harry Potter* movies (Dir. Chris Columbus 2001, 2002; Alfonso Cuarón 2004; Mike Newell 2005; David Yates 2007 and 2009) and *The Golden Compass* (Dir. Chris Weitz 2007). What is new here, as I see it, is not the reproduction of isolated fairy-tale symbols and images in new contexts, but that their reutilization in branding "new" products often rests on the marketability of mixing and parodying these iconic bits.

At the same time, the film industry continues to capitalize on the remake of well-known tale types. In 2010, just before Disney announced that it would no longer produce animated fairy-tale films, *Tangled* put more spunk and romance into the "Rapunzel" tale. Along with the much-hyped Warner Bros. *Red Riding Hood* (Dir. Catherine Hardwicke), the more modest CBS *Beastly* (Dir. Daniel Barnz) was released in 2011. Catherine Breillat's *Sleeping Beauty* and Julia Leigh's *Sleeping Beauty*, produced respectively in France and Australia, were also both distributed in 2011, offering differently sexualized live-action adaptations of the classic tale. In 2012 alone, two "Snow White" adaptations, Universal's *Snow White and the Huntsman* (Dir. Rupert Sanders) and Relativity's *Mirror Mirror* (Dir. Tarsem Singh), are in the theaters along with the Disney rerelease of its 1991 *Beauty and the Beast* in 3-D; the SyFy movie *Witchslayer Gretl* circulates on TV and online; trailers announce another action-filled sequel, *Hansel and Gretel: Witch Hunters* (Dir. Tommy Wirkola) and the battle-filled Warner Bros. production, *Jack the Giant Slayer* (Dir. Bryan Singer, producer of *X-Men*); *Pinocchio* (Dir. Tim Burton), *Cinderella* (Dir. Mark Romanek), *Order of the Seven* (Dir. Michael Gracey), a live-action "Snow White" from Disney, and *Maleficent* (Dir. Robert Stromberg) are in preproduction as I write. This is hardly a comprehensive list.[5]

To make a specific intervention in the debate in which scholarly and other knowledge communities are engaged over today's fairy-tale films, this chapter considers the choices and effects of mixing fairy tales—their fragments and tale types—not with each other, but with other narrative genres. Recognizing the fragmentation of the fairy tale, as it is visible in current configurations of the fairy-tale web, *and* the central role that not just individual tales but competing notions of the fairy tale play in the encoding, decoding, and remaking of popular culture, I focus on generic remix in order to map out: (a) distinctive worlds the fairy tale in combination with other genres projects in contemporary globalized film culture; (b) specific histories, social forces, and knowledges at work in their economy of genres; and (c) divergent positions the films are staking out in the culture and industry of entertainment.

Is this generic complexity of fairy-tale films new? I certainly do not mean to contrast it with some "pure" practice of filmic genre or of the fairy tale. As Rick Altman shows in *Film/Genre* (1999), genre labels such as the "musical" or the "western" emerge "by apparently incidental borrowing from several unrelated genres" (34), and at the same time "Hollywood labours to identify its pictures with multiple genres, in order to benefit from the increased interest that this strategy inspires in diverse demographic groups" (57). As for literary or cinematic fairy tales, they—and indeed almost all narratives longer than a headline or a joke—make use of more than one genre and in ways that are specific to the tales' cultural and historical situatedness. At stake in my analysis are relationships of tension or harmony—the clashing or the blending of different genres in a text. In classic fairy-tale films, the fairy tale blends into and integrates itself with other filmic genres. In *Snow White and the Seven Dwarfs* (Dir. David Hand 1937), the fairy tale and the musical are not in tension but rather flow "naturally" and harmoniously into each other; their shared distance from realism seems complementary. In *The Wizard of Oz* (Dir. Victor Fleming 1939) the transitions between the realistic Kansas sections of the film and the magic world of Oz are carefully mediated and explained in a way that allows everything in the fantasy section to be explained in realist terms (that is, as Dorothy's feverish dream). Some recent films, though, make a point of pushing the generic complexity of their narratives into the foreground. Disney's *Enchanted* (Dir. Kevin Lima 2007), for instance, creates a passage between a fairy-tale world and a realistic one and exploits the two worlds' differences to a comic effect as a kind of meta-commentary on the historic suppression of realism in earlier Disney productions of fairy-tale films.

In chapter 2 when I simply called *Enchanted, Pan's Labyrinth, Bluebeard,* and *Hansel and Gretel* "fairy-tale films," I did so in response to significant generic cues and referred to the movies' generic complexity—their fairy-tale mixes with comedy, war, costume drama, horror and other film genres—only instrumentally, as it supported these films' staged readings of the fairy tale, their different projections of the fairy-tale world. However, the film industry's multiple labels for three of these films already reference their being marketed to various audiences and their weaving together of various coded expectations.[6] It is to foreground this generic multivocality—the different worlds, knowledges, and genre economies these films put into play—that I will return to two of these big-budget films, *Enchanted* and *Pan's Labyrinth*, and then discuss two independent films, *Year of the Fish* (Dir. David Kaplan) and *Dancehall Queen* (Dir. Rick Elgood and Don Letts) that bring different investments to the fairy-tale remix.

My overall question here is, how does thinking of the fairy-tale genre today as a web whose hypertextual links do not refer back to one authority or central tradition impact my approach, as a folklorist and cultural critic, to filmic fairy-tale remixes? Metacritically, this chapter seeks to activate links in the globalized web of folk and fairy tales to three specific points girding contemporary genre analysis as John Frow synthesizes: "Texts—even the simplest and most formulaic—do not 'belong' to genres but are, rather, uses of them . . . [so that] they refer not to 'a' genre but to a field or economy of genres, and their complexity derives from the complexity of that relation" (2006, 2); not only do these "genre systems form a shifting hierarchy" (71), but when they mix we need to ask "what are the conditions that make this possible?" (40); and if genre is a process, it is important to address not only "genericity" (Heidmann and Adam 2010) but "genrification," or "the institutional forces that govern the determination and distribution of classification and value" (Frow 2006, 137). In approaching how fairy-tale elements mix with other genres in contemporary films, what concerns me is the social significance of this generic complexity, its sociohistorical conditions, and its hierarchical interplay or economy. Most of all, by asking specific questions of these genre remixes, I seek to account for filmic uses of the fairy tale's story powers in ways that attune us to divergent effects, histories, and investments. How do the reality effects produced by generic incongruities match up with the fantasies that support our everyday worlds? How are the conditions and effects of hybridizing the fairy tale different from those of creolizing it on the big screen? And how do these generic economies call to specific audiences?

MIXING GENRES AND WORLDS TO DIFFERENT REALITY EFFECTS

In this section, I revisit *Enchanted* and *Pan's Labyrinth*, recent popular, big-budget films that generically mix fairy-tale elements as a major part of their appeal but do not rely on a single fairy-tale plot to do so; my focus is on the storyworlds this genre remix produces. To say that generic strategies involve an economy of genres means, first, that generic choices have values attached to them, and, second, that making those choices involves taking a position in relation to other choices and values. For Frow, the consequences of generic choice bear upon the construction of one's sense of reality: "genres create effects of reality and truth which are central to the different ways the world is understood. . . . The semiotic frames within which genres are embedded implicate and specify layered ontological domains—implicate realities which genres form as a pre-given reference" (2006, 19). Frow playfully lists a few of our "generically projected worlds," including the tabloid press world, the world of the picaresque novel, the world of the Petrarchan sonnet, the world of the curse, the world of the television sitcom, "and so on, as many worlds as there are genres" (86–87). While I use the term "storyworld" throughout to highlight its narrative construction, Frow's understanding of "world" applies here: "a relatively bounded and schematic domain of meanings, values, and affects" that "generates reality-effects specific to it" and is generically framed (85–86).

One of the most prominent forms of genre mixing in recent fairy-tale films is the parodic strategy of undercutting fairy-tale conventions by contrasting them humorously with realist ones. The Walt Disney Company's *Enchanted* begins with a scene that evokes the "my prince will come" expectations of Disney's *Snow White* and *Sleeping Beauty* (Dir. Clyde Geronimi 1959) classics, but then the fairy-tale princess, Giselle, finds herself unexpectedly exiled from the two-dimensional animated world and having to survive as an exaggeratedly naive woman in the unfriendly world of New York City. The relationship between the cartoon Disney fantasy and the realist New York setting is apparently one of stark oppositions—pastels decorating the heroine's idyllic relationship with nature and the fulfillment of romance in one space and genre, versus grays cementing regular New Yorkers' routine dealings with work, dirt, and vermin in the other. As each of the fairy-tale characters emerges into New York from the enchanted world of Andalasia, his or her arrival is represented as a traumatic experience. The city takes the place of the unfamiliar forest where classic fairy-tale heroines and heroes used to be tested, but at first what is tried is not the characters' mettle so much as their sense of genre. Giselle mistakes a thief for a helper, her Prince (James Marsden) mistakes public utilities workers for peasants, and both show an alarming propensity to launch into song during the middle of a conversation. The climax of this incongruity comes in Giselle's musical housecleaning number in New York, a grotesque parody of the housecleaning song in *Snow White* that had already been more subtly parodied in the film's cartoon section.

Underlying this clash of genres, however, is an economy that reunites them. *Enchanted*'s parodic strategy eventually yields to a return to Disney's familiar fairy-tale expectations, even though Giselle changes from a Sleeping Beauty/

Snow White innocent persecuted heroine to the rescuer of her "true love" in a dragon-slaying scene at the top of the Empire State Building. This mélange of Disney's *Sleeping Beauty, King Kong* (Dir. Merian C. Cooper and Ernest B. Schoedsack 1933), and *Shrek* hinges on a role reversal that is hardly transformative. That the dragon is female recalls and plays off the female dragon in *Shrek*, and in a way naturalizes the irrationality of the kidnapping of Robert, Giselle's New York love interest. That the monstrous dragon is only the final metamorphosis of the monstrously powerful older female Narissa, the Queen who does not want to relinquish her power to her son Prince Edward, prompts us to ask who or what is a King Kong threat nowadays. Finally, while Giselle risks her life to save Robert, it's the sidekick chipmunk Pip (voice by Jeff Bennett in Andalasia and by Kevin Lima in New York) who saves the day in the climax of the film's rehabilitation of city vermin as animal helpers.

So we can't even say that Giselle performs the heroic rescue expected of the Prince Charming stereotype. She is charming, and that's it. In this and all too many other ways, *Enchanted* merely pays lip service to feminism. While becoming more three dimensional and making choices for herself, Giselle continues to be a cheerful and fashionable housecleaning helpmate, whose actions never question the institution of marriage. The film parodies Disney's earlier representations of Snow White and Sleeping Beauty—the princesses who sing but have nothing to say, who engage in cheerful housework and exhibit fashions on hourglass figures, who know their prince will come—but it ultimately seeks only to bring new glamour and power to the Disneyfied fairy-tale princess image and her romantic plot. Furthermore, it does so by valorizing the Disney Princess and antifeminist choices in the figure of Morgan, the girl child in New York City, who—as I discuss in chapter 2—is presented as the moral compass in the film. As the initially bifurcated storyworlds come together, one of their reality effects is to affirm, as Linda Pershing and Lisa Gablehouse have noted, "faux feminism," whereby "fragments of feminist ideas are trivialized or subsumed within a dominant discourse of traditional gender roles" (2010, 154).[7]

The film's continuity with the Disneyfication of the fairy tale harnesses its gender ideology to a commercial economy of which Morgan is hardly the only happy consumer. *Enchanted* blatantly advertises Disney's "princess" franchise, a multi-billion-dollar business that sells toys, DVDs, dolls, and clothes for girls and women, as well as Disney weddings. In the transporting song-and-dance scene set in Central Park, the commodification of the fairy tale today as an escapist or compensatory fiction is naturalized, or more precisely spectacularized. Early in the film, New Yorkers are shown to scoff at the "ever ever after," but in this scene they (as representatives of *Enchanted*'s mainstream Euro North

PLATE 26. Central Park as Fantasy World in *Enchanted* (1)

American audiences) are also shown to love pretending they are in its make-believe world, whether this means dressing up for an exclusive and expensive costume ball, dressing up and paying for a "fairy-tale" wedding, or flocking to a children's performance of "Rapunzel" (ATU 310) featuring a young girl with fake long tresses spilling out of a miniature tower in the park—another teaser, or advertisement, for *Tangled* (Dir. Nathan Greno and Byron Howard 2010), the Disney computer-animated film that was then in preproduction. It is no wonder that Giselle's song and charm seduce the New York lawyer who is her skeptical prince figure, as well as *all* the park-goers. The ball, the wedding, and the other make-believe scenarios naturalize the appeal of fantasy and display the power of magic for sale in the contemporary world.

As Central Park turns into Disney World, there is no parody here, but a *Fantasia*-like (Dir. James Algar, Samuel Armstrong. Ford Beebe, Norman Ferguson, Jim Handley, T. Hee, Wilfred Jackson, Hamilton Luske, Bill Roberts and Paul Satterfield 1940) spectacle of commercialized dreams for which girls and women dress up. The film's insistent clash of worlds and genres merely consolidates a normative project that exploitatively deploys "faux feminism" to the same ends as Cathy Lynn Preston sees in *Ever After*: to "retrieve the romantic possibilities of 'true love' for the generation currently raised in the aftermath/afterglow of second-wave feminism and post-Marxist critique" (2004, 200).[8]

As we know, DreamWorks produced *Shrek* and its sequels starting in 2001 in an effort to contest Disney's corporate monopoly (Zipes 2006a, 211). This struggle for power among producers of today's fairy-tale films is actually dramatized as a mise en abyme from the competitor's perspective in one of *Shrek's* early scenes, as we see unruly fairy-tale or fantasy characters like Pinocchio, the

PLATE 27. Central Park as Fantasy World in *Enchanted* (2)

ogre, the damsel in distress, and the talking donkey fighting to free themselves from the normalizing and self-aggrandizing project of one ruler's fantasy. And the commercial success of the *Shrek* films has indeed challenged Disney enough for it to produce *Enchanted* as an attempt to reassert its shaken monopoly on the cinematic fairy tale.[9] But the parodic strategies that Disney and DreamWorks employ in comically mixing genre conventions, then deploying them to bolster a specific social use of the fairy tale as genre, are not that different.

Like *Enchanted*, the *Shrek* films start by comically disrupting what is commonly understood as a classic—meaning clichéd rather than traditional in folkloristic terms—fairy-tale frame. Each of the three *Shrek* films (as seen in chapter 2) begins with the same stereotypical scenario as its pre-text and framing device: the rescue of the maiden in the tower, or the damsel in distress motif that a romanticized and Disneyfied image of the fairy tale has canonized. And in each film, that rescue explodes into parody. However, while the parodied rescue scenes draw on a satirical demystification of fairy-tale formulas and motifs already active in popular culture, the effect is merely humorous and transient, because the alliance of fairy tale and romance still ends up ruling the stories' closure and emotional hold. *Enchanted* seems to have learned from the *Shrek* films this strategy of initially parodying the idealization of romance in earlier fairy-tale films only to end up celebrating the same set of conventions. The presence of this strategy in both franchises—and in subsequent films such as *Mirror Mirror*—testifies to some impact of feminist critique on the production and reception of fairy-tale films, on the one hand, and to the underlying strength of the gender ideology that feminists have sought to contest, on the other.

This pattern of parodying and then celebrating enchantment in these films may finally be less about the fairy tale than about the ideological power and contradictions in romance itself. Each of these films exposes the tension between fantasy and realism in the conventions of popular, formulaic romance, which combines strongly repetitive plots, a highly predictable set of complications, and a nearly obligatory happy ending with a demand for full-bodied characters—or at least engaging and convincing ones. The parodies of fairy-tale conventions in these films echo this contradiction between the demands of plot and characterization. In fact, the films' jokes distance the main characters from their fairy-tale prototypes for their viewers in a way that resembles what Sigmund Freud calls the "bribe" that the joke teller offers the listener to allow the utterance of hostile or obscene material (1960, 100). The parodies express a disavowal of belief in fairy-tale fantasies that opens up the space for rehearsing those very fantasies; since the films have declared that they and their audiences do not take them seriously, they and their audiences can go ahead and repeat them. Thus this parodic strategy may owe the success evident in its repetition to the way it conspiratorially establishes the tellers' and the listeners' agreement to indulge in the guilty pleasures of unreconstructed romantic fantasy.

Like Frow, Mark Bould connects genre choice to world construction when he argues that the critical potential of the genre of fantasy lies in its making obvious the inevitability and inescapability of such constructions, in contrast to the invisibility that cloaks the generic strategies involved in maintaining our everyday sense of reality: "what sets fantasy apart from much mimetic art is a frankly self-referential consciousness . . . of the impossibility of 'real life'" (Bould 2002, 83). Angela Carter wrote that the fairy tale "positively parades its lack of verisimilitude" (1990, xi). But through the institutionalization of the fairy tale as children's literature, the critical potential Bould would attribute to this parading of artifice has been, for the most part, carefully subordinated to didacticism. The fairy tale has had to teach its child reader a lesson about the real adult world, and our enjoyment of the pleasures of fairy-tale imagination has had to be justified by its ultimate performance of its real-world duty. Because of that history, the relationship between a fairy tale world and a realist world also has something to do with relationships between children and adults.

The choice to contrast fairy-tale and realist elements with each other in the telling of a story or the making of a film necessarily involves taking a position about make-believe and reality in relation to pleasure and duty and to childhood and maturity. In *Enchanted*, these oppositions collapse into the all-embracing economy of consumer capitalism, and the adults are finally infantilized by their embrace of the happily-ever-after romance fantasy. Although the *Shrek* films successfully take up arms against the Walt Disney Company's dominance of the fairy-tale film industry, they certainly do not equally contest the dominance of conventional romantic fantasy or didactic rhetoric. In both *Shrek* and *Enchanted*, the deliberate parodic contrast between fairy-tale convention and realistic representation is not sustained because the values attached to the genres—the generic worlds that have been called upon—are not really at odds with one another at all. The gestures of rebellion, whether they are against patriarchal convention or corporate convergence, are only pretexts setting up the eventual triumphant celebration of family values and consumerism.

At the other end of the spectrum in terms of the way it constructs and sustains a contrast between fairy tale and realistic generic worlds is Guillermo del Toro's R-rated *Pan's Labyrinth*. No recent film raises the stakes involved in the generic economy of the fairy tale higher. Its double plot sets the fairy-tale narrative of the voice-over frame and the young protagonist Ofelia against the historical narrative, set in 1944 Spain, that is the world of all of the other, adult characters in the film. Both worlds are dangerous and brutal: one is not a fantasy escape from the harsh realities of the other. During the climactic confrontation at the heart of the labyrinth between Ofelia and her monstrous stepfather, the fascist Captain Vidal, the fact that Vidal cannot see the magical Faun to whom Ofelia is speaking is never afforded the straightforward explanatory power one might expect: that Vidal sees what is really there, and Ofelia is only imagining her fairy tale. Instead, the scene dramatizes the abyss that separates the two narrative worlds—their mutual incomprehensibility to each other.[10]

Nonetheless, the worlds act upon each other. While Vidal's bullet kills Ofelia in the historical world, in the fairy-tale world it completes the choice to save her newborn brother—rather than sacrifice him, as the Faun has commanded her—that earns her the return to her true, royal home. Thus Ofelia's fairy-tale worlds, the one of her magic tasks and the one of Princess Moanna's origin, are not insulated from the adults' reality, but constitute alternatives to it. And Ofelia's belief in the magical world is surely no more delusional than Vidal's faith in his own favorite story, the story of the honorable death of a soldier passed on to him from his father, which he pathetically expects the community he has tortured and terrorized during his life to pass on to his son. Stories in this film have profound effects and tie together generations, but no hierarchy of genres sorts out the choices they offer.

Pan's Labyrinth features two strong female protagonists (Ofelia and Mercedes [Maribel Verdú], Vidal's head servant and secret supporter of the anti-Fascist rebels), but its debt to feminism has less to do with the critique of gender ideology than with that critique's realization of the fairy tale's power. Del Toro does not strip the fairy tale of its didacticism. Ofelia's story—her disobedience

PLATE 28. Neither world is safe in *Pan's Labyrinth*

and sacrifice—certainly has an ethical point. Rather, del Toro separates the fairy tale's moral force from the condescension that so often attends the encryption of adult rules in fairy-tale situations. The fears and anxieties so strongly depicted in a film like *The Wizard of Oz* are no longer insulated, not so much from the children who view it—remember how notoriously frightening that film has been to many a young child—as from the adults invited to pass off the Wicked Witch of the West (Margaret Hamilton) as mere make-believe. *Pan's Labyrinth* allows no subordination and separation of its sometimes-nightmarish fairy tale from the nightmare of history.

Del Toro's achievement bears comparison to Angela Carter's treatment of fairy tale conventions and traditions in *The Bloody Chamber*, but these artists' generic mixes are tellingly different from each other. Instead of the rapprochement between fairy tale and Gothic that Carter achieves through eroticism, del Toro uses the resources of cinematic horror, a genre he has praised as a form of "naive surrealism" that sets itself against commercial culture's pathological denial of darkness and death. By calling horror cinema's surrealism "naive," del Toro does not mean that it is for children, but that unlike the surrealist movement of the early twentieth century, it does not bracket itself from popular culture through the ironic distance afforded by an elite or avant-garde posture. He claims that his predilection for depicting monsters participates in "no postmodern irony whatsoever." The strategy of merging fairy tale and horror, and then making them the emotional and thematic partners of historical realism, insists upon the intellectual seriousness of these forms of popular cultural production that have been conventionally trivialized.[11]

Some generic remixes of the fairy tale that may initially seem surprising are supported by a certain structural or formulaic homogeneity of genres. Think for instance of the television series *Grimm* and *Once Upon a Time*, which first competed for American viewers' attention on NBC and ABC respectively in the 2011–12 season.[12] While they both bring fairy-tale characters into realistic settings and play with a number of genres, such as legends and family drama, *Grimm*'s genre bending primarily mingles fairy tales with crime dramas while *Once Upon a Time* turns in the direction of soap operas. On the one hand, already in the 1970s, focusing on character types and functions, folklorist Tekla Dömötör concluded that the analogies between heroic as well as antagonist figures, "supernatural" tasks, helpers, and outcomes in the two genres "undoubtedly show that the detective novel is a direct descendent of the Volksmärchen," specifically the tale of magic (ATU 300–749), "perhaps not a legitimate one, but a child all the same" (Dömötör 1975, 335).[13] On the other hand, in her introduction to *The Virago Book of Fairy Tales*, Angela Carter noted how "the excessive wealth of some of the characters, the absolute poverty of others, the excessive extremes of good luck and ugliness, of cleverness and stupidity, of vice and virtue, beauty, glamour, and guile, the tumultuous plethora of events, the intense and inharmonious personal relationships" and more "are characteristics of the fairy tale that link it directly to the contemporary [1980s] television soap opera" (1990, xx). Texts that combine fairy tales and pornography or erotica also rely on the generic homogeneity—their abstraction of human relations and bodies as well as their exploration of conforming to and transgressing norms—of apparently clashing genres, an alikeness that Angela Carter sought to counter in her critical and fictional writings, Catherine Orenstein noted in *Red Riding Hood Uncloaked: Sex, Morality, and the Evolution of a Fairy Tale* (2002), and recent shorts such as the Belgian *Black XXX-mas* (Dir. Pieter Van Hees 1999) and the Singaporean *A Wicked Tale* (Dir. Tzang Merwyn Tong 2005) put in new evidence.

A different kind of thematic and structural analogy operates in the mix of realism and fairy tale animating *Year of the Fish* (written and directed by David Kaplan 2007) and *Dancehall Queen* (written by Suzanne Fenn, Don Letts, and Ed Wallace, and directed by Rick Elgood and Don Letts 1997), both of which cast real-world social injustices and problems as "Cinderella" stories that are

definitely not child friendly in their language, themes, or imagery.[14] Like Tom Davenport's *Ashpet* (1990; DVD 2005) or *Hansel and Gretel* (1977; DVD 2005), which Americanize the Grimms' tales, setting them in twentieth-century Appalachia, *Year of the Fish* and *Dancehall* are independent, low-budget movies that are markedly located, one in New York City's Chinatown, the other in Kingston, Jamaica. And they are, as Jack Zipes remarks of Davenport's live-action films, "interested in how people survive oppression, particularly, how they survive with pride and a sense of their own dignity" (foreword to www.davenportfilms .com/pages/cl_zipespage.html). These films demand we suspend our disbelief to the extent that they offer happy endings to the dispossessed in storyworlds that purposefully have a naturalistic specificity. My analytical focus here is on how, in their mixing "Cinderella" with realism, Kaplan's and the Elgood-Letts films tap into the folktale and fairy tale as genres that are now inextricably commingled (in the "hybrid genre" we call "fairy tale") but are not simply coterminous with each other in terms of history or expectations. I will argue that this disjuncture is accommodated differently in each case, and that this difference has to do with specific histories of genre and place in which *Year of the Fish* and *Dancehall Queen* intervene as well as with the specific economies of entertainment to which the films contribute.

Both *Dancehall Queen* and *Year of the Fish* approach "Cinderella" as a tale of transformation that centers in the optative mood on issues of labor *and* sexual

PLATE 30. Marcia in *Dancehall Queen*

abuse. As such, each film breaks away from the Disneyfied romance-centered vision of Charles Perrault's "Cendrillon" and links up instead with narratives that folklorists have long classified as related tale types, the more commonly known plot of domestic mistreatment on the part of the heroine's stepmother, "Cinderella" (ATU 510A); and "Peau d'âne" or "Donkeyskin" (ATU 510B), a story centered on the mistreated heroine's escaping sexual abuse on the part of her father.[15] In the films, the two plots are brought together in ways that refuse to separate problems of labor injustice from those of sexual labor in heteropatriarchal capitalist economies.

Shot entirely in twenty-first-century New York City's Chinatown, with a pan-Asian cast, Kaplan's *Year of the Fish* features Ye Xian (Vietnamese American An Nguyen) who has, in order to help her elderly father, migrated from China only to find herself contracted to work off her passage to the United States in the euphemistically called "massage parlor" run by Mrs. Su (Tsai Chin, who played the mother in *The Joy Luck Club* [1993], Madame Wu in *Casino Royale* [2006], and Helen Rubinstein in *Grey's Anatomy* [2007]).[16] Naive, young, and deprived of her passport (which Mrs. Su holds hostage), Ye Xian nevertheless refuses to service the parlor's clients sexually, which results in her having to clean, shop, and cook for Mrs. Su, her "girls," and her brother Vinnie (Lee Wong), whose lurking around Ye Xian disturbingly progresses into sexual harassment and a barely disguised proposal for bride purchase. As Mrs. Su, the "cruel stepmother" Madam, sums it up for Ye Xian, "you are in a new country now, and all that old Chinese dignity stuff doesn't mean anything anymore. . . . In America, without money there is no dignity."

Shot in Kingston, Jamaica, in the 1990s, with an entirely Jamaican crew and cast, Elgood and Letts's *Dancehall Queen* introduces Marcia (Audrey Reid), a thirty-year-old street vendor who cannot make ends meet for her and her daughters without Larry (Carl Davis) lending a not-so-disinterested hand to help with the bills and, most significantly, the older girl's education. The film opens with scenes of conflict: one where Marcia has to compete with a violent newcomer, Priest (Paul Campbell), for her usual spot on the sidewalk to sell merchandise; the other where her older daughter, the fifteen-year-old Tanya (Cheryne Anderson), is having to fend off "Uncle" Larry's lechery. These economic and sexual threats rapidly escalate into irremediable violence as Priest kills Marcia's friend, Sonny, and Larry violates Tanya. Marcia's life, in and out of her ghetto home, is shattered. Furthermore, Marcia's "going with the program," whether it is Priest's injunction not to talk to the police about the murder or Larry's claims over her daughter, ends up making her even more vulnerable. Priest stalks Marcia not only to make sure that her younger brother, Junior, won't talk to the police about the murder, but also to force her into a sexual relationship. And Larry leaves them out to dry once Tanya refuses to have anything further to do with him, saying, "I want to see how you will manage without Santa Claus." While her age and lack of innocence make her an unlikely damsel in distress, Marcia's hard work and collusive victimization are the building blocks of her Cinderella persona.

The two films, *Year of the Fish* and *Dancehall Queen*, also trace their respective protagonist's path from oppression to redemption in folk and fairy-tale style, with helpers and tests paving the way for her recognition; however, these paths are quite different, as powerfully marked throughout by the different musical scores, the "shimmering, fairy-tale feel" (Kaplan 2007) of Paul Cantelon's piano compositions versus Wally Badarou's pulsing reggae songs performed by Beenie Man, Bounty Killer, General Degree, and other artists. In *Year of the Fish*, Ye Xian is offered help before she even realizes how much of a problem she is going to have to face as a young woman and illegal immigrant.

PLATE 31. The Magic Fish in *Year of the Fish*

Drawing on the a ninth-century Chinese "Cinderella"—one that is often identified as the oldest version we have access to in manuscript form, and an illustrated children's book, *Yeh Shen: A Cinderella Story from China* (1982), makes it easily accessible in English—Ye Xian's help comes from a fish, who is also surreally the narrator (David Lee) of the whole film, "I will tell you what I saw."[17] The care that Ye Xian bestows on the fish in turn bonds him to her so that even after the fish has been killed and consumed by the greedy Mrs. Su and her minions, his spirit protects her from losing herself in the $-exchange economy. She has passed the test. Further help comes along the way from socially marginal characters such as a homeless old man, the sex worker who still wishes for love, and three women working in Auntie Yaga's garment factory. Most dramatically, the fairy-godmother figure in the film is Auntie Yaga (Randall Duk Kim),[18] a sexually and ethically ambiguous larger-than-life character who in the guise of a fortune-teller gives Ye Xian the fish in the first place and, later, having listened to bones of the fish expressing his gratitude to the girl, provides a new dress for Ye Xian to go to the Chinese New Year celebration. By the end of the film, Ye Xian has proven herself brave—not letting herself be commodified in the massage parlor but also not letting herself be stopped by the white-, red-, and no-faced guardians of Auntie Yaga's factory—and, as her father's spirit tells her, her ancestors are proud of how she has retained her dignity. Johnny, the struggling musician with whom she has fallen in love, recognizes her value and frees her from her servitude to Mrs. Yu. In the film's storyworld, a surreally rotoscoped Chinatown,[19] Ye Xian's holding on to her ancestors, values, and traditions, as represented in the ancient tale, is affirmed as a survival tool that does not allow her to break free from poverty as an (illegal) immigrant, but does protect her from being fully reified or nullified by exploitation.

While Marcia's helpers are easily identified in *Dancehall Queen*, her tests and her identity are not so straightforward or openly conforming to traditional values as they are in *Year of the Fish*. Left alone to provide for her family and spurned by Tanya (who candidly states, "You made me into a whore, mamma"), Marcia is faced with the realization of how her collusion with an exchange economy based on sexual exploitation did nothing much to alleviate their financial burden or offer her daughters a better future. Help does not come to her, but she does recognize Tanya's rebellion as inspiration for her own transformation, and upon noticing "how ordinary" the dancehall queen Olivine (Patrice Harrison) looks in her day clothes, Marcia sees an opportunity for herself to assume a radically different persona in a new space, the dancehall.[20] As she secretly practices new dance moves and designs her own flashy dancehall costumes, Marcia finds a "magic" helper (or fairy godmother) in Miss Gordon (Pauline Stone Myrie), the dressmaker. Rather than drawing on a Caribbean version, *Dancehall Queen* localizes the tropes we expect in a Cinderella tale: clothes, beauty, secret identity at the dance, competition, and recognition play significant roles in the unpromising heroine's transformation. The tasks Marcia poses for herself are to try on a different persona, to perform in a role that will earn her respect, to use her own resources to better her own and her family's lives. Eventually, Marcia cleverly gets rid of both Priest and Larry in one swoop, and, in her Mystery Lady guise, she successfully competes with Olivine for the Dancehall Queen title and the exorbitantly large cash prize that goes with it. By the end, Marcia has proven herself brave—not letting herself be commodified in the dancehall but also not letting herself be controlled by rapacious men—and, as her Tanya and Miss Gordon tell her, her family as well as the other disenfranchised people in the dancehall are proud of how she has proven her cleverness and their dignity.

The intertextual links of "Cinderella" with *Year of the Fish* and *Dancehall Queen* are varied and strong, but what is at stake in their genre mixing and for whom? Aptly described by one reviewer as "a small film with large ambitions . . . challenging the contemporary fairy tale to raise issues of human trafficking and human worth" (Yamashiro 2011, 178), *Year of the Fish* (re)activates an intertextual link with the "Yeh Shen" tale for American audiences as an

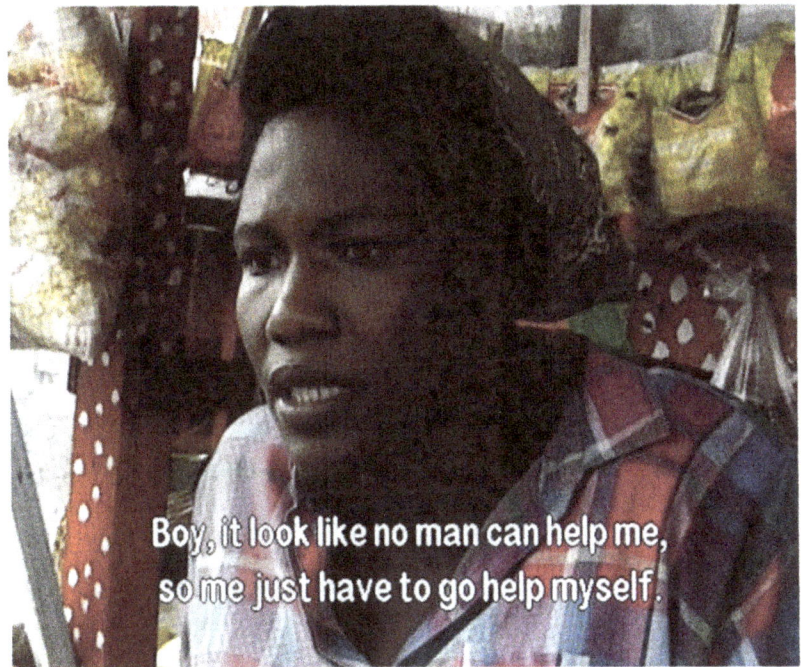

PLATE 32. Marcia's realization in *Dancehall Queen*

invitation to resist the assimilation logic of capitalism and pay homage to the resistance that immigrant communities harbor.[21] It does so as I have shown by affirming (what the film adopts as) Chinese folktale and belief traditions in contrast to the hegemonic expectations we have of "Cinderella" as a glittery fairy tale in which the innocent persecuted heroine rises (back) up to princess status in a usually all-white court. A strong tension between uses of folk and fairy tales that sustain social justice and uses that sustain commodification is, thus, at the heart of Kaplan's imaginative project, and, in the end, I argue, attending the resolution of this tension is a contradiction. As the film blends Chinese narrative and belief traditions into a fairy-tale script, issues of labor and sexual exploitation give way to the familiar "my prince will come" plot. While the film challenges the hegemony of a commodified Euro-American fairy tale by updating the ancient Chinese tale and showcasing its relevance in the United States today, at the same time it also subordinates cultural alterity to the overarching appeal of the fairy-tale film as romantic comedy and to a severely limited version of the American dream. Supporting this Americanized fantasy, at least two ideological

PLATE 33. Ye Xian and her helpers in *Year of the Fish*

structures are at work in the *Year of the Fish*'s generic mix: individualism and heteronormative romance.

Throughout the film Ye Xian is identified as exceptional. Verbally, this is affirmed at the start of the film when Mrs. Su scolds the young woman for thinking she is superior to the other parlor workers and then, much later, when the foreman says to the women working in Auntie Yaga's sweatshop, "this woman [Ye Xian], she has nothing to do with you." Visually Ye Xian's attire also distinguishes her from the provocatively dressed girls in the massage parlor: she wears the same unisex raincoat—its red hood an allusion to another well-known tale—and shapeless clothes for most of the film. After the plainly dressed factory workers have bathed and clothed her in what Ye Xian describes as "a blue dress with tear drops, color of sky, color of sea," the same women escort her down the streets of Chinatown to the big celebration they will not be attending.[22] Of course, the heroine's qualities are, in folk and fairy tales alike, contrasted starkly with those of antagonists and false heroines, and the heroine's natural beauty and dress externalize her moral qualities. We know to expect this, but here the social hierarchy is filmically *naturalized* rather than called attention to, as it was in older folktales (for instance, the ones collected by Giuseppe Pitrè in Sicily) where the storyteller would remark of the successful heroine, "So, she remained happy and content / While we still can't pay the rent" (Zipes and Russo 2009, 35).[23]

PLATE 34. Helpers escort Ye Xian in *Year of the Fish*

Perhaps even more symptomatic of the contradictions in *Year of the Fish* is that the blue dress is not simply key for others to see Ye Xian's worth, but it is held as the measure of her desire.[24] Earlier in the film, her looking longingly out of her little room to the open sky visually signaled Ye Xian's aspirations for a different life. Taking initiative to pursue them, she saves the fish bones, disobeys Mrs. Su's orders, and dares to face the mysteriously powerful Auntie Yaga in her hellish garment factory. What is made of her actions and desire? Auntie Yaga tells her to go to the New Year celebration: "maybe you'll find what you are looking for." Ye Xian's agency, as well as her aspirations for freedom from servitude and sexual violence, is instantly reduced to the prospect of her meeting with her love interest, Johnny Pan (Ken Leung, who then played Miles Straume in the TV series *Lost* [2008–10]). The scene at the Chinese restaurant that follows has all the tropes of the dance scene in which the princess appears in her true splendor to the prince who only has eyes for her, and this "magically" turns the modern localization of a Chinese tale into the ethnic flavoring of a hegemonic American romantic comedy script.

In the end, Ye Xian will deserve to be rescued: Johnny recognizes her exceptional resilience, beauty, and dignity, even in the squalid parlor of sexual trafficking, and his grandmother pays off the heroine's debt to Mrs. Su. As the magical-fish narrator tells us in the end, Ye Xian and Johnny "will not be rich, but have a chance to be happy." Once Auntie Yaga identifies romantic "love"

PLATE 35. Romantic bliss in *Year of the Fish*

as Ye Xian's only desire, we never have a chance to know what more she might have wanted, and the possibility for meaningful social, rather than individual, transformation is off the table. In fact, Auntie Yaga threatens to "bite off her teats" if Ye Xian ever returns to the exploitative factory again, and a quick final scene gestures toward explaining Mrs. Su's systematic violation of human rights as the outcome of personal grief. As the American dream of liberty and happiness the immigrant Ye Xian tenuously holds on to is decoupled from any expectation of social justice and economic change, a stereotypically heteronormative fairy-tale romance also displaces the desire for social justice the film's beginning inspired.[25]

My point here is not to detract from the ambition of Kaplan's *Year of the Fish* as a twenty-first-century adaptation of "Cinderella." It is, first, to show up a limitation or contradiction that goes hand in hand with marketing considerations, the pressures on this beautiful independent film that disputes Mrs. Su's axiom, "in America without money there is no dignity," to conform to primarily American audiences' expectations of "Animation—Fantasy—Romance." Second, it is to show that the sociohistorical conditions enabling creative genre mixing matter to the generic hierarchy at work in the hybrid cultural product and its effects. If global designs and commerce create opportunities for genre mixings, considering their economy of agency and representation helps to address what is at stake and for whom in the remix.

Kaplan chose to work the Chinese "Yeh Shen" into his film because the *Year of the Fish* focuses on and is an homage to the people of New York City's Chinatown. In other words, the histories and gritty realities of a specific group's immigration to the United States make activating this intertextual and generic link not only possible but also appropriate for Kaplan; however, there is no telling from the film how active this link is for the people of Chinatown that are imaginatively represented in the film. As he states in his commentary, the director was well aware of the plethora of "Cinderella" versions, and he "loosely based" his film on the ninth-century Chinese one because it has "wonderfully strange, unique details" (such as the fish as magical helper) compared to the well-known Perrault tale, and so "it seemed to make sense to take this ancient Chinese story and set it in modern-day Chinatown" (Kaplan 2007). Whether it is through the film's rotoscoping animation or its musical score, Kaplan's deliberate vision is to "situate the film somewhere half between reality, the reality of the street scenes and the reality of Chinatown, the gritty underbelly reality, and balance that with this kind of magical fairy-tale story, where strange things happen, magical things happen." As he integrates the Baba Yaga character from Russian folklore as well as details from Baba Yaga stories such as the Bright Day, the Red Sun, and the Dark Night into his film, Kaplan applies his extensive knowledge of and interest in folktale symbolism; at the same time, this collage or multicultural approach can be read as one indicator of how the balance tips toward the fairy tale and its magic as the film's overarching investment in a genre or reality effect. Kaplan's investment in hybridizing the fairy tale is further corroborated by his other brilliant fairy-tale shorts, such as the alluring *Little Red Riding Hood* (1997; 2007 DVD) and the disturbing *The Frog King* (1994; 2007 DVD). His investment in re-creating fairy-tale magic is also brought home by the "storybook closure" (Kaplan 2007) of *Year of the Fish*, a framing sequence in which the magical-fish narrator says "good night" not only to Ye Xian and Johnny but also to Mrs. Su, Auntie Yaga, the massage parlor girls, and others. These vignettes offer a glimpse into the characters beyond their involvement with Ye Xian as antagonists or helpers; they also deliberately link with the charm of a popular American children's book, *Goodnight Moon*.

In contrast, I see the generic mix in *Dancehall Queen* as rearticulating hegemonic scripts more "from the perspective of local histories" (Mignolo 2000, 41) and for Jamaican audiences first, while seeking also to appeal to a broader public. Grounding the creolization of the fairy tale in this film are Marcia's representation as trickster rather than innocent persecuted heroine in the storyworld's sexual *and* labor economies, and the remix of "Cinderella" in Jamaican dancehall culture. As such, the film locates itself first in narrative and living traditions of Jamaica; it also transforms the glittery image of the fairy-tale princess, playing it out as the hypersexual dancehall queen, but also deploying it to the celebration of a counterworld in which social justice is fulfilled, even if only temporarily.

In its DVD version, the title of *Dancehall Queen*'s first scene is "Best Behavior," referring most literally to the dialogue when, just before he protects Marcia from Priest's bullying, Sonny asks, "Marcia, you sure you asked him nicely?" and she replies, "Sonny, I was on my best behavior." What neither Sonny nor Marcia knows is that Priest is not there to take over her vendor's spot but to establish contact in preparation for murdering Sonny, who is a problem for Larry in his landowner fight against "squatters." Marcia is unknowingly a pawn in Priest's *and* Larry's game from the start, and the game involves much more than her household's well-being. As she and we, the audience, find out much later in the film from Larry who wants to show off to her in her dancehall persona, this is a game in which the rules of profit and accumulation apply equally to land, labor (as seen in Larry's go go club as well as in his "delegation" of murder to hired help), and sex relations. Marcia reacts to this revelation of systemic violence with horror, but effectively hides it from Larry. She is forming a plan of her own based not only on her realization that "boy, it look like no man can help me so me just have to help myself," but activating her decision to "make a change."[26]

Marcia's success depends not on her being good or kind—though, like Ye Xian and many other Cinderellas, she is that too in her own way—but on her becoming a trickster figure in the West African Anansi tradition that lives on in Jamaica. As she explains later to Tanya, about her dancehall guise, "That's not me but I have a plan that's going to make life better for all of we." Refusing to be a willing participant in Priest's and Larry's game (their heteropatriarchal and exploitative violence), she plays *with* their rules and turns the tables on them. "Who you see is who I am" she tells Larry, for instance, when he first meets her in her dancehall guise; to him, from then on, she is "Sexy Bitch," and to his detriment he never bothers to ask her name or find out who she actually is. By performing to the roles Priest and Larry expect of her and by playing to these men's appetites within the limits she defines, Marcia cleverly leads them to fight each other, which eventually results in her being free of both of them, without her engaging in violence. Marcia brings that same savvy refusal to be manipulated to her actions in the dancehall. In Jamaica today, this is a space where "ghetto youth (the black lower-class masses)" engage in "active cultural production . . . and attempt to deal with the endemic problems of poverty, racism, and violence" (Stolzoff 2000, 1), a space where—as the raunchy dance sequences

PLATE 36. Marcia makes a change in *Dancehall Queen*

in the film portray—women's bodies are also hypersexualized.[27] In the film's dancehall scene, Marcia's power springs not simply from her hard work, expert dancing, and sexy performance, but from her refusal to let herself be managed by a guy or commodified. Center stage in her mind is the purpose to change things. We see this most clearly when she wins the Dancehall Queen contest: her getting the trophy and title is primarily the means to some financial independence. Olivine remains the "true" Dancehall Queen, as Marcia tells her when she returns the trophy to her; what Marcia wants—relief from financial dependence as well as respect—escapes the confines of the dancehall: "There's a whole world out there waiting, and I'm going to get some."

As I read *Dancehall Queen*, it is Marcia's trickster persona and participation in dancehall culture that rearticulate the "Cinderella" tale from a contemporary Jamaican experience, rather than it being a "Cinderella" tale about that experience. This is especially visible in the film's "recognition" scene, which traditionally is the moment when, thanks to her successfully passing the shoe test, the Cinderella figure is recognized by villains and suitor alike to be the splendidly clothed mystery beauty who had awed them all at the ball. In Georges Méliès's 1899 short film, *Cendrillon* (Cinderella), this moment of truth was validated by the fairy's instant makeover of the girl in rags, and then Cinderella's ascension to royalty was celebrated outside of the church by the villagers' dancing. In 1998, almost a century later, *Ever After*'s "Cinderella goes unknown to the ball" (Uther 2004, 293) sequence was disrupted by a warped "recognition" scene within it, where the stepmother recognizes the Comtesse Nicole de Lancret as Danielle and reveals she is not a noblewoman; at that point Danielle's awesome appearance as Nicole is no longer regarded (even by her prince) as a marker of her inner beauty or nobility, but brands her as an impostor, reversing the function of recognizing the heroine for who she is. We know that in the end Prince Henry sees her worth in spite of class differences and marries her to everyone's delight, especially since Danielle seems to have traded utopia for romance.[28]

In full-on melodrama style, *Dancehall Queen* stages an equivalent of the *Ever After* recognition-reversed scene at the crucial time of the competition for the Dancehall Queen title. Olivine has found out that the Mystery Lady is nothing more than "an ordinary street vendor," someone she believes has no place competing with her on the dance floor, and she lets her opponent as well as the dancehall crowd know. Marcia's initial reaction is to call the competition off as she appears to be ashamed of who she is, whether we take that to be the dancehall persona she wants to keep from her family and neighbors, or the poor hard-working single-mother persona she sought to escape in the dancehall. At this point of crisis, the social power of dancehall culture takes over to reframe the fairy tale and bring about *Dancehall Queen*'s distinctive happy ending. Tanya, who has already accepted her mother's double life, asks Marcia in disbelief, "After all this work, money, sacrifice, you are going to call it quits?" She also points out that Olivine must be going through all this trouble because she recognizes Marcia's talent. When Miss Gordon brings in the unexpected news about the crowd in the dancehall, "Everyone knows, and they love it!," Tanya chimes in encouraging Marcia to compete: "It's for all of we." The competition takes place, and the majority vote of the people in the dancehall goes, not surprisingly, to Mystery Lady/Marcia, the defiant and talented underdog with whom they identify.

If Marcia's success is a given in the "Cinderella" tale, what stands out in the outcome of *Dancehall Queen* is how her victory empowers other underdogs as well as herself: her daughters, materially; her supporters—"the people who have big dreams," in the words of Beenie Man, the real-life dancehall celebrity who is MC and organizer of the fictional competition—less tangibly, but still meaningfully. She walks back to her home with them, and, even as the people cheer for

PLATE 37. At the competition in *Dancehall Queen*

PLATE 38. Marcia the winner with her people in *Dancehall Queen*

her, her ordinary dress signals she is still one of them, she is celebrated as being a part of them.

Tellingly, the film, which is filled throughout with reggae music, opens and closes with the same song. "It's a dancehall thing!" a man's voice announces at the very start of the film, while the camera introduces us to a Kingston neighborhood by interspersing shots of Marcia pushing her stall down the streets and Beenie Man singing a song he seems to have just written the lyrics to while sitting on a crate on the sidewalk, surrounded by Rastafarian and Black Power symbols (including a map of Africa, Emperor Selassie, and Malcolm X). It is the "Dance Hall Queen" song, which refers to Marcia by name, that praises her— "so full a etiquette and yuh so clever"—and anticipates her becoming a legendary dancer thanks to Selassie's design and her talent for arousing men. By the time the dressed-up Beenie Man and Chevelle Franklin sing the song for Marcia on stage at the end of the film, she has become that legendary character—and in a way proven her royal status—but her performance and her cleverness have also undone the script in which she seems more of an object of desire than a trickster.

If, as scholar Carolyn Cooper (2004) suggests, Jamaican dancehall culture is a "world of make-believe," where new social identities are self-consciously embodied and performed, Marcia is a heroine within it and for her ghetto community in *Dancehall Queen*'s storyworld because that "make-believe" is not insulated from labor and other social problems in Kingston and, at the same time, because the "make-believe" of dancehall culture is fully embraced, even paraded, as having some political force.[29] That *Dancehall Queen* creolized and reframed "Cinderella" tropes within these specifically located cultural practices as well as within Anansi narrative traditions speaks to a generic economy that not only privileges a Jamaican audience but also effectively provincializes the fairy tale as romantic comedy. With music, dance, and the theme of social justice as its primary appeal, *Dancehall Queen* set sales records in Jamaica ($215,000) and, for a small film, was also quite successful in the United Kingdom (£98,000 box office) and in the United States ($162,000 in its first three weeks), countries with large Jamaican diasporic populations.[30]

To the beat of the title song, the theatrical trailer for *Dancehall Queen* juxtaposes over-the-top dancehall costumes and dance moves with dramatic and violent scenes in Marcia's life, as the following titles run across the screen: "... a journey ... / ... into the world of ... DANCEHALL / ... the survival story ... / ... of a strong ... JAMAICAN WOMAN ... / ... in a world ... where the code ... is TOUGHER than TOUGH / ... will she win ... or will she lose ... / DANCEHALL QUEEN." Beenie Man's voice-over delivers these same lines, concluding, "It's a dancehall thing!" In contrast, the DVD preview, which also features the title song but includes dancehall scenes only, at that and some of the tamer ones, announces in standard English voice-over: "Dancehall Queen. Jamaica's No.1 theatrical release. A modern-day Cinderella story backed by a pulsating reggae soundtrack. *Dancehall Queen* will captivate your heart and soul, Jamaican style." The DVD showcases both trailers. Blending their two marketing strategies, and perhaps adding a touristic appeal, the tagline of the DVD cover also reads, "*Dancehall Queen* is a modern-day Cinderella story, with no Prince Charming, but one very strong woman, backed by a pulsing reggae soundtrack and the scintillating sights of Kingston, Jamaica." On the IMDb website, the film's genre is "drama."

I take this coexistence of the multiple generic cues in the production and marketing of *Dancehall Queen* as a starting point to consider how questions of genre mixing relate to genrification, the ongoing process by which various institutional forces (often at odds with one another) assign a place and value to a (filmic) text in relation to competing and changing genre systems (Frow 2006, 137–39). As Rick Altman points out, this process, in the US studio economy especially but not exclusively, aims to multiply, rather than limit, a movie's generic affiliations in order to attract more and different kinds of audiences (1999, 123–43). From the side of mainstream film production and marketing, genre mixing is nothing new but, as I noted earlier in this chapter, self-conscious mixing of the folk and fairy tale with other genres as a tactic of "*fertile juxtaposition*" (Altman 1999, 136) is currently on the rise. Furthermore, along with the messages of distributors and the labels of the film industry, audiences, reviewers, and critics have a crucial say in the process of genrification, often bringing to the table a commitment to strong genre recognition as opposed to weak and multiple generic affiliations. It is in the process of genrification that the concept of genre as marketing label or even horizon of expectations may clash most clearly with that of genres as "knowledge nets" (Frow 2006, 85) or portals to certain types of storyworlds in which different knowledge communities have strong investments.

What makes a film a "fairy-tale film"? Answers vary quite dramatically. It matters, first of all, that there is no such category for the US film industry, and if this is the genre system we are working with (for example, comedy, western, drama, horror, science fiction, family, etc.), "fantasy" is by default the umbrella genre. Since the American Film Institute (AFI) defines fantasy as "a genre where live-action characters inhabit imagined settings and/or experience situations that transcend the rules of the natural world," films as different as *King Kong* (1933), *The Wizard of Oz* (1939), *It's a Wonderful Life* (1946), and *The Lord of the Rings: The Fellowship of the Ring* (2001), are listed among the AFI top 10 in the genre. While recognizing the potential for overlap, film critics who take their cue from this system see fairy-tale films—as distinct from sword and sorcery or epic fantasy—as a subgenre of fantasy (Butler 2009, 43–76). And yet reviewers and audiences alike are quick to recognize films that fall into the drama or comedy genres as "fairy-tale films."

For Jack Zipes, whose critical work has been foundational to historicizing the fairy tale as well as institutionalizing fairy-tale studies, "a fairy-tale film is any kind of cinematic representation recorded on film, on video tape, or in digital form that employs motifs, characters, and plots generally found in the oral and literary genre of the fairy tale, to re-create a known tale or to create and realize cinematically an original screenplay with recognizable features of the fairy tale" (Zipes 2011, 9). Zipes's capacious definition works in many ways for me, especially since he grounds it in the understanding that the fairy tale "as a genre is not 'pure,'" and that it "also borrows from other genres" (9).[31] But it is based on a different genre system that unlike the AFI's runs across media to include the oral folktale, the literary fairy tale, advertisements, opera, graphic novels, poems—all of which could contribute to a fairy-tale film. Relying on yet another genre system, Pauline Greenhill in "Folklore and/on Film" contrasts fairy-tale films that "incorporat[e] traditional culture as part of a fictional narrative" to ethnographic documentaries, vernacular films, and "fictional films produced by indigenous individuals and communities, about their traditional and popular culture" (2012, 484). Here, while spanning across AFI categories like horror and psychological melodrama (Greenhill and Matrix 2010, 8–9), fairy-tale films are characterized as "cinematic" or "filmic folklore" (Zhang 2005; Sherman and Koven 2007) and are also distinguished from indigenous or insiders' fictional films (see Wood 2008). Greenhill's four useful categories, which she is careful to say sometimes intersect, operate "at the cusp of folklore and film" mapping genre onto yet a different set of concerns about and across cultures more so than Zipes's terminology does.

My point is neither to critique these definitions of fairy-tale film nor to propose an alternative one. It is to recognize how the overlapping of genres *and* the mixing of genre systems are operative in the very process of genre making, and how within this process—and in a particularly heightened way, for filmic genres—scholars are inevitably in competition with other institutions and knowledge communities. It is to dwell on how what we call "fairy-tale film" is contested territory—already at the intersection of several genre systems across institutions, media, scholarly disciplines, and cultural traditions—which in turn has implications for how to approach the fairy-tale web geopolitically and methodologically.

I believe the critical challenges and promises that mixing across genre systems poses are all too often bypassed in favor of a process of fairy-tale genrification, where "the continuity of a generic name may disguise real discontinuities in its content as it passes from one system to another" (Frow 2006, 131). This is perhaps most obvious in what Zipes describes as the twentieth-century canonization of specific tales—from "Cinderella" and "Little Red Riding Hood" to "Aladdin" and "Ali Baba and the Forty Thieves" (2011, 19)—to represent "the fairy tale" in children's literature, film, and critical practices.[32] As we know, this history of cultural and generic appropriation or "rough translation" (Chakrabarty 2007, 17) is much older than film, still pervasive, and global. To describe the process of "folkloristic activity in the British Empire," for instance, Sadhana Naithani imagines a "digitally animated visual of the world map," where collected narratives from Asia, Africa, and Australia reach "a tiny island in the northern part of the globe, from where they go out as books" destined primarily for the European continent (Naithani 2010, 12); in many of these books, the native or vernacular genres have been obliterated for the purposes of translatability into "folktales" and "fairy tales." In *Legendary Hawai'i and the Politics of Place: Tradition, Translation, and Tourism* (2007), I outline an analogous process by which the *mo'olelo* or (hi)stories of the Hawaiian nation become affiliated with "legend" and especially "fairy tale" in the process of consolidating the US annexation of Hawai'i at the turn of the twentieth century.

Thus my concern with this practice of appropriation has informed the question I posed in this chapter, how does thinking of the fairy-tale genre today as a web whose hypertextual links do not refer back to one authority or central tradition impact my approach to filmic fairy-tale remixes? Extrapolating from Naithani's conclusion to her book on colonial and postcolonial folkloristics

PLATE 39. "Cinderella" by Chan-Hyo Bae (2008). Reproduced with permission of the artist.

(Naithani 2010, 115–28), the challenge I seek to meet as a critic in the Euro-American tradition of fairy-tale and folktale studies is to take on the intercultural dynamics and transnational scope of story power as a field of "disjunctions," or unequal links, striving not to naturalize the privilege of one genre system but rather to learn from generic contestation across various cultural traditions and geopolitical sites. The "fairy-tale film," like the fairy tale, emerges in the contact zone, more precisely, in multiple contact zones.[33] In Dani Cavallaro's words, for instance, the exchange between fairy tale and anime is a dialogical journey: "As anime is capable of mutating as a result of its encounter with the fairy-tale tradition, so the latter enjoys a tantalizing opportunity for self-reinvention as a result of its imaginative appropriation by anime" (Cavallaro 2011, 104).[34] Within this approach, storytellers, writers, filmmakers, artists, and critics inhabiting other generic and cultural traditions present statements and questions for us in the Euro-American fairy-tale discourse to address. One such perspective on "fairy tale" as a site of intercultural and transnational disjuncture comes from Chan-Hyo Bae, a Korean artist living in London. His series, *Existing*

PLATE 40. "Beauty and the Beast" by Chan-Hyo Bae (2009). Reproduced with permission of the artist.

in Costume, visually embodies racial, gendered, and class estrangement from the fairy-tale glamorizing of royalty and the more specific fantasy of British royalty, an estrangement that in turn disfigures naturalized privilege. Particularly telling in Chan-Hyo Bae's view is the homology between British portraiture of royalty as powerfully strong and fairy-tale heroines' aspirations to royal status: for him, both tell (hi)stories that "lead their readers to accept a fixed conclusion or thought," to accept the ruling order and the power of the West (www. saatchionline.com/photomam). That's why his generic mix disrupts both the photographic medium and the European oil portrait style, as the photographer in drag enters the scene of (de)Orientalized parody.

What I sought to do in this chapter, and in the spirit of meeting the critical challenge I outlined above, was to approach four contemporary filmic fairy-tale remixes as an opportunity to focus on genre economies rather than simply genre mixing. In this framework, genres—like genre systems—are not only mutually constitutive of one another but operate according to hierarchies of value that are historically shifting, though often naturalized. With *Enchanted* and *Pan's*

Labyrinth, I showed interest in the values that are at work in the blending or colliding of generic worlds, the power relations that frame their production and reception. By focusing on how *Year of the Fish* and *Dancehall Queen* do not represent the folktale and fairy tale as coterminous in terms of history or expectations, I put in relief the located heterogeneity that continues to inhabit what we call fairy tale. Throughout, my purpose was to emphasize competing social uses of the folk and fairy tale in these contemporary mainstream and independent films as a way into asking what is at stake and for whom in contemporary filmic fairy-tale remix. The contemporary remix in fairy-tale film has to do not with one clash but with clashes of values that are far from being played out. If we are critically invested in contesting the implicit hierarchy of genre systems that support the globalized genrification of fairy-tale magic, we have as much to learn from the genre's creolization as we do from its hybridization.

4

Resituating *The Arabian Nights*

Challenges and Promises of Translation

[Scheherazade] avait un courage au-dessus de son sexe, de l'esprit infiniment avec une pénétration admirable. Elle avait beaucoup de lecture et une mémoire si prodigieuse, que rien ne lui était échappé de tout ce qu'elle avait lu. Elle s'était heureusement appliquée à la philosophie, à la médecine, à l'histoire et aux arts; elle faisait des vers mieux que les poètes les plus célèbres de son temps. Outre cela, elle était pourvue d'une beauté extraordinaire, et une vertu très solide couronnait toutes ces belles qualités.

Le vizir aimait passionnément une fille si digne de sa tendresse. Un jour qu'ils s'entretenaient tous deux ensemble, elle lui dit: "Mon père, j'ai une grâce à vous demander; je vous supplie très humblement de me l'accorder."
—*Les mille et une nuit*, 1704, Antoine Galland's translation of *Alf layla wa-layla* (fourteenth- or fifteenth-century Arabic MS of Syrian origin now in the Bibliothèque Nationale de France)

Scheherazade was possessed of a degree of courage beyond her sex, joined to an extent of knowledge, and degree of penetration that was truly astonishing. She had read much, and was possessed of so great a memory, that she never forgot anything, she had once perused. She had applied also, with much success, to philosophy, to medicine, to history, and to the arts; and made better verses than the most celebrated poets of the time. Besides this, her beauty was incomparable; and her virtuous disposition crowned all those valuable qualities.

The Vizier was passionately fond of so deserving a daughter. As they were conversing together one day, she addressed him with these words. "I have a favor to ask of you, my father. And I entreat you not to refuse me."
—*Arabian Nights*, 1802, Edward Forster's translation of Galland's translation

[The vizier's] older daughter, Shahrazad, had read the books of literature, philosophy, and medicine. She knew poetry by heart, had studied historical reports, and was acquainted with the sayings of men and the maxims of sages and kings. She was intelligent, knowledgeable, wise, and refined. She had read and learned. One day she said to her father, "Father, I will tell you what is in my mind."

ARABIAN NIGHTS, 1990, Husain Haddawy's translation of Muhsin Mahdi's edition of *Alf layla wa-layla* (fourteenth- or fifteenth-century Arabic MS of Syrian origin now in the Bibliothèque Nationale de France)

Adaptations of the *Arabian Nights* play out a related but different economy of wonder genres from the one I explored in chapter 3, and crucial to their global production and reception for several centuries now has been the mostly naturalized work of translation, as standing in for adaptation and constructing the "Orient" as other. Thus when I teach the *Arabian Nights*, I find it particularly important—even if and in a way even more because I am ignorant of the Arabic language—to do so in ways that call attention to the politics of translation (Spivak 1993; Venuti 1998) but also foster a "culture of translation" (Shankar 2012, 141).[1] In my classes, this means analyzing at least selections from different English-language translations to foreground how their varied poetics inflect the representation of characters, social world, style, and the supernatural in *Arabian Nights*. I do this to denaturalize appropriative misreadings and stereotyping, and also to reinforce the understanding that translation—like storytelling, like reading, and like adapting—always involves interpretation and transformative choices. I have found that looking at how Edward Forster, Edward William Lane, John Payne, Richard Burton, Powys Mathers, Husain Haddawy, and (most recently) the Malcolm C. and Ursula Lyons team introduce Shahrazad, the bold heroine and wonderful storyteller of *The Thousand and One Nights/ Arabian Nights*, to their readers is, for instance, a good place to start. She is an extremely well read woman in all translations, but in turn she is also beautiful, wise, polite, sweetly eloquent, incomparable, well bred, phenomenal at memorizing book knowledge, avid as a book collector, or active in learning from books and sayings. Whether the translators are working from Arabic manuscripts, Antoine Galland's immensely influential French translation, or other French and English texts; what their knowledge of and investment in Arabic language and cultures are; and to which Euro-American discursive paradigms (fantasy, ethnology, erotica, Arabic literature) they contribute also matters, and so we try to get at least a rudimental understanding of the translators' varied historical contexts, positionalities, and legacies. The point being not to become experts in the *Arabian Nights* but to gain and put to work a stronger awareness of what translation is: an act of reading and rewriting that the discourse of (in)fidelity often obscures;[2] "a necessary impossibility" (Spivak 2005, 105), meaning an impossible task and an indispensable practice; an act of social engagement and recontextualization, whatever its politics and uses (Tymoczko 2010).

Generally speaking, some ways for those of us in cultural and narrative studies to promote this kind of culture of translation more widely are to foreground the workings of translation in the construction of literary and generic systems, whether national or transnational, rather than relying on their invisible labor (Lefevere 1992a; Venuti 2000; Schlump 2011); to consider how translation into a hegemonic language like English affects at-risk languages (for example, St-Pierre 2000; Kuwada 2009b; Aiu 2010) and how translating from and back into colonizing languages can function as resistance or activism (for example, Christie 2009; Kuwada 2009a); to learn/actively use languages other than English and produce translations as a form of activism or resistance to a "multiculturalism that goes hand in hand with monolingualism" (Spivak 2010, 38); to be attentive to the strategies and practices of translation, not to evaluate them as reproductive acts, but to discriminate among their transformative effects.[3]

In this chapter, as I give my attention to the transformative strategies of a few contemporary adaptations of the *Arabian Nights* in North America, I am particularly interested in reflecting on four aspects of translation. One, while they produce different sets of expectations, translation and adaptation are both acts of reading and rewriting, and "rewriters create images of a writer, a work, a period, a genre, sometimes even a whole literature" (Lefevere 1992b, 5). My discussion will shuttle back and forth between translation as adaptation and adaptation as translation because the way that translation and adaptation have been heavily imbricated with each other in the history of the *Arabian Nights*' production and reception necessarily impacts how we receive new adaptations today. Two, in paying attention to how translations and adaptations of the *Arabian Nights* relocate it within a universalizing hierarchy of Western wonder genres, and how in Indo-European languages the act of translation is consistently associated with movement of meaning across space, I focus on the strategies of "transporting" and "displacing" characters as symptoms of this geopolitical shift. Three, because translation always figures ethical and political choices, I am especially interested in translations-adaptations of the *Arabian Nights* operating in the violent climate of pre- and post-9/11, specifically their ideologies of representation and the antagonistic or humanist bent of their poetics. And four, translation has done and continues to do violence to subaltern/colonized/Orientalized cultures, but translations and adaptations also enable us to act on the imperative of becoming more response-able to the diversity of knowledge and artistic systems of stories (King 2005) across conceptual and cultural horizons.

ADAPTATION AS DOMESTICATING TRANSLATION: THE GENIE AS PAWN IN THE QUEEN'S CHECKMATE

Aired in the United States on January 29, 2012, "Fruit of the Poisonous Tree," the eleventh episode of the first season of ABC's television series *Once Upon a Time*, offers one example of how the generic and cultural othering of *Arabian Nights* works in a monological popular-culture framework. This episode transports a Genie presumably from the *Arabian Nights* (Giancarlo Esposito) into the Disney-like fairy-tale land that in the TV show parallels the Storybrooke "realistic" world, in order to provide a backstory for the making of the wicked Queen (Lana Parilla playing Snow White's stepmother and Mayor Regina's otherworldly person) and for Storybrooke's reporter Sidney Glass (the Genie's alter ego). As a way into the larger discussion of *Arabian Nights*' relation to Western fairy tales in twenty-first-century adaptations, I focus here on the role of the Genie in the "Snow White" plot and on what his role tells us about the hierarchy of magic represented by the lamp's wishes, on the one hand, and the queen's wiles, on the other.

Snow White's father, King Leopold (Richard Schiff), who has inadvertently summoned the Genie of Agrabah by rubbing a magic lamp he found near the shore, somewhat surprisingly states he wants nothing for himself when informed of his three wishes.[4] The King nevertheless makes two wishes, one to set the Genie free and the other to grant him the third and final wish. The Genie is delighted with his freedom, but states he will never use his wish based on his knowledge of how the 1,001 wishes he granted have all ended badly; instead, he plans to use his freedom from the lamp to find "true love."

The Genie's image and the script he is written into after this initial encounter hold few surprises, in spite of his freedom and the change in settings. The Genie of Agrabah—an explicit reference to Disney's *Aladdin* movie (1992)[5]— wears the obligatory turban; his colorful clothing, curly goatee, and accentuated eye makeup give him a mysterious, exotic, and somewhat feminized look. Having accepted the invitation to stay in King Leopold's kingdom, he immediately

PLATE 41. The King and the lamp in *Once Upon a Time*

falls for his benefactor's wife, Snow White's stepmother. While the Queen's skin may not be "as white as snow," meaning she does not have the innocence of Snow White and cannot ultimately replace Snow White's mother in the King's heart, her beauty is enough of a lure to enslave the dark-skinned Genie to the Queen. Significantly, Regina is wearing an off-white gown when they first meet under the special apple tree she has brought to the palace grounds, and (for the first season of *Once Upon a Time*) in both Storybrooke and King Leopold's kingdom, Sidney/the Genie is the only nonwhite character and actor. Another "Snow White" motif, from the Grimms' version, makes its appearance when the Genie gives the Queen a gift, a beautiful mirror so she can see herself as he does, as "the fairest in the land." That they continue to meet near the apple tree reinforces the connection with the "Snow White" tale but also with the Garden of Eden scene, especially when a two-headed viper comes into the plot and the Genie, while still appearing wise and honorable, starts to act deviously with the King and foolishly with the Queen. Having eaten the fruit of Regina's apple tree, the Genie is clearly domesticated into a storyworld where he has no special powers and elicits no fear or wonder.[6]

Spectators are likely to realize that Regina is manipulating the Genie much earlier than he does. Under Regina's spell, the Genie believes she needs saving so he kills King Leopold only to realize too late that she has played him and that the two-headed viper of Agrabah she chose as their weapon points clearly to him as the King's assassin. Confronted by the Queen's explicit statement that he "is

PLATE 42. The scene of temptation in *Once Upon a Time*

no longer of any use" to her, the Genie defiantly brings out the magic lamp and makes his wish to "be with [her] forever, to look upon [her] face forever." That wishes always end poorly is confirmed when the Genie finds himself once more a prisoner, this time of Regina's looking glass.

This scene of wish fulfillment run amok connects intertextually with the *Arabian Nights* as well as with "Snow White." In "The Story of the Fisherman and the Demon" (Haddawy 1990, 30–66), the fisherman cleverly tricks the powerful being who wants to kill him into returning to the jar from which the fisherman had freed him.[7] Regina, like the fisherman, deceives the Genie into doing what she wants, but he poses no threat to her and is only susceptible to her guile because he is in love with her. The magic mirror in which the *Once Upon a Time* Genie is imprisoned also recalls the most popular "Snow White" narratives, the Grimms' and Disney's, but in contrast to them its voice and image are recognizably those of a character we know has an intensely personal attachment to the Queen. In particular, the Genie's dark features stand out against the pale mask in the Disney mirror, as does the Genie's anguish against Disney's dispassionately abstract figure in the mirror. The not-so-wise Genie in the *Once Upon a Time* mirror will continue to confirm the power of Regina's beauty to her, and in Storybrooke he will continue to do her bidding as Sidney, the editor of the *Daily Mirror*.[8] Clearly, the Queen from the "Snow White" tale wins the power game in "Fruit of the Poisonous Tree" all around, and within *her* story the

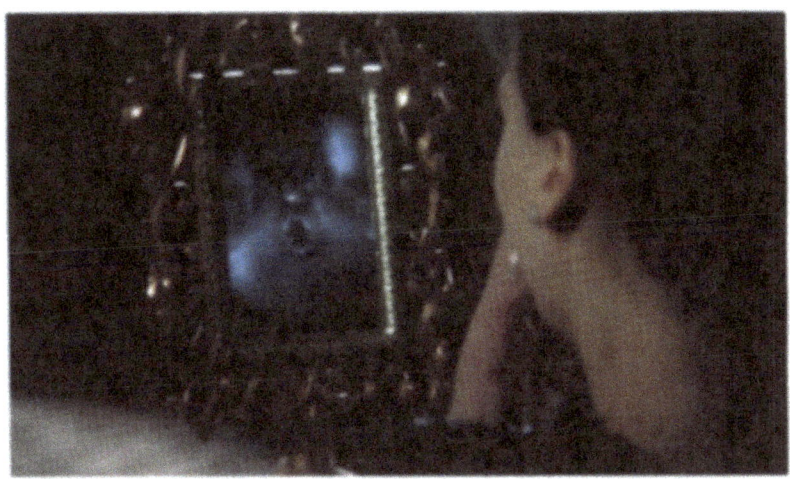

PLATE 43. The Genie in Regina's mirror in *Once Upon a Time*

violent, because emotional and foolish, Genie of the *Arabian Nights* is enslaved to her and faces her contempt.[9]

In this fairy-tale/*Arabian Nights* remix, the traditional "Snow White" tale has been altered by Regina's plotting to kill her husband, but the function of the Genie in the "Snow White" adaptation is narratively clear and fitting: he serves as her magic helper, though magic refers more to his being than to his actions. In contrast, the matter of how this Genie in *Once Upon a Time* relates to the *Arabian Nights* narratives remains vague and also somewhat extraneous to most spectators' expectations. After all, "Fruit of the Poisonous Tree" features the Genie as one of the iconic images from *Aladdin* the movie, not "The Story of Aladdin and the Wonderful Lamp," and the link I made earlier with "The Story of the Fisherman and the Demon" is likely to be perceived by many viewers of the show as rather esoteric. Overall, this episode of *Once Upon a Time* transports the Genie as a narrative prop into the storyworld of the "Snow White" fairy-tale adaptation and capitalizes, in its visual and thematic tropes, on the generalized familiarity its target audience has with an *Arabian Nights* phenomenon that, over centuries, has transformed *Alf layla wa-layla* or *The Thousand and One Nights* into the globalized *visual* production of an exoticized magic that embodies both eroticism and deviousness. Before turning to an analysis of other North American contemporary *Arabian Nights* adaptations, I will offer a brief synthesis of this translation or transformative rewriting process across cultures, languages, and media, and then link two specific aspects of it to the critical questions this chapter explores.[10]

THE TRANSLATION-ADAPTATION OF *THE NIGHTS* AND THE EVERYDAY POLITICS OF MEDIA TEXT

About *The Thousand and One Nights* in European culture, Francesco Gabrieli wrote in 1947 that following Antoine Galland's early eighteenth-century "free version" of it in French, "the West came to be submitted to the reign of the Eastern tale and fable" (Gabrieli [1947] 2010, 426). This is an accurate statement in that *The Thousand and One Nights*, almost as popular as the Bible in Europe during the eighteenth and nineteenth centuries, was widely read in its various translations and adaptations (Irwin 2004a), and that it influenced fashion and art (as seen in the writings of Edgar Allan Poe, George Lord Byron, Charles Dickens, and Robert Louis Stevenson, to name only a few English-language examples). But true? Only if one takes Gabrieli's point to mean that the West fell under the spell of what it construed, in Orientalist fashion (Said 1978), to be "the Eastern tale and fable" and continued to refashion into the European and then globalized cultural phenomenon of *The Arabian Nights* (Marzolph 2007, 30).

The textual history of *The Thousand and One Nights* and the transnational cultural morphing of the *Arabian Nights* are immensely complex. Here are the basics of what I learned from reading scholars as well as teaching the tales in translation (Haddawy 1990; Irwin [1994] 2004a; Marzolph and van Leeuwen 2004; Marzolph 2007; Chraïbi 2007; Marzolph 2008; Nurse 2010; Warner 2012). Including stories that generally portray a Muslim storyworld from the medieval or Abbasid and Mamluk period, but are mainly from Indian, Persian, and Arabic (Syrian and Egyptian) traditions and date back to manuscripts from the ninth to the fourteenth centuries, *The Thousand and One Nights* was never simply one book, in manuscript or print form, and it was never in print until Antoine Galland published it in a French adaptation (1704–15) in twelve volumes. It was generically eclectic (integrating jokes, epics, legends, and didactic and wonder tales) but projected for the most part the values of a mercantile class (Chraïbi 2004);[11] its storyworld portrayed characters from various religions and parts of the world; and at its core covered some two hundred nights of storytelling, never a thousand and one. It is by now widely known that Antoine Galland added the tales most immediately associated with the *Arabian Nights*, such as "Aladdin and the Wonderful Lamp" and "Ali Baba and the Forty Thieves," having heard them from Syrian Maronite storyteller Hanna Diyab in Paris; known as the "orphan tales" (Gerhardt [1963] 2010), these were not in Arabic manuscripts until, for instance, "Aladdin" was translated from Galland's French writings. Characteristic of the collection are its *khurafat* (amazing or fantastic narratives dealing with the supernatural), ransom tales, and their embeddedness in frame stories, often multiply layered, as they are offered by several characters turned intra- but also extradiegetic narrators in Shahrazad's tales to Shahriyar.

Issues concerning the global circulation and popularity of *The Thousand and One Nights* are just as complicated as its textual history. Partly because of its vernacular and folkloric features, *The Thousand and One Nights* was definitely not considered a masterpiece in the context of the rich traditions of classic Arabic literature, but it has been revalued and adapted in the second half of the twentieth century, especially in Egyptian, Syrian, Lebanese, and Palestinian literary texts. In European literature, specific intertextual links with stories from *The Thousand and One Nights* are active as early as in Giovanni Sercambi's *Novella d'Astolfo* (circa 1400) and Ludovico Ariosto's *Orlando Furioso* (1516–32),[12] and more tenuous links in early collections of fairy tales such as Giovan Francesco Straparola's *Le piacevoli notti* (1550–53) and Giambattista Basile's *Lo cunto de li cunti* (1634–36) suggest story trafficking across cultures and continents had an impact long before Galland's translation/adaptation. In the nineteenth century, European adaptations of *The Thousand and One Nights* were also translated into non-European languages, including Hawaiian, not necessarily with an Orientalist bent (Bacchilega and Arista 2007), and Japanese (Sugita 2006), eliciting new fantasies and further adaptations by writers, illustrators, and filmmakers, including contemporary anime artist Hayao Miyazaki. Even the basics about *The Thousand and One Nights* are exceedingly complex.

For my limited purposes here, I am interested specifically in two aspects of this baggy history of translations and exchanges as intersecting in current adaptations of the *Arabian Nights* and their production of wonder. First, the *Arabian Nights'* transformation into a "media text" of visual culture; second, the relationship between histories and fantasy that such adaptations construct, especially in a post-9/11 globalized culture. My focus in tracking these links is to explore whether and to what extent Western adaptations of the *Arabian Nights* contribute to a renewed politics of wonder that demands *re*translating across media and cultures so as to decouple Orientalist or stereotypical associations and resituate story power within cultural and historical specificities.

What am I calling a media text? A specific formation of popular cultural memory, "media text" is what Karin Kukkonen describes as Roland Barthes's *déjà lu* or "already-read," the "conventions and codes established through *other* texts" to identify a "source text," in this case the *Arabian Nights* without actually reading it (Kukkonen 2008, 262, my emphasis). While the *Arabian Nights* through translations and adaptations has continued to be transformed world-wide over the last three hundred years, in the twentieth century the book "ceased to be part of the common literary culture of adults" (Irwin [1994] 2004a, 274; see also Nurse 192–93); however, its confinement to children's literature was at the same time balanced by its popularization in film where the wonders of technology capitalized on those of the stories. As early as 1899 with George Albert Smith's *Aladdin and the Wonderful Lamp*, 1902 with Ferdinand Zecca's *Ali Baba et les Quarante Voleurs*, and 1905 with Georges Méliès's *The Palace of the One Thousand and One Nights*; then with Lotte Reiniger's 1926 *The Adventures of Prince Achmed* and *The Thief of Bagdad* in 1924 (US production directed by Raoul Walsh, starring Douglas Fairbanks) and in 1940 (UK production directed by Ludwig Berger, Powell, and others), and on to Disney studio's animated 1992 *Aladdin*, characters, motifs, and landscapes associated with *The Thousand and One Nights* dazzled adults and children (Irwin 2004b; Zipes 2011; Butler 2009). With films as its most prominent aspect,[13] but also with illustrations, television shows, Halloween costumes and toys, flying-carpet images, and more recently video games, visual culture has contributed a great deal to our twenty-first-century experience of the *Arabian Nights* phenomenon as a media text.

As media text, the *Arabian Nights* has been increasingly reduced to Aladdin, Ali Baba, and Sindbad since these are the heroes of action movies and children's cartoons. Because it clashes with such structures of adventure and action stories (Butler 2009, 61), Shahrazad and Shahriyar's[14] frame narrative is conspicuously absent from screen adaptations, with Hallmark Entertainment's *Arabian Nights* (2000) as a rare exception in which, however, the brave and wise heroine is domesticated to American family values (Orme 2010c). As media text, the *Arabian Nights'* main props are eclectically "Oriental," and in Robert Irwin's words, they "signal fantasyland. As Ray Harryhausen remarked: 'When you are making a picture about the *Arabian Nights*, there are certain things you are going to have which are repetitious, like a sword and a turban'" (Irwin 2004b, 24).[15] Genies, magic lamps and rings, flying carpets; splendor, astounding riches, the legendary Roc bird (as seen in the 1962 *Uncle Scrooge* comic "The Cave of Ali Baba); and—when the images are not for children only—sexual pleasures have become the wonders that brand this *Arabian Nights* world.

This kind of fantasy connects very little with the histories of the diverse peoples who produced *The Thousand and One Nights* or with the history of the tales as they migrated and impacted a range of cultures and literatures over the centuries. Nevertheless, coinciding with a time of intellectual secularism in Europe, the publication of Galland's *Les mille et une nuit* [sic] has had quite a lasting legacy outside of the Arab world as it constructed not only an exotic and sumptuously imaginary space of magical riches but also a pseudo-ethnographic knowledge of the people that by the nineteenth century European powers—especially, though not exclusively, Britain and France—sought to colonize. What does a fictional text tell us about the people who produced it? A lot, which should not, however, be confused with the people's "nature" or be replacing their actual histories, contributions to world civilization, and lived realities. What "if the tales compiled by the Brothers Grimm, however evocative, were all that were known of German literature and were considered all that was needed for an understanding of the German people?" (Kabbani 2004, 26). What's more, to a substantial degree, the producers of the *Arabian Nights* and its storyworld were its European translators or, better, adaptors who—we can say in retrospect—in the process participated in popularizing a multidisciplinary discourse about the people of/fictionalized in the *Arabian Nights* and thus contributed to the reproduction of a limited inventory of dehumanizing tropes and the naturalization of Orientalist disciplinary practices to manage these "strange" people.[16]

Within *The Thousand and One Nights*, Shahrazad refers to her tales as "strange and lovely" or as "strange and amazing" (in Haddawy's translation (1990) see for example 18 and 25), which I would say connects with the production of a state of wonder she is seeking to elicit in Shahriyar so as to open him up to respond to the unexpected, in particular to what he does not expect of women and in himself—and, metanarratively, with the wonder the narrator of an oral or written version of the tales wants to elicit in listeners or readers. However, as Europeans came to enjoy these wonder-filled entertainments in the eighteenth and nineteenth centuries, they also insisted on "a political vision of reality whose structures promoted the difference between the familiar (Europe, West, "us") and the *strange* (the Orient, the East, "them")" (Said 1978, 43, my emphasis). Etymologically as well as culturally, in French, English, Italian, and other European languages the "strange" is the "stranger," and even today the *Arabian Nights* as media text plays a formative role in what passes for outsiders' "knowledge," that is, our sanctioned ignorance of the so-called Orient, of the Middle-Eastern or Arabic stranger. In this media text, and at large in the Hollywood imaginary, the "other" who is from the Arab world automatically becomes a Muslim: barbaric, violent, and devious if male; oppressed, licentious, and devious if female (Shaheen 2003; Cooperson 1994).[17]

This has been going on for a long time, and not without protests. It is well known, for instance, that in response to complaints from the American-Arab Anti-Discrimination Committee (ADC), Disney Studio revised the most offensive lines in the "Arabian Nights" song that opened *Aladdin* (1992).[18] But following the September 11, 2001, hijackings and attack on the Twin Towers, anti-Muslim sentiments have escalated in the United States, and the conflation of "Arab" with "Muslim" and "violent Muslim stereotype" has further fantastically become equated with "terrorist."[19] Anti-Islamic hate crimes went to being the "second highest reported among religious-bias incidents" in 2001, the FBI reported, and these statistics remain unchanged in their 2010 report.[20]

This violence brings a new gravity to the deployment of *Arabian Nights* tropes in the public sphere, popular culture, and everyday usage.[21] I will point just to one "Ali Baba" example. At the time US troops were withdrawing from Iraq after almost nine years of war, Fox News' Geraldo Rivera wrote a blog entry for December 16, 2011, titled "Back in Iraq with U.S. Soldiers on the Journey Home," where he reminisced: "When looters we called Ali Baba's began tearing apart Baghdad shortly after our triumphant March 2003 invasion, we hoped it was just an exuberant display of long-suppressed freedom from tyranny." This reference signals not only how popular the association of thief and Arab is, but how well the *Arabian Nights* media-text iconic figure serves the purposes of profiling and dehumanizing.[22] The question of where the actual responsibility lies for looting not only the banks, hotels, and government buildings, but the museums of Baghdad in 2003 is successfully deflected here thanks to the tacit understanding that it is in the nature of these people to be violent and steal. Reports on these violent events taking place at a time of chaos in a city of several million vary, and a May 2003 article in the German newspaper *Süddeutsche Zeitung* covered the story that, according to Iraqi witnesses, some American soldiers instigated the plundering themselves, saying "Go in, Ali Baba, it's all yours!" (Sommerfeld 2003).[23] Yet another German newspaper reported a more violent use of the epithet on the part of American troops in 2003, which resulted in an Amnesty International's request that there be a further investigation of possible violation of human rights.[24] While it is hard to assess the reliability of sources documenting the specifics of its circulation, it is clear that "Ali Baba" became for American troops at the time an almost generic term for Iraqi looters.

Antoine Galland, who introduced "Ali Baba and the Forty Thieves" into the *Arabian Nights* Western canon, is clearly not the one responsible for such vilifying contemporary usage. Galland's intervention as a translator and adaptor was not only vastly influential but also complex and sustained by admiration, not racism.[25] Its unforeseeable effects point simultaneously to how in the production of the *Arabian Nights* phenomenon there is no single use or project, just as there isn't in the history of the fairy-tale genre in general, and to how the expropriation of *Arabian Nights'* wonders has been and continues to be naturalized or masked by their branding as "exotic" or "other." In his presentation on the *Arabian Nights* at the 2010 American Folklore Society meeting, Ulrich

Marzolph (2010) productively connected political and textual concerns in this way: "For the purpose of my presentation, disregarding or neglecting the fact that Muslim terrorists are not representative of Islam as a whole is equal to regarding the world of the *Thousand and One Nights* as a legitimate playground for Western fantasy while disregarding their highly complex and diverse character." He concluded that the " 'experts'—whether those of Islam or those of the *Thousand and One Nights*—hold the key to preventing the solidification and further growth of biased notions." Marina Warner's 2012 visionary book, *Stranger Magic*, takes on this project by making the case that "reading the *Nights* as a case study in the contact zones of history offers a path towards changing preconceptions about Arabs, Islam, and the history and civilization of the Middle and Near East" (Warner 2012, 26). In whatever ways we can, we all—not just scholars, but artists, readers, fans, bloggers, and spectators—have a responsibility to counter this politics of inequality.

In the next two sections, the main question I will be asking of specific *Arabian Nights* adaptations is whether and how they contest this naturalized and vilifying imaginary, especially in light of the escalation of Islamophobic violence in a post-9/11 cultural economy. Because peoples and their cultures are equated wholesale with one another in the limited language of exoticizing, and because their stories function in a hierarchical economy of genres, my query extends to metanarrative considerations: how do these adaptations figure the *Arabian Nights* in relation to the modern genre of the fairy tale, or what is their story-power relation? Metacritically, this chapter seeks to activate links in the folk and fairy-tale web to three specific points about translating/adapting/deploying *Arabian Nights* across cultures and media: translation is an ethical and political act that "does not merely reflect existing knowledge, it can also . . . construct knowledge, much of which becomes the foundation of representation" (Tymoczko 2010, 16), and this applies just as much to adaptation; any discussion of the *Arabian Nights* today will benefit from taking into account the interplay of visual and verbal codes and tropes (Ouyang 2003; Kukkonen 2011) in an intertextuality that is not only intermedial but also immersed in the everyday politics of culture, and if stories "need not report on real life, but clear the way to changing the experience of living it" (Warner 2012, 27), the stakes of such a transformation are dramatically high within the *Arabian Nights* with its life-or-death outcome as well as in the everyday politics of its global circulation today. Do these adaptations contest the popularization of *Arabian Nights* as repository of vilifying stereotypes? Do they reproduce the iconic wonders we have come to expect in *Arabian Nights*, and to what purposes? Do they activate other links that invite us to approach the tales, and the worlds they come from, in and with wonder, and how? The next two sections ask these questions of two North American adaptations, respectively a comic-book series and a play, both of which make explicit reference to current events and struggles in the Middle East.

TRANSLATION AS TRANSPORTING AND DISPLACING CHARACTERS: FANTASIES OF DIPLOMACY, VIOLENCE, AND USURPATION

Fables, Bill Willingham's series of comics and the winner of multiple Eisner awards, is ten years old in 2012 and going strong. Published by Vertigo, a subsidiary of DC Comics known for its adult themes, issues of *Fables* appear monthly and are then republished in trade volumes, of which the first eleven comprised a complex "journey of connected stories" that over six years took readers down what its creator called "The Fables Road" (Willingham 2008a, 178). The journey has since successfully continued (as I write this chapter, issue #114 is for sale, and there are at least seventeen volumes), and the road has forked, expanding the *Fables* "universe" to other series, such as *Jack of Fables* (2006–), *Cinderella from Fabletown with Love* (2009–), and *Fairest* (2012–). Authored by Willingham in its entirety and illustrated by many artists (Mark Buckingham most prominently, but also Lan Medina, Steve Leialoha, Charles Vess, Mark Wheatley, and others), *Fables* features fairy-tale characters and nursery-rhyme/fantasy beings who call themselves Fables and, unbeknownst to the Mundies (mundane humans, akin to "muggles" in the *Harry Potter* series) in New York City, have lived there for centuries in the underground community of Fabletown.[26] As the title of the first volume, *Legends in Exile*, announces (Willingham 2002), because the mysterious and powerful Adversary invaded their Homelands and many kingdoms, the Fables sought refuge in "this dreary mundane place: the one world the Adversary seemed to take no interest in" (84). Needless to say, this truce did not last long: over the many volumes, not only is the Adversary revealed to be Geppetto, Pinocchio's and other wooden puppets' creator, but also there is an "all-out war" between Fabletown and the Adversary's Empire in which the various Fables prove their different kinds of heroism. In the process, the exiled-in-New-York Fables interact with "Arabian Fables," and I will analyze the ideology of these encounters between characters, but also between narratives, against the backdrop of the series' intertextual politics.

As seen in Karin Kukkonen's study of *Fables*'s iconography (2008; 2011), Adam Zolkover's analysis of bodies and sexuality (2008), and Jack Zipes's critical comments on how comics tend to minimize the "resistant quality of the fantastic" (2009b, 87), this series has definitely attracted the attention of folklorists as well as narrative and fairy-tale scholars. Of particular interest to me is the playfully ironic genre mixing of the Fables' adventures and their backstories with urban fantasy, murder mystery, war and love tales, especially as it impacts characterization and metanarrative. We see this in Bigby Wolf who, if there is such a role in the Fables ensemble, plays the main hero. He is the sheriff of Fabletown in the beginning, then frontline and monstrous warrior in the war with the Adversary, and eventually Snow White's devoted husband; he is described as "a monster and a brute, but a reformed one, now on the side of the angels" ("Who's Who in Fabletown," in Willingham 2008b, 6); he is the conflation of many storied wolves and can switch back and forth into his powerful animal body, while his human look is that of a scruffy, unshaven dark-haired man who's always lighting up. His "big bad wolf" image is clearly linked to fairy tales: his experience as predator and then prey of the hunter in the Grimms' "Red Riding Hood" version makes a cameo appearance in Bigby's backstory, "The Runt" (Willingham 2006a, 79). But his masculinity and heroism are just as much related to werewolf legends as to a range of "mythic" narratives, including that of the underdog, the cowboy outlaw, the World War II American soldier, and the Bogart-like detective. As Mark Hill noted, "Bigby's connection with a horrific past, as well as his current honorable conduct, only strengthens his connection to an American heroic imagination fueled by stories of redemption and second chances found within the mythology of Jesse James" (Hill 2009, 184).

Worldly politics are never far from comics, and *Fables* is no exception. This association fueled much controversy when in *Wolves* (Willingham 2006c), following the defeat of the Empire's invading army of wooden soldiers, Bigby declared to the Adversary/Geppetto, "Fabletown has decided to adopt the Israel template in whole" (76 and 144). "The Israel Analogy," as per the episode's title, is thus delivered: "Israel is a tiny country surrounded by much larger countries dedicated to its eventual total destruction. . . . They stay alive by being a bunch of tough little bastards who make the other guys pay dearly every time they do anything against Israel. . . . Every time you [Geppetto with your huge Empire] hurt us [Fabletown] we're going to damage you much worse in return. . . . You're the only one who can end the cycle" (76–77 and 144).[27] Geppetto shows no fear ("Are you near to being done? I'd like to go back to sleep," says the old man knowing that he and Pinocchio are protected by spells, 76 and 144), but, in order to punish him for "the wooden soldier raid against Fabletown" (77 and 144), Bigby proceeds to detonate dozens of bombs and destroys Geppetto's home and the magic grove from which he made his puppets. In response to the online controversy that followed the publication of this issue, Willingham, while declaring himself pro-Israel, also unequivocally asserted that *Fables* was "not going to be a political tract" (qtd. in Sternberg 2011, a post on the conservative team blog of the David Horowitz Freedom Center) and made it clear in various interviews that the "Israel analogy" was Bigby's: "we've already established that historically, he [the character] went to war several times, and was involved in World War I and II. He would be the type of character who would think along those lines" (Willingham and Robinson 2007). It is hard to say how much such statements depend on the increased power of fans' say in convergence culture, but the "Israel analogy" is not the only instance in which Willingham's characters perform so-called antiliberal, if not Zionist, politics.[28]

Having characters stand on the soapbox or perform specific ideologies is nothing new in comics or other artistic practices. My interest in bringing up these controversies and explicit references to worldly conflicts lies in how they intersect with my dual focus of analysis: how the interactions between the citizens of Fabletown in New York City and the so-called Arabian Fables dramatize ideology, and how the metanarrative aspect of this politics unfolds; that is, what is the commentary that *Fables* makes on competing storytelling traditions? Significantly, in the *Fables* storyworld these interactions revolve mainly around the alliance of Fables across geopolitical lines to resist and defeat the powerful Empire: they are both diplomatic and military relations. More specifically, in *Arabian Nights (and Days)* (volume 7, 2006b), Sinbad [*sic*] is an envoy from Baghdad to Fabletown, and in the prequel graphic novel *1001 Nights of Snowfall* (Willingham 2006a), Snow White goes to King Shahryar (spelling in *Fables*) as ambassador of the European Fables. My argument is that rather than an exchange, these encounters envision either a terrorist or ancillary construction of Arabian Fables; these interactions also propose a "stagist" (Chakrabarty 2007) revision of historical intertextuality, meaning that the *Arabian Nights* is imagined as "not yet" there compared to the European fairy tale. This hierarchical economy of genres is established through very different strategies and links to the *Arabian Nights*; however, overall, transporting the jinnî to Fabletown and Snow White to the *Arabian Nights*' frame tale results in an ironic reversal of Gabrieli's words ([1947] 2010), "the West came to be submitted to the reign of the Eastern tale and fable"; that is, it enacts the submission of *Arabian Nights* to the reign of the Western Fables and tales.

When in the first chapter of *Arabian Nights (and Days)*, Prince Sinbad and his adviser Yusuf arrive in Fabletown to pursue a diplomatic mission, they are in a fancy white limousine, from which harem slaves emerge in a procession that is vaguely reminiscent of the *Arabian Nights* dream scene in Federico Fellini's film *Amarcord* (1973).[29] In typical *Fables* ironic style of clashing expectations, Flycatcher, the janitor (also "Frog Prince of Old," 2006a, 4), is the only one there

PLATE 44. Page 15. From *Fables: Arabian Nights (and Days)* © Bill Willingham & DC Comics. Used with Permission.

to greet the diplomatic party, and certainly not in the manner to which Sinbad is accustomed. "Who **are** you, western dog, and why are you the only one here to greet me? Where are the courtiers and wazirs and sundree **grandees** of high office?" asks Sinbad (2006b, 15).[30] Prince Charming, the mayor of Fabletown at the time, has forgotten about the envoy's arrival, and making things worse, the Fables that Sinbad encounters have trouble understanding his English. Sinbad and his entourage are finally given rooms, but the tension mounts as Prince Charming calls his guests "damned slave traffickers" (20).

Issues of language and cultural norms are thus immediately foregrounded. How much of each other's words the two leaders actually understand is not that clear. While all dialogue is in English for the reader, the difference in font style alerts us to when the characters are speaking Arabic, and the chapter's title, "Broken English," points to challenges in the storyworld's communication. When King Cole is called upon as interpreter and go-between, his Arabic translates into flowery English on the page, and some communication flow is established. Later in the story arc the slaves' and Sinbad's English-language misnomers are occasion for some comic relief. Also visually emphasizing the clashing of cultural norms or "larger social horizons of knowledge and experiences—the "social minds" of the Oriental and Western fairy tale characters" (Kukkonen 2011, 48)—are the different icons framing the pages or panels that present the Arabic Fables' perspective or focalization (stylized minarets and patterns, as seen in plate 44 and partially in plate 46) or Fabletown's official and security concerns (eagle emblem, guard in uniform, as seen in plate 45).

In contrast, when in *1001 Nights of Snowfall* Snow White travels as "envoy from a small community of fabled refugees" to the "far-off demon-haunted land of magnificent jeweled cities," the language of communication is not even mentioned. Clad in Victorian travel dress, Snow White presents "her credentials, with all appropriate ritual and courtesies, at the palace of the ruling Sultan, where she is received well, as befitted the import of her mission." However, "Then she is escorted to a most comfortable suite of rooms, whereupon she was fed, bathed, rested, and thereafter ignored" (Willingham 2006a, 9). After weeks of being more "prisoner than honored guest" (10), Snow White decides to do away with "courtly manners" and starts throwing tantrums, "frightening the servants from her sight" (10). When as a result of these antics there finally is a response to Snow White's demand that she see the Sultan, the Wazir approaches her by unceremoniously stating, "You are a most troublesome woman!" (10), and asking, "what sort of backward people would send a woman as their envoy?" (11).

While Snow White's and Sinbad's diplomatic missions start out quite differently, in both cases the Arabian Fables' treatment of women is at issue: in one scenario, Prince Charming morally condemns Sinbad for having a harem; in the other, the Wazir will not hear of diplomacy coming out "of a woman's devil-painted mouth" (2006a, 12). This common Orientalist trope that locates gender inequality and women's oppression outside of Western modernity establishes at once where subjectivity and civilization reside, whether it is with modern-day Fabletown or its "once upon a time" Snow White envoy.[31]

What is also established in the first few pages of both volumes is that as Willingham's readers we can easily fall back on our knowledge of the *Arabian Nights* media text. The *Arabian Nights* as media text in Western and now global-ized popular culture has functioned most lavishly in its visual tropes, and this is the case in *Fables* as well: we recognize Sinbad's turban, Yusuf's sinister sil-houette and hooked nose, the scimitars, the flying carpets that identify Sinbad's scenes in the comics' top gutter, the huge and powerful jinnî that is released in *Arabian Nights (and Days)*, the veiled yet sexy women of the harem, the "sump-tuous garments of silk and gauze" (2006a, 12) in which Snow White is veiled and draped in preparation for her seeing the Sultan. These are the visual "work-ings of imprecise intertextuality" (Kukkonen 2008, 262), of a popular cultural memory that extracts the *Arabian Nights* from its history and works to reinforce what we think we know.

The structural pitting of the two male Arabian Fables in Willingham's *Ara-bian Nights (and Days)* (2006b) against each other as opposite types is equally predictable. Sinbad is the Other who is well meaning and curious about Western cultural systems and quickly moves toward assimilation: he plays chess with King Cole, he appreciates the discursive subtleties of their conversations in Ara-bic and makes progress with his English, and of course he liberates his slaves giving them the opportunity to return as free citizens to Baghdad or remain in Fabletown. He is a mimic man with no critical edge, of the kind that Thomas Babington Macaulay fantasized about in the "Minute on Education," which in 1835 advocated the adoption of English (replacing Sanskrit and Arabic) for edu-cation in colonial India.[32] Yusuf, to the contrary, is consistently double-tongued, acts suspicious of Fabletown, and as proponent of a binary logic reminds Sinbad "we should join them [Fabletown], but only in the way that the conqueror joins the conquered" (2006b, 35). Once he suspects being crossed by Sinbad, whom he sees succumbing to Fabletown's ways, Yusuf does not hesitate to resort to jinn magic in order to reassert the power of the Arabic Fables over "western dev-ils" (50).[33] Particularly interesting in connecting the *Arabian Nights* fantasy with a more contemporary fantasy of Middle Eastern innate deviousness are the pan-els in which the jinnî who is doing Yusuf's bidding in a US-military-occupied Baghdad takes on the appearance of a slave girl whose sexual lure is an asset

PLATE 45. Page 90. From *Fables: Arabian Nights (and Days)* © Bill Willingham & DC Comics. Used with Permission.

PLATE 46. Page 51. From *Fables: Arabian Nights (and Days)* © Bill Willingham & DC Comics. Used with Permission.

both for the jinnî to elude the scrutiny of a US patrol and also trick Baghdadian conspirators (56–60). Sinbad is educable, transitioning to becoming more civilized; his treacherous adviser is not, and it is implied that his type never will be. Eventually, once Sinbad declares he had no intention or "invention" (in his "broken English") to be at war with Fabletown, he is redeemed in the eyes of Prince Charming and King Cole and instated by them as "the new major of Fabletown East" (88). That his title of Prince is hardly used in the dialogue suggests that his becoming mayor of this mirror Fabletown is much more of an honor.[34]

Just as the Arabian Fables are ancillary to Fabletown's "true" (that is, unqualified or absolute) heroes and political power, their magic is easily overcome in *Arabian Nights (and Days)* by Fabletown's Frau Totenkinder, "the Black Forest witch who used to live in a gingerbread house" (2006b, 4). Her spells detect that Sinbad and Yusuf have brought with them a "**d'jinn**," who—she explains to Beast, the new sheriff of Fabletown—is "**exactly** like a genii, Mr. Beast. 'Genii' is just a corruption of the proper term" (41). In this chapter ironically titled "D'jinn & Tonic with a Twist," Frau Totenkinder is clearly presented as the authority on jinn when she informs Beast and readers that jinn are "close to 97 percent" magic (41), much more powerful than sorcerers, and they are "wild things with no sense of good or evil" (42) who can grant wishes, "**any** wishes" (41). They cannot be stopped or killed, continues Frau Totenkinder but, as "Sulymon the Wise" did when he cleverly cajoled them into shrinking themselves into small bottles, they can be tricked. While Frau Totenkinder's magic is not strong enough to defeat or trick the jinnî himself, her exposition previews the means by which she will succeed. Cunningly, she works not on the jinnî, but on Yusuf, and she distorts his wording when he makes his wishes known to the powerful being. While Yusuf believes he has sent the jinnî on a mission to destroy his enemies in Baghdad as well as Fabletown leaders, which will put him in command, Frau Totenkinder has turned Yusuf's words against him so that the jinnî—unbeknownst to his master—goes off to destroy Yusuf's secret allies in Baghdad, comes back to "**devour** [Yusuf]—slowly and oh so **very** painfully" (73), and with the third wish is eventually contained again in his small bottle.

Grandmotherly and apparently fragile Frau Totenkinder, who is often shown knitting or drinking tea, is no match in many ways for the jinnî or d'jinn. However, like Regina in *Once Upon a Time*, she is clever and cunning enough to prevail; the witch of the West, whether she is young and beautiful or old and wrinkly, will defeat the overly emotional, powerful but slavish Other.[35] Furthermore, while Yusuf and Sinbad have trouble with the English language, her magic translates across language barriers and she effectively pulls off a ventriloquizing trick in Arabic. Metanarratively, one could say that the demonic and spectacular magic of the *Arabian Nights* succumbs to the more domestic and behind-the-scenes magic of the Euro-American fairy tale, but this intertextuality has a political valence as well. As shown in the disproportionate size of the jinnî and the witch in the two images (plates 47 and 48), Frau Totenkinder is also another figure for the "Israel Analogy," according to which mighty strength will not lead to victory.

What will lead to victory from Bigby's perspective, we know, is the determination to be "tough little bastards," which Frau Totenkinder has no trouble with in spite of her meek appearance; I would add that as the workings of Orientalism in history have shown, constructing a system of knowledge about the Other also contributes to her success. "They grant wishes, **any** wishes. Let's say I had one and wished for Fabletown to be destroyed—or New York—or **America**" (2006b, 41; plate 47), explains Frau Totenkinder to Beast to help him imagine just how powerful the jinnî is. The words in the panel refer to the witch's hypothetical wish, but the image suggests the jinnî's actualization of the violent wish in New York City, which at one level evokes the real-world tragedies of 9/11 and at another anticipates Yusuf's wishes to take over Fabletown. Frau Totenkinder's focalization of the jinnî offers an aggrandized and violent portrait of jinn, who instead in the *Arabian Nights* stories are mortal (in fact, a carelessly flung date stone hits and kills one in "The Story of the Merchant and the Demon" [Haddawy 1990, 17]) and can be malevolent, indifferent, or benevolent in dealing with humans (Marzolph and van Leeuwen 2004, 534–37; Warner 2012, 44–53). While the jinn "add the energy of unpredictability" (Warner 2012, 44) to the plots in the *Arabian Nights*, Frau Totenkinder's terrorist construction of what jinn are and do determines the development of the whole *Arabian Nights (and Days)* plot, and given this conceptualization it is no surprise that her work is done and Fabletown is safe only once the jinnî is returned to and sealed in the bottle. Her words and clever imagination as power/knowledge control the jinnî much more fully than Yusuf ever can, constructing the magic being from the start as a serious threat to Fabletown and then engaging to disarm him.[36]

In a way, I am suggesting that the interdependence of words and images in these two panels (plates 47 and 48) somewhat undermines the legitimacy of Frau Totenkinder's view of the jinnî's powers as terrorist because—in the absence of any further decoupage or breaking down of the panel into differently focalized scenes—it is presented as a construct of her imagination to which Beast, Prince Charming, and the other political authorities of Fabletown grant absolute authority. But despite this deconstructive opening, overall Frau Totenkinder is celebrated in *Arabian Nights (and Days)* as the unpromising hero of the "Israel Analogy," enacting metanarratively the superiority of an unassuming fairy-tale

PLATE 47. Page 41. From *Fables: Arabian Nights (and Days)* © Bill Willingham & DC Comics. Used with Permission.

PLATE 48. Page 74. From *Fables: Arabian Nights (and Days)* © Bill Willingham & DC Comics. Used with Permission.

magic over the impressive wonders of the *Arabian Nights*. While the size of their icons in the comics' top gutter is equal, the discursive power of the gingerbread-house magic (plate 47) not only overcomes but also *inscribes* that of the flying-carpet magic that marks the Arabian Fables scenes (plates 44, 46, and 48). And this is visually confirmed when we consider the "braiding" (*tressage*) of plates 47, 46, and 48 (Willingham 2006b, 41, 51, 74), that is, the linking as a series of these discontinuous panels "through non-narrative correspondences" (Groensteen 2007, ix), for example, visually through the jinnî's size, fierceness, and color. In this series, we see the magic-carpet icon appearing in the top gutter as a spatial or character-function marker (these images concern the Arabian Fables) in two panels, but the "social horizon of knowledge and experiences" or "social mind" of the Arabian Fables figures only in the lateral framing of plate 46, and (if we consider the series of three panels sequentially in the volume) it is braided into or enveloped by the witch's panel first (plate 47) and then by a deceptively un-framed—that is, naturalized and universalized—panel (plate 48). Here, Frau Totenkinder, from the bottom right corner of the page where she stands with King Cole, verbally asserts her overwhelming power as "an old back-country witch" by belittling Yusuf and "his dutiful demon," the jinnî.

In contrast to *Arabian Nights (and Days)*, 1001 *Nights of Snowfall* (Willingham 2006a) does not engage in openly political analogies—possibly because, as I mentioned earlier, its time frame is that of Fabletown's "once upon a time"—and its economy of genres is based on a richer intertextual relationship with the *Arabian Nights*, even as, I argue, its revisionist framework problematically reduces the storytelling power of Shahrazad (or Scheherazade as she appears in the graphic novel).

When the Grand Vizier finally grants the ambassador Snow White "a private audience with the Sultan," a "crafty look" has come into his eyes (Willingham 2006a, 12). Clued in by the title of the volume and the setting, readers already know that the so-far unnamed Sultan is "King Shahryar," the crazed tyrant who tells Snow White he has already sent one thousand brides of his to their death after their wedding night. As Shahryar and Snow White converse, readers who know the *Arabian Nights* frame narrative are made aware of what Snow White has and has not in common with the legendary heroine whose role she is about to play. A "proper woman of demure manners," Snow White, like Shahrazad, is "possessed of subtle cunning" (14) and exhibits poise, wit, and courage. Like Shahrazad, Snow White has a political mission, but it is a diplomatic one to bring about an alliance between the Arabian Fables and Fabletown against the Adversary; unlike Shahrazad, Snow White is a foreigner who is unaware, until he tells her, of Shahryar's experience of betrayal and its horrific consequences on the lives of his subjects. Unlike Shahrazad (and unlike the Snow White heroine in the Grimms' or Disney's tales), this Snow White is not a virgin and is divorced. Both Shahrazad and Snow White in their respective frame narratives ask the Sultan's permission to tell him a tale and embark in long-lasting storytelling therapy.

Willingham's frame tale, "A Most Troublesome Woman" (in 2006a, 7–22, 55, 85, 136–40), indicates a rather unusual level of engagement in American popular culture with the themes and structure of the *Arabian Nights* and its narrative frame. Featuring continuous verbal text with sumptuous illustrations by Charles Vess and Michael William Kaluta, Willingham's frame tale is also in its page layout set apart from the stories that Snow White tells, which feature a range of illustrators—including John Bolton, Mark Buckingham, Tara McPherson, and Jill Thompson—but are all in comics style. By the end of the first installment of the frame tale, the image of Snow White has also undergone quite a transformation. And both images provide significant distance between Snow White the ambassador and storyteller (plates 49 and 50) in this graphic novel and, respectively, the Snow White with whom readers of the comic-book series *Fables* are familiar (plate 51; Willingham 2002, 9) and the one whose story Snow White as Shahrazad tells King Shahryar (plate 52; Willingham 2006a, 23).

The multiplying of Snow White images is, on the one hand, a sign of how the graphic novel is less constrained than the comic-book series by the need to offer readers great ease of character identification, which presenting over and over again a distinctive body type, facial features, and dress for each main character produces (Lefèvre 2011, 16); on the other hand, the transformation of the Victorian-dressed Snow White into her *Arabian-Nights*-like persona exemplifies Snow's great "artifice and subterfuge" (21)—visually signaled by the images' same color palette—as she seeks to entertain and persuade the deadly Sultan not only to spare her life but also to heed to the political alliance she has come to propose between their countries. The image of Snow White as harem-like storyteller shows us not only how the Sultan sees her but also, metanarratively, channels for readers with previous knowledge of the *Arabian Nights* frame tale (which Shahryar has in part just summarized for Snow) that of the wonderful Shahrazad, just as to most readers the events in the first story that Snow White/Shahrazad tells clearly indicate it is a sequel to and disturbing reading of the traditional "Snow White and the Seven Dwarves" tale. At the same time, there is a marked contrast between the storyteller Snow White's Orientalized masquerade and her image in John Bolton's illustrations of the story she tells—illustrations that oscillate between the Disney-like homage of the cover (plate 52) and the evocation of a (differently Orientalized) East Asian sensual-and-dangerous trope, of

PLATE 49. Page 9. From *Fables: 1001 Nights of Snowfall* © Bill Willingham &
DC Comics. Used with Permission.

the *Crouching Lion, Hidden Dragon* (Dir. Ang Lee 2000) wuxia style, and the visual disassociation between these two Snow Whites is key to the storyteller's enchantment of her listener as she draws the Sultan into her fictional storyworld.

While she responds in more ways than one to the Sultan's request, "Tell me
your tale, Snow White" (Willingham 2006a, 21), it is crucial for Snow White/
Shahrazad to establish some narrative distance, to provide her stories with a fictional and fantasy-like patina coating her experience and the messages she wants
to convey: "Know, O King of the Age, that long ago and far away, a beautiful

maiden was rescued from varied trials and tribulations by a handsome prince" (Willingham 2006a, 24). The same strategy ("It is said, O wise and happy King, that once there was a prosperous merchant . . .") (Haddawy 1990, 17) allowed Shahrazad in the *Arabian Nights* to change the Sultan's absolutely dark outlook on women and life, showing him that "revenge is ultimately unsatisfying" (Willingham 2006a, 55) without calling his own murderous practices directly into question. In his use of the *Arabian Nights'* frame tale, narrative embedding,[37] and therapeutic slant, Willingham—the writer we know has *Arabian*

PLATE 51. Page 9. From *Fables: Legends in Exile* © Bill Willingham &
DC Comics. Used with Permission.

THE FENCING LESSONS

∗⋅-⋅—∗-⋅-∗

In which a wedding gift is given,
bad doings are discovered,
and two neighboring kingdoms begin
to beat the drums of war.

ILLUSTRATED BY JOHN BOLTON

PLATE 52. Page 23. From *Fables: 1001 Nights of Snowfall* © Bill Willingham &
DC Comics. Used with Permission.

Nights on his mind (however novel its metanarrative setting may be for the Snow White character from Fabletown)—shows remarkable wit and craft.

1001 Nights of Snowfall also skillfully adapts another storytelling strategy on which Shahrazad's success in the *Arabian Nights* depends, and that is her wide range of stories and genres. "Fencing Lessons" is a post-HEA tale of intrigue and revenge; "Christmas Pies" is also a trickster tale, but the protagonists are forest animals as in Aesop's fables; tales about losing everything to war ("A Frog's-Eye View"), growing up ("The Runt"), abusing one's powers or using them to help others ("The Witch's Tale" as well as "Fair Division") follow. Women—just as in the tales Shahrazad told the Sultan—are not consistently treacherous or trust-worthy, and what it means to be a hero shifts from tale to tale. It is the exposure to this multiplicity of experience that, in the setting of both frame narratives, counters Shahryar's belief that "there is not a single chaste woman anywhere on the entire face of the earth" (Haddawy 1990, 10; repeated almost verbatim in *1001 Nights of Snowfall* [Willingham 2006a, 20]) and the cycle of violence that such absoluteness demands. In the graphic novel, the illustrators' styles further convey a spectrum of experiences by constructing multiple storyworlds in different color palettes and line drawings. At the same time, many of the tales that Shahrazad and Snow White tell cluster around themes of revenge, loss, transformation, and the deception of appearances that—in their varied treatments—speak to the King. And while all the stories told to Shahryar work to extend and eventually redeem the life of their tellers, Shahrazad and Snow White, some of them function as "ransom tales" (Gerhardt 2010) within embedded narrative frames. The first of several examples occurring in the *Arabian Nights* is "The Story of the Merchant and the Demon" (Haddawy 1990, 17–19) in which three sheiks save the merchant's life by each telling a "strange and amazing" (22) story to the Demon; and in *1001 Nights of Snowfall*, acknowledging "The Witch's Tale" she has just heard as "an amazing story " (Willingham 2006a, 112), Red Rose decides to save the old and weak witch by taking her with them as she and her sister, Snow White, flee from the Adversary. While of course the elaborate art of narrative variation and repetition in the *Arabian Nights* cannot be matched in Willingham's compact graphic novel, *1001 Nights of Snowfall* does seriously engage not with the iconic wonders of the *Arabian Nights*—the genie, the flying carpet—but with the wonder that Shahrazad's stories inspire in the Sultan and in readers.

However, while *1001 Nights of Snowfall* celebrates the storytelling power of the *Arabian Nights*, it does so by having Snow White and the other Fabletown heroes temporarily take over its fictional landscape. Snow White replaces Shahrazad; the tales Snow White tells provide backstories for Bigby, Fly Catcher,

Snow White herself, King Cole, and Frau Totenkinder; and Snow White's political goal has everything to do with Fabletown's security and future. Contrary to the jinnî in *Arabian Nights (and Days)* whose relocation to Fabletown could only result in his defeat as an enemy, Snow White in the *Arabian Nights* is the victorious hero who charms Shahryar and redeems her own life even though, after three years or a 1001 nights of storytelling, she must admit to having run out of stories "of giants and dragons and cursed princesses" (Willingham 2006a, 136). Snow White has not only won him over, helping the Sultan emerge from his rage, but has also won, or disarmed him, by exposing him—in his words—as "a fraud" (136) who for a while had been only pretending to be unchanged because he wanted more stories. Note how, in contrast to most illustrations of Shahrazad and Shahriyar in bed together,[38] one of the final images in *1001 Nights of Snowfall* represents the Sultan in a subservient and lower position in relation to the comfortable and in-control Snow White (plate 53).

Furthermore, that Snow White has taken over not by appropriating the stories of *Arabian Nights* but by usurping Shahrazad's power is evident when the comic-book Scheherazade (spelling as in *Fables*) makes her entrance at the very end of *1001 Nights of Snowfall*. She is the Wazir's daughter who is fated to be King Shahryar's new bride when Snow White leaves, and Snow White has the last word when she gives Scheherazade some advice, "He likes stories" (Willingham 2006a, 140). This is a clever ending, which many of my students enjoy in its symmetry and playfulness, but it is also a sleight of hand that claims for the Euro-American Fables Shahrazad's inventiveness and wisdom, and, fictionally, reverses the intertextual history of exchanges between older *Arabian Nights* stories and the emergent fairy-tale genre in early-modern Europe. While she has her own stories to tell, this Scheherazade can only mimic the inventive and clever Snow White, or act after the fact and in her shadow. Just as their body language in the illustration (plate 54) suggests a mother-child composition,[39] symbols in the verbal description of the two—"She [Scheherazade] was a woman, like Snow White, bright with exceeding fairness and grace and beauty, but where Snow was the rising sun, she was the somber twilight" (Willingham 2006a, 140)—consolidate a hierarchy. I have called this a "stagist" revision of intertextual history because in this case too, European modernity comes "to non-European peoples . . . as somebody's way of saying 'not yet' to somebody else" (Chakrabarty 2007, 8).

"Fabletown is where as adults we keep our fairy tales after the invasion of the Adversary," commented Jason Adaniya in one of my classes, capturing the deep hold that Willingham's series *Fables* has on many young and not so young inhabitants of our "mundane and quite unmagical world" (Willingham 2006a,

PLATE 53. Page 137. From *Fables: 1001 Nights of Snowfall* © Bill Willingham &
DC Comics. Used with Permission.

PLATE 54. Page 139. From *Fables: 1001 Nights of Snowfall* © Bill Willingham & DC Comics. Used with Permission.

6). We read and enjoy *Fables* because it actively resists the exile of the imagination from the everyday world of business and traffic, and it does so, according to Willingham's preview in the introduction to *1001 Nights of Snowfall*, by providing "modern day adventures" to characters from folklore and fairy tales that, Willingham eagerly reassures us, we "already know" (6). So nostalgia and comfort ("Grab a comfy seat and make yourself at home. We'll be starting the story in a moment," 6) are both important elements in the reenchantment that *Fables* offers. It is, therefore, not surprising that the characters adults participating in globalized pop culture already know best—Snow White, the Big Bad Wolf, the Witch, Prince Charming—are its central protagonists, even when they link up with the *Arabian Nights*. What is more striking to me is how the *Fables* series is also, and perhaps centrally, a fictional response to 9/11, where resistance to the "invasion of the homelands" justifies war and where Fabletown's moral and world-making superiority (in its Israel analogy or its re/dislocating of Arabs strategies) is absolutely upheld.

ADAPTATION AS *RETRANSLATING* STORIES, *REORIENTING* AUDIENCES, AND *IMPROVISING* FOR WONDER

As with *Fables'* graphic narrative, the work of adaptation in Mary Zimmerman's play, *The Arabian Nights*, involves a shift from telling to highly selective showing, visually dramatizing the passing of time, description, and thoughts; however, like a movie and unlike a comic book, a stage production transforms not only the verbal into visual but also print into the audible (Hutcheon 2006); as a performance, it also involves a direct interaction with its audiences in the theater. A member of the Lookingglass Theatre Company, Zimmerman is a professor of performance studies at Northwestern University and a prolific adapter of classics such as Ovid's *Metamorphoses* for the stage (which won her the Tony Award in 2002 for Best Direction of a Play) and of operas for the Metropolitan's new stage productions *and* its *Live in HD* series (for example, Gioacchino Rossini's *Armida* with Renée Fleming, 2009–10). When working with non-dramatic texts, Zimmerman is well known for her use of improvisation and live-audience involvement as well as her Reader's Theater style. This means that several plays she has adapted and directed are also available in print, which has allowed me to teach *The Arabian Nights* (Zimmerman 2005a, abbreviated as *TAN* from now on) in courses on fairy-tale adaptations, in which when we read her script in the classroom we are confronted with another level of adaptation—back from the stage to the printed page but with new possibilities for reading

PLATE 55. Photo by Sean Williams. Design by Ted Studios. Courtesy of Lookingglass Theatre Company.

out loud and performance in an instructional setting.[40] The play, *The Arabian Nights*, premiered in Chicago in 1992, as Zimmerman has often stated, "in the shadow of the first Gulf War." In a 2011 interview, she continued, "I was distressed by the discourse surrounding The Middle East at the time. In order to persuade people to go to war against others, you have to convince them that the others are truly different, not quite human, not quite 'like us.' In *The Arabian Nights*, the characters are actually very familiar sorts, although we find them in somewhat exotic trappings" (Zimmerman and Markowitz 2011).[41] In the book, the play is framed on one end by an epigraph, quoting the tenth-century Arab geographer Muqadassi [sic] or Muqaddasi, in praise of a thriving ancient Baghdad, and at the other by the final lines the whole cast repeats several times, "And the nights over Baghdad were whiter than the days" (*TAN*, 130), to evoke the bombing of the Iraqi city during Operation Desert Storm in 1991. Stage directions call in this final scene for "the sound of air-raid sirens and of static on a distant radio and the rising of the wind" (130), with the whole company "sink[ing] to the ground" and "roll[ing] away . . . like dead leaves in the wind," until the wind stops and "everyone is still" (131).[42] In between these two (dramatically opposite and temporally distant from each other) views of the city, the fictional storytelling the play brings to life seeks to give us more than a glimpse of the talent, elegance, and knowledge that Muqaddasi ascribed to Baghdad and its people. John Wat, who directed a 2005 high school production of the play in Honolulu, recalls how he and his students "talked about the idea that with US bombs dropped on the Tigris and Euphrates river valleys, it was like 'we' were bombing the cradle of our own civilization" (e-mail communication).[43]

To bring this humanist message to audiences and readers, Zimmerman deploys several strategies in her adaptation of *The Arabian Nights*, resulting in what I am calling a *retranslation* that offers its target audiences antihegemonic ways to connect with *The Arabian Nights* that differ from the usual icons of its media text version. This *retranslation* is not aimed at establishing or recreating cultural authenticity. Zimmerman works for her adaptation from E. Powys Mathers's translation, *The Thousand and One Nights* (specifically in the Routledge and Kegan Paul 1986 edition)—a not so fashionable multivolume text in the English language that is itself a translation of the French and very fanciful version of the *Nights* by Joseph Charles Victor Mardrus (1899–1904). I take it that by choosing Mathers as her canvas, Zimmerman implicitly acknowledges the convoluted history of *Arabian Nights* translations and takes responsibility— from her position as an American woman in the early 1990s adapting *The Arabian Nights* for the stage with no specific investment in Arabic culture or knowledge of Arabic—for working within a culture of translation as well as against its Orientalist tradition.[44] Because Zimmerman's motivation is to *move* her North American public away from dehumanizing stereotypes, exercising the impulse to think outside of the "*Nights* as media text" box necessarily involves intervening in the discourse of Orientalism, thus claiming no representational purity, and she does so aiming to produce an appreciation of *The Arabian Nights* as a masterful treatment of the life-saving quality of stories, an artwork of salutary significance to all humans. Her *retranslation* is meant to loosen a fixed image of *The Arabian Nights* and the diverse kinds of people who produced it, just as Shahrazad's storytelling in *The Arabian Nights* succeeds in undoing Shahriyar's all-negative image of women and his blood for blood logic.

Shahrazad in *The Arabian Nights*, Zimmerman in her play, and Scheherazade in Zimmerman's play proceed "gently and fictionally" to move—emotionally and epistemologically—their respective, fictional and live, audiences.[45] One of Shahrazad's strategies that Zimmerman adapts in her play is to tell tales that are rhetorically varied though thematically linked; significantly, they are selections from *The Arabian Nights* that are not well known to the general public. Retranslating, in this case, means surprising audiences and readers with stories they are unfamiliar with and yet cultivating a relationship between these fictional tales and their listeners/readers that fosters "empathy" as a way to reorient us in the social world.

For instance, the storytelling action from *The Arabian Nights'* frame narrative that is dramatized in Act 1 of the play extends to a few nights only, during which Shahryar and audiences in the theater listen to the following "new" stories:

- the tale of Harun al-Rashid, the famous and wise caliph of Baghdad (who in Scheherazade's tales is a mirror image of the sultan Shahryar could be) going to visit the madhouse (*TAN*, 10–38) in which the Madman tells Harun about his marriage with Perfect Love—

- "The Madman's Tale," which is the "Story of the Second Lunatic"[46] in *The Arabian Nights*, mixed with the witty verbal sparring from "The Porter and the Three Ladies of Baghdad"—as a result of which Harun has him freed "for the sake of this story" (37);

- and "The Perfidy of Wives" (40–74), the tale of the Jester's wife and her four lovers (the Pastrycook, the Butcher, the Greengrocer, and the Clarinetist), framing the tales they each tell Harun al-Rashid to redeem their own lives;

- "The Pastrycook's Tale" (49–53), a version of "The Ruined Man Who Became Rich Again through a Dream" from *The Arabian Nights*;

- "The Butcher's Tale" (53–63), a version of "A Contest of Generosity";

- "The Greengrocer's Tale," or "The Wonderful Bag" (64–67), a version of "'Alî the Persian";

- and "The Clarinetist's Tale" (69–74), a version of "How Abu Hasan Brake Wind."

Most of these tales in Act I are successful ransom tales that do not present themselves as moralities or as tales of magic. Via the tales and the narrators to whom she delegates, Scheherazade dares to challenge Shahryar's totalizing or monological worldview and to present varied, even simultaneously different perspectives on deceit, virtue, sex, fortune, and transformation. The humor that animates many tales of *The Arabian Nights* also plays a big part in Act I of Zimmerman's play, dramatizing conflicts and confronting the self-important or powerful with their images in funhouse mirrors, but working less toward satire and more toward establishing chance and human frailty as great equalizers. These jocular tales are just that, an invitation to play, rather than to stick with the set rules and moves of a violent game: while death is inevitable, sentencing other humans to death is shown to be madness. At the start of the first night of storytelling, Shahryar "unsheathes his curved knife, and holds it up to [Scheherazade's] throat" (7); but by the end of Act I, Shahryar, Scheherazade, and Dunyazade are "rolling with laughter" and, while Shahryar still "raises his knife to Scheherazade," he ends up kissing her and letting the knife be taken from him (74).

PLATE 56. Pictured: Jason Ellinwood and Gilani Moiseff in *The Arabian Nights*, by Mary Zimmerman. Mid-Pacific Institute School of the Arts, Honolulu, 2005. Courtesy of Dir. John H. Y. Wat.

PLATE 57. Pictured: Susaan Jamshidi, Barzin Akhavan, Andrew White, and David Catlin in *The Arabian Nights,* Written and Directed by Mary Zimmerman. Photo by Sean Williams. Courtesy of Lookingglass Theatre Company.

Scheherazade's life is still at risk, but the mood is different in Act 2, which begins on "the five hundred and first night" and with Shahryar asking to "hear words of wisdom from you [Scheherazade]" (75). In Act 2, retold and partly retold tales from *The Arabian Nights* include "The Tale of 'Azîz and 'Azîza," "Tawaddud," "The Mock Caliph," "The Prince and the Tortoise," "Qamar al-Zamân and Budûr," "'Alâ al-Dîn Abu'l-Shâmât," "Hard-Head and His Sister Little-Foot," and "Ishâq of Mosul and the Lost Melody." The generic range of this selection again significantly contests the impoverished canon of *Arabian Nights* as media text, and the stories' variations on the themes of love, power, grief, and knowledge likewise contribute to draw Shahryar out of his repetition compulsion. Harun al-Rashid's encounter with Sympathy the Learned (adapted from "Tawaddud") is key to advancing Shahryar's transformative journey, not only because it mirrors that of Shahryar with Scheherazade, but also because Sympathy the Learned— who displays extraordinary knowledge of the Koran and religion, "things of the body and the world" (82), and riddling, putting to shame his top (male, of course) sages at court—refuses Harun's marriage proposal by asserting, "Kings do not need Sympathy. She must lie with those less fortunate" (92). In the tales that follow ("The Mock Caliph" and "'Azîz and 'Azîza") Scheherazade confronts Shahryar with reflected images of his own grief, which is no longer about being betrayed but also about, as Zimmerman explains, the "killing off of his own ability to re-engender ... and regenerate himself" (Zimmerman 2009), and opens him up to desiring change or self-transformation. "How perfect just to be someone else" (*TAN*, 108) becomes not impersonating or ventriloquizing the Other, but recognizing the Other within oneself as well as recognizing that fictions provide humans with a space to try out new possibilities. While I have only sketched how Zimmerman's and her cast's selections work in this adaptation, I hope to have conveyed how the play takes advantage of the collection's generic range and how refreshing its *re*translation and engagement with the narrative variety, sophistication, and power of *The Arabian Nights* are.[47]

"Scheherazade, marvelous girl, you have lifted the veil from my heart," Shahryar finally exclaims (122). The goal of the play is to dramatize how Shahryar's experience of multiple possibilities through stories saves him, but it is also to transport us, audiences in the theater and readers, and to lead us away from our prejudices. As such, the tales become portals to knowledge, not to knowledge about Shahryar as the Other, dehumanized tyrant and enemy, but about ourselves as we are, like him, moved.

Working with a second strategy of adaptation, Zimmerman's stage directions, choreography, and casting facilitate this emotional and epistemological reorientation by immersing us in a space that is fluid and a human subjectivity that is plural. "The play is best suited to a thrust stage with the audience sur-rounding" it; "all of the performers [musicians included] remain in full view of the audience throughout the play, sitting or lying on pillows . . . rising to join the action as needed"; "the action is continuous; scenes and locations overlap and dissolve into one another" (*TAN*, "A Note on Staging," xv). In Reader's Theater style, when Scheherazade begins to tell her first tale to Shahryar, the shift from frame narrative to embedded tale is performed aurally (rather than spatially) as she and Harun Al-Rashid, a character and focalizer in her tale, speak a few lines together ("Let us go at once," 12); after that, one ring of the finger cymbals will signal moving from the scene of the frame tale to the storyworld of one of Scheherazade's tales, and the triangle chime signals the arrival of dawn and of Scheherazade's ordained (but then postponed) death.

Furthermore, just as carpets overlap on the stage, actors have several parts, "adding a bit of costume as they play a new role" (xv); the man performing as Shahryar, for instance, also plays Mock Khalifah and 'Azîz. However, playing out a multiplicity of personae in one body does not empty the subject of conflicts or result in obvious pairings: Zimmerman suggests that different actors, for example, play Shahryar and Madman, or Scheherazade and Sympathy the Learned. In other words, visual and auditory experiences on stage are set up to represent *The Arabian Nights'* wonderful stories as "airy suspension bridge[s]" where "traffic moves in both directions" (Warner 1994, 24)[48] between normative reality and its transforma-tion, and to cultivate the audience's abilities to perceive human subjects relationally (rather than as unchangeable essences or in binary oppositions).

That storytelling is a form of social interaction of consequence is reinforced in the play by characters' comments about stories they are telling or listening to. The mise-en-scène of such evaluative comments (for example, Harun says "This is an excellent tale indeed" [53] in response to the "The Tale of the Pastrycook," and Scheherazade and Clarinetist announce, "I have a story even more absurd—if you will hear it!" [68]) works to break down Shahryar's absolute authority to kill the teller Scheherazade if the tale is not to his liking. Following the telling of "A Contest of Generosity," the audience is encouraged to be part of this articulation of varied responses to storytelling, and members of the cast ask people in the theater to indicate, by clapping, who are their favorite or "most generous" characters. By breaking the fourth wall, Zimmerman further involves the public not as specta-tors but as human beings whose life choices are—like Shahryar's—animated by narratives and fantasies, and whose prejudices have harmful consequences.

Attuning Shahryar to wonder in his life and the audience to a (somewhat) de-exoticized sense of wonder is a third and final strategy of adaptation by which Zimmerman's *The Arabian Nights* engages in a humanist *re*translation of *The*

Arabian Nights stories that seeks to undermine the us/them logic informing what has become the "war on terror."[49] When she is no longer under the threat of death, Scheherazade asks in the play for permission to tell one more story, the tale of "The Forgotten Melody" (122). In it, the great musician Ishak of Mosul describes his reaction upon hearing the performance of the forty-third song composed by an even more accomplished musician of earlier times, Maabad of al-Hijaz; in Ishak of Mosul's words, "the walls moved closer in to listen. . . . And time was frozen in my blood, and I left the prison of my skin and became other than myself" (124). He believes he will never forget such an extraordinary song, but when he tries to play it himself—and for himself since he wants to keep the song as his greatest possession—he is unable to. Determined to search for "his" lost melody, the musician is on a quest across the desert when he is approached by three young women who tell him they too know the song, having overheard it from the harem on the night it was performed for Ishak of Mosul. They know how greedy he is, so before singing the song, they make him promise to "willingly sing it and every other song you know to whomever you may meet upon the road" (127). The three women then sing and dance, "and the vault of heaven came closer in to listen, and the stars began to dance, and the river and all its life began to dance" says Ishak of Mosul (127). What the audience experiences is the women's *silent* dance on stage, which Zimmerman's notes tell us is "made up of the ordinary gestures of everyday life—perhaps tying a shoe, spreading a cloth, etc. Slowly, and at first clumsily, Shahryar joins them" and so does Scheherazade and every other member of the company (*TAN*, 127–28).

The adapted tale and the on-stage performance of the "lost melody" serve, I believe, multiple functions in Zimmerman's play. First, within the frame narrative in which Scheherazade's storytelling has been a lifesaver, hearing and responding to Ishak of Mosul's tale give Shahryar two related opportunities: in his own silent dance performance, he shows that he is finally ready to move from the fictionality of "story time" back into the flow of life in the everyday; his capacity to tune into the "silent music" shows that his appreciation of the many strange and wonderful experiences and lives in Scheherazade's tales will not be confined to the realm of performance, but extend to his everyday choices. The Scheherazade of this play is a successful teacher, who like the Shahrazad in Haddawy's English-language translation "had read and learned" (1990, 11) and who is perhaps testing here whether Shahryar's epistemological and emotional transformation is *habitus* forming and, at the same time, how capable he is of improvising in response to the good and bad surprises that life inevitably holds.

Second, that Zimmerman's notes list only a couple of possible movements for the "silent dance" performance suggests there is no one melody that is wonderful to all or for good, and metanarratively it reinforces the important role of improvisation in Act 1's trickster tales adapted from *The Arabian Nights*, in Scheherazade's storytelling as she adapts her tales in response to Shahryar's signs of interest or boredom, and in the writing and staging of the play itself. The actors' improvisation is most prominent in the performance of "The Wonderful Bag," in which two characters enumerate the imaginary contents of the bag, and Zimmerman encourages them to come up with "outrageous" lists (of which two examples are given in *TAN*, 133–39). But improvisation is overall integral to the process by which Zimmerman adapts nondramatic texts. For her, "the script does not precede the production, but rather 'grows up' simultaneously with it" under the pressure of three factors: the designs for the play, the cast, and "the events and circumstances of the world during the rehearsal period of the play" (Zimmerman 2005c, 26). Writing the script "in the hours between rehearsals," she strives to be attentive to the actors' physical improvisations, to the narrative she is adapting, and to creating a text that is "open to the world, part of the world," responding to the events that are in the news at the time, that she and the cast bring with them to rehearsals.

For *The Arabian Nights* play, in particular, we already know which events were on Zimmerman's mind at the time when she and the Lookingglass Theatre Company in 1991 were engaged in rehearsals and adaptation; since then, this poetics of improvisation has resulted in productions with different music and tighter scripts, but also in shows that have continued to vary, even if slightly, to put pressure on the dehumanizing rhetoric of "holy wars" wherever it comes from.[50] For his 2005 production of Zimmerman's play, director John Wat utilized "a process in rehearsal called 'discoveries.' Anyone working on the production is encouraged to 'discover' something related to the play and share it with the cast. For example, the girl who played Sympathy the Learned, found all the Christian equivalents to the list of prophets from the Koran. . . . I do think the story of Sympathy the Learned was especially effective at presenting some facets of Islamic knowledge, belief systems, and customs. And I think it was also an effective exploration or critique of 'professed' knowledge and true knowledge and wisdom" (e-mail communication to author, April 30, 2012).[51]

Third, the "Lost Melody" tale and the silent performance of its song also work to shift the audience out of "story time" and back toward rejoining the everyday. While the finale's evocation of Baghdad's bombing in 1991 reconnects us to the news and world events, the silent dance embodies an everyday with which, it is implied, we have lost touch, an everyday that has its own melodies and surprises, *habitus*, and improvisations. In its generic and emotional range, Scheherazade's storytelling has prepared us, like Shahryar, to participate in our own—and different—scenarios with renewed appreciation. This small-scale wonder of the everyday is—despite the exotic costumes and setting—then serving a de-Orientalizing function in the play. What we (may be moved to) feel is wonderful has nothing to do with flying carpets or jinn, but with reviving our participation in our ordinary home worlds. Contributing to this de-Orientalizing of wonder is also Zimmerman's deployment of the Lookingglass Theatre Company's multicultural cast. While there is no pretense to the characters having some sort of authentic look, my students' reactions to the play and to the illustrations in the book suggest that this multicultural casting can work against, on the one hand, the reduction of diversity in the Middle East to one Arabic image or Muslim stereotype and, on the other, can work to undermine the preconception that "the others are truly different, not quite human, not quite 'like us'" (Zimmerman and Markowitz 2011). And this is the prejudice that Zimmerman sought to intervene against by *retranslating The Arabian Nights* for North American audiences as "one of the great masterpieces of world literature."

■   ■   ■

The adaptations of *The Arabian Nights* I discussed in this chapter have all been not only North American but also mainstream in the fields of popular culture and performance arts. While all exhibit some degree of sophistication in their poetics that deserves scholarly attention, their politics of adaptation is tame, at the most embracing a humanist approach to de-exoticize wonder—much tamer, for instance, than that of the creolizing projects I analyzed in chapters 1 and 3. If my discussion of these adaptations projects a rather limited and precarious sense of a de-Orientalizing poetics of wonder, this is not only because there is nothing here about the wealth and range of recent adaptations produced in the Middle East or by Arabic artists, but also because the currency of Ali Baba stereotypes is powerful, and the tragic consequences of war are very much with us. Scheduled performances in Chicago of another theatrical adaptation, *The Thousand and One Nights* (dramatized and directed by Tom Supple, staged in summer 2011 at the Luminato Festival in Toronto and the Edinburgh Festival, and featuring an all-Middle-Eastern cast) were canceled after several members of its pan-Arabic cast had problems with US visas.[52] I take it as a good sign in this climate that high school students today have the opportunity to perform in Zimmerman's play and cultivate their improvising skills as one strategy to contest the pernicious naturalization of the us/them rhetoric.[53]

The Politics of Wonder

Wonder has no opposite; it springs already doubled in itself, compounded of dread and desire at once, attraction and recoil, producing a thrill, the shudder of pleasure and of fear. It names the marvel, the prodigy, the surprise as well as the responses they excite, of fascination and inquiry; it conveys the active motion towards experience and the passive stance of enrapturement.

MARINA WARNER

"Dom, did you think about your third wish?'
"No"
"Take your time"

FIONA, THE FAIRY, and DOM in *La fée / The Fairy* 2011

You probably know this tale, but it's worth retelling.

One winter, when the snow was deep, a poor boy had to go outside with his sled to gather wood. After he had finally collected enough wood and had piled it on his sled, he was so frozen he decided not to go home right away. He thought he would instead make a fire to warm himself up a bit. So he began scraping the snow away, and as he cleared the ground he discovered a small golden key. Where there's a key, he knew, there must also be a lock. So he dug farther into the ground and found a little iron casket. If only the key will fit! he thought. There must be precious things in the casket. He searched and searched, but could not find a keyhole. Then, finally, he noticed one, but it was so small he could barely see it. He tried the key, and fortunately it fit. So he began turning it in the keyhole.

And now we must wait until he unlocks the casket completely and lifts the cover.
That's when we'll learn what wonderful things he found.

This is my own amalgamation of two English-language translations, Maria Tatar's and Jack Zipes's, of "The Golden Key" in the Brothers Grimm collection. I like retelling this tale and have done so in class as well as at scholarly meetings because it does, in a minor key, what Angela Carter associated with fairy tales in general: to quote her again, while providing "the most vital connection we have with the imaginations of the ordinary men and women whose labour created our world," these tales "positively parade [their] lack of verisimilitude," and they exhibit, perhaps even instigate, "heroic optimism." I also enjoy retelling it because it helps to reflect on the poetics of wonder.

What I mean here by *wonder*, as I extrapolate it from reading "The Golden Key," should resonate with the texts and ideas I discussed in earlier chapters of this book. If you are familiar with the tale in German or in another language, please keep in mind the words as you know them, especially what translates as "wonderful things," because to what extent this resonance carries across to the so-called equivalents of the English-language "wonder" in German, Dutch, Italian, French, Portuguese, Spanish (*wunder, wonder, meraviglia* or *incanto* or *prodigio, merveille, maravilha, asombro* or *maravilla*), or for that matter Hawaiian (*kamaha'o*) and other non-European languages, varies and matters.[1]

Something I noticed in three recent translations of "The Golden Key" into English is that the final sentences of the tale do not only enact the movement from storyworld to the scene of storytelling but also shift from the past tense to the present and future. For Zipes, "So, he began turning it, and now we must wait until he unlocks the casket completely and lifts the cover. That's when we'll learn what wonderful things he found" (Zipes 1987, 289). In Maria Tatar's wording, the final sentences read: "Now, he's started turning it, and we'll just have to wait until he finishes unlocking the casket and lifts the lid. Then we'll know what kinds of wonderful things can be found in it" (Tatar 2010, 251). And in Matthew Price's rendition, "And now we'll just have to wait until he has unlocked it all the way and raised the lid. Then we'll discover what wonderful things are tucked away inside" (Price 2011, 290). This metanarrative shift in space and time—bridging action in the storyworld with the storytelling situation—is what makes retelling the tale worth it for me. This shift marks, without naming it, the transformative process that inhabits the tale, a transformation that seeks to bring about *wonder* as its effect and affect on listeners and readers.

Wonder throughout the Grimms' tale animates the boy's actions starting from the moment when he questions, because he is too cold to make it home, the wisdom of trying to complete his assignment right away. So to survive he

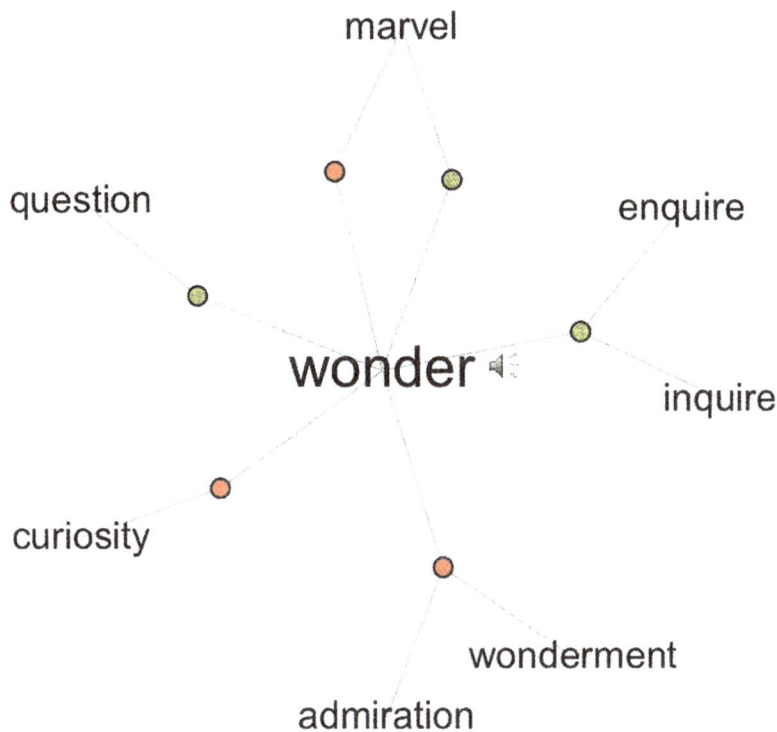

marvel

question

enquire

wonder

inquire

curiosity

wonderment

admiration

wanders off task, he then marvels in finding something unexpected, he speculates and anticipates possibilities, he acts on his curiosity, and he inquires further. He is experiencing wonder as a state or emotion (nouns are marked in red in the online *Visual Thesaurus*) and he is wondering, acting out on his desire for something more (verbs are marked as green); his knowledge of the world (he knows to clear the snow covering the earth) opens him up to being in awe of what it unexpectedly offers; he is open to the change, in his being and his actions, to which the encounter with wonder exposes him. This feeling and action of wonder are not the same as "the wonderful things" that are contained in the little casket but rather have everything to do with the boy's encounter with and curiosity about something unexpected or other in his experience of the world. Whether his actions result in his surviving, we are not told, and the word "casket" has its own ambivalent connotations, but we know that his knowledge, curiosity, and openness to the world are part of this boy's survival kit.

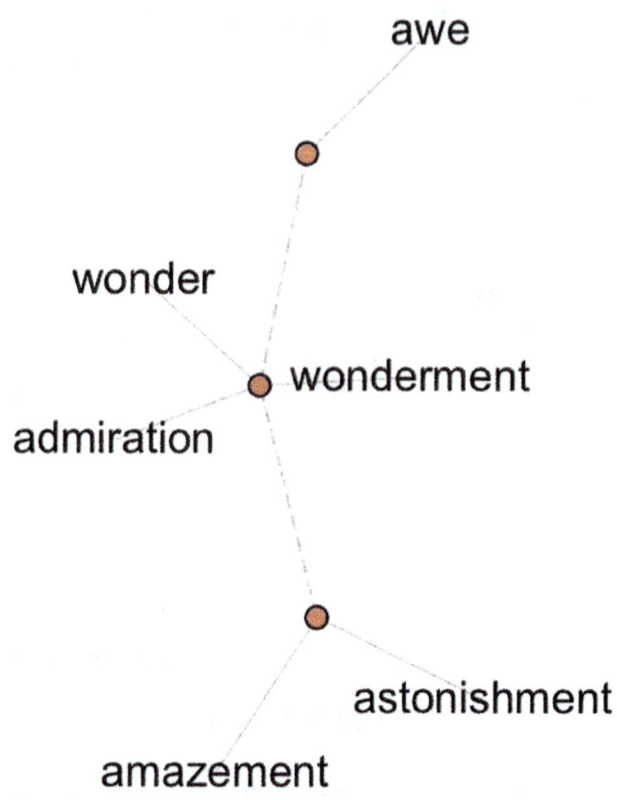

awe

wonder

wonderment

admiration

astonishment

amazement

As listeners/readers of the Grimms' tale, "we" are interpellated by the storyteller to relate to the boy's experience but at a distance, not so much readying ourselves to enjoy "the wonderful things" with him, but to wonder about the difference between what he may find and what we will or can "learn," between what he "found" and what we will or may "feel" or "know." "We," the tellers/narrators/ translators and listeners/readers, are not the ones to find the "wonderful things"; we are the ones whom the storyteller/narrator conducts toward reflecting on the experience of wonder. We are alerted, in that pregnant moment when the boy in the tale is about to uncover "wonderful things," to the power of the unexpected or amazing, the inexplicable, the "other"—whether it be our mortality or the miraculous—in our own experiences of the world and of stories. This awakening is an invitation that never ceases to attract humans' attention.

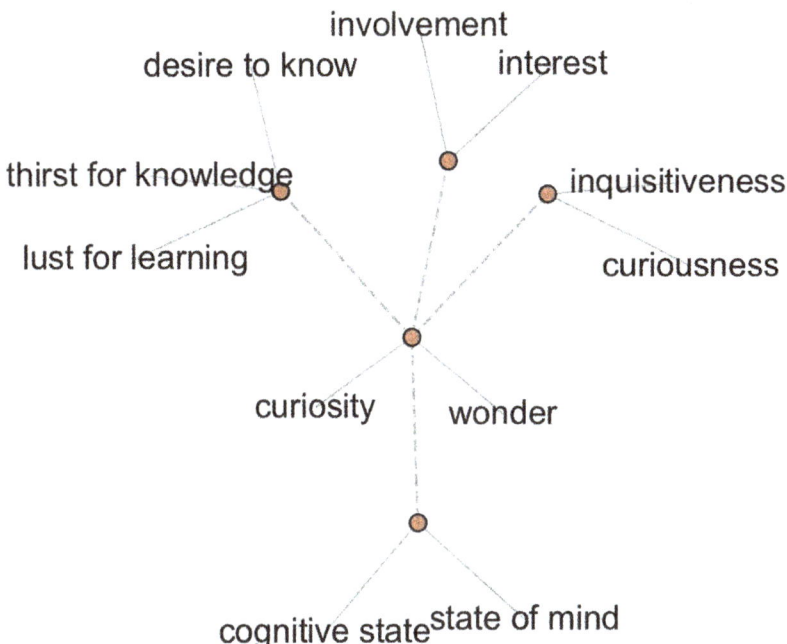

involvement
desire to know   interest

thirst for knowledge   inquisitiveness

lust for learning   curiousness

curiosity   wonder

cognitive state state of mind

Perhaps this is why Anne Sexton's disenchanting volume *Transformations* (1971) begins with the poem "The Gold Key," a response from the self-proclaimed "middle-aged witch" to "The Golden Key" tale that Marie Hassenpflug had told the Grimms and that the Grimms placed as the last one in their 1815 edition of the *Kinder- und Hausmärchen*. As we close their book, the Grimms' finale can be read as encouraging each of us—children and adults—to exercise our curiosity, to find our own golden key to the stories, to unlock our own sense of wonder in the Grimms' fairy tales. Noel Daniel writes in his brief commentary, "the ending of the [Grimms'] final tale seems to say, 'You, too, are part of the process. Take it from here'" (in Price 2011, 289). Which is, of course, what Sexton did with a vengeance, recognizing the significance of the tale's appeal to wonder at the same time that she acted on the desire to transform what the commodification of the Grimms' book—the iron casket of stories and human destinies—had fixed or reified as wonderful things or outcomes. Lighting up a side effect of the Grimms' Disneyfied enchantment in the United States of the 1950s and 1960s, Sexton asked her readers, "Are you comatose? / Are you undersea?" (1971, 1).

Her poem ends by introducing her own book as a transformative site for reading the Grimms with an eye to wonder. Sexton, like Angela Carter, Guillermo del Toro, and many fairy-tale adapters including the Grimms in their times, was looking to renew wonder in its complexity as both state and action, in response to the unfamiliar, the unexplained, the easily overlooked detail or way of being in our worlds, our stories, and within us, and calling for our own active— and, even more so, activist—responses to and participation in the process of storytelling and interpretation.

■   ■   ■

As I noted in the introduction, fairy tales are also referred to, though less commonly, as "wonder tales" because they can produce this complex effect and because historically in Europe they emerge in part from the secularization of medieval miraculous tales and the transformation of pagan beliefs. Wonder's association with the numinous has implications for thinking about the fairy tale as a genre.

One could say that in its very emergence at the turn of the eighteenth century as a newly named modern genre in Europe, the secular *conte de fées* emancipated the fairy (*fée*) as a powerful, experienced woman from the patriarchal control of the church *at the same time* that it subordinated wonder to magic, to what the modern fairy could make happen rather than what nature, numen, or fortune produced.[2] Within modernity, the cause-and-effect logic of science and rationalism was expected to explain away the unexpected or astounding, replacing it with its human-made wonders. With modernity, wonder as an "unsettling pathos" that opens up inquiry, as Mary-Jane Rubenstein puts it in *Strange Wonder: The Closure of Metaphysics and the Opening of Awe* (2009, 4), was objectified as "wonders" that could be possessed.[3] And within this logic, the means of wonder, that is, magic, became a trick or childlike make-believe rather than the outcome of a way of knowing and being in the world. Furthermore, from the perspective of a stagist historicism, narratives from other cultures that sought to elicit wonder were enlisted either to the production of primitivism in the service of coloniality or to the modern production of an exoticized/eroticized magic.

Are today's adaptations transforming the fairy-tale genre? Madame d'Aulnoy did just that when she adopted the term *conte de fée* to write literary wonder tales in which the female fairy (not Fortune or the Church) was in control; Antoine Galland's adaptations did so in the early eighteenth century with his appropriation of *The Thousand and One Nights*; the Grimms, though hardly alone, did it in the nineteenth, and Georges Méliès at the turn of the twentieth century; the Angela Carter generation did it in the late twentieth; there are many more examples. Does the politics of wonder play a transformative role in today's adaptations?

Significantly, most of the narrative texts I discuss in this book do not represent wonder or wonders; rather, they work in different modes and media to cultivate our taste for wonder and attune us to its power in fairy tales. I have read these adaptations as contestations of an impoverished poetics of magic that the Disneyfied fairy tale codifies and as symptomatic of a renewed, though hardly cohesive, poetics and politics of wonder in the contemporary cultural production and reception of fairy tales. As such, they are activist responses to and *potentially* transformative adaptations of the fairy tale as hegemonically put to work in globalized consumer popular culture. I say "potentially" because their effects depend on our reading practices, our openness to forming a different *habitus*. And, for scholars of the fairy tale, they depend on our willingness to engage the question, "How does [this] story change people's sense of what is possible, what is permitted, and what is responsible or irresponsible?" (Frank 2010, 75), with an ear to how storytellers from varied locations of colonial difference turn to the folk and fairy tale for making "the impossible possible" (Hopkinson and Nelson 2002).

There are many more such texts, I believe. Reading adaptations of *The Thousand and One Nights/Arabian Nights* in Middle Eastern and Indian literatures as well as from the Arabic diaspora would certainly activate different links in the fairy-tale web from the ones I highlighted in chapter 4. Such literary and filmic relocations range from Elias Khoury's *Gate of the Sun* (1998; trans. 2006), Githa Hariharani's *When Dreams Travel* (1999), Tahir Shah's *In Arabian Nights: A Caravan of Moroccan Dreams* (2008), *The Arabian Nights* a children's book written by Wafa' Tarnowska and illustrated by Carole Hénaff (2010) to Nacer Khemir's films including *Baliseurs du desert* (1984), Moufida Tlatli's *The Silences of the Palace* (1994), and the Egyptian movie *Scheherazade, Tell Me a* Story (Dir. Yousry Nasrallah 2009).[4] I am only scratching the surface here, and my list is limited to adaptations that are produced or accessible in English or French.

In other contemporary literary traditions, a direct engagement with the fairy tale may be less common. This seems to be the case in Oceania, for instance, where I believe artists in various media (e.g., the multimedia epic drama, *Holo mai Pele*, by Hālau o Kekuhi; the feature film *The Land Has Eyes*, directed by Vilsoni Hereniko; the anthology of modern *mo'olelo*, *Don't Look Back: Hawaiian Myths Made Anew*, edited by Christine Thomas; Robert Sullivan's graphic novel *Maui: Legends of the Outcast*) are *more* interested in revitalizing and popularizing homegrown wonder genres and indigenous epistemologies in order to decolonize the telling of stories and history both. While the translation of

European fairy tales and of the *Arabian Nights* into Hawaiian had its influence on nineteenth-century Hawaiian literature (Bacchilega 2007), generally speaking, the fairy tale is not a genre of choice in Hawaiian adaptation projects today, possibly because the reframing of Hawaiian *mo'olelo* as fairy tale continues to have currency in popular imagination to disparaging effects (for example, Disney's *Lilo and Stitch*).

Regardless, what is being tapped to cultivate our sense of wonder is a local tradition behind or beside the fairy-tale's poetics of magic and/or the fiction's meshing with local legends and emplaced knowledges. In this book, I have pointed to creolized texts in particular as doing this, but I am also noticing it in a few Euro-American literary texts as well. Téa Obreht's *The Tiger's Wife* (2011) and Eowyn Ivey's *The Snow Child* (2012) come to mind and deserve critical attention. And experimental writers of speculative fiction—among them, Kelly Link, Margo Lanagan, and Theodora Goss—are also proposing to replace magic-gone-stale with a contemporary and ironic sense of wonder. Just as some visual artists today produce "conflicted mosaics" that "draw on an assortment of fairy-tale fragments to evoke a sense of wonder" associated, for Zipes, with "otherness or realms of estrangement" (2012, 137).

So there is, indeed, much more to be done with and about the poetics and politics of wonder in contemporary fairy tales. This book makes one foray into what Christine A. Jones and Jennifer Schacker aptly describe as the "tangled webs" constituted by the "collective histories of literary tales and entextualized oral traditions," webs "whose many tendrils interlock and whose patterns change depending on the vantage point from which one looks at them" (2012, 37). It is an activist foray in its own way. And its purpose is to induce us, as fairy-tale readers/fans/scholars, to intensify our attention to the significance of orality and located epistemologies in multimedia fairy-tale traditions and to the relationship of folk and fairy tales with other cultures' wonder genres.

◼   ◼   ◼

Fairy-tale studies have been and continue to be a much-contested field. While the main struggle in the early twenty-first century no longer seems to be between psychological and sociological approaches, the debates continue, from my perspective, to have everything to do with how we conceptualize the genre's history in relation to a politics of inequality. It is in this larger context that my book calls for the need to provincialize the Euro-American literary fairy tale and seeks to contribute, in Haase's words, to decolonizing fairy-tale studies.

The recent polemics surrounding Ruth B. Bottigheimer's book, *Fairy Tales: A New History* (2009),[5] offer a testing ground to think about what this means and why it matters. In 2009, Bottigheimer's book articulated an exclusively book-centered approach to the genre. Scholars in Europe and North America from various disciplines have already responded critically or negatively, at conferences and in writing, to this framework, the basic reaction being that literary intertextuality plays an important part in the transmission of fairy tales, but not to the exclusion of an oral tradition.[6] Without engaging the specifics of Bottigheimer's claims—something other folklorists and literary critics have done admirably and persuasively—I want to foreground the metadiscursive regime her claims support, specifically how her work participates in a discourse that regulates what and who can be defined as "modern."

Very briefly, what does *Fairy Tales: A New History* claim? First, in Bottigheimer's words, "folk invention and transmission of fairy tales has no basis in verifiable fact" (1), and this alone for her is evidence of its absence. Second, in the "new" book-based history of fairy tales that should replace this "once upon a time" fantasy of the oral tradition, "the ubiquitous and mysterious folk and nursemaids remain, but as consumers of fairy tales rather than as producers" (103). Third, early-modern Italian authors play a crucial role that has gone relatively unacknowledged in the "invention" of the genre; I quote: "Straparola created the form. Basile provided much of the content that later authors adopted. Together, they created the basis for Europe's fairy tale tradition" (74). French authors, Charles Perrault and the aristocratic women fairy-tale writers of the late seventeenth/early eighteenth century, borrowed from and edited the Italians, and the Brothers Grimm in nineteenth-century Germany perfected this tradition of collecting and rewriting "oral" tales that were actually of bookish lineage. As Bottigheimer states succinctly in her conclusion: "In a large sense the international spread of fairy tales can be explained within a history of predominantly Italian creation, French editing, and German re-editing that took place in a context of commercial mechanisms within book distribution networks" (107).

Such are the claims *in nuce*.[7] My purpose in what follows is to outline how accepting or not Bottigheimer's approach to the genre's origins has consequences for how we think of the folk's—that is, ordinary persons' and especially subaltern groups'—role in the production and consumption of culture; how we envision fairy tales on a global scale today; and what we think our responsibilities as scholars are.

1. What are the consequences of identifying an exclusively literary and European pedigree for the fairy tale, as Bottigheimer does in *Fairy Tales: A New History*? In addressing this question, my first point is to foreground how Bottigheimer's approach is very much a déjà vu when we consider the ideological

and discursive framework that enables it. By reducing the history of the fairy-tale genre to that of a few authored books and also by limiting the definition of fairy tale to what she calls "rise plots," Bottigheimer's work participates in a metadiscursive regime that Richard Bauman and Charles Briggs have historicized for us in *Voices of Modernity: Language Ideologies and the Politics of Inequality*, that is, an ideological framing of language, narrative, and expressive culture that champions the modern in opposition to and at the expense of what and who is identified as the premodern. I suggest that Bottigheimer's history of the fairy tale exclusively as a modern genre replicates and reinforces such a framework wherein the premodern, in and outside of Europe, is equated with the oral, necessarily marked as a lack in opposition to literacy and print, and by extension to individual subjectivity. Thus designated to the premodern, some people are—within this conceptualization of language and culture—deprived of history since history is limited to written documentation; if they have a voice in history, expert writers whose selections of how to represent them assume unquestionable authority always mediate that voice.

So when Bottigheimer writes, "Rise fairy tales are a product of that quintessential engine of modernity, the printing press," this seemingly matter-of-fact statement participates in a larger and powerful discourse that has represented modernity as strictly literate as well as simply European, and has configured the difference between oral and print traditions into a strategy of control and domination. Why does this matter? Whether the fairy-tale genre is considered exclusively within European and literary history or as a genre whose ties to expressive cultures and comparative literatures are inflected by global dynamics, has significant implications for ascribing a place in history for subaltern knowledge or for knowledges in the plural.

For instance, accepting as Bottigheimer does that "class-ascension-via-magic" is the primary if not only defining scope of the fairy-tale plot also has ethical and political consequences. In Bottigheimer's narrative, only literate storytellers, literary authors, were capable of imagining and articulating these tales of empowerment of the poor through magic. Jeana Jorgensen already foregrounded the "power imbalance" underlying this scenario when she asked: "Does this mean that rise tales feature poor protagonists who cannot progress without magical aid from others because elite taletellers believe illiterate populations incapable of exercising agency?" (2007b, 24). This "power imbalance," I find, is even further inscribed in Bottigheimer's representation of folk or subaltern subjects, whose "dreams of improving their lot," she says, "could only be a dream," for they are ready consumers of fairy tales as "escapist narratives" (93). The poor, and by extension other subaltern groups, from women to colonized peoples, were—and are, is the implication—helpless to effect change, hopelessly dependent, apparently unable to narrate their own desires—and furthermore duped by entrepreneurial authors to buy this story and its magic as placebo and then reproduce it as their own. This image of the fairy tale certainly runs counter to other empowering visions of fairy tales as narratives that work to undo privilege and injustice. Bottigheimer's claims for the structure and social function of fairy tales are also challenged by the research-based observation Lee Haring made that "so many Indian and Australian aboriginal tales [which Bottigheimer's circular logic of definition would not accept as fairy-tale related] are in descending structure with unhappy endings" and by overwhelmingly numerous examples of storytelling practices, fairy tales included, as coded resistance to structures of power. Bottigheimer naturalizes escapism, and thereby social conservatism, as a definitive characteristic of fairy tales as narratives for, but not by, subalterns. And yet in social interaction, the authority of fairy-tale telling is negotiated everyday.

2. How does the story that Bottigheimer tells relate to today's fairy-tale practices? If today's fairy-tale web is constituted by intertextual, hybrid, competing, and multimedia cultural practices, neither establishing a longer pedigree for the fairy tale canon (that is, moving from Perrault-the Grimms-Disney to Straparola-Basile-Perrault-the Grimms) nor defining this pedigree as purely literary speaks to contemporary fairy-tale practices at all. As Dan Ben-Amos reminded us on the radio, Bottigheimer's history does not connect with the "general observation of social behavior and artistic performance," which shows people telling and retelling stories to one another in both nonliterate and literate societies (Ben-Amos and Bottigheimer 2009).

One could say, on Bottigheimer's behalf, that her argument is about the origins and not the contemporary fairy tale. But isn't one of the tasks of history to connect the present to the past, to make the past usable and relevant in the present and to make us accountable as historical agents in the present for the stories we tell about the past? Notably, Bottigheimer's "new" history begins in the 1500s and takes us up to the mid-1800s with the Grimms, but no further. The implication is that whether we approach the fairy tale as folklorists, literary critics, or cultural historians, our domain is the past—preferably a bookish past that is insulated from the present. By ignoring contemporary fairy-tale practices of production, transmission, reception, and reproduction that do not privilege the book as direct or only source, Bottigheimer's kind of history implicitly dismisses them and, more importantly, abdicates our responsibilities as scholars to the present.

3. How are scholars in folklore and fairy-tale studies already counter-ing a purely author-centered and European-centered history of the genre in ways that do not support the same politics of inequality that characterize Bottigheimer's approach? And what have they/we been saying about who de-cides, in the face of varied performances and traditions, what is a fairy tale, what should be relevant to its history, what it means to people in different social circles and locations?[8]

While I do *not* believe we already have a history of the fairy-tale genre that works wonders or magic, I can easily refer to scholarship that has changed my own approach and informed my own research; and there are many other examples of course to be made. Reflecting critically on the opposition of oral versus printed words as an example of how the politics of othering and domi-nation is constitutive of modernity sets in motion an epistemological reloca-tion of thinking, of knowledge, of stories in action. I have learned this from Kay Stone's undoing of the Grimms' authority through storytelling, from Kay Turner's queering of that same authority, from scholars of Hawaiian and other indigenous studies working on oral traditions as well as from Walter Mignolo's work on coloniality and Ngũgĩ wa Thiong'o's discussions of orature (2012). And large projects in which folklorists and literary scholars located in different regions participate—such as the *Greenwood Encyclopedia of Folktales and Fairy Tales* (2008)—have provided the groundwork for more interdisci-plinary and transnational work.[9] One North American folklorist provocatively asked in 1998, "if comparative literature eliminates elitism and periodiza-tion . . . [w]hat would a true comparative literature look like?" His response was promising, also for those of us who are thinking about fairy tales today: "Using translations and ethnographies, comparative literature can take as its field both oral and written literatures in literary systems around the world" (Haring 1998, 37); not in an imperialist way, but one that shows "how literary and folkloric texts are embedded in their social context" and how "the diversity of artistic systems is an irreplaceable laboratory for an understanding of the nature of verbal art" (1998, 41). I recognize in Lee Haring's proposal a poetics that is sociopolitically situated and a comparativism that seeks not to bolster Eurocentrism.[10]

A new cartography of knowledge and genres is pivotal to effecting such a dis-placement. In *The Story-Time of the British Empire*, Sadhana Naithani points out that "in modern colonization, [the] transformed oral expressive culture of dif-ferent peoples . . . is a loop that ran [and runs] across many regions, languages, and readers." Thus she calls for a transnational approach to folktales and fairy tales that would defy the silences of colonial folkloristics and recognize LORAL (local/oral) perceptions of history. For others, relocating knowledge also means recognizing visual culture as a nonlinguistic semiotic system that impacts the storytelling of oral as well as literate societies; Teresia Teaiwa's article in an issue of *PMLA* makes this case for Oceania but does not limit its currency to one region or specific cultures alone. For instance, quoting Joy Harjo and drawing on "Native/American Digital Storytelling: Situating the Cherokee Oral Tradition within American Literary History," Lisa Brooks also in *PMLA* suggests that if "along with the Web, texts, petroglyphs, and wampum belts, the land itself is part of the 'spiral on the road to knowledge'" (2012, 314), "a new path for mapping American literary history" (313) opens up.

Because the fairy-tale web as reading and writing practice reaches back in history to multiple story-weaving traditions where not all links are or were equal, it seems we cannot be too attentive to the power structures that inform the relationship of fairy tale to folktale and literary traditions, other wonder genres, comparative literatures, and social history, or for that matter, to the fantasies that structure our sense of the real. Bottigheimer's approach conflates the project of writing the history of a genre with establishing a longer and exclusively literary pedigree for a European literary fairy-tale canon. In doing so, this approach limits our view of fairy tales as cultural practices in the past as in the present because it a priori condemns those who are deemed illiterate or ignorant in print culture to being captive consumers of the stories that are told about them. Decolonizing fairy-tale studies, as Haase has argued for, requires debunking this and other hierarchical binaries. Or, as folklorist Henry Glassie put it, "A better history would speak of the engagement of wills, of the interaction of traditions, each fraught with value, all driving toward their several visions of the future" (1995, 396).

Broadly speaking, such a history of and reorientation toward genre—any genre—demand a framework of "relation" to engage in the hard work of "crossing conceptual horizons" (as Paul Lyons suggests, taking his cue from Louis Owens, in the project of unmaking American Pacificism). Many scholars are already doing this work to reeducate themselves across disciplines and from different positionalities. And many of us in folktale and fairy-tale studies are aware of how buying into a European books-only history of the fairy tale means giving up on the social dynamics that keep people from all walks of life telling and retelling wonder tales across media, locations, and cultures. At stake in the question of fairy-tale origins are matters of power, authority, agency, and more basically human subjectivity that are simply bypassed in a European history of the fairy tale narrowly constructed around books only, and of modernity as severed from colonialism and coloniality.

Learning from the emergent poetics of those who are rewriting the fairy tale from located, counterhegemonic and decolonizing perspectives leads me to think that if there is to be a "new" history, it will have to be one that opens us up to transnational, transdisciplinary, multimedial, and perhaps most importantly collaborative projects.[11]

NOTES

NOTES TO INTRODUCTION

1. When I was writing this book, some of the comments were available on the "Media" link of Goldstein's website. As *Fairy Tales Transformed?* goes into production, those links are no longer available, but the blogs are easily accessible online. In dealing with electronic texts in a scholarly project, I have become more acutely aware of the ephemeral accuracy of their citations.

2. "I put up the series on JPG.com to get some feedback and had no idea what would happen next. Hundreds of blogs from all over the world posted the series. My web site was overloaded and thousands of e-mails came in congratulating me. There has also been quite a lot of controversy and discussion over a couple of the pieces. I welcome any interpretation of the work even though I disagree with much of it" (Goldstein, "About the Series," www.fallenprincesses.com/, accessed on June 8, 2011). The photos have since been exhibited in Vancouver (October 15–November 15, 2009) at the Buschlen Mowatt. The two most controversial pieces are "Jasmine" and "Red Riding Hood," which many bloggers see as reproducing racial and body stereotypes rather than disenchanting archetypes. See Li Cornfeld's analysis of "Not-So-Little Red Riding Hood" for an argument based on both visual studies and fairy-tale studies that shows how Goldstein's photograph "solicits scorn and pity," thus controversy, but also puts the issue of control over her body as Red Riding Hood's fare, with no wolf around (Cornfeld 2011).

3. Kay Turner's essay, "Playing with Fire: Transgressions as Truth in Grimms' 'Frau Trude,'" invites a radically different reading of enchantment in fairy tales (in Turner and Greenhill 2012, 248), a reading on which I intend to reflect more and learn from.

4. "Many of the most important differences that emerge from setting [fairy tales] in their historical contexts relate to the sense of wonder that is fundamental

to fairy tales, which indeed are often known technically as 'wonder tales'"
(Ziolkowski 2006, 64).

5. Another term that speaks to fairy tales' poetics and their relations to a
specific social context as well as genre system is "marvels" or *merveilles* (see
Seifert 2001).

6. "The verb 'to wonder' communicates the receptive state of marveling as
well as the active desire to know, to inquire" (Warner 1994, xx).

7. Grammatically, the optative mood expresses hope or desire—a favorable
outcome—in relation to the proposition the speaker is making. It is easily identi-
fiable in languages such as ancient Greek, Sanskrit, German, and Navajo. In the
English language, its function is taken by "may . . . ," "let's," or "would that . . ."
expressions and by some types of subjunctives. It may help to think of the optative mood as opposite of the imprecative mood, with curses positing an unfavor-
able outcome; grammars inform us that both are volitive moods that express the
speaker's desire for or commitment to having something happen or not.

8. This is how the first poem, "The Gold Key," in Sexton's collection ends.
The poem metaphorically takes off of No. 200 in the Grimms' collection *Kinder-
und Hausmärchen*, a tale in which the protagonist—a poor and curious boy—is
using a small gold key to open a mysterious iron casket. Published in the 1815
edition, this tale was told to the Brothers Grimm by Marie Hassenpflug. See
Zipes (1987, 288–89). I return to this tale in the epilogue.

9. Donald Haase's "Feminist Fairy-Tale Scholarship," the introduction to
Fairy Tales and Feminism: New Approaches (2004), traces the history and trajectories of some thirty years of such criticism.

10. "We might alternatively christen them the Angela Carter generation,
in that Carter's extensive work on the traditions of the fairy tale—as author,
editor, and critic—was preeminently influential in establishing a late twentieth-
century conception of the tales, the influence of which has continued into the
new millennium" (Benson 2008, 2), writes Stephen Benson who, marking the
publication of *Contemporary Fiction and the Fairy Tale*, organized, with Andrew
Teverson, a significant conference in April 2009, "The Fairy Tale after Angela
Carter." Selected and revised papers from that meeting constitute a special issue
of *Marvels & Tales: A Journal of Fairy-Tale Studies* (vol. 24, no. 1, 2010), also guest
edited by Benson and Teverson.

11. Focusing on Angela Carter's and other English-language fairy-tale adaptations that emerged from this cultural climate, my earlier book, *Postmodern
Fairy Tales: Gender and Narrative Strategies* (1997), analyzed their folkloric intersections and ideological underpinnings.

12. Transmedial phenomena are "non-specific to individual media" (Wolf 2005, 253); this can apply to formal devices, such as repetition; specific traits that different media have in common during a specific time period; or themes that are treated in verbal, visual, and multichanneled media (Wolf 2005). The genre of the fairy tale, in its form and content, is a transmedial phenomenon, but I refer to it more often as a "multimedial" phenomenon to stress the multiplicity of semiotic systems that retell fairy tales and also to point to the "intermedial" move across genres that its adaptations require.

13. For Ashliman's websites, see www.pitt.edu/~dash/folktexts.html and www.pitt.edu/~dash/folklinks.html#electronictext. Maintained from 1996 to 2006, Folklinks is a companion piece to his book, *Folk and Fairy Tales: A Handbook* (2004). Ashliman provided a wealth of links to folktale and fairy-tale indexes, directories, electronic texts, journals, reference tools, and sites in various European languages. The *Enzyklopädie des Märchens* consists of fourteen volumes published over the last sixty years, and it has an electronic index database; see www.user.gwdg.de/~enzmaer/. For the Snow White site, see http://comminfo.rutgers.edu/professional-development/childlit/snowwhite.html, accessed June 18, 2011.

14. This is according to the WebCounter statistics that appear on Ashliman's sites. On June 18, 2011, the number was 3,351,177. The site details its popularity going from 100,000 visitors in October 1998 to 3,000,000 in January 2010. Folklinks (1996–2006) is part of the larger Electronic Texts site, which continues in 2011 to be updated.

15. The award-winning *Journal of Mythic Arts* appeared on the Endicott Studio site from 1997 to 2008 and, the editors state, remains available in the site's archive as an online resource "to readers both old and new" for several years to come. http://endicottstudio.typepad.com/about/, accessed June 16, 2011.

16. www.surlalunefairytales.com/, accessed June 15, 2011.

17. "For more than 20 years, Endicott has supported a wide variety of mythic projects, events, and publications in the U.S. and U.K.—while at the same time raising money for charities assisting homeless, abused, and at-risk children," we are told in "About the Endicott Studio." http://endicottstudio.typepad.com/about/.

18. "I do not make a profit from this site which I have created strictly for educational and entertainment purposes. The minimal money received from my association with Amazon.com helps to defray the personal expenses I incur from research and maintenance of this site. I became an Amazon.com associate primarily to help the site's visitors locate recommended books," writes Heidi Heiner. www.surlalunefairytales.com/introduction/heidi.html.

19. From its incipit, according to Heiner's statement about the site, Sur-LaLune went from 2 MB to 235 MB in 2007. The Disclosure Statement on her blog includes the following: "This small revenue helps finance SurLaLune and keeps it free and available to thousands of readers around the world each day of the year. Last time I did the math I made about 50 cents (USD) an hour for my work through affiliate links. So no, I'm not getting rich, but my expenses are covered sufficiently to hopefully keep the site going for many years to come." www.surlalunefairytales.com/disclosure.html, accessed June 17, 2011.

20. See Community Statistics, http://surlalunefairytales.yuku.com/forums/1#.TfvfvcoTO8o, accessed June 16, 2011.

21. Subtitled "Maria Tatar's Forum for Storytelling, Folklore, and Children's Literature," Tatar's blog often features fairy-tale materials. See http://blogs.law.harvard.edu/tatar/, accessed June 17, 2011. Blogging from San Diego, California, Michael Lundell describes himself as an "Academic type working on the 1001 Nights, also known as The Arabian Nights, with a focus on Muhsin Mahdi and Richard F. Burton." http://journalofthenights.blogspot.com/, accessed November 9, 2012. The Fairy Tale Films Research Group was, in Pauline Greenhill's words, "created as part of research conducted by Cristina Bacchilega, Pauline Greenhill, Steven Kohm, Sidney Eve Matrix, Cat Tosenberger, and Jack Zipes, funded by the Social Sciences and Humanities Research Council of Canada, called Fairy Tale Films: Exploring Ethnographic Perspectives," www.facebook.com/groups/fairy.tales.films.research/, accessed February 20, 2013.

22. While this is the most common message conveyed by the images of "Disney Princes," there are several versions, as seen for instance on FunPic.hu and ComicsAlliance.com.

23. Related to these images is also the spoof of a *Cosmopolitan* magazine image feature, titled "Dating Advice from Disney Princesses," which on CRACKED.com is said to have more than a million viewers as of November 2012 and also elicited over 350 comments. See www.cracked.com/funny-4485-classic-disney-movies, accessed November 9, 2012.

24. Preston analyzes the 1998 movie *Ever After*, the 2000 FOX network special *Who Wants to Marry a Millionaire?*, and women.com.

25. Valente had previously made the novel available in its entirety on the web for free. Apparently, she was not hopeful about a publisher wanting it, especially since the text had a previous life as a fiction within a fiction in another novel of hers for adults. The novel received high praise on various websites. An online advertisement for the product includes a review by Cory Doctorow, "co-editor of the popular weblog BoingBoing and the author of *Little Brother*, *Wastelands: Stories of the Apocalypse*, and several other books," that begins: "Valente's *The Girl Who*

Circumnavigated Fairyland in a Ship of Her Own Making: sweet fairytale, shot through with salty tears—magic!" www.amazon.com/Girl-Circumnavigated-Fairyland-Ship-Making/dp/1250010195/ref=sr_1_1?s=books&ie=UTF8&qid=13 57335110&sr=1-1&keywords=Girl+Who+Circumnavigated+Fairyland+in+a+Ship+of+Her+Own+Making, accessed June 19, 2011.

26. See David Harvey's *The Condition of Postmodernity* (1989) for a compelling analysis of space-time compressions as bound with a different phase of capitalism and their impact on cultural production.

27. Since 1996, Disney distributes Studio Ghibli films globally, now in DVD and Blu-Ray formats as well. In 2006, in a multi-billion-dollar deal, Disney bought Pixar, whose six computer animated films grossed more than $3.2 billion worldwide, according to movie tracking research firm Box Office Mojo. Things are more complicated with Disney's competitor, DreamWorks: since 2009, DreamWorks has a distribution agreement with Disney, but not (at the time of my writing this) for DreamWorks Animation, still distributed by Paramount, or for distribution in India.

28. In Ovid's etiological tale, the exceptionally skilled Arachne, whose weaving threatens the goddess Athena's fame, is transformed into the first spider as a punishment. My thanks to Christy Williams for commenting on how communal spider webs in nature appear to have multiple centers and pointing me to how giant webs are visualized in popular film, such as *The Lord of the Rings* and *Arachnophobia*.

29. Bauman (2004, 4) is commenting here on how Bakhtin describes the dialogic relation between texts as "a contact of personalities and not of things" (Bakhtin 1986, 162).

30. I will mention only a few key English-language researchers in these areas: Elizabeth W. Harries, Nancy Canepa, Graham Anderson, William Hansen, Jan M. Ziolkowski, Bill McCarthy, Carl Lindhal, Ulrich Marzolph, Saree Makdisi, and Felicity Nussbaum.

31. Folklore, even when the state relies on it to construct its past or its future, gets relegated, in Antonio Gramsci's words, to the "provincial," where it is exploited for hegemonic purposes but it remains inferior to the so-called "universal."

32. Mignolo underlines how coloniality is a "disturbing concept" because— like Immanuel Wallerstein's modern world-system approach—it exposes the imbrication of modernity with colonialism. For a discussion of how Mignolo positions his theory in relation to Immanuel Wallerstein, Slavoj Žižek, and Édouard Glissant, see "The Geopolitics of Knowledge and the Colonial Difference" (Mignolo 2002b). What I like of Mignolo's approach is how he connects place

and thinking into a geopolitics of knowledge and how he limns the place of orality in constituting what he calls the "coloniality of power."

33. Analyzing the convergence of coloniality, capitalism, and modernity in the sixteenth century, Mignolo attributes to the period a "colonization of time" that results in the invention of the dark Middle Ages, and a "colonization of space" as the construction of Old and New worlds (Mignolo 2002a, 940). We could say with Harvey that this process corresponded with a first stage of capitalist time-space compression. But Mignolo's approach emphasizes that rather than emerging after modernity or alongside with it, colonialism is constitutive of modernity, of its capitalist economy and ideologies.

34. Frank De Caro and Rosan Augusta Jordan's *Re-Situating Folklore: Folk Contexts and Twentieth–Century Art* (2004) and Kevin Paul Smith's *The Postmodern Fairy Tale* (2007) offer useful, and quite different, frameworks for the purposes of categorization.

NOTES TO CHAPTER 1

1. For Linda Hutcheon, adaptation as a product is "an announced and extensive transposing of a particular work or works" (7).

2. "Tout texte est un *intertexte*; d'autres textes sont présents en lui à des niveaux variables, sous des formes plus ou moins reconnaissables: les textes de la culture antérieure et ceux de la culture environnante; tout texte est un tissu nouveau de citations révolues" (in Barthes's entry for the *Encyclopaedia universalis*, 1985, vol. 17: 996–1000).

3. Calling attention to a form of metatextuality, particularly illuminating within fairy-tale studies at large, is Vanessa Joosen's focus on "the interaction between [fairy-tale] retellings and fairy-tale criticism," where the intertextual dialogue is "constructed in the reading process and not necessarily in the writing process" (2011, 17).

4. For two readings, also in dialogue with each other, of Carter's story, see the opening section of my essay "Extrapolating from Nalo Hopkinson's *Skin Folk*" (2008) and Michelle Ryan-Sautour's "Authorial Ghosts and Maternal Identity in Angela Carter's 'Ashputtle *or* The Mother's Ghost: Three Versions of One Story' (1987)."

5. Heidmann's publications on intertextuality and fairy tales provide ample evidence of how productive her approach is. In *The Irresistible Fairy Tale*, Zipes also recognizes the significance of Heidmann and Adam's "dynamic notion of genericity" but notes "that they do an injustice to folklorists as well as themselves by excluding the study of oral influences and folklore in their study of

Perrault's tales" (Zipes 2012, 45 and 46). I agree with Zipes that we have everything to gain by considering how oral tales as well as other forms of expressive culture participate in the dynamics of both genericity and intertextuality. Having had this conversation with Ute Heidmann, however, I believe that while oral sources are not her focus, her approach does not a priori "exclude" them or preclude their inclusion. One of the reasons I see Heidmann turning away from analyzing Perrault's relation to the oral tradition is that contributions in France to Perrault studies were, for a time at least (for example, Marc Soriano and Paul Delarue), very much focused only on that tradition, marginalizing Perrault's links to the literary. This could lead to an interesting discussion of how different folklore studies in the United States and ethnology in Europe are as well as to how fairy-tale studies reconfigures the oral/print divide.

That said, my point here is that Heidmann's project is—as Zipes also states—"to reestablish Perrault's tales as literature" (Zipes 2012, 48).

6. These are only some of the more visible threads in the tissue, or links in the web of possibilities, especially since readers and discursive communities come to Carter's text from different knowledge bases, interests, and cultural contexts, which may lead some to recognize in "Ashputtle" connections with other Carter texts, others to recall personal experiences of grief, and others yet to focus on her dialogue with Jack Zipes or her anticipations of Judith Butler's arguments.

7. Zipes draws on Constantine Verevis for the analytical concept of "remake," and their combined approach resonates with mine especially in considering how genres and remakes or adaptations "depend on a network of historically variable relationships" (Verevis 2006, 87, qtd. in Zipes 2011, 15). However, the term applies best to cinema and can be limiting in other media.

8. "The affordances of language, pictures, movement, and music complement each other, and when they are used together in multi-channel media, each of them builds a different facet of the total imaginative experience: language narrates through its logic and its ability to model the human mind, pictures through their immersive spatiality and visuality, movement through its dynamic temporality, and music through its atmosphere-creating, tension building and emotional power" (online, n.d., par. 38, last modified January 13, 2012).

9. Stam, who is writing specifically to filmic adaptations of novels, concludes his dynamic statement about how adaptations redistribute energies: "the linguistic energy of literary writing turns into the audio-visual-kinetic-performative energy of the adaptation in an amorous exchange of textual fluids" (2005, 46). The intertextual exchanges to which I want to bring our attention turn on intimate histories of discursive and material relations, but in a contestatory mode.

See also *Adaptation and Appropriation* by Julie Sanders. I choose for the most part not to use the term "appropriation" for several reasons. As Zipes points out in *The Enchanted Screen*, "Whatever [artistic and technical] mode used, the adaptation always involves an expropriation and appropriation" (10). Property and propriety are indeed, I agree with Zipes, at stake in the conceptualization, process, and product of appropriation, and that makes it interesting. However, if some form of "appropriation" is inevitable in adaptation, I find it more productive to look at what specific strategies are deployed and uses it is put to in the process rather than using the catchall "appropriation." Another problem is that "reappropriation" talks back to "appropriation," but when the process began is hard to say; my approach is to think of located and activist responses instead as framed by historically changing dynamics. In a parallel move, Verevis writes, "cinema constantly remakes itself, but whether this is understood as homage, imitation or theft depends . . . upon historically specific technologies such as copyright law and authorship, film reviewing and exhibition practices" (2006, 170).

10. Nalo Hopkinson was born in Jamaica in 1960, the daughter of a Guyanese and a Jamaican; she lived in Guyana, Jamaica, and Trinidad until the age of sixteen when she moved to Connecticut and then to Toronto, where she has lived for many years. Her father was the late Guyanese poet and playwright Slade Hopkinson. She has a master's degree in writing popular fiction from Seton Hill University, has been writer in residence at Clarion Workshops, and is currently an associate professor in the Department of Creative Writing at the University of California–Riverside. The department's website provides the following information: Hopkinson "is a recipient of the John W. Campbell Award, the World Fantasy Award, the Gaylactic Spectrum Award, and a two-time recipient of the Sunburst Award for Canadian Literature of the Fantastic." Hopkinson is one of the founding members of the Carl Brandon Society, whose mission is "to increase racial and ethnic diversity in the production of and audience for speculative fiction." www.carlbrandon.org/about.html. Hopkinson is also a talented "craftsperson," as she wittily refers to herself in "Maybe They're Phasing Us In: Re-Mapping Fantasy Tropes in the Face of Gender, Race, and Sexuality" (2007), producing fabric designs, collages, and mini art installations. She discusses "My Little Pony Girl" in this 2007 talk as a 3D installation that talks back at racist color coding and objectification in pop culture.

Several essays focus on Nalo Hopkinson's intervention in science fiction and spec-fic: see Smith (2009) and *Extrapolations* 46, no. 3 (2005). For ongoing information about Nalo Hopkinson and her writing, see http://nalohopkinson.com/.

11. "Fisherman" can be read as extrapolating from "The Shift of Sex" (ATU 514). This intertextual link or adaptive move is one of many for a story that calls to be read in the genre contexts of erotica and queer erotica.

12. For this section on *Skin Folk*, I draw on my previously published essay in *Contemporary Fiction and the Fairy Tale*, edited by Stephen Benson (Wayne State University Press, 2008). There I experimented with inserting "text bubbles" to visualize intertextuality as a secondary orality, while suggesting a (hypertextual) web of stories. While the earlier essay develops a reading of transformation and creolization in Hopkinson's collection, here I focus on creolization more specifically in relation to relocation.

13. These "skin folk" are expressions of belief and are part of religious and ritual systems that Hopkinson's fiction does not necessarily replicate or revive but supplements and carries on into the future.

14. "Whereas transformations above all mark the magic of European fairy tales before the *Arabian Nights*, flight distinguishes the fantasies of the latter" (Warner 2012, 332). Warner's examples are Perrault's and the Grimms' collections where characters "remain grounded" (333), and she contrasts these to tales by Marie-Catherine d'Aulnoy and other "Orientalizing writers" whose protagonists are "so gleefully taken off into the skies"; Warner argues that this "aerial freedom emulates that of the *Nights* even as she agrees with Anne Duggan that these writers were adapting the stage machinery of courtly plays and festivals in France and Italy (333).

15. Hopkinson has over the years articulated various definitions of science fiction and fantasy, always in relation to each other, definitions that—she insists—are not meant to replace each other. In "A Reluctant Ambassador from the Planet of Midnight," she writes: "one of the things that fantasy and science fiction do is to imaginatively address the core problem of who does the work. Science fiction looks at technological approaches to the problem, and at all the problems the solutions create. You know, the discovery that a computer isn't exactly a labor-saving device. . . . Fantasy looks at the *idea* of work. Instead of using technology, it uses magic. But both are labor-saving devices" (2010, 346–47).

16. Warner is referring here to her first reading of Angela Carter's "The Bloody Chamber."

17. See Hopkinson's keynote address, "A Reluctant Ambassador from the Planet of Midnight," at the 2010 International Conference of the Fantastic in the Arts for her response to RaceFail 2009 and how science fiction and fantasy approach race. For more information on RaceFail 2009, Hopkinson sends readers to Rydra Wong's LiveJournal blog at http://rydra-wong.livejournal.com/146697.html.

18. Trapped in prescribed scripts that pass for "human," Hopkinson's characters are transformed as they recognize a more complex reality, reconnect with "a context of blackness and Caribbeanness" (Hopkinson and Mehan 2004, 8), and visualize or become visible as the trickster within. When, having been touched by an Anansi figure, the protagonist of "Something to Hitch Meat To" "help[s others] peel off the fake skins" (42), and Hopkinson's language does again invoke a true/false binary opposition, it is more productive to read this transformation not so much from within a Euro-American framework for gendered subjectivity but as an echo of Frantz Fanon's unmasking whiteness and uncovering "black skin."

19. Creolization, Lee Haring has pointed out, works as agency in woman-centered folktales of the Indian Ocean, especially when such storytelling is approached from within the islands' history (2004). A key text on "creolization" is Edward Brathwaite's *The Development of Creole Society 1770–1820* (1971). For work in a more broadly postcolonial context, see Robert Young, *Colonial Desire: Hybridity in Theory, Culture, and Race* (1995). For discussions of creolization's conceptual "potential for folklore studies and cultures in a postmodern global perspective" (Elaine J. Lawless, "From the Editor" 3) and its enabling "us to see not simply 'hybrids' of limited fluidity, but new *cultures in the making*" (Robert Baron and Ana C. Cara, "Introduction: Creolization and Folklore—Cultural Creativity in Progress," 5) see the *Journal of American Folklore* special issue (winter 2003); Lee Haring's extensive work on the subject, and Simon Bronner's essay on Lafcadio Hearn (2005).

I am aware of only three essays on Hopkinson's fairy-tale intertexts so far. Hennard Dutheil de la Rochère's essay (2009b) and mine are in productive conversation with each other. Natalie Robinson's essay, "Exploding the Glass Bottles: Constructing the Postcolonial 'Bluebeard' Tale in Nalo Hopkinson's 'The Glass Bottle Trick'" (2011), while somewhat derivative in its discussion of Perrault's and Grimms' intertexts in "The Glass Bottle Trick," develops the short story's important link with the Anansi tale, "Yung-Kyung-Pyung."

20. *Code sliding* is a term from linguistics; I am more familiar with *code switching*. Whether it is Hopkinson's or certain linguists' coinage, code sliding is less mechanical than code switching, I think, perhaps more suggestive both of the ease with which Creole enacts linguistic hybridity and the slipperiness of language beyond individual intention. "Creolization is a slippery concept" (2003, 88), writes Robert Baron in an essay that analyzes different metaphors for creolization, such as "compound," "convergence," "coalescence," "coagulation," all involving "catachresis, the provision of a term where one is lacking in our vocabulary" (89).

21. As Hennard Dutheil de la Rochère also notes, "In Hopkinson's postcolonial variation on the ["Bluebeard"] story, the sign of the husband's strangeness and monstrosity no longer lies in his blue beard but in his denial of his skin colour: in a nut (or egg) shell, the disgust provoked by Bluebeard's beard has turned to self loathing" (2009b, 224). Our references to Frantz Fanon work well together.

22. "The creole languages spoken in the regions of the New World that received slaves are all Signifyin(g) discourses aimed at 'decomposing and deporting' the language of the other through double entendres, puns, verbal tricks and plurality of meanings. It is relevant to note that while creoles derive most of their lexicon from the master's tongue, be it French, English, Spanish or Dutch, lexemes were not only deshaped but reshaped and their meaning often skewed as they were made to fit within an African-based grammatical grid and a creole setting" (De Souza 2003, 343–44). In a 2011 interview, Hopkinson stated, "Caribbean language has its own roots, its own linguistic integrity, its own modes of speech. Part of it is that writing in vernacular helped me to understand what speech does and to see what has happened to English, having been imposed on the Caribbean people and then the Caribbean people taking it and making it their own."

23. In her 1991 talk, "Bra Rabbit Meets Peter Rabbit: Genre, Audience, and the Artistic Imagination: Problems in Writing Children's Fiction," children's-literature author Jean D'Costa described her experience as a child with "high" and "low" culture at home and in the educational system. Children raised on Anansi and Br'er Rabbit trickster tales were likely to encounter Peter Rabbit, Roald Dahl, Jack London, and other adventure tales in school. But "the printed folktales (Grimm, Perrault, Andersen)" D'Costa writes, "have to compete directly with the local oral tradition and may form less of a classroom staple. I have, for example, read or heard European folktales at home along with Anancy stories; my peers at primary school heard a few of the European tales in school and, typically for a small rural community, heard none at home" (D'Costa 1990, 257–58).

24. This strategy can be read as "traditional referentiality"—the text's metonymic invoking of an enormously larger sociocultural context and echoing of multiple traditions and performances—and its linguistic codes (see Foley 2008). For a discussion that seeks to "intervene in discussions of oral vs. print transmission with an eye to re-situating 'folklore and literature' within the larger dynamic of cultural politics" see Bacchilega 2012.

25. While recognizing that his art addresses a larger and varied audience, Māori poet Robert Sullivan refers to wanting his people to have "the best seats in the house" (2003). This kind of poetics is not uncommon among indigenous

and other nonhegemonic writers, and it requires a reorientation on the part of critics as well.

26. This detail links Hopkinson's story also with the Grimms' Bluebeard tale, "Fitcher's Bird," where a sorcerer, disguised as a beggar, tricks one sister after another into his power: "he had only to touch her, and that compelled her to jump into his basket" (Zipes 1987, 182). In the end, in an ironic reversal, the clever heroine makes use of a basket herself to trick her husband into freeing the women she has, unbeknownst to him, brought back to life.

27. See De Souza's essay on Anansi tales in the Caribbean "for the African continuities that can be traced in the New-World Anancy tales," and "the fluctuancy of the folktale as an art form" (2003, 341).

28. I have not consulted other published versions of the tale so I cannot say the order of the three girls' names in Jekyll is representative in any way. Comparing Hopkinson's text to Jekyll's, the change in the order of the names is significant.

29. Hennard Dutheil de la Rochère's and my reading of the duppies are aligned, but she concludes: "In the process of cultural reinscription as a literary equivalent of the voodoo ritual, Perrault also comes back to life radically transformed, furnished with a new dark skin, sensual female body and rich Creole voice that can speak meaningfully in the present and from an extra-European perspective; thus, Hopkinson's intertextual dialogue with her predecessor simultaneously pays homage to the permanence of Perrault's stories and gives them renewed relevance as they travel through time, space and culture" (2009b, 227–28).

30. Grace Dillon's readings of Hopkinson would be definitely relevant. Dillon's essay takes as its starting point that "fantasy, sf, and speculative fiction often rely on so-called 'cautionary tales' to depict dystopic worlds where the lavish embracing of advancing western technologies leads to environmental decay. And, increasingly, tellers of cautionary tales are juxtaposing the technologically compromised order with native and indigenous worldviews" (2007, 23). In her introductory remarks in the *Walking the Clouds* collection, Dillon also singles Hopkinson's techniques out as "placing the reader in worlds that split apart the colonizer-versus-colonized binary that occurs in much sf" (2012, 99).

31. And in 2012, *Skin Folk* was announced to be going into production as a movie featuring "three tales of supernatural horror" set in New Orleans in the near future (see www.youtube.com/user/skinfolkmovie. Prod. Asli Dukan; Dirs. Asli Dukan and M. Miguel Jerez) and based on Nalo Hopkinson's spec-fic (though I cannot tell at this point if it is based specifically on her homonymous collection).

32. See Benson's *Cycles of Influence* (2003), chapter 2, "Theory in Tales: Cycles, Levels, and Frames."

33. See Harries (2001, 15–16); her distinction between simple and complex tales has been extremely productive in the discussion of fairy-tale gendered traditions.

34. The author of several novels about contemporary life (*Stirfry* 1994; *Hood* 1995; *Landing* 2007; *Room* 2010), historical fiction (*Slammerkin* 2000; *The Sealed Letter* 2008), short stories *(Kissing the Witch* 1997; *The Woman Who Gave Birth to Rabbits* 2002; *Astray* 2012), and radio plays, Emma Donoghue was awarded the 1997 American Library Association's Gay, Lesbian and Bisexual Book Award for Literature for *Hood*. Her novel, *Room*, won many awards, among them, the Hughes and Hughes Irish Novel of the Year, the Rogers Writers' Trust Fiction Prize (for best Canadian novel), the Commonwealth Prize (Canada and Caribbean Region), a Salon Book Award for Fiction, an NPR Best Book of 2010, a *New Yorker* Reviewers' Favorite, Bloomberg's 2010 Top Novel, and *The Week* magazine's Top Book 2010. Donoghue has also published several books of literary history, including *Passions between Women: British Lesbian Culture, 1668–1801* (New York: HarperCollins, 1995) and *Inseparable: Desire between Women in Literature* (New York: Knopf, 2011); and is the editor of several anthologies, starting with *Poems between Women: Four Centuries of Love, Romantic Friendship, and Desire* (New York: Columbia University Press, 1997), published in the United Kingdom as *What Sappho Would Have Said: Four Centuries of Love Poems between Women* (London: Hamish Hamilton, 1997). This information draws on her official website, www.emmadonoghue.com, which also contains a lively FAQ section.

35. Based on the Grimms are "The Tale of the Shoe" ("Cinderella"), "The Tale of the Apple" ("Snow White"), "The Tale of the Handkerchief" ("The Goose Girl"), "The Tale of the Hair" ("Rapunzel"), "The Tale of the Spinster" ("Rumpelstiltskin" and, Donoghue adds, similar stories of magical helpers), "The Tale of the Cottage" ("Hansel and Gretel"), and "The Tale of the Skin" ("Donkeyskin"). Hans Christian Andersen's "Thumbelina" is identified as the main pretext for "The Tale of the Bird" on Donoghue's website, but several readers have told me they associate it with Charles Perrault's "Bluebeard"; two more tales revise Andersen: "The Tale of the Brother" ("Snow Queen") and "The Tale of the Voice" ("Little Mermaid"). "The Tale of the Rose" adapts Madame LePrince de Beaumont's "Beauty and the Beast," and "The Tale of the Needle" adapts Perrault's "Sleeping Beauty."

36. Steven Gin and I presented a version of this multimedia presentations at the MLA meeting in Los Angeles (January 2011) and another at the "The Grimm

Brothers Today: *Kinder- und Hausmärchen* and Its Legacy 200 Years After" conference in Lisbon (June 2012).

37. The reference here is not so much to witches in history, but to stepmothers, Frau Trude figures, the old woman in "Hansel and Gretel," the false brides and wise women in fairy tales. Diane Purkiss argues, "The witch offers opportunities for both identification and elaborate fantasy, standing in supportive or antagonistic relation to the contemporary feminist-activist-historian inscribing her" (1996, 10).

38. See Jack Zipes's important historical work connecting witches and fairies to ancient goddesses and beliefs ("Witch as Fairy/Fairy as Witch: Unfathomable Baba Yagas" in Zipes 2012, 55–79) and the wide-ranging explorations in *Des fata aux fées* of female power in fairy tales (Hennard Dutheil de la Rochère and Dasen 2011). Zipes writes about the transformation of pagan goddesses in the Western world into the Greco-Roman goddesses and fates, which in turn transformed into witches and fairies as well.

39. Quotations are from the HarperCollins paperback edition of *Kissing the Witch* (Donoghue 1999).

40. Of the first tale in Donoghue's collection, "The Tale of the Shoe," Karlyn Crowley and John Pennington also write: "We see how Donoghue evokes the residue of the Perrault and Grimms tale—even with the early reference to the dove—yet she revises the old tales into an original retelling" (2010, 307).

41. "The Tale of the Kiss" is "not based on any source text, but suggested by various folk motifs about oracles and magic helpers, discussed in Marina Warner's *From the Beast to the Blonde*" (www.emmadonoghue.com/writings/short-story-listing.htm#FairyTales).

42. See Orme's "Mouth to Mouth" (2010a) essay for a much fuller and insightful reading of this tale.

43. The agreement between the two women, however, does not guarantee the "false" princess a happy ending. After her prince dies before she's given him an heir, to pursue her ambition she goes "wandering the world again in search of a crown [she] could call [her] own" (80), and that leads her to becoming the stepmother in "The Tale of the Apple."

44. As Ann Martin writes, "such indeterminacy poses difficulties for a reader trained to expect illumination as the significance of the plot, and especially of its politics, by the end of the story" (2010, 13). If readers expect Donoghue's tales to be LGBTQ identity-affirming tales, they may be frustrated.

45. In a personal communication, Donoghue stated she had not gone back to look at Lang's book at the time of writing the dedication; her memory was of "Pinkel and the Witch."

46. As David Waldron's *The Sign of the Witch: Modernity and the Pagan Revival* (2008) delineates, Neo-Paganism has undergone radical changes in its twentieth-century history and is a highly diversified movement that ranges from New Age spirituality and the 1968 WITCH (Women's International Terrorist Conspiracy from Hell) Marxist group to eco-feminism and an eclectic paganism that is more commonly commodified in popular culture. Ronald Hutton's *The Triumph of the Moon: A History of Modern Pagan Witchcraft* (1999) is a particularly influential study, but the literature on witchcraft and contemporary Paganism is vast, and I am only scratching the surface here.

My point is only to connect with the uses this counterculture makes of fairy tales. Magliocco writes: "Folk narratives—myths, legends, ballads, and especially *Märchen*, or magic tales, furnish Neo-Pagans with much of the sources material for their rituals. . . . Reclaiming's Witch camp is often organized around one particular myth or folktale. In *The Twelve Wild Swans* (2000), Starhawk and Hilary Valentine explain why they have chosen to use the eponymous tale (AT 451 "The Girl in Search of Her Lost Brothers") as a template for the transformative process of Witch camp" (Magliocco 2004, 142). And many Neo-Pagans "report childhood fascinations with myths, legends, and folktales, and an attraction to contemporary literary forms, such as fantasy and science fiction, which make use of the devices of the *Märchen* (169).

In making this connection between *Kissing the Witch* and Neo-Paganism, I am not arguing that it is a Neo-Pagan text—even as the illustrations in the Hamish Hamilton edition could perhaps encourage such a reading—but that Donoghue's collection participates in contemporary adaptive strategies of folk and fairy tales that are not only literary and that link these tales to alternative belief systems.

47. "Fa'agogo are our fairy tales," says McMullin. They "utilize historical characters but are informal night time stories, whereas tala are less informal" (e-mail to Robyn Oishi, quoted with permission by Oishi and McMullin both). Richard Moyle, whose collection *Fāgogo: Fables from Samoa in Samoan and English* influenced McMullin, writes: "There exists in Samoan folklore a type of story called *fāgogo*, told mostly at night, privately, inside individual homes" (Moyle 1981, 7).

48. Dan Taulapapa McMullin was born in Samoa and, after having grown up there as well as in California, Hawai'i, and Europe, he currently lives in California as well as in Apia, Samoa. His short film *Sinalela* won the 2002 Honolulu Rainbow Film Festival Best Short Film Award. McMullin's poetry is widely anthologized, most recently in *Sovereign Erotics: A Collection of Two-Spirit Literature* (University of Arizona Press, 2011) and *Mauri Ola: Contemporary Polynesian*

Poems in English (2010), edited by Albert Wendt, Reina Whaitiri, and Robert Sullivan. His performance poem, "The Bat," and other early works received a 1997 Poets&Writers Award from The Writers Loft. He edited in 2011 a new anthology of contemporary Pacific writing, *Nafanua*, for Ala Press of Hawai'i. McMullin's artwork has been exhibited at the De Young Museum, the Gorman Museum, the Bishop Museum, the Peabody Essex Museum, Fresh Gallery Otara, Galeria de la Raza, Cambridge Museum, NYU's A/P/A Gallery, and the United Nations. For further information see www.taulapapa.com/.

49. An accompanying note says that "The One-Eyed Fish" is "taken from writings for a sound installation titled *The Resurrection of Tigilau* at Galeria de la Raza, a series of Samoan traditional and original narratives of resurrection and transformation" (McMullin 2003, 115). While I italicize the Samoan word *fa'afafine*, Dan Taulapapa McMullin does not, and he also uses different spellings that I reproduce when quoting. Also note that the protagonist's name in the unpublished short story is "Sinavela." The general meaning of *vela* in Samoan is "cooked"; in an e-mail communication with Robyn Oishi, the writer specifies, "vela meaning hot as in ashes" (December 1–2, 2011). My thanks to Robyn Oishi and to Dan Taulapapa McMullin for permission.

50. In Oceania, tattooing is reclaimed as *tatau*, and for Wendt, one of the most prominent and influential novelists and intellectuals in Oceania, as *Tatau Samoa*, a specifically Samoan art form. See also Teaiwa. "The women's tattoo is called a malu," writes Wendt who explains many meanings of *tatau* and *malu* (86–87) also to point out that "to better understand postcolonial literature . . . you have to know the indigenous language and culture of the writer producing that literature in English" (88). This is an obvious and important point that, since I do not know the Samoan language, I negotiate in this section of my chapter by listening not for what I know, but to become more attuned to what I don't. To clarify that the point is not about race, in this same essay, Wendt also writes: "It is incorrect to think that you cannot be tataued unless you are Samoan or connected by blood and title to Samoan aiga" (95) and goes on to speculate about what is at stake for humans in undergoing a tatau.

51. Mayer notes, "There are strong associations between fa'afafine and the animal world" (2008, 19), and that transforming into a spider enables or produces Sinalela's love story.

52. Samoan American poet and scholar Caroline Sinavaiana writes, "When the Samoan archipelago was summarily divided and seized in 1900 by Germany and the United States, an ancient covenant was called into question. Despite millennia of tending to our islands and ourselves, to island neighbors and

trading partners near and far across the great ocean, we Samoans suddenly found ourselves on different sides of an imaginary boundary. The nine western islands were renamed Western Samoa by Germany, and the seven eastern islands called "The US Naval Station Tutuila," and later "American Samoa" (Sinavaiana forthcoming).

53. In *Sinalela* there is a critical reference to how Samoan children are in a touristic economy reduced to selling the garlands. In a 2009 interview conducted by poet and fiction-writer Sia Figiel, McMullin describes his narrative poetics: "For me painting and making visual art is a high form of storytelling and grows out of my poetry, theatre, screenwriting and performance, and what you, Sia, call the suifefiloi of our narrative, the 'weaving' together of garlands of our stories, the island and the urban" (McMullin and Figiel 2009). McMullin's documentary in progress *Ula: The Garland*, was presented at the 2011 South Auckland Pacific Arts Summit and described on their blog as an "important piece of Pacific art history [that] documents interviews with a huge range of Pacific creative practitioners from the US, Cook Islands, Fiji, Samoa and Aotearoa," http://2011pacificartssummit.wordpress.com/category/film/.

54. *ALTERNATIVE: An International Journal of Indigenous Peoples* is one of the journals that since 2005 "showcase[s] themes of indigenous knowledge and epistemologies, differing indigenous methodologies, research ethics, critiques from an indigenous perspective, and analyses of the challenges facing indigenous peoples in the 21st century" (Smith, foreword to the journal's inaugural issue, 2005). *Alter*Native and alter-Native (neither is my coinage) are small but powerful markers of how indigenous perspectives change meaning-making or language games.

55. In Samoan language dictionaries *lela* corresponds to the English word, "that." Sinalela also translates Cinderella in Samoan, as several of my students pointed out when we were reading McMullin.

56. The short story "Auntie Sinavela" provides further evidence of McMullin's interest in providing an activist response to the Grimms specifically. I thank the author for sharing the manuscript with me and look forward to its publication.

57. In discussing definitions of "queer," Turner and Greenhill note how fairy tales, like emergent literatures, address "concerns about marginalization, oddity, and not fitting into society generally. Queerness embraces more than sex/gender/sexuality to deal with the problematics of those who for various reasons find themselves outside conventional practices. As Lee Edelman defines the term, *queerness* 'marks the excess of something always unassimilable that troubles the relentlessly totalizing impulse informing normativity' (Dinshaw et

al. 2007, 189). Such excess is discoverable in the traditional fairy tale" (Turner and Greenhill 2012, 4–5). I agree, especially if "fairy tale" here—as I believe it is—refers to wonder tales in oral and print traditions across cultures.

1. See Catherine Tosenberger's "Homosexuality at the Online Hogwarts: Harry Potter Slash Fanfiction" (2008).

2. The year 2012 marked the two hundredth anniversary of the publication of the Brothers Grimm's *Kinder- und Hausmärchen*, which brought about several scholarly conferences; the publication of Philip Pullman's fascinating retellings of *Fairy Tales from the Brothers Grimm: A New English Version* (2012) and Jack Zipes's edition of the Grimms' translation/adaptation by Edgar Taylor, *German Popular Stories* (2012); and an intensification of the fairy-tale film hype, with articles about fairy tales and fairy-tale films and TV shows in the *Wall Street Journal* (Gidwitz 2012) and *The New Yorker* (Acocella 2012).

3. See www.sarahsawyer.com/2012/01/upcoming-fairy-tale-films/#comments. The blogger, Sarah Sawyers, according to the Bio information, is a member of American Christian Fiction Writers and seeks to "promote Christian speculative fiction wherever she can." Some of the discussion in response to upcoming fairy-tale films expressed concerns about their "darkness."

4. While I am critical of the Disneyfication of the fairy tale, my everyday experience and my students also make me aware of how viewers of Disney are hardly passive and remake these films in their own minds, focusing on their disturbing aspects as well as developing unintended messages. Kay Stone's illuminating essays in the 1980s about fairy tales and women point to how doing more ethnographic work on the reception of Disney, especially since the early 1990s with their "new" fairy-tale films, is important. In this chapter, however, I am focusing on the staging of fairy-tale reading and reception in four films, and not on actual reception.

5. Note that del Toro's *Pan's Labyrinth* is in Spanish with English-language subtitles; Catherine Breillat's *Bluebeard*, which I discuss later, is in French with English-language subtitles; and *Hansel and Gretel* is in Korean with English-language subtitles. I will be quoting from these translations throughout, occasionally adding some commentary of my own for the French.

6. Donald Haase's important essay, "Hypertextual Gutenberg," provides a critical foundation for Christine Kotecki's analysis of Disney's style of fairy-tale adaptation in contrast to Guillermo del Toro's in *Pan's Labyrinth*. Kotecki observes that "Disney's *Snow White* replicates the print medium in its opening

scene" and how "his dependency on the authority of his source text is also ex-emplified by the fidelity with which the Grimms' Snow White character is tran-scribed into a newer medium" (2010, 239). Like Haase, Kotecki sees Disney's adaptation style as a form of negotiation between the well-established print me-dium and the emergent cinematic one. Significantly, she also notes how Disney not only gained "credibility" by adapting the Grimms' printed tale specifically in the *Snow White* film, but also acquired legal rights by producing the "replicated" or animated book tale for the screen.

7. The bibliography on Disney fairy tales and on the Disney industry is ex-tensive. Particularly relevant here is Thomas Leitch's "The Adapter as Auteur: Hitchcock, Kubrick, Disney" (2005).

8. Julie Andrews performs the queen mother's voice in the *Shrek* series.

9. I do not want to suggest that playing with Disney princesses can only re-sult in producing consumers. Children's play does subvert social scripts all the time. The question is how toys and stories contribute to or impede this play. See Karen E. Wohlwend's "Damsels in Discourse: Girls Consuming and Produc-ing Identity Texts through Disney Princess Play" for a sophisticated analysis of structured creativity in a kindergarten writing workshop in which Disney princesses are "animated" by the children as characters in their plays. The chil-dren were Disney princess fans but not passive consumers in these activities, where they creatively addressed their frustration with the passivity of the prin-cess roles. As one child said, describing her doll, "She really is a princess, but I am pretending she's a super-hero" (Wohlwend 2009, 75).

10. I quote from Guillermo del Toro's commentary track accompanying the film. The "Director's Notebook" DVD feature further provides some insight into del Toro's process as a visual artist translating across media.

11. In a similar vein, Jacqueline Ford takes the scene "to suggest that fairy tales are here summoned to reinforce a fantastic element's reality status" (Ford 2011, 392). For Ford, the large insect is a mantis, and she provides an interesting reading of its symbolism.

12. Laura Hubner (2007) also notes the significance of disobedience in *Pan's Labyrinth* and associates it with the sexual transgression symbolized in several fairy tales.

13. See Paul Julian Smith (2007) and also Jacqueline Ford (2011).

14. Kotecki's main argument is to "suggest that *Pan's Labyrinth*'s blend of fairy-tale motifs and references to popular film and culture displays a 'hyper-textual' aesthetic" (2010, 235), with which I agree. What's relevant here are her observations about Ofelia's multiple hypotexts, especially *Alice in Wonderland* (244–45 and 249) and multiple roles in the film. Kotecki identifies Ofelia as

an embodied or "reincarnating tale," but also as a storyteller and, based on her use of the book and the chalk, as a "writer-storyteller" (250). In this "writer-storyteller" role, Ofelia is in my view rewriting the script into which the Faun and the Book of Crossroads had written her.

15. See chapter 3 for this discussion.

16. Haase's two essays reference historical, life-writing, and critical literature concerning children, fairy tales, and war.

17. According to del Toro in his commentary to the film, "violence makes you more susceptible to fantasy, and fantasy makes you more vulnerable to the violence."

18. For this and more information, see Flach Film press releases. "Pour Jean-François Lepetit, le créateur de Flach Film, 'l'idée est d'adapter de façon contemporaine des contes qui résonnent dans l'imaginaire collectif.' Ces films seront, dotés d'un budget d'environ 1,2M€ chacun, aussi bien destinés à la télé (Arte) qu'au cinema," www.flachfilm.com/presse/presse/news/flach-film-adapte-des -contes-populaires-pour-arte-septembre-2009-1.html. This loosely translates into how these films are to adapt in a contemporary fashion tales that resonate in the collective imaginary; each film has a limited budget (approximately 1.2 million euros) and is made for both television and distribution in the theaters. Flach Film's TV department is directed by Sylvette Frydman, who after working with Breillat went on to coproduce *Le petit poucet* (2011) for ARTE.

19. In Katharine Young's narratological framework, one world—that of the *told* narrative—is called "taleworld," while the other—that of the *telling* of the tale—is the "storyrealm" (1987). I find this distinction helpful, generally speaking, but I will be referring to the "storyrealm" as the mise-en-scène of reading, both to underscore the cinematic choice of the director to stage the narration and to avoid the potential confusion of "storyworld" (which I am configuring as comprised of the two tales the movie as a whole tells us) with "storyrealm." On the page, the names of the four characters in the film (Marie-Catherine, Anne, Catherine, and Marie-Anne) are already confusing enough.

20. Douglas Keesey's chapter "Sisters as One Soul in Two Bodies" (in Keesey 2009) discusses Breillat's film *A ma soeur!* (translated as *Fat Girl*) and others in which the French director focuses on the complicity and rivalry between two young sisters. Just as in *Bluebeard*, the relationship in *Fat Girl* between the "rebellious Anaïs and a more conformist Elena played itself out in Breillat's relationship with her sister Marie-Hélène" (49). Breillat also playfully makes a point of this parallel when discussing both movies.

21. See Keesey (2009, 56–57).

22. The title page we are shown clearly identifies the publisher of this edition of Perrault's fairy tales, Eugène Ardant in Limoge. While this revised edition for children, and specifically Christian children, was published in numerous editions starting in 1867, an Ardant volume for children was also issued as late as in the 1930s. I have so far not been able to find the specific edition shown in the movie or to identify the engraver, except to note that he is not the popular Gustave Dorè.

23. Angela Carter's *The Bloody Chamber* resonates here. Of the bloody chamber in "Bluebeard," Breillat said: "As a very young girl, I was drawn to the image of the [murdered] wives hanging in the room—I love this image of the eternally fresh blood that was like a mirror under them. That, to me, is a vision of the eternity of women" (Breillat and Anderson 2010).

24. For Muñoz, disidentification describes "the survival strategies the minority subject practices" (1999, 4); it "scrambles and reconstructs encoded messages; it exposes the universalizing and exclusionary aspects of the message and recircuits it to account for/include/empower minorities identities and identifications" (31). Here the minority subject is the girl child in a world of large, socialized, and heteronormative adults.

25. In contrast with Perrault's text where the heroine's brothers come to the rescue, in Catherine's reading it is two "musketeers"; in Perrault's tale, one of the brothers is identified as a musketeer.

26. Maria Tatar's book, *Secrets beyond the Door: The Story of Bluebeard and His Wives* (2004) and Stephen Benson's chapter "Craftiness and Cruelty: A Reading of the Fairy Tale and Its Place in Recent Feminist Fictions" in *Cycles of Influence* (2003) marked an important shift in the critical discussion of "Bluebeard." See also Casie Hermansson's *Bluebeard: A Reader's Guide to the English Tradition* (2009) and Shuli Barzilai's *Tales of Bluebeard and His Wives from Late Antiquity to Postmodern Times* (2009).

27. As she states in the same interview with Maria Garcia, "I have always liked the courage of bold, young girls, and it is always the youngest girl in the family who is the boldest. No doubt this is true because I had an older sister and I had to be bolder than she was" (Breillat and Garcia 2011).

28. "Catherine has attained what she sought and resembles the strong, chaste Judith in the great oil paintings by Lucas Cranch the Elder and Fede Galizi, who portray her after she has slain the Assyrian general Holfernes—his head on a table of plate" (Zipes 2012, 52). I agree with Zipes that Breillat's film contests Perrault's tale and patriarchal visualizations of it, but I see her also troubling reversals of it within feminist discourse.

29. Lisa Johnson emphasizes how Breillat identified representing "the point of view of shame" as a specific feminist contribution to envisioning love in cinema. Johnson writes: "Like Sedgwick, Breillat is not using shame morally, either as a threat about what happens to bad girls or as something to be overcome. Rather, shame functions as an element of experience that can be explored. For Breillat, since shame and other "taboo" or degraded elements and affects are integral parts of the fullness of sex acts, the exploration and engagement of those elements may themselves work toward restoring 'female dignity' . . . not so much because the exploration removes shame but because it acknowledges and spends time with shame" (Johnson 2004, 1376).

30. Hermansson (2009, 16–17, 142–43, 217n34).

31. There is very little music in the *Bluebeard* film, actually none in the attic scenes of reading. The "Kyrié Eleïsson" is performed by the Jeune Coeur du Limousin, directed by Annette Petit. Given that Catherine and Marie-Anne in the 1950s storyworld are respectively wearing red-and-white and blue-and-white gingham, the association between Marie-Anne and Bluebeard, the two characters who die, is made at least visually, though of course the more or less saturated blue, its symbolism, and the characters are quite different. Similar is the power play, the rivalry and affinity both, that animates the Catherine/Marie-Anne and Marie-Catherine/Bluebeard relationships.

32. Barunson and CJ are also known to Euro-American audiences for producing and distributing *The Good, the Bad and the Weird* (2008) and *Mother* (2009).

33. Pil-Sung Yim attributes this to Korean audiences' lack of familiarity with the fantasy genre. See "Hansel & Gretel director Yim Pil-Sung darkens film's childlike utopia" in Straight.com (April 23, 2009). Available on DVD, the film is also on Netflix and YouTube.

34. See for example "Hansel and Gretel" reviews on Twitchfilm (August 26, 2008), http://twitchfilm.com/reviews/2008/08/k-film-reviews-hansel-and-gretel.php; AsianMovieWeb, www.asianmovieweb.com/en/reviews/hansel_and_gretel.htm (n.d.); VideoVista (April 2009), www.videovista.net/reviews/april09/hansgret.html; *Variety* (October 2008), www.variety.com/review/VE1117938665/.

35. While the budget for *Enchanted* is estimated at $85 million on IMDB.com, the estimate is €13.5 million (some $20 million) for *Pan's Labyrinth*, $4 million for *Hansel and Gretel*, and $2.4 million for *Bluebeard*.

36. See Zipes's chapter, "Abusing and Abandoning Children: 'Hansel and Gretel,' 'Tom Thumb,' 'The Pied Piper,' 'Donkey-Skin,' and 'The Juniper Tree,'" for an excellent mapping of how filmmakers have, since the early twentieth century, "devised many different strategies to address the problematic actions of the

parents, the cruelty of the witch, and the search for a safe and happy home" in the Grimms' "Hansel and Gretel" tale (2011, 197).

37. Whether they are ghosts or not, Young-Hee, Man-Bok, and Jung-Soon maintain their appearance as children, unless they are in the dark, dusty room behind a surreal blue door where Young Hee's face looks horrifically aged and sad. It is in this room that Eun-Soo finds a whole library of the children's notebooks, recording their frustrated hopes for a happy home.

38. While in the flashback the three siblings are unable to help this child, in the scene where the serial killer has attacked Eun-Soo they succeed.

39. "Any hard-and-fast distinction between witches and ogres ultimately fails," as Marina Warner details in *No Go the Bogeyman* (1998, 12). In this book "about fear" (4), Warner explores the figure of the ogre across time and arts, fantasies of devouring, and lullabies as well as humorous responses to fear of being swallowed by the dark or death. She does so in ways that foreground gendered fears and plots as well as what is different about these fears in the modern world. Her analysis of ogres in this book also foregrounds how in Freudian psychoanalysis, the crimes of the father figure—Kronos or Laius—are minimized compared to the crime of the son, Zeus or Oedipus (see 69). Because Warner's book pursues a creatively productive conversation between visual arts and scholarship, I find it particularly fertile reading for thinking about the remediation of fairy tales in film.

40. The music is by well-known composer Lee Byung-Woo, who also provided the score for other Korean films, including *The Red Shoes*, *The Host*, *Voice of a Murderer*, *Mother*, and *Haeundae*.

41. Francisco Vaz da Silva's brilliant paper, "Hansel and Gretel across Media: A Transcultural Perspective" (2012), offers a complex reading of the film that, in conversation with a draft of my chapter, presents a different take on the "trail of rabbits." Vaz da Silva reads the bear as a positive force in opposition to the rabbits. I find this intriguing, but I am not sure I see it as a structural binary, especially since the rabbits as forest spirits may very well have a positive and different role from the ones in the distorted children's fantasy world.

42. Sunkyung Cho teaches at the Some Institute of Picture Book (SI) in Seoul, Korea; a picture book artist, he is also the director of the Some Press. His blog, www.chosunkyung.blogspot.com/, includes images from his picture books (e.g., *The Humpback and the Fairies*, 2007; and *Underground Garden*, 2005) as well as self-portraits and an interview about his work and poetics as an illustrator. My thanks to Sangho Chung for interpreting the interview for me.

1. In the first few paragraphs of this chapter and in its second section I re-contextualize ideas and words from the essay that John Rieder and I coauthored, "Mixing It Up: Generic Complexity and Gender Ideology in Early Twenty-First Century Fairy Tale Films" (2010). My thanks to John Rieder for his collaboration first and now his permission to recast our work.

2. That the Cinderella character in this 20th Century Fox film production is played by pretty but not Hollywood beautiful Drew Barrymore further increases the potential for audience identification.

3. In her essay "The Shoe Still Fits: *Ever After* and the Pursuit of a Femi-nist Cinderella," Christy Williams brings further insight to the film's feminism manqué (2010). I know of two other essays that discuss the economy of genres in *Ever After* and raise important questions of cultural value. John Stephens and Robyn McCallum (2002) focus on the hybridization of fairy tale and uto-pia in the film; their argument pits postmodern ideology and poetics against a feminist humanism, reinforcing a binary opposition that does not neces-sarily characterize fairy-tale intertextuality today. Elisabeth Rose Gruner (2003) analyzes how the dynamics of history and fairy tale in the film deauthorize a male-dominated tradition.

4. Whether the term "fairy-tale pastiche" stays in the critical vocabulary of fairy-tale and folklore studies or not, Jorgensen's essay opens up new possibilities for discussing the dynamics of social power within these popular-culture texts, in their relationship to literary and oral tales, and in the uses we as scholars make of our disciplinary authority.

5. Not only do these "Snow White" films play visually off of other fairy-tale films, but, as seen in *Mirror Mirror* most vividly, some also mix in and parody fairy-tale fragments from other tales. In fact, *Puss in Boots* (Dir. Chris Miller) short-circuits the distinction I just drew. Produced by DreamWorks animation in 2011, this film is titled after the trickster tale of which Giovanni Francesco Straparola, Giambattista Basile, Charles Perrault, and the Grimms gave us dif-ferent renditions, but it completely ignores the tale's plot. This animated *Puss in Boots* capitalizes instead on the popularity of Antonio Banderas and his feline avatar in *Shrek Two*; and to the mix of fairy-tale and nursery-rhyme icons (Puss meets with Jack and Jill as well as Humpty Dumpty), it adds more celebrity voices, including Guillermo del Toro's (Moustache Man) and Salma Hayek's (Kitty Softpaws). In Altman's terms, this is an example of how "Hollywood reg-ularly eschews genre logic for production and publicity decisions, in favour of series, cycles, remakes, and sequels" (Altman 1999, 115).

6. *Enchanted* is classified as comedy, family, fantasy, musical, romance; *Pan's Labyrinth* as drama, fantasy, war; *Hansel and Gretel* as drama, fantasy, horror, mystery. *Bluebeard* is "fantasy" only, but the French film system does not privilege multiple genre affiliations. Within this official classification "fairy tale" is simply conflated into the larger "fantasy" label, as I discuss later. Rick Altman's *The American Film Musical* also offers an important discussion of how *heterogeneous* the genre of the musical is, with the "fairy-tale musical," "the folk musical," and the "show musical" coexisting in tension with one another (1987).

7. See the section "Faux Feminism: Disney's Response to the Women's Movement," especially 152–53, in Linda Pershing's and Lisa Gablehouse's insightful essay (2010).

8. Christy Williams details how in *Ever After* the film's "narrative and visual framing implicitly validates the authority of [the Grimms'] version, thus undermining the feminist ideology of the entire film" (2010, 105).

9. *Shrek* grossed $120 million during its first weekend in 2001. *Enchanted* grossed approximately the same in four months.

10. Kristine Kotecki (2010), Tracie Lukasiewicz (2010), Jennifer Orme (2010b), John Rieder and I (2010), and Jack Zipes (2008) hold distinctly different interpretations of the relationship between Ofelia's fairy-tale world and the realistic 1944 storyworld set in Spain. While he upholds the willful Ofelia as child hero, Zipes's characterization of the fairy-tale world as fantasy (into which Ofelia "*wills herself*" [2008, 238]) is a fairly common reaction on the part of reviewers. Kotecki discusses how the film's multiple endings are an "approximation" of hypertextualization that "sidesteps an authoritative discounting of the filmic magic and signals to the audience to claim this authority for themselves" (2010, 251).

11. As John Rieder noted, "Here a second comparison to Carter suggests itself. While Carter's prodigious erudition allowed her to retell well-known fairy tales by drawing on their less-well-known folkloric genealogies, Del Toro constructs a synthesis of cinematic and pictorial traditions, alluding with equal virtuosity to Arthur Rackham and Francisco Goya (see DVD Director's Commentary). For both Carter and del Toro, the point is that this allusiveness not only positions their own work in relation to the traditions they invoke, but also re-positions the genres they work with" (Bacchilega and Rieder 2010, 35).

12. *Once Upon a Time* was first aired in the United Kingdom in February 2012.

13. Nadya Aisenberg, among others, developed the analogy in the chapter "Myth, Fairy Tale and the Crime Novel" of *Common Spring: Crime Novel and Classic* (Bowling Green, OH: Bowling Green University Popular Press, 1979).

14. Note that while Chinese characters accompany the English-language title at the start of *Year of the Fish*, the dialogue in Kaplan's film is entirely in English.

In *Dancehall Queen*, characters speak in English as well in Jamaican Creole, and most of the songs are in the Creole. The film has English-language subtitles, and I quote from those. The lyrics of the title song are not subtitled in the beginning scene of the film.

15. While there are increasingly more discussions and adaptations of it now that incest is less of an unspeakable topic, "Donkeyskin" is not part of the fairy-tale canon for children. It is, however, clearly put in conversation with "Cinderella" in anthologies and other pedagogically oriented fairy-tale texts such as Maria Tatar's *Classic Fairy Tales* and *Folk and Fairy Tales*. For critical analysis, see Marina Warner's "The Runaway Girls: Donkeyskin I" and "The Silence of the Fathers: Donkeyskin II," in *From the Beast to the Blonde* (1994), and Helen Pilinovsky's "Donkeyskin, Deerskin, Allerleirauh: The Reality of the Fairy Tale" (2007).

16. "Not every Cinderella story set in Manhattan is 'Enchanted,'" wrote Bill White in his review. He continues, "The story might be a fairy tale, but the treatment is from the gutter, its streetwise dialogue disturbingly incongruous with the Cinderella tale. Still, *Year of the Fish* works as a downbeat tale of a modern-day indentured servant who arrives in America with dreams of prosperity and finds herself the property of unscrupulous slavers" (White 2008). This is not the only review that stresses how this is not a film for children.

17. In 2011, the San Francisco artist Jane R. Willson produced and curated *The Shocking Truth of Cinderella*, an exhibition at the San Francisco Main Public Library that featured the tale of Yeh Shen and many other "Cinderella" stories across cultures. See http://sfpl.org/index.php?pg=1007602401 and www.youtube.com/watch?v=dy-7-b8JJ6Y for highlights. My thanks to Jack Zipes for sharing this information with the Fairy Tale Film Research Group.

18. Wearing different makeup of his own devising, Randall Duk Kim also plays the Foreman and the Old Man. He narrated Disney's *Mulan* special edition DVD (2004) and has, in addition to doing TV and film, been a Shakespearean actor for several decades.

19. Kaplan talks about his use of rotoscoping not to produce a "clean-edged, graphic-novel look" (as Richard Linklater does in *Scanner Darkly*), but a "sloppy painterly look" that is both like watercolor and oil painting (director's commentary). He is also clearly aware of how rotoscoping also contributed to the magic quality of early Disney films, including *Snow White and the Seven Dwarves*. Reviewer Diva Velez commented, "Adding to the sense of fantasy is the rotoscope animation that places a layer of unreality to some of the sleazy aspects of the story, namely the brothel and lends a storybook-like presence to the hunch-backed grotesque, Auntie Yaga, as well as Ye Xian's love-at-first-sight encounter with the Prince Charming of the story" (Velez 2008).

20. In *Billboard: The International Newsweekly of Music, Video, and Home Entertainment*, the full-page advertisement for the film's release described dancehall culture as characterized by "outrageous fashions, innovative dance steps, a distinct vernacular" and dancehall music as "present day [1997] Jamaican Reggae, voicing the young (and the not so young) population's concerns, conflicts, fantasies, and frustrations, while sometimes offering escapist, humorous observations of oppressive situations" (Meschino 1997).

21. For a reading that foregrounds "resistance and self-definition" as key to *Year of the Fish*, see Zipes (2011, 191–92).

22. Kaplan's use of a hand-held camera and rotoscoping made it possible to shoot more freely in the streets of Chinatown, even during the parade, thus allowing for a fuller image of life in the neighborhood and also maintaining throughout the film the anonymity of people in the streets. See City Room for "Live from New York, It's (an Animated) Chinatown" by Jennifer 8. Lee (*New York Times*, August 27, 2008), http://cityroom.blogs.nytimes.com/2008/08/27/live-from-new-york-its-an-animated-chinatown/.

23. "Sicilian storytellers of the nineteenth century, no matter how much magic, fantasy, transformation, and humor were contained in their tales, always brought their listeners back to reality at the end. The endings or codas reveal how the storytellers were well aware of their own condition and the impossibility of realizing their fantasies. . . . Happiness was a fiction" (Zipes, 2009a, 17). Glauco Sanga (2010) also discusses these codas within a structural analysis of the relationship between myth and fairy tales. My thanks to Luisa Del Giudice for making this essay available to me.

24. "*Year of the Fish* packs more sadness than the familiar fairy tale but offers its own fantastical delights. Ye Xian's party dress, made of teardrops, suits her—and her story—perfectly," writes Jeannette Catsoulis in her *New York Times* review (2008).

25. Countering the reading I have just offered, one could say there is an honesty about this low-key, sweet ending that does not pretend to make romance last forever or result in the disappearance of all "real" problems. I do agree that the "ever after" is refreshingly undercut in this happy ending.

26. The DVD's sixth scene is titled "Marcia Makes a Change."

27. As Sandra Duvivier notes about the movie, "Infused with reggae, beats, DJing, and audience participation/dancing, dancehall's salience in *Dancehall Queen* lies in its dialectic function: as a subversive space of black subjectivity, especially among the masses; and a patriarchal site in which the black female body, though celebrated, is arguably sexualized" (Duvivier 2008, 1115). My referring to the dances in the movie as "raunchy" is definitely a personal reaction

from an outsider's perspective and, as my analysis shows, is not intended to take away from the critical force of dancehall in the film. About dancehall's gender politics—as well as its class politics and its local/global meanings—the debate within Caribbean studies is ongoing. In his discussion of *Sound Clash: Jamaican Dancehall Culture at Large* by Carolyn Cooper (New York: Palgrave Macmillan, 2004), for instance, Mike Alleyne writes: "Carolyn Cooper's work over the past decade presents consistent resistance to reactionary impulses of rejection and condemnation of dancehall, exposing dangerous essentialisms and generalizations which actually damage popular cultural analysis as a whole. As she has demonstrated in *Sound Clash*, recognition of textual depth and skillful application of creative license do not automatically sanction what many may view as vulgarity and obscenity, both of which remain open in any case—and beyond the Jamaican context as well—to significant personal interpretation. There can be no pretense whatsoever that dancehall has not challenged the boundaries of social morality, but in so doing it has also exposed alarming hypocrisies and fractures along moral borderlines" (Alleyne 2006, 155). The October 2006 issue of *Small Axe* is devoted to a discussion of dancehall culture and Cooper's reading of it; she responds in "At the Crossroads—Looking for Meaning in Jamaican Dancehall Culture: A Reply" (Cooper 2006). Dancehall songs have also been criticized as homophobic; however, see Nadia Ellis's "Out and Bad: Toward a Queer Performance Hermeneutic in Jamaican Dancehall" (Ellis 2011).

28. See Christy Williams especially for her discussion of Danielle's hyper-femininity—at the royal ball and whenever she dresses as the noblewoman Nicole—as "masquerade" (2010, 105–8), a gender and class performance that is key to her happy ending as Prince Henry's wife. For a different interpretation that however builds on Williams's insights, see Zipes (2011, 186–88).

29. While I am in no position to comment on the complexities, outside of the film, of the social power of Jamaican dancehall culture, it continues to play a significant role in living traditions and popular culture. In *Wake the Town and Tell the People: Dancehall Culture in Jamaica* (2000), which Duvivier calls "one of the groundbreaking works on dancehall culture," Norman Stolzoff writes, "Dancehall . . . is the most potent form of popular culture in Jamaica. For Jamaica's ghetto youth (the black lower-class masses), from among whom come its most creative artists and avid fans, dancehall is their favorite recreational form. Yet dancehall is not merely a space of passive consumerism. It is a field of active cultural production, a means by which black lower-class youth articulate and project a distinct identity in local, national, and global contexts; through dancehall, ghetto youth also attempt to deal with the endemic problems of poverty, racism, and violence" (qtd. in Duvivier 2008, 1116).

30. The film was originally shot in DVC for some £350,000 (approximately $500,000) (Deutschman 2002) or JMD 35,390,673 according to the IMDb.com figures; it broke all sales records in Jamaica at the time, surpassing the cult classic, *The Harder They Come*. It is by some accounts the most watched Jamaican film in Jamaica, and yet local sales in the theaters were not sufficient to cover production costs. It was released on DVD in September 1998.

31. Zipes's reliance on Jessica Tiffin's "identifying fairy tale by texture" gives me pause. Tiffin's book *Marvelous Geometry: Narrative and Metafiction in Modern Fairy Tale* makes in my view very significant contributions to the analysis of twentieth-century fairy tales. However, I find her definition of fairy-tale texture as "render[ing] a fairy tale intrinsically familiar" (2009, 7) problematic; furthermore, as one reviewer noted, for Tiffin the texts that qualify as fairy-tale adaptations "must clearly retain fairy tale structures rather than simply include fairy-tale motifs and must deliberately accept the marvelous and the fairy tale's 'flatly textured sparsity of tone'" (Orme 2012, 27).

32. In his discussion of Euro-American "*The Arabian Nights* in Film Adaptations," Robert Irwin echoes Edward Said's observation of how they are filled with Orientalist fantasies and for the most part targeted at children (Irwin in Marzolph and van Leeuwen 2004, 22–25).

33. This approach can take film critics in numerous directions. For instance, David Butler productively points to the difference between "wonder film," a category that was in use in the United Kingdom during the 1920–50 period, and "fantasy" in the United States since both genres identified *The Thief of Bagdad* (1924 and 1940) films (Butler 2009, 34–36).

34. See Bill Ellis's "Fairy Tales as Metacommentary in Manga and Anime" (2012).

NOTES TO CHAPTER 4

1. This is not to underestimate the work of translation in the global circulation of literature and cultures more generally. I focus on translation when we read European "classic" fairy tales as well, but this focus is heightened when we discuss *The Arabian Nights* because its translations are even more naturalized and their political implications particularly current.

2. For a discussion of Galland and translation as la belle infidèle, see Larzul 1996, particularly 20–24.

3. Pertaining to the *Arabian Nights*, more specifically, significant work has been done on its translations as Orientalist texts (Kabbani 2004; Sallis 1999; Schacker 2003) and on its translations into non-Western languages and cultures (Cohen 2005; Sugita 2006; Geider 2007; Bacchilega and Arista 2007; and more).

4. That jinn grant only three wishes is a modern expectation that became popular in the aftermath of films like *The Thief of Bagdad* (1940).

5. No connection is made between the Genie and the jinnî or daemon/demon from the Arabic tradition. Here the principal association is with Disney's *Aladdin*, as I have mentioned, where the Genie (Robin Williams) is an important but comic figure. In the animated movie, Aladdin uses his third and final wish to grant the Genie his freedom, and the Genie goes off to explore the world. For the relationship between *Aladdin* and the *Thief of Bagdad* movies, see Cooperson (1994).

6. See Anne Duggan's paper on the verbal and visual construction of the genie in French- and English-language translations of *The Arabian Nights* for the insights into the racializing and disempowering of the daemon or jinnî as he is translated into the genie. She too remarks on the domestication of Disney's Genie.

7. The fisherman expresses his disbelief to the demon: "By the Almighty name, tell me whether you really were inside the jar. . . . You are lying, for this jar is not large enough, not even for your hands and feet" (Haddawy 1990, 35). The jinnî or demon turns into smoke and begins to enter the jar to show that he was not lying, and the fisherman seals the jar. This is not however how the tale ends. The fisherman frees the demon once more in exchange for the promise of a reward. The demon kicks the jar away into the sea this time and then keeps his promise to help the fisherman become rich.

8. For Giancarlo Esposito, as he explains it in an interview, the character Magic Mirror, into which the Genie morphs, is more complex as he tells Regina the truth, though in veiled terms, whether she wants to hear it or not, and she is compelled to listen because of their personal attachment. Esposito sees the three characters he plays as quite different, and the development of the series may well confirm that (Reiher 2011). It seems to me that both Magic Mirror and Sidney Glass function as Regina's shadow.

9. For Lawrence Venuti and other scholars, the protocols and values of the target language and system are adopted in a "domesticating translation" in order to minimize the strangeness of the source text or concept (Venuti 1995). In contrast, a "foreignizing translation" refuses to obscure the differences of the source text, which may well result in a less readable or transparent translation. Maria Tymoczko (2010) has questioned the simple opposition of these two types of translation by pointing out that a translation can domesticate some aspects of the source text but foreignize others and also by refusing to equate foreignizing translations with resistance.

10. In order to underscore that the Arabic manuscripts and publications are quite different from their European-languages adaptations, I point to *The One Thousand and One Nights* (Arabic texts that were translated) in somewhat stark

contrast to the title *The Arabian Nights (Entertainments)*. However, the flow of stories and titles is much more complex than my schematization allows for, and to prove that, Galland's trend-setting French text was titled *Les mille et une nuit*. When I focus on adaptations, I will refer to *Arabian Nights* or more simply to *Nights*.

11. Setting it in parallel with the tradition of "mirrors for princes," Chraïbi writes, "*The Arabian Nights* represents a manual of basic rules in manners and customs for young merchants" (Chraïbi 2004, 6).

12. However, recently the *Orlando Furioso* intertextual link is understood to connect with the *101 Nights* because of the beauty contest that is not present in the *1001 Nights*. See Marzolph and Chraïbi (2012).

13. In "The *Arabian Nights*, Visual Culture, and Early German Cinema," Donald Haase (2007) discusses how not only was the *Arabian Nights* "a focal point in the development of visual culture" in the twentieth century, but literary commentary on reading the *Arabian Nights* in late nineteenth- and early twentieth-century Germany highlighted the visual and spectacular aspects of the experience.

14. Spellings vary. I will in my own prose adopt Shahrazad and Shahriyar, but use the adaptor's spelling when discussing individual texts.

15. Ray Harryhausen produced three animated Sindbad movies (1958, 1974, and 1977).

16. "Depicting Eastern peoples, however colorful their attire or exotic their habitat, as intrinsically slothful, violent, sexually obsessed, and incapable of sound self-government made it seem justified, even imperative, for the imperialist to step in and rule them" (Kabbani 2004, 28).

17. Jack Shaheen is also the author of *Reel Bad Arabs: How Hollywood Vilifies a People* (2001, revised edition 2009) and *Guilty: Hollywood's Verdict on Arabs after 9/11* (2008), and has received the American-Arab Anti-Discrimination Committee's "Lifetime Achievement Award." He analyzed over nine hundred Hollywood films in *Reel Bad Arabs*.

18. "Oh, I come from a land, from a faraway place, where the caravan camels roam," was originally followed by "Where they cut off your ear, if they don't like your face. It's barbaric, but hey, it's home," then changed to "It's flat and immense, and the heat is intense. It's barbaric, but hey, it's home." While the original lines referenced male violence, the new ones pointed to heat, the heat of the desert, but also possibly the hotness of its female inhabitants: one stereotype replaces another. For readers of German, Ulrich Marzolph discusses this change in "Das Aladdin-Syndrom. Zur Phänomenologie des narrativen Orientalismus" (449–62) published in *Hören, Sagen, Lesen, Lernen: Bausteine zu*

einer Geschichte der kommunikativen Kultur, Festschrift Rudolf Schenda, edited by Ursula Brunold-Bigler and Hermann Bausinger (Bern: Peter Lang, 1995). See "Arab Stereotypes and American Educators" by Marvin Wingfield and Bushra Karaman (1995) on how stereotypes in popular culture affect Arab American children in US schools; this article was published in 1995 and revised after the September 11, 2001, attacks.

19. In a 2010 interview, Jack Shaheen pointed out that anti-Muslim feelings in the United States "escalated after 9-11 and there are several reasons why it has escalated. One is the fact that we fail to distinguish between the 19 non-American Arab Muslim terrorists, and the seven-plus million American Muslims that had nothing to do with 9-11. . . . The destruction . . . was not committed by American Muslims. So why are we condemning and attacking them?"

20. Anti-Islamic religion incidents grew "by more than 1,600 percent over the 2000 volume. In 2001, reported data showed there were 481 incidents made up of 546 offenses having 554 victims of crimes motivated by bias toward the Islamic religion." www.fbi.gov/about-us/cjis/ucr/hate-crime/2001.

21. In Marzolph's words, "The Western perception of the Muslim world has long been dominated by stereotypical notions of the East as a sensual paradise, most aptly expressed in the notion of the *Arabian Nights*. In recent times, this image is tainted by partial and biased notions of the Muslim world as the ultimate harbor of universal terrorism that is particularly opposed to the basic values defining the West such as the freedom of speech and democracy. Needless to say that both views are equally simplistic in disregarding the complexity and diversity of the phenomena concerned" (Marzolph 2010).

22. Noting that Ali Baba was not one of the forty thieves in the *Arabian Nights* tale does little to get at the substance of the problem, but it does reinforce the point that the practice of reading the actual tales is *not* what sustains these stereotypes.

23. George Paxinos's translation of Walter Sommerfeld's article reads, "The most surprising detail in all reports was the assertion that American soldiers often made the looting possible at all, by breaking open or unlocking well-protected doors and then animating bystanders to plunder: "Go in, Ali Baba, it's all yours!"—shouted the Americans, say Iraqi eyewitnesses." Sommerfeld is professor of Oriental philology in Marburg.

24. An Amnesty International report cited an article published in *Dagbladet* by Line Fransson with pictures of Iraqi detainees on whose chests "the words 'Ali Baba—Haram(i)' (which means Ali Baba—thief) in Arabic" had been written. www.dagbladet.no/nyheter/2003/04/25/367175.html. Amnesty International UK director, Kate Allen, said: "If these pictures are accurate, this is an

appalling way to treat prisoners. Such degrading treatment is a clear violation of the responsibilities of the occupying powers. Whatever the reason for their detention, these men must at all times be treated humanely" (AIUK, posted on April 25, 2003).

25. Warner writes of Galland as "an admirer and advocate of Middle Eastern culture" who "started a course in Arabic at the Sorbonne" (Warner 2012, 15). It is well known that he had a gift for languages (Turkish, Arabic, and Persian) and was a dedicated scholar in addition to being a collector of Oriental artifacts for the king.

26. Snow White, Cinderella, Beauty, Beast, Red Riding Hood, Bluebeard, Pinocchio, Baba Yaga, the Snow Queen, Boy Blue, Mowgli and Bagheera, King Cole, and characters from *The Wizard of Oz* like the flying monkey Bufkin are all "Fables." Other legendary or fantasy characters are also evoked visually: C. S. Lewis's lion, Aslan; Cervantes's Don Quixote and Sancho Panza; Alice and the white rabbit all make appearances in the first volume. Some of these, as Willingham notes in an interview (Willingham and Robinson 2007), can only be visual allusions because of copyright restrictions; he refers specifically to the *Narnia* books and also to *Peter Pan* in the United Kingdom.

27. Since a complete script to this volume of *Fables* is provided (Willingham 2006c, 131–59), I quote from both the graphic and the verbal narrative.

28. In that same volume, when Bigby and Snow marry, King Cole asks the groom "wilt thou love her, comfort her," and the bride "wilt thou obey him and serve him, love" (Willingham 2006c, 97 and 157), and this unfazed reproduction of vows that normalize gender inequality also brought about a number of readers' complaints.

29. This intertextual link possibly extends to the later scene in which Sinbad's former slaves, parading their exotic dress, flirt with Flycatcher (the Woodland Building's janitor and former Frog Prince), reminiscent of the street vendor's dream sequence with a visiting sultan's harem in Fellini's film.

30. "The use of different fonts, enlarged, presented in bold or in a different color, gives the written text a visual and emotional quality" (Kukkonen 2011, 37). Thus, though when quoting from *Fables* I cannot retain all font differences, I have included bold lettering.

In combining visual and verbal narrative, comics and graphic novels are hybrid media or graphic narratives that make use of features from other media in distinctive ways. Scott McCloud's *Understanding Comics: The Invisible Art* (1993) is by now the ABC for comic-book storytelling, guiding us to recognize the verbal and visual strategies by which time, space, perspective, and emotion are negotiated and represented in this hybrid art form. The US-based literature on comics and intermedial narrative has since grown exponentially, and English-language translations from other critical traditions are also impacting the field. Work by Mieke Bal, Hilary Chute, Pascal Lefèvre, Geert Vandermeersche and Ronald Soetaert, Thierry Groensteen, Jared Gardner, and David Herman has shaped my thinking about intermedial narrative and my rudimentary comic-book literacy. I refer to Karin Kukkonen's essays in particular because they read *Fables* as a case study to "unlock insights on comics as vehicles for narration, and as multimodal medium" (2011, 48). In my own analysis, I focus on mise-en-scène and focalization in panels, the interaction of verbal and visual elements, the breakdown (or decoupage) of narrative into distinct panels, what happens in the gutter, the visual or paradigmatic association of panels that are not close to one another, and in a very limited way the effect of different drawing styles.

31. Willingham's introduction to the volume dates the events in *1001 Nights of Snowfall* to "at least a century before the events depicted in the first issue of the regular FABLES comic book series" (2006a, 6). While Snow White's attire when she arrives in Shahryar's [sic] land is pictured as Victorian, verbally the graphic novel begins, "Once upon a time, as all stories of this type must begin" (9).

32. Macaulay ([1835] 1965) (in)famously wrote, "We must at present do our best to form a class who may be interpreters between us and the millions whom we govern,—a class of persons Indian in blood and colour, but English in tastes, in opinions, in morals and in intellect." Another passage of his is a stellar example of what Paul Lyons (2006) calls sanctioned and "willful ignorance" as well as of its power since Macaulay's proposal of education reform in India was approved in March 1835: "I have no knowledge of either Sanscrit [sic] or Arabic. But I have done what I could to form a correct estimate of their value. I have read translations of the most celebrated Arabic and Sanscrit works. I have conversed, both here and at home, with men distinguished by their proficiency in the Eastern tongues. I am quite ready to take the oriental learning at the valuation of the orientalists themselves. I have never found one among them who could deny that a single shelf of a good European library was worth the whole native literature of India and Arabia. The intrinsic superiority of the Western literature is indeed fully admitted by those members of the committee who support the oriental plan of education." I should qualify that in 1835 India was not directly subject to British rule but to that of the East India Company, and also that my critical observations have less to do with the outcome of colonial education in India than with Macaulay's assumptions in arguing for it.

33. From the Arabic, jinn is the plural transliteration of jinnî (male singular) and jinniyya (female singular).

34. When King Cole goes with Sinbad back to what he believes is a "city under occupation" to set up "a new Fabletown," he is surprised to find out that the "true Baghdad" (Willingham 2006b, 91) is free and hidden from the Adversary. That Sinbad kept it a secret all through his stay in Fabletown confirms he may be reliable, but he is sly; of course, that is true of Prince Charming and other Fables too. In other volumes, the Baghdad that Sinbad rules over is referred to as "the magical version" ("Who's Who in Fabletown," in Willingham 2008b, 6). That both Ali Baba and Aladdin ask to host King Cole on his first evening there is but one small example of Willingham's tongue-in-cheek playfulness.

35. In much Orientalist literature, jinn are "depicted as possessing great powers but a weak mind—in other words, a great creative potential but a less developed intellectual capacity. The latter characteristic results from their emotional responding to their impulses" (Marzolph and van Leeuwen 2004, 536).

36. In the end, the harm the jinnî could have done (had Frau Totenkinder not modified his charge) is used as leverage by Prince Charming and King Cole in the "trial" they subject Sinbad to before releasing him from prison and reinstating him as the legitimate leader of the Arabian Fables.

37. Told by the "Hansel and Gretel" witch, "The Witch's Tale" is further embedded within the "Diaspora" tales that Snow White is telling the Sultan; this is a common strategy in *The Arabian Nights*.

38. In the first known illustration related to the *Arabian Nights*, the frontispiece for the 1706 English-language translation of Galland's French text, the two are shown in Western style sitting in bed together and at the same height. This image was widely reproduced. However, Thomas Dalziel's frontispiece for the *Illustrated Arabian Nights' Entertainments* (1864–65) and the illustration by Léon Carré for the prologue of J. C. Mardus's *Nights* (1926–32) are but two examples among many where Shahrazad is placed well below the Sultan. See Kobayashi (2006) for discussion of these and other representations of Shahrazad.

39. Not surprisingly since the focus is not on the so-called Arabian Fables, missing in Willingham's graphic novel is Shahrazad's younger sister, Dunyazad, who is both helper to and apprentice of Shahrazad in the *Nights* and eventually marries Shahriyar's younger brother. To some extent, the illustration of Snow White and Scheherazade by Vess and Kaluta evokes the relationship between the two sisters in the *Arabian Nights*, but ascribing the role of the wiser Shahrazad to Snow White and that of Dunyazad to the childlike and naive Scheherazade.

40. The Northwestern University Press edition of *The Arabian Nights* includes a brief production history, notes on the play's staging and casting, the transcript of an improvised scene, and stills from two different productions of the play.

41. Since 1992, Zimmerman's play has been produced in many North American cities by the Lookingglass Theatre Company ensemble as well as by other companies. Commenting on the 2009 production that Zimmerman's Lookingglass Theatre Company did with the Berkeley Repertory Theatre and Kansas City Repertory Theatre is also Zimmerman's statement: "We first produced *The Arabian Nights* in 1992 in the shadow of the first Gulf War. It remains for us an attempt to embody the remarkable richness of one of the great masterpieces of world literature. In spite of time, distance and the rhetoric of difference, we find in these characters and tales—over and over—ourselves" (Zimmerman, www.lookingglasstheatre.org/content/thearabiannights). In the interview with Joel Markowitz concerning a 2011 production at the Arena in Washington, DC, Zimmerman noted production changes starting with the 2009 show that seek to further the play's critique of Orientalism: "In the original, when the audience came in the set was already established—rugs, lamps, ottomans were all visible. We were already in the exotic sort of nostalgic fantasy of the Old Araby. That seemed utterly impossible this time around and utterly impossible to present that setting as anything but a construction. So now when the audience comes in, everything is covered with white muslin as though in storage. It is all rather quiet, rather bleak. A bare, modern light bulb hangs over the stage. Then two fellows come in and their first move is to cover that light bulb with a filigreed lamp then everything becomes musical, riotous; we see the set unfold as the cast uncovers its elements, kicks out carpets, arranges things. We always did that arranging, but the elements were visible from the beginning in the old days."

42. The epigraph reads: "Baghdad, in the heart of Islam, is the city of wellbeing, in it are the talents of which men speak, and elegance and courtesy. Its winds are balmy and its science penetrating. In it are to be found the best of everything and all that is beautiful. From it comes everything worthy of consideration, and every elegance is drawn toward it. All hearts belong to it, and all wars are against it" (*TAN*, unnumbered page).

43. Wat also mentions, "I have seen a production of *The Arabian Nights* which leaves out the air-raid ending. To me, that makes no sense because it removes what I think is an important layer of meaning" (e-mail communication).

44. Given Zimmerman's investment in valorizing the *Arabian Nights* as a quintessential text of "world literature," her specific choice of Mathers could have something to do with the influence of Mardrus's translation on writers like Marcel Proust (see Marzolph and van Leeuwen 2004, 637–38 and 682). Style, the tales included in Mathers's text, availability, twentieth-century idiom, and the relative unfamiliarity of the general public with this translation could also be factors. Of Mardrus's text, Jorge Luis Borges wrote, and I quote in

translation, "It can be said that Mardrus did not translate the book's words but its scenes: a freedom denied to translators, but tolerated in illustrators. . . . I do not know if these smiling diversions are what infuse the work with such a happy air, the air of a far-fetched personal yarn rather than a laborious hefting of dictionaries. But to me the Mardrus 'translation' is the most readable of them all—after, Burton's incomparable version, which is not truthful either. . . . It is [Mardrus's] infidelity, his happy and creative infidelity, that must matter to us" ([1999] 2010, 422–23).

45. I quote here from Zimmerman's "Empathy through Storytelling," as she refers to Shahrazad's approach to saving Shahriyar, helping him out of his trauma and back into the real world.

46. For the *Arabian Nights* tales on which Zimmerman draws, I provide titles from *The Arabian Nights Encyclopedia*. In some cases the titles Zimmerman gives to the tales (*TAN*, "A Note on Casting," 141) clearly draw on titles that translators, editors, and scholars gave to stories in the *Arabian Nights*. In other cases identifying the corresponding tale in the *Nights* requires reading familiarity with the collection or at least some detective work.

47. The Lookingglass Theatre Company's "core values," as explained on their web page, http://lookingglasstheatre.org/content/explore_productions/mission, are collaboration, transformation, and invention, and Zimmerman confirms that members of the cast participated in the selection of tales, bringing in their favorites from the *Arabian Nights*, and that she also chose some tales specifically to match the talents of the actors.

48. Warner is writing about fairy tales and their bridging "learned, literary, and print culture" with the "oral, illiterate, people's culture" in this passage; she continues, referring to "Bluebeard" and "Beauty and the Beast," that "while romancing reality, [the fairy tale is] deeply concerned with undoing prejudice" (Warner 1994, 24). Given the thematic associations between "Bluebeard" and the *Arabian Nights'* frame narrative, I hope my application of her metaphor to Zimmerman's *The Arabian Nights* is not out of place.

49. An articulation of this logic that seems particularly relevant here is White House spokesperson Marlin Fitzwater's comment in 1991 after the NATO coalition bombing in Baghdad resulted in a number of "civilian casualties": "We don't know why civilians were at that location, but we do know that Saddam Hussein does not share our sanctity for human life" (*New York Times*, February 14, 1991, www.nytimes.com/1991/02/14/world/war-gulf-white-house-fitzwater-s-statement-bombing-building-iraq.html).

50. Praising the 2009 revival of the play in Chicago, this reviewer captures the humanist poetics and effect of the 1991 original production: "It was the time

of the first Gulf War, when Iraq's cultural identity, thanks to both its merciless dictator and the needs of his Western antagonists, had been rendered in the media and the halls of government as a hostile, homogenous antithesis of light, art and freedom. By reminding everyone of our shared cultural roots—and by demonstrating the Arabian heritage of humor and wisdom—Zimmerman and her young, just-graduated cohorts seemed—almost alone—to be pulling back a black veil and letting in the humanity" (Jones 2009). Another reviewer in 2008 wrote of the play's production in Berkeley: "First devised during the Gulf War 16 years ago, Mary Zimmerman's revived *The Arabian Nights* arrives at another moment when some positive appreciation of Islam and the Arabic world is particularly welcome. Not to mention nearly three hours of exhilarating, imaginative theatrical escape—always desirable, but especially soothing at present" (Harvey 2008).

51. Wat, who has a PhD in performance studies from Northwestern University and chose to produce *The Arabian Nights* because of his "admiration for [Zimmerman's] aesthetic work," specifies that "the oldest students in the play were born in 1987 so they probably did not have much in the way of personal memories or thoughts about [the First Gulf] war. On the other hand, they were certainly cognizant of the 9/11 (2001) attacks and the second Gulf War (2003) in the spring of 2005 when we worked on the production." About their "discoveries," he states: "We discussed the ironies of the conflicts between Muslims, Christians and Jews given that the three religions all derive from the Abrahamic tradition. We talked about the irony that Arabs and Israelis are both semitic peoples, essentially 'cousins,' and that they use what is essentially an identical greeting, salaam/shalom, which means 'peace.' We discussed Arabic contributions to science, mathematics, art, music, architecture, culture, etc. We discussed how much of classical knowledge was preserved by Arabic cultures through the European Dark Ages" (e-mail communication with author). Wat recalls that some parents and the school's principal were concerned with the play's sexual rather than political themes.

52. Some news coverage says the artists were denied visas. The announcement of "postponement" that the Chicago Shakespeare Theater issued reads: "The production, which was scheduled to open this week at Chicago Shakespeare Theater, had its premiere earlier this month at Luminato Festival in Toronto, Canada, but delays in the issuance of U.S. visas make it impossible for the company to perform its scheduled engagement in Chicago. From the time the company of artists from across the Arabic-speaking world assembled in Egypt for rehearsals earlier this year (before relocating to Morocco due to the uprising

in Cairo) proper and timely procedures were followed to secure permission for the company to enter the United States."

53. The publication of Zimmerman's script enables these productions. I saw the one in Honolulu in 2005, and its showcasing of students' creativity was striking. An Internet search for Fall 2011 shows that Mineral Wells High School Ram Theater in Texas and Beloit Memorial High School Theater in Wisconsin produced the play in November 2011; Estero High School in Florida is producing Dominic Cooke's *Arabian Nights* in 2012.

NOTES TO EPILOGUE

1. I know that the equivalence breaks down in Italian, for instance, and I expect it will in other languages as well. It is worth exploring these differences, which can only be done through cultivating more critical conversations and collaborations across linguistic and scholarly traditions.

2. See Ziolkowski (2006) and Zipes (2001 and 2012) for the commingling of Christian legends and folktale in medieval Europe that fed into the fairy-tale genre. The figure of the fairy developed as a modernized and secularized version of the powerful *fata* of antiquity. For a recent and very rich analysis of this complex process from ancient to contemporary texts, see *Des fata aux fées*, edited by Martine Hennard Dutheil de la Rochère and Véronique Dasen (2011).

3. Rubenstein's presentation of the etymologies and meanings of wonder is very rich and corroborates philosophically and linguistically Warner's interpretation of wonder. Also particularly interesting as we think about the wonder tale's relation to other genres is Rubenstein's reference to Thaumas (wonder) in Hesiod's *Theogony* and his progeny: both Iris, the rainbow, *and* the Harpies (2011, 11). My thanks to John Zuern for pointing me to Rubenstein's book.

4. This is a promising focus of research. While scholars in feminist studies and Middle Eastern literatures write about these texts, Vassilena Parashkevova's is one of the few essays I know of addressing fairy-tale studies scholars specifically.

5. For the final part of this epilogue, I draw on "Authorizing Fairy-Tale History? Disciplinary Debates and the Politics of Inequality," the paper I delivered at the American Folklore Society meeting in 2010.

6. See Catherine Velay-Vallantin, Francisco Vaz da Silva, Jan Ziolkowski, Dan Ben-Amos, Linda Lee, and Lewis Seifert in the "Critical Exchanges" section in *Marvels & Tales* 20 (2006): 276–84 and the "Reflections on the 2006 Annual Meeting of the American Folklore Society in Milwaukee" in the *ISFNR*

Newsletter (March 2007): 17–26. The fall 2010 issue of the *Journal of American Folklore* (vol. 123, no. 490) also features this debate as it grew out of a session organized by Dan Ben-Amos at the Milwaukee meeting of the American Folklore Society in 2006. Most recent is Jack Zipes's "Sensationalist Scholarship: A 'New' History of Fairy Tales," Appendix A in *The Irresistible Fairy Tale* (2012, 157–73).

7. From the assertion that Venetian writer Straparola single-handedly "invented" the modern genre of the fairy tale to the simplistic equation of "the lack of evidence" with "evidence of lack," the enormity of Bottigheimer's claims is staggering, since like a magic wand they are supposed to wave away the very possibility of orally transmitted fairy tales before the sixteenth century and also implicitly taint as "bookish" or print-derived their later circulation as documented in the nineteenth and twentieth centuries. The promise of this "new" magic garnered Bottigheimer's book an unusual (if temporary) degree of visibility in the public sphere, including articles in the *Chronicle of Higher Education*, the *New York Times*, and *The Guardian*, and an interview with the Australian ABC Radio National.

8. When it comes to folklore studies specifically, Bottigheimer's claims are buttressed by her representation of a hegemonic belief in the "unlettered country folk" on the part of collectively fantasizing folklorists, straw men who even today apparently never consider the interaction of oral and written texts. In other words, the soundness of this new history is predicated on exiling the findings of contemporary folklorists to the realm of outdated ideas, to fantasy, that is, outside of history. As for literary scholarship, perhaps, rather than providing us with a new perspective on the history of the fairy tale, Bottigheimer's book takes us back to a time when intertextuality meant source studies only, literary history was centered on major authors, genre was a plot container, interdisciplinary work was anathema, and interpretation the exclusive purview of scholars and literati.

9. In her recent response to "revisionist folktale scholars" who champion the priority of printed over oral texts, I particularly appreciated Christine Shojaei Kawan's statement: "No modern scholar would of course deny that the interaction between oral and written literature was underplayed by folklorists in most of the nineteenth and early twentieth centuries and that printed works have exerted considerable influence on tale tradition in many places" (Shojaei Kawan 2011, 299). Folklore studies as a discipline has distinctive histories and methodologies across nations, but as seen in the *Companion to Folklore Studies* (2012), ignoring or dismissing the interaction between oral and written texts is not a prevalent approach.

10. It should be clear I do not believe we need to limit ourselves to reading folk and literary texts *alone* in the fairy-tale web, that is, to the exclusion of other cultural productions.

11. Astutely, one of the confidential readers of this manuscript suggested I address the "'impossibility' of comparative fairy-tale studies on a global scale." This scholar asked, "How do we train the next generation of scholars?" and "Do we still need specialists in national languages and literatures, or will they be displaced by a new generation of scholars who think globally, even when it means sacrificing precision and depth?" These questions bring home the importance of language skills and cultural knowledge in our scholarship. I hope to have championed their importance and to have been mindful of my limitations. Meeting the challenge of truly comparative fairy-tale studies may never be a reality, and my point is not to think of a worldwide fairy-tale web, but a worldly one. The process of writing this book has only intensified my conviction that collaboration across national and disciplinary boundaries is key to the future of our inquiry and conversations.

WORKS CITED

Acocella, Joan. 2012. "Once Upon a Time: The Lure of the Fairy Tale." *The New Yorker* (July 23): 73–78.

Adaniya, Jason. 2009. In-class comment. English 480: 21st-Century Fairy-Tale Adaptations. University of Hawai'i at Mānoa. Fall.

Aiu, Pua'alaokalani D. 2010. "Ne'e Papa i ke Ō Mau: Language as an Indicator of Hawaiian Resistance and Power." In *Translation, Resistance, Activism*, edited by Maria Tymoczko, 89–107. Boston: University of Massachusetts Press.

Alcoff, Linda Martín. 2007. "Mignolo's Epistemology of Coloniality." *CR: The New Centennial Review* 7 (3): 79–101.

Allen, Chadwick. 2007. "Rere Kē / Moving Differently: Indigenizing Methodologies for Comparative Indigenous Literary Studies." *Studies in American Indian Literatures* 19 (4): 1–26.

Alleyne, Mike. 2006. "Inside Out: Dancehall and the 'Re-Cooperation' of Meaning." *Small Axe* 21 (October): 150–60.

Altman, Rick. 1987. *The American Film Musical*. Bloomington: Indiana University Press.

———. 1999. *Film/Genre*. London: British Film Institute.

Anderson, Graham. 2000. *Fairytale in the Ancient World*. New York: Routledge.

Apter, Emily. 2006. *The Translation Zone: A New Comparative Literature*. Princeton, NJ: Princeton University Press.

Ashliman, D. L. 2004. *Folk and Fairy Tales: A Handbook*. Westport, CT: Greenwood Press.

Atwood, Margaret. 1983. *Bluebeard's Egg: Stories*. Toronto: McClelland and Stewart.

Bacchilega, Cristina. 1997. *Postmodern Fairy Tales: Gender and Narrative Strategies*. Philadelphia: University of Pennsylvania Press.

———. 2007. *Legendary Hawai'i and the Politics of Place: Tradition, Translation, and Tourism*. Philadelphia: University of Pennsylvania Press.

———. 2008. "Extrapolating from Nalo Hopkinson's *Skin Folk*: Reflections on Transformation and Recent English-Language Fairy-Tale Fiction by Women." In Benson, *Contemporary Fiction and the Fairy Tale*, 178–203.

———. 2011. "Fairy Tales in Literature and Film Today: Feminist or Not, for Whom Do They Work?" In *Les réécritures du canon dans la littérature féminine de langue anglaise*, edited by Claire Bazin and Marie-Claude Perrin Chenour, 35–51. Textes et genres IV. Nanterre: AIR.

———. 2012. "Folklore and Literature." In Bendix and Hasan-Rokem, *A Companion to Folklore Studies*, 447–63.

Bacchilega, Cristina, and Noelani Arista. 2007. "*The Arabian Nights* in the *Kuokoa*, a Nineteenth-Century Hawaiian Newspaper: Reflections on the Politics of Translation." In Marzolph, *The Arabian Nights in Transnational Perspective*, 157–82.

Bacchilega, Cristina, and John Rieder. 2010. "Mixing It Up: Generic Complexity and Gender Ideology in Early Twenty-First Century Fairy-Tale Films." In Greenhill and Matrix, *Fairy Tale Films: Visions of Ambiguity*, 23–41.

Bae Chan-Hyo. 2008/2009. *Existing in Costume: Fairy Tale Project*. Photographic collection.

———. 2012. "Work: *Existing in Costume: Fairy Tale Project*." Saatchi Online. www.saatchionline.com/photomam Accessed on November 17, 2012.

Bakhtin, Mikhail. 1986. *Speech Genres and Other Late Essays*. Translated by Vern W. McGee. Edited by Caryl Emerson and Michael Holquist. Austin: University of Texas Press.

Baron, Robert. 2003. "Amalgams and Mosaics, Syncretisms and Reinterpretations: Reading Herskovits and Contemporary Creolists for Metaphors of Creolization." *Journal of American Folklore* 116 (Winter): 88–115.

Baron, Robert, and Ana C. Cara, eds. 2003. *Journal of American Folklore* 116 (459). Special issue on Creolization.

Barthes, Roland. 1981. "Theory of the Text." In *Untying the Text: A Post-Structuralist Reader*, edited by Robert Young, 31–47. London: Routledge and Kegan Paul.

———. 1989. "From Work to Text" (1971). In *Modern Literary Theory: A Reader*, edited by Philip Rice and Patricia Waugh, 166–71. London: Edward Arnold.

———. 1993. *Mythologies*. Translated by Annette Lavers. London: Vintage.

Barzilai, Shuli. 2009. *Tales of Bluebeard and His Wives from Late Antiquity to Postmodern Times*. London: Routledge.

Basile, Giambattista. 1986. *Lo cunto de li cunti* (1634–36). Edited and translated by Michele Rak. Milan: Garzanti.

———. 2007. *The Tale of Tales, or Entertainment for Little Ones*. Translated by Nancy L. Canepa. Foreword by Jack Zipes. Illustrated by Carmelo Lettere. Detroit: Wayne State University Press.

Bauman, Richard. 2004. *A World of Others' Words: Cross-Cultural Perspectives on Intertextuality*. Malden, MA: Blackwell.

Bauman, Richard, and Charles L. Briggs. 2003. *Voices of Modernity: Language Ideologies and the Politics of Inequality*. Cambridge: Cambridge University Press.

Beaumont, Jeanne Marie, and Claudia Carlson, eds. 2003. *The Poets' Grimm: Twentieth-Century Poems from Grimm Fairy Tales*. Ashland, OR: Story Line Press.

Bell, Elizabeth, Linda Haas, and Laura Sells, eds. 1995. *From Mouse to Mermaid: The Politics of Film, Gender, and Culture*. Bloomington: Indiana University Press.

Ben-Amos, Dan, and Ruth B. Bottigheimer. 2009. "Debating Fairy Tales." Ramona Koval, presenter. ABC National Radio, July 8.

Bendix, Regina, and Galit Hasan-Rokem, eds. 2012. *A Companion to Folklore Studies*. London: Blackwell-Wiley.

Benson, Stephen. 2003. *Cycles of Influence: Fiction, Folktale, Theory*. Detroit: Wayne State University Press.

Benson, Stephen, ed. 2008. *Contemporary Fiction and the Fairy Tale*. Detroit: Wayne State University Press.

Bernabé, Jean, Patrick Chamoiseau, and Raphaël Confiant. 1993. *L'eloge de la créolité / In Praise of Creoleness*. Translated by M. B. Taleb-Khyar. Paris: Gallimard.

Bernheimer, Kate, ed. 2010. *My Mother She Killed Me, My Father He Ate Me: Forty New Fairy Tales*. New York: Penguin.

Bettelheim, Bruno. 1976. *The Uses of Enchantment: The Meaning and Importance of Fairy Tales*. New York: Knopf.

Birkeland, Eric. 2009. In-class comment. English 480: 21st-Century Fairy-Tale Adaptations. University of Hawai'i at Mānoa. Fall.

Block, Francesca Lia. 2000. *The Rose and the Beast: Fairy Tales Retold*. New York: HarperCollins.

Bolter, Jay David, and Richard Grusin. 2000. *Remediation: Understanding New Media*. Cambridge, MA: MIT Press.

Borges, Jorge Louis. [1999] 2010. "The Translators of *The Thousand and One Nights*." Translated by Esther Allen. In *The Arabian Nights: A Norton Critical Edition*, edited by Daniel Heller-Roazen, 409–26. New York: Norton.

Bottigheimer, Ruth B. 2009. *Fairy Tales: A New History*. Albany: State University of New York Press.

Bould, Mark. 2002. "The Dreadful Credibility of Absurd Things." *Historical Materialism* 10 (4): 51–88.

Bourdieu, Pierre. 1993. *The Field of Cultural Production*. Edited by Randal Johnson. New York: Columbia University Press.

Brathwaite, Edward Kamau. 1971. *The Development of Creole Society (1770–1820) in Jamaica*. Oxford: Clarendon Press.

Breillat, Catherine, and Melissa Anderson (interviewer). 2010. "Q&A with *Bluebeard*'s Catherine Breillat: On Sisterly Love, Sadomasochism, and Serial Killing." *Village Voice*, March 2. www.villagevoice.com/2010-03-02/film/q-a-with-bluebeard-s-catherine-breillat/. Accessed on December 12, 2011.

Breillat, Catherine, and Maria Garcia (interviewer). 2011. "Rewriting Fairy Tales, Revisiting Female Identity." Interview by Maria Garcia. *Cineaste* 36 (3): 32–35. www.cineaste.com/articles/rewriting-fairy-tales-revisiting-female-identity-an-interview-with-catherine-breillat. Accessed on January 19, 2012.

Breillat, Catherine, and Glenn Kenny (interviewer). 2009. "Some Words about Bluebeard with Catherine Breillat." Mubi.com. October 31. http://mubi.com/notebook/posts/some-words-about-bluebeard-with-catherine-breillat. Accessed on December 12, 2011.

Bronner, Simon J. 2005. "'Gombo' Folkloristics: Lafcadio Hearn's Creolization and Hybridization in the Formative Period of Folklore Studies." *Journal of Folklore Research* 42 (2): 141–84.

Brooks, Lisa. 2012. "The Primacy of the Present, The Primacy of Place: Navigating the Spiral of History in the Digital World." *PMLA* 127 (2): 308–16.

Broumas, Olga. 1977. *Beginning with O*. Yale Series of Younger Poets, 72. New Haven, CT: Yale University Press.

Brown, Laura S. 1995. "Not Outside the Range: One Feminist Perspective on Psychic Trauma." In *Trauma: Explorations in Memory*, edited by Cathy Caruth, 100–112. Baltimore: Johns Hopkins University Press.

Brown, Margaret Wise. 2007. *Goodnight Moon* (1947). Illustrated by Clement Hurd. New York: HarperCollins.

Butler, David. 2009. *Fantasy Cinema: Impossible Worlds on Screen*. London: Wallflower Press.

Butler, Judith. 2004. *Undoing Gender*. New York: Routledge.

Cardigos, Isabel. 1996. *In and Out of Enchantment: Blood Symbolism and Gender in Portuguese Fairytales*. Folklore Fellows' Communications No. 260. Helsinki: Suomalainen Tiedeakatemia (Academia Scientiarum Fennica).

Carney, Jo. 2012. "Aimee Bender's Fiction and the Intertextual Ingestion of Fairy Tales." *Marvels & Tales: Journal of Fairy-Tale Studies* 26 (2): 221–39.

Carter, Angela. 1983. "Notes from the Front Line." In *On Gender and Writing*, edited by Michelene Wandor, 69–77. London: Pandora Press.

———. 1993. *American Ghosts & Old World Wonders*. London: Chatto & Windus.

———. 2006. *The Bloody Chamber and Other Stories*. 1979; London: Vintage.

Carter, Angela, ed. 1990. *The Virago Book of Fairy Tales*. London, Virago.

———. 1993. *The Second Virago Book of Fairy Tales*. London, Virago.

Castells, Manuel. 1996. *The Rise of the Network Society*. Malden, MA: Blackwell.

Catsoulis, Jeannette. 2008. "A Chinatown Fairy Tale." Review of *Year of the Fish*. *New York Times*, August 28. http://movies.nytimes.com/2008/08/29/movies/29fish.html. Accessed March 2, 2012.

Cavallaro, Dani. 2011. *The Fairy Tale and Anime: Traditional Themes, Images, and Symbols at Play on Screen*. Jefferson, NC: McFarland.

"The Cave of Ali Baba." 1962. Art by Carl Barks. *Uncle Scrooge #37*. New York: Walt Disney Dell Comics.

Chakrabarty, Dipesh. 2007. *Provincializing Europe*. Rev. ed. Princeton, NJ: Princeton University Press.

Cho Sunkyung. 2007. *Hansel and Gretel*. Art Work.

Chraïbi, Aboubakr. 2004. "Situation, Motivation, and Action in the *Arabian Nights*." In Marzolph and Leeuwen, *The Arabian Nights Encyclopedia*, 1:5–9.

———. 2007. "Galland's 'Ali Baba' and Other Arabic Versions." In Marzolph, *Arabian Nights in Transnational Perspective*, 3–16.

Christie, Stuart. 2009. "Translating Sovereignty: Corpus Retranslation and Endangered North American Indigenous Languages." *Translation Studies* 2 (2): 115–32.

Cohen, Matthew Isaac. 2005. "*Thousand and One Nights* at the Komedie Stamboel: Popular Theatre and Travelling Stories in Colonial Southeast Asia." In *New Perspectives on [the] Arabian Nights: Ideological Variations and Narrative Horizons*, edited by Wen-Chin Ouyang and Geert Jan van Gelder, 103–14. New York: Routledge.

Cooper, Carolyn. 2004. "Lady Saw Cuts Loose: Female Fertility Rituals in the Dancehall." *Jamaica Journal* 27 (2–3): 13–19. Also "Lady Saw Cuts Loose: Female Fertility Rituals in Jamaican Dancehall Culture." In *Proceedings of the Dancing in the Millennium Conference, Washington, DC, July 2000*, edited by Juliette Crone Willis. www.jouvay.com/interviews/carolyncooper.com. Accessed February 20, 2012.

———. 2006. "At the Crossroads—Looking for Meaning in Jamaican Dancehall Culture: A Reply." *Small Axe* 21 (October): 193–204.

Cooperson, Michael. 1994. "The Monstrous Births of 'Aladdin.'" *Harvard Middle Eastern and Islamic Review* 1:67–86.

Coover, Robert. 1969. *Pricksongs and Descants, Fictions*. New York: Dutton.

Coppola, Maria Micaela. 2001. "The Gender of Fairies: Emma Donoghue and Angela Carter as Fairy Tale Performers." *Textus: English Studies in Italy* 14 (1): 27–142.

Cornfeld, Li. 2011. "Shooting Heroines: On Dina Goldstein's Fallen Princesses." Talk at the "From Portraits to Pinups: Representations of Women in Art and Popular Culture" conference, Brooklyn Museum, May 13.

Cross, Heather. 2005. "Bloomingdale's 2005 Holiday Window Displays." *New York City Travel.* December 13. http://gonyc.about.com/od/christmassights/ss/2005_bloomies.htm.

Crowley, Karlyn, and John Pennington. 2010. "Feminist Frauds on the Fairies? Didacticism and Liberation in Recent Retellings of 'Cinderella.'" *Marvels & Tales: Journal of Fairy-Tale Studies* 24 (2): 297–313.

Datlow, Ellen, and Terri Windling, eds. 1997. *Black Swan, White Raven.* New York: Avon.

———. 1999. *Silver Birch, Blood Moon.* New York: Avon.

D'Costa, Jean. 1990. "Bra Rabbit Meets Peter Rabbit: Genre, Audience, and the Artistic Imagination; Problems in Writing Children's Fiction." In *Caribbean Women Writers: Essays from the First International Conference,* edited by Selwyn Reginald Cudjoe, 254–62. Wellesley, MA: Calaloux.

De Caro, Frank, and Rosan Augusta Jordan. 2004. *Re-Situating Folklore: Folk Contexts and Twentieth-Century Art.* Knoxville: University of Tennessee Press.

Dégh, Linda. 1994. "Magic for Sale: Märchen and Legend in TV Advertisement." In *American Folklore and the Mass Media,* 34–53. Bloomington: Indiana University Press.

Del Toro, Guillermo. 2007a. *Featurette: The Director's Notebook.* 2-disk DVD.

———. 2007b. *Pan's Labyrinth: Director's Audio Commentary.* 2-disk DVD.

De Souza, Pascale. 2003. "Creolizing Anancy Signifyin(g) Processes in New World Spider Tales." In *A Pepper-Pot of Cultures: Aspects of Creolization in the Caribbean,* edited by Gordon Collier and Ulrich Fleischmann, 339–63. Amsterdam: Editions Rodopi.

Deutschman, Yvonne. 2002. "Filming Begins on ONE LOVE Starring Ky-Mani Marley, Cherine Anderson, and Vas Blackwood." November 8. www.ydeutschman.com/article1.htm. Accessed March 4, 2012.

Dillon, Grace. 2007. "Indigenous Scientific Literacies in Nalo Hopkinson's Ceremonial Worlds." *Journal of the Fantastic in the Arts* 18 (1): 23–41.

Dillon, Grace, ed. 2012. *Walking the Clouds: An Anthology of Indigenous Science Fiction.* Tucson: University of Arizona Press.

Dimock, Wai Chee, and Bruce Robbins, eds. 2007. *Special Topic: Remapping Genre.* PMLA 122 (5).

Dinshhaw, Carolyn, Lee Edelman, Roderick A. Ferguson, Carla Freccero, Elizabeth Freeman, Judith Halberstam, Annamarie Jagose, Christopher Nealon, and Nguyen Tan Hoang. 2007. "Theorizing Queer Temporarlities: A Roundtable Discussion." In "Queer Temporalities," edited by Elizabeth Freeman. Special issue, *GLQ: A Journal of Lesbian and Gay Studies* 13 (2–3): 177–95.

Dömötör, Tekla. 1975. "Folktales and the Detective Story." Translated by Elizabeth Tucker and Antony Hellenberg. *Folklore Forum* 8 (1): 335–43.

Donoghue, Emma. 1997. *Kissing the Witch.* London: Hamish Hamilton.

———. 1999. *Kissing the Witch: Old Tales in New Skins.* New York: HarperCollins.

Do Rozario, Rebecca-Anne C. 2011. "Australia's Fairy Tales Illustrated in Print: Instances of Indigeneity, Colonization, and Suburbanization." *Marvels & Tales: Journal of Fairy-Tale Studies* 25 (1): 13–32.

Driskill, Qwo-Li, Chris Finley, Brian Joseph Gilley, and Scott Lauria Morgensen, eds. 2011. Introduction to *Queer Indigenous Studies: Critical Interventions in Theory, Politics, and Literature,* 1–28. Tucson: University of Arizona Press.

Duggan, Anne E. 2011. "Du génie à l'éfrit: Apparitions fantastiques dans les contes des *Mille et une Nuits.*" Paper presented at the "Apparitions fantastiques" conference. Angers, November 24–26.

Duvivier, Sandra. 2008. "'My Body Is My Piece of Land': Female Sexuality, Family, and Capital in Caribbean Texts." *Callaloo* 31 (4): 1104–21.

Elliott, Kamilla. 2003. *Rethinking the Novel/Film Debate.* Cambridge: Cambridge University Press.

Ellis, Bill. 2001. *Aliens, Ghosts, and Cults: Legends We Live.* Jackson: University of Mississippi Press.

———. 2012. "Fairy Tales as Metacommentary in Manga and Anime." In Jones and Schacker, *Marvelous Transformations,* 503–8.

Ellis, Nadia. 2011. "Out and Bad: Toward a Queer Performance Hermeneutic in Jamaican Dancehall." *Small Axe* 35: 7–23.

Enzyklopädie des Märchens. Berlin: Walter de Gruyter.

Fabian, Johannes. 1983. *Time and the Other: How Anthropology Makes Its Object.* New York: Columbia University Press.

Figueroa, Esther. 2005. Personal Communication.

Foley, John Miles. 2008. "Navigating Pathways: Oral Tradition and the Internet." *Academic Intersections* 2. http://pathwaysproject.org/AI-article/1-Abstract.html. Accessed on April 30, 2012.

Ford, Jacqueline. 2011. "'Cover Your Eyes and Count to a Hundred': Freud's *Uncanny* and Guillermo del Toro's *Pan's Labyrinth.*" In Kérchy, *Postmodern Reinterpretations of Fairy Tales,* 383–402.

Frank, Arthur W. 2010. *Letting Stories Breathe: A Socio-Narratology*. Chicago: University of Chicago Press.

Freud, Sigmund. 1960. *Jokes and Their Relation to the Unconscious*. Translated and edited by James Strachey. New York: Norton.

Frow, John. 2006. *Genre*. New York: Routledge.

———. 2007. "'Reproducibles, Rubrics, and Everything You Need': Genre Theory Today." *PMLA* 122 (5): 1626–34.

Gabrieli, Francesco. 2010. "The *Thousand and One Nights* in European Culture" (1947). Translated by Daniel Heller-Roazen. In *The Arabian Nights: A Norton Critical Edition*. Translated by Husain Haddawy. Edited by Daniel Heller-Roazen, 426–33. New York: Norton.

Gaiman, Neil. 1998. "Snow, Glass, Apples" (1994). Reprinted in *Smoke and Mirrors: Short Fictions and Illusions*, 325–39. New York: HarperCollins.

García, Pedro Javier Pardo. 2005. "Beyond Adaptation: Frankenstein's Postmodern Progeny." In *Books in Motion: Adaptation, Intertextuality, Authorship*, edited by Mireia Aragay, 223–42. Amsterdam: Rodopi.

Geider, Thomas. 2007. "Alfu Lela Ulela: The *Thousand and One Nights* in Swahili-Speaking East Africa." In Marzolph, *The Arabian Nights in Transnational Perspective*, 183–200.

Gerhardt, Mia Irene. 2010. "From *The Art of Storytelling*" (1963). In *The Arabian Nights: A Norton Critical Edition*, edited by Daniel Heller-Roazen, 433–42. New York: Norton.

Gidwitz, Adam. 2012. "In Defense of Real Fairy Tales." *Wall Street Journal*, October 14. http://blogs.wsj.com/speakeasy/2012/10/14/the-forest-beckons-the-magic-of-real-fairy-tales/. Accessed on February 23, 2013.

Gillain, Anne. 2003. "Profile of a Filmmaker: Catherine Breillat." In *Beyond French Feminisms: Debates on Women, Politics, and Culture in France, 1981–2001*, edited by Roger Célestin, Eliane DalMolin, and Isabelle de Courtivron. New York: Palgrave Macmillan.

Gin, Steven. 2011/2012. "Reading *Kissing the Witch* Intertextually." Flash presentation. Presented at the MLA Meeting in Los Angeles (January 2011) and at "The Grimm Brothers Today: *Kinder- und Hausmärchen* and Its Legacy 200 Years After" conference in Lisbon (June 2012).

Glassie, Henry. 1995. "Tradition." *Journal of American Folklore* 108 (430): 395–412.

Goldstein, Dina. 2012. *Fallen Princesses*. www.dinagoldstein.com/fallen-princesses.com. Accessed on November 2, 2012.

Goss, Theodora. 2006. *In the Forest of Forgetting*. Gaithersburg, MD: Prime Books.

Gottschall, Jonathan, et al. 2008. "'Beauty Myth' Is No Myth: Emphasis on Male-Female Attractiveness in World Folktales." *Human Nature* 19 (2): 174–88.

Greenhill, Pauline. 2012. "Folklore and/on Film." In Bendix and Hasan-Rokem, *A Companion to Folklore Studies*, 483–99.

Greenhill, Pauline, and Sidney Eve Matrix. 2010. "Envisioning Ambiguity: Fairy Tale Films." In Greenhill and Matrix, *Fairy Tale Films: Visions of Ambiguity*, 1–22.

Greenhill, Pauline, and Sidney Eve Matrix, eds. 2010. *Fairy Tale Films: Visions of Ambiguity*. Logan: Utah State University.

Groensteen, Thierry. 2007. *The System of Comics*. Translated by Mark Beaty and Nick Nguyen. Jackson: University Press of Mississippi.

Gruner, Elisabeth Rose. 2003. "Saving 'Cinderella': History and Story in *Ashpet* and *Ever After*." *Children's Literature* 31: 142–54.

Haase, Donald. 1998. "Overcoming the Present: Children and the Fairy Tale in Exile, War, and the Holocaust." In *Mit den Augen eines Kindes: Children in the Holocaust, Children in Exile, and Children under Fascism*, edited by Viktoria Hertling, 86–99. Amsterdamer Publikationen zur Sprache und Literatur 134. Amsterdam: Rodopi.

———. 1999. "Yours, Mine, or Ours? Perrault, the Brothers Grimm, and the Ownership of Fairy Tales" (1993). Reprinted in *The Classic Fairy Tales: A Norton Critical Edition*, edited by Maria Tatar, 353–64. New York: Norton.

———. 2000. "Children, War, and the Imaginative Space of Fairy Tales." *The Lion and the Unicorn: A Critical Journal of Children's Literature* 24: 360–77.

———. 2004. "Feminist Fairy-Tale Scholarship." In *Fairy Tales and Feminism: New Approaches*, 1–36. Detroit: Wayne State University Press.

———. 2006. "Hypertextual Gutenberg: The Textual and Hypertextual Life of Folktales and Fairy Tales in English-Language Popular Print Editions." *Fabula* 47: 222–30.

———. 2007. "The *Arabian Nights*, Visual Culture, and Early German Cinema." In Marzolph, *The Arabian Nights in Transnational Perspective*, 245–60.

———. 2010. "Decolonizing Fairy-Tale Studies." *Marvels & Tales: Journal of Fairy-Tale Studies* 24 (1): 17–38.

———. 2011. E-mail message to author. June 24.

Haase, Donald, ed. 2004. *Fairy Tales and Feminism: New Approaches*. Detroit: Wayne State University Press.

———. 2008. *Greenwood Encyclopedia of Folktales and Fairy Tales*. 3 vols. Santa Barbara, CA: Greenwood.

Haddawy, Husain, trans. 1990. *The Arabian Nights*. Based on the text edited by Muhsin Mahdi. New York: Norton.

Haring, Lee. 1998. "What Would a True Comparative Literature Look Like?" In *Teaching Oral Traditions*, edited by John Miles Foley, 34–45. New York: Modern Language Association.

———. 2003. "Techniques of Creolization." Special Issue: Creolization. *Journal of American Folklore* 116 (Winter): 19–35.

———. 2004. "Cultural Creolization." *Acta Ethnographica Hungarica* 49 (1–2): 1–38.

———. 2007. *Stars and Keys: Folktales and Creolization in the Indian Ocean*. Bloomington: Indiana University Press.

———. 2012. "Creolization Invisible in Plain Sight." Paper presented at the American Folklore Society meeting. New Orleans, October.

Harries, Elizabeth W. 2001. *Twice Upon a Time: Women Writers and the History of the Fairy Tale*. Princeton, NJ: Princeton University Press.

Harvey, David. 1989. *The Condition of Postmodernity*. Cambridge, MA: Blackwell.

Harvey, Dennis. 2008. "The Arabian Nights." Review of *The Arabian Nights*. Dir. Mary Zimmerman. *Variety*. December 2. www.variety.com/review/VE1117939135?refcatid=33. Accessed on April 14, 2012.

Hauʻofa, Epeli. 2008. *We Are the Ocean: Selected Works*. Honolulu: University of Hawaiʻi Press.

Heidmann, Ute. 2008. "La Barbe bleue palimpseste: Comment Perrault recourt à Virgile, Scarron et Apulée en réponse à Boileau." *Poétique* 154: 33–54.

———. 2011. "Expérimentation générique et dialogisme intertextuel: Perrault, La Fontaine, Apulée, Straparola, Basile." *Féeries* 8: 45–69.

Heidmann, Ute, and Jean-Michel Adam. 2010. *Textualité et intertextualité des contes: Perrault, Apulée, La Fontaine, Lhéritier . . . .* Paris: Édition Classiques Garnier.

Heiner, Heidi Ann, ed. 2010a. *The Frog Prince and Other Frog Tales from Around the World*. Lexington: SurLaLune Press.

———. 2010b. *Rapunzel and Other Maiden in the Tower Tales from Around the World*. Lexington: SurLaLune Press.

———. 2011. *Bluebeard: Tales from Around the World*. Lexington: SurLaLune Press.

———. 2012. *Cinderella: Tales from Around the World*. Lexington: SurLaLune Press.

Hennard Dutheil de la Rochère, Martine. 2009a. "Queering the Fairy Tale Canon: Emma Donoghue's *Kissing the Witch*." In *Fairy Tales Reimagined: Essays on New Retellings*, edited by Susan Redington Bobby, 13–30. Foreword by Kate Bernheimer. Jefferson, NC: McFarland.

———. 2009b. "Rattling Perrault's Dry Bones: Nalo Hopkinson's Literary Voodoo in *Skin Folk*." *Les Carnets du Cerpac* 8: 211–33.

Hennard Dutheil de la Rochère, Martine, and Véronique Dasen, eds. 2011. *Des fata aux fées: Regards croisés de l'Antiquité à nos jours*. Études de Lettres 289. Lausanne: Revue Études de Lettres.

Hereniko, Vilsoni, and Rob Wilson, eds. 1999. *Inside Out: Literature, Cultural Politics, and Identity in the New Pacific.* Lanham, MD: Rowman and Littlefield.

Hermansson, Casie. 2009. *Bluebeard: A Reader's Guide to the English Tradition.* Jackson: University Press of Mississippi.

Hill, Mark C. 2009. "Negotiating Wartime Masculinity in Bill Willingham's *Fables.*" In *Fairy Tales Reimagined: Essays on New Retellings,* edited by Susan Redington Bobby, 181–95. Foreword by Kate Bernheimer. Jefferson, NC: McFarland.

Hines, Sara. 2010. "Collecting the Empire: Andrew Lang's Fairy Books (1889–1910)." *Marvels & Tales: Journal of Fairy-Tale Studies* 24 (1): 39–56.

Hopkinson, Nalo. 2000. "Red Rider." In *Tellin' It Like It Is: A Compendium of African Canadian Monologues for Actors,* edited by Djanet Sears, 11–14. Toronto: PUC Play Service.

———. 2001. *Skin Folk.* New York: Warner Books.

———. 2003. *Skin Folk.* Toronto: Caribbean Tales Production. CD.

———. 2007. "Maybe They're Phasing Us In: Re-Mapping Fantasy Tropes in the Face of Gender, Race, and Sexuality." *Journal of the Fantastic in the Arts* 18 (1): 99–107.

———. 2010. "A Reluctant Ambassador from the Planet of Midnight." *Journal of the Fantastic in the Arts* 21 (3): 339–50.

———. N.d. "Code Sliding." http://nalohopkinson.com/writing/nonfiction/about_writing/code_slide. Accessed February 24, 2013.

———. N.d. "Dark Ink: Science Fiction Writers in Colour." nalohopkinson.com/essay_dark_ink. Accessed on March 14, 2013.

Hopkinson, Nalo, and Paul Jarvey (interviewer). 2011. "Interview with Nalo Hopkinson." *Canadian Science Fiction Review* 1 (3). http://aescifi.ca/index.php/non-fiction/34-interviews/471-nalo-hopkinson. Accessed on April 30, 2012.

Hopkinson, Nalo, and Nick Liptak (interviewer). 2010. "Nalo Hopkinson's Other World." *The New Yorker.* January 8. www.newyorker.com/online/blogs/books/2010/01/nalo-hopkinsons-other-world.html#ixzz0c4Ne1uoj. Accessed on May 6, 2012.

Hopkinson, Nalo, and Kellie Magnus (interviewer). 2005. "Writing Is Believing." *Caribbean Beat: The Caribbean's Favourite Glossy Magazine* 73 (May/June). www.meppublishers.com/online/Caribbean-beat.

Hopkinson, Nalo, and Uppinder Mehan, eds. 2004. *So Long Been Dreaming: Postcolonial Science Fiction and Fantasy.* Vancouver, BC: Arsenal Pulp Press.

Hopkinson, Nalo, and Alondra Nelson (interviewer). 2002. "Making the Impossible Possible: An Interview with Nalo Hopkinson." *Social Text* 20 (2): 97–113.

Hubner, Laura. 2007. "*Pan's Labyrinth*, Fear, and the Fairy Tale." "Fear, Horror, and Terror at the Interface: First Global Conference." Oxford, England. October 10. Available at Inter-Disciplinary.net. www.inter-disciplinary.net/ati/fht/fht1/hubnerpaper.pdf.

Hutcheon, Linda. 2006. *A Theory of Adaptation*. New York: Routledge.

Hutton, Ronald. 1999. *The Triumph of the Moon: A History of Modern Pagan Witchcraft*. Oxford: Oxford University Press.

Ince, K. 2006. "Is Sex Comedy or Tragedy? Directing Desire and Female Auteurship in the Cinema of Catherine Breillat." *Journal of Aesthetics and Art Criticism* 64 (1): 157–64.

Irwin, Robert. 2004a. *The Arabian Nights: A Companion*. 1994; London: Tauris Parke.

———. 2004b. "The *Arabian Nights* in Film Adaptations." In Marzolph and Leeuwen, *The Arabian Nights Encyclopedia*, 1:22–25.

Jekyll, Walter. 1907. *Jamaican Song and Story: Anancy Stories, Digging Sings, Ring Tunes, and Dancing Tunes*. London: Published for the Folk-Lore Society by D. Nutt.

———. N.d. *The Project Gutenberg EBook of Jamaican Song and Story*.

Jenkins, Henry. 2008. *Convergence Culture: Where Old and New Media Collide*. Rev. ed. New York: New York University Press.

Johnson, Lisa. 2004. "Perverse Angle: Feminist Film, Queer Film, Shame." *Signs: Journal of Women in Culture and Society* 30 (1): 1361–84.

Jones, Chris. 2009. "'Arabian Nights' at Lookingglass a Cascade of Life-Affirming Stories." Review of *The Arabian Nights*. Dir. Mary Zimmerman. *Chicago Tribune*. May 31. http://leisureblogs.chicagotribune.com/the_theater_loop/2009/05/Arabian-nights-at-lookingglass-a-cascade-of-lifeaffirming-stories.html. Accessed on April 14, 2012.

Jones, Christine A., and Jennifer Schacker, eds. 2012. *Marvelous Transformations: An Anthology of Fairy Tales and Contemporary Critical Perspectives*. Peterborough, ON: Broadview Press.

Joosen, Vanessa. 2011. *Critical and Creative Perspectives on Fairy Tales: An Intertextual Dialogue between Fairy-Tale Scholarship and Postmodern Retellings*. Detroit: Wayne State University Press.

Jorgensen, Jeana. 2007a. "A Wave of the Magic Wand: Fairy Godmothers in Contemporary American Media." *Marvels & Tales: Journal of Fairy-Tale Studies* 21 (2): 216–39.

———. 2007b. "Reflections on the American Folklore Society Annual Meeting 2006." ISFNR Newsletter, March: 23–4.

Justice, Daniel Heath, and James H. Cox. 2008. "Queering Native Literature, Indigenizing Queer Theory." *SAIL: Studies in American Indian Literatures* 20 (1): xiii–xiv.

Kabbani, Rana. 2004. "*The Arabian Nights* as an Orientalist Text." In Marzolph and Leeuwen, *The Arabian Nights Encyclopedia*, 1:25–29.

Kaplan, David. 2007. "Director's Audio Commentary." DVD Gigantic Pictures.

Keesey, Douglas. 2009. *Catherine Breillat*. Manchester: Manchester University Press.

Kérchy, Anna, ed. 2011. *Postmodern Reinterpretations of Fairy Tales: How Applying New Methods Generates New Meanings*. Lewiston, NY: Edwin Mellen Press.

King, Thomas. 2005. *The Truth about Stories: A Native Narrative*. Minneapolis: University of Minnesota Press.

Kobayashi, Kazue. 2006. "The Evolution of the *Arabian Nights* Illustrations: An Art Historical Review." In *The Arabian Nights and Orientalism: Perspectives from East and West*, edited by Yuriko Yamanaka and Tetsuo Nishio, 171–93. New York: I. B. Tauris.

Kotecki, Christine. 2010. "Approximating the Hypertextual, Replicating the Metafictional: Textual and Sociopolitical Authority in Guillermo del Toro's *Pan's Labyrinth*." *Marvels & Tales: Journal of Fairy-Tale Studies* 24 (2): 235–54.

Kukkonen, Karin. 2008. "Popular Cultural Memory: Comics, Communities and Context Knowledge." *Nordicom Review* 29 (2): 261–73.

———. 2011. "Comics as a Test Case for Transmedial Narratology." *SubStance* 40 (1): 34–52.

Kuwada, Bryan Kamaoli. 2009a. "How Blue *Is* His Beard? An Examination of the 1862 Hawaiian-Language Translation of 'Bluebeard.'" *Marvels & Tales: Journal of Fairy-Tale Studies* 23 (1): 17–39.

———. 2009b. "To Translate or Not to Translate: Revising the Translating of Hawaiian Language Texts." *Biography* 32 (1): 54–65.

Lang, Andrew. 1968. *The Orange Fairy Book*. 1906; New York: Dover.

Larzul, Sylvette. 1996. *Les traductions francaises des Mille et une Nuits: Étude des versions Galland, Trébutien et Mardrus*. Paris: L'Harmattan.

Lefevere, André. 1992a. *Translating Literature: Practice and Theory in a Comparative Literature Context*. New York: Modern Language Association.

———. 1992b. *Translation, Rewriting, and the Manipulation of Literary Fame*. New York: Routledge.

Lefèvre, Pascal. 2011. "Some Medium-Specific Qualities of Graphic Sequences." *SubStance* 40 (1): 14–33.

Leishman, Donna. 2000. "Does Point and Click Interactivity Destroy the Story? The Convergence of Interactivity with Narrative." www.6amhoover.com/destroystory.htm. Accessed on May 6, 2012.

Leitch, Thomas. 2005. "The Adapter as Auteur: Hitchcock, Kubrick, Disney." In *Books in Motion: Adaptation, Intertextuality, Authorship*, edited by Mireia Aragay, 107–24. Amsterdam: Rodopi.

———. 2008. "Adaptation Studies at a Crossroads: A Review Article." *Adaptation Studies* 1 (1): 63–77.

Louie, Ai-Ling. 1982. *Yeh Shen: A Cinderella Story from China*. Illustrated by Ed Young. New York: Philomel.

Lukasiewicz, Tracie D. 2010. "The Parallelism of the Fantastic and the Real: Guillermo del Toro's *Pan's Labyrinth / El Laberinto del fauno* and Neomagical Realism." In Greenhill and Matrix, *Fairy Tale Films: Visions of Ambiguity*, 60–78.

Lyons, Paul. 2006. *American Pacificism: Oceania in the U.S. Imagination*. New York: Routledge.

Macaulay, Thomas Babington. [1835] 1965. "Minute on Education." February 2, 1835. In *Bureau of Education: Selections from Educational Records, Part I (1781–1839)*, edited by H. Sharp, 107–117. Calcutta: Superintendent, Government Printing, 1920. Reprint: Delhi: National Archives of India, 1965. www.columbia.edu/itc/mealac/pritchett/00generallinks/macaulay/txt_minute_education_1835.html. Accessed March 31, 2012.

Magliocco, Sabina. 2004. *Witching Culture: Folklore and Neo-Paganism in America*. Philadelphia: University of Pennsylvania Press.

Maguire, Gregory. 1995. *Wicked: The Life and Times of the Wicked Witch of the West*. New York: HarperCollins.

Maitland, Sara. 2009. "The Wicked Stepmother's Lament" (1987). Reprinted in *Folk and Fairy Tales*, edited by Martin Hallett and Barbara Karasek, 130–35. 4th ed. Peterborough, ON: Broadview Press.

Makinen, Merja. 2008. "Theorizing Fairy-Tale Fiction, Reading Jeanette Winterson." In Benson, *Contemporary Fiction and the Fairy Tale*, 144–77.

Martin, Ann. 2010. "Generational Collaborations in Emma Donoghue's *Kissing the Witch: Old Tales in New Skins*." *Children's Literature Association Quarterly* 35 (1): 4–25.

Marzolph, Ulrich. 2007. "Arabian Nights." In *EI: The Encyclopaedia of Islam Three Preview*. Leiden: Brill, 30–40.

———. 2008. "Arabian Nights." In Haase, *Greenwood Encyclopedia of Folktales and Fairy Tales*, 1:55–60.

———. 2010. "What *Nights?* Expert Knowledge vs. Lay Perception of the World's Most Famous Story Collection." Paper presented at the American Folklore Society meeting. Nashville, TN.

Marzolph, Ulrich, ed. 2007. *The Arabian Nights in Transnational Perspective.* Detroit: Wayne State University Press.

Marzolph, Ulrich, and Aboubakr Chraïbi. 2012. "The Hundred and One Nights: A Recently Discovered Old Manuscript." *Zeitschrift der Deutschen Morgenländischen Gesellschaft* 162: 299–316.

Marzolph, Ulrich, and Richard van Leeuwen, eds. 2004. *The Arabian Nights Encyclopedia.* 2 vols. Santa Barbara, CA: ABC-Clio.

Mayer, Sophie. 2008. "This Bridge of Two Backs: Making the Two-Spirit Erotics of Community." *SAIL: Studies in American Indian Literatures* 20 (1): 1–26.

McAra, Catriona, and David Calvin, eds. 2011. *Anti-Tales: The Uses of Disenchantment.* Cambridge: Cambridge Scholars.

McCloud, Scott. 1993. *Understanding Comics: The Invisible Art.* New York: HarperCollins.

McMullin, Dan Taulapapa. 2001. *Coming of Age in Amelika.* Asian/Pacific/American Gallery. New York University. Fall. www.apa.nyu.edu/pacific/gallery/Mcmullin.txt.

———. 2003. "The One-Eyed Fish." In *Oceania in the Age of Global Media,* edited by Peter Britos, 113–15. Special issue of *Spectator* 23 (1).

———. 2004. *A Drag Queen Named Pipi and Other Poems.* Honolulu: Tinfish Press.

———. 2011a. "Fa'afafine Notes: On Tagaloa, Jesus, and Nafanua." In *Queer Indigenous Studies: Critical Interventions in Theory, Politics, and Literature,* edited by Qwo-Li Driskill, Chris Finley, Brian Joseph Gilley, and Scott Lauria Morgensen, 81–94. Tucson: University of Arizona Press.

———. 2011b. "Monsieur Cochon." In *Nafanua: Works from Writers and Artists Who Attended the 10th Festival of Pacific Arts in American Samoa,* edited by Dan Taulapapa McMullin, 38–42. Honolulu: Ala Press.

McMullin, Dan Taulapapa, and Robyn Oishi. 2011. E-mail correspondence. December 1–2.

McMullin, Dan Taulapapa, and Sia Figiel (interviewer). 2009. "Seabird Tales: The Pacific Paintings of Dan Taulapapa McMullin." *Art and Australia Magazine* 46 (4). www.artaustralia.com/article.asp?issue_id=187&article_id=181. Accessed on May 8, 2012.

Meder, Theo. 2008. "Internet." In Haase, *Greenwood Encyclopedia of Folktales and Fairy Tales,* 2:489–95.

Meschino, Patricia. 1997. "*Dancehall Queen*: The Song, the Soundtrack, the Movie." *Billboard*, July 19, 65.

Mignolo, Walter D. 2000. *Local Histories/Global Designs: Coloniality, Subaltern Knowledges, and Border Thinking*. Princeton, NJ: Princeton University Press.

———. 2002a. "The Enduring Enchantment: (Or the Epistemic Privilege of Modernity and Where to Go from Here)." *South Atlantic Quarterly* 101 (4): 927–54.

———. 2002b. "Geopolitics of Knowledge and the Colonial Difference." *South Atlantic Quarterly* 101 (1): 57–96.

Mignolo, Walter D., and Madina Tlostanova. 2007. "The Logic of Coloniality and the Limits of Postcoloniality." In *The Postcolonial and the Global*, edited by Revathi Krishnaswamy and John Charles Hawley, 109–23. Minneapolis: University of Minnesota Press.

Moyle, Richard, ed. and trans. 1981. *Fāgogo: Fables from Samoa in Samoan and English*. Auckland, NZ: Auckland University Press.

Muñoz, José Esteban. 1999. *Disidentifications: Queers of Color and the Performance of Politics*. Minneapolis: University of Minnesota Press.

Mustich, Emma. 2011. "Are Dark Fairy Tales More Authentic? Disney and Others Are Chasing Dollars, Not Keeping It Real, One Expert Argues." Salon.com. August 20. www.salon.com/ent/movies/feature/2011/08/20/fairy_tale_movies. Accessed on February 5, 2012.

Naithani, Sadhana. 2008. "Colonialism." In Haase, *The Greenwood Encyclopedia of Folktales and Fairy Tales*, 1:222–26.

———. 2010. *The Story-Time of the British Empire: Colonial and Postcolonial Folkloristics*. Jackson: University Press of Mississippi.

Napier, Susan J. 2006. *Anime from Akira to Howl's Moving Castle: Experiencing Contemporary Japanese Animation*. Rev. ed. New York: Palgrave MacMillan.

Ngũgĩ wa Thiong'o. 2012. *Globalectics: Theory and the Politics of Knowing*. New York: Columbia University Press.

Nurse, Paul McMichael. 2010. *Eastern Dreams*. Toronto: Viking.

Opie, Iona, and Peter Opie. 1980. *The Classic Fairy Tales*. Oxford: Oxford University Press.

Orenstein, Catherine. 2002. *Little Red Riding Hood Uncloaked: Sex, Morality, and the Evolution of a Fairy Tale*. New York: Basic Books.

Orme, Jennifer. 2010a. "Mouth to Mouth: Queer Desires in Emma Donoghue's *Kissing the Witch*." *Marvels & Tales: Journal of Fairy-Tale Studies* 24 (1): 116–30.

———. 2010b. "Narrative Desire and Disobedience in *Pan's Labyrinth*." *Marvels & Tales: Journal of Fairy-Tale Studies* 24 (2): 219–34.

———. 2010c. "Stories to Live By: Re-Framing Scheherezade in *Arabian Nights* the Mini-Series." In *Beyond Adaptation: Essays on Radical Transformations of Original Works*, edited by Phyllis Frus and Christy Williams, 144–55. Jefferson, NC: McFarland.

———. 2012. Review of *Marvelous Geometry: Narrative and Metafiction in Modern Fairy Tale*, by Jessica Tiffin. *Marvels & Tales: Journal of Fairy-Tale Studies* 26 (2): 271–73.

Ouyang, Wen-Chin. 2003. "Metamorphoses of Scheherazade in Literature and Film." *Bulletin of the School of Oriental and African Studies, University of London* 66 (3): 402–18.

Palmer, Paulina. 2004. "Lesbian Gothic: Genre, Transformation, Transgression." *Gothic Studies* 6 (1): 118–30.

Parashkevova, Vassilena. 2010. "*When Dreams Travel*: Mirrors, Frames, and Storyseekers in Githa Hariharan's Retelling of the *Arabian Nights*." *Marvels & Tales: Journal of Fairy-Tale Studies* 24 (1): 86–98.

Perrault, Charles. 2002. *The Complete Fairy Tales in Verse and Prose. L'Intégrale des Contes en vers et en prose: A Dual-Language Book* (1694 and 1697). Edited and translated by Stanley Appelbaum. Mineola, NY: Dover.

Pershing, Linda, and Lisa Gablehouse. 2010. "Disney's *Enchanted*: Patriarchal Backlash and Nostalgia in a Fairy Tale Film." In Greenhill and Matrix, *Fairy Tale Films: Visions of Ambiguity*, 137–56.

Pilinovsky, Helen. 2007. "Donkeyskin, Deerskin, Allerleirauh: The Reality of the Fairy Tale." *Journal of Mythic Arts, Endicott Studio*, Spring. Revision of print article in *Realms of Fantasy* 2001. www.endicott-studio.com/rdrm/fordnky.html. Accessed on February 10, 2012.

Poniewozik, James. 2009. "The End of Fairy Tales? How Shrek and Friends Have Changed Children's Stories." In *Folk and Fairy Tales*, edited by Martin Hallett and Barbara Karasek, 394–97. 4th ed. Peterborough, ON: Broadview Press.

Powell, Timothy B., William Weems, and Freeman Owle. 2007. "Native/American Digital Storytelling: Situating the Cherokee Oral Tradition within American Literary History." *Literature Compass* 4 (1): 1–23.

Preston, Cathy Lynn. 2004. "Disrupting the Boundaries of Genre and Gender: Postmodernism and the Fairy Tale." In Haase, *Fairy Tales and Feminism*, 197–212.

Price, Matthew, with Noel Daniel, trans. 2011. *The Fairy Tales of the Brothers Grimm*. Edited by Noel Daniels. Cologne: Taschen.

Pullman, Phillip. 2012. *Fairy Tales from the Brothers Grimm: A New English Version*. New York: Viking Penguin.

Purkiss, Diane. 1996. *The Witch in History: Early Modern and Twentieth-Century Representations*. New York: Routledge.

Reiher, Andrea. 2011. "*Once Upon a Time*'s Giancarlo Esposito on the Magic Mirror and Evil Queen's 'Interesting Relationship.'" Zap2it. October 30. http://blog.zap2it.com/frominsidethebox/2011/10/once-upon-a-times-giancarlo-esposito-on-the-magic-mirror-and-evil-queens-interesting-relationship.html. Accessed on March 31, 2012.

Rich, Adrienne. 1972. "When We Dead Awaken: Writing as Re-Vision." *College English* 34 (1): 18–30.

Rivera, Geraldo. 2011. "Back in Iraq with U.S. Soldiers on the Journey Home." www.foxnews.com/on-air/geraldo/blog/2011/12/16/Geraldo-back-iraq-us-soldiers-journey-home#ixzz1pRDB7VL1. Accessed on March 18, 2012.

Robinson, Natalie. 2011. "Exploding the Glass Bottles: Constructing the Postcolonial 'Bluebeard' Tale in Nalo Hopkinson's 'The Glass Bottle Trick.'" In McAra and Calvin, *Anti-Tales: The Uses of Disenchantment*, 253–61.

Röhrich, Lutz. 2011. *Folktales and Reality*. Translated by Peter Tokofsky. Bloomington: Indiana University Press. Cambridge: Cambridge Scholars Publishing.

Rowe, Karen E. 1999. "To Spin a Yarn: The Female Voice in Folklore and Fairy Tale" (1986). Reprinted in *The Classic Fairy Tales: A Norton Critical Edition*, edited by Maria Tatar, 297–308. New York: Norton.

Rubenstein, Mary-Jane. 2009. *Strange Wonder: The Closure of Metaphysics and the Opening of Awe*. New York: Columbia University Press.

Rushdie, Salman. 1990. *Haroun and the Sea of Stories*. London: Granta Books.

———. 1992. *The Wizard of Oz*. London: British Film Institute.

Rutledge, Gregory E. 2002. "Nalo Hopkinson." DigitalCommons@University of Nebraska–Lincoln. http://digitalcommons.unl.edu/englishfacpubs/25. Accessed May 1, 2012.

Ryan, Marie-Laure. N.d. "Narration in Various Media." In *The Living Handbook of Narratology*, edited by Peter Hühn et al. Hamburg: Hamburg University Press. http://hup.sub.uni-hamburg.de/lhn/index.php/Narration_in_Various_Media. Accessed on February 17, 2013.

———. 2004. "Introduction." In *Narrative across Media: The Languages of Storytelling*, edited by Marie-Laure Ryan, 1–40. Lincoln: University of Nebraska Press.

Ryan-Sautour, Michelle. 2011. "Authorial Ghosts and Maternal Identity in Angela Carter's 'Ashputtle *or* The Mother's Ghost: Three Versions of One Story' (1987)." *Marvels & Tales: Journal of Fairy-Tale Studies* 25 (1): 33–50.

Said, Edmund W. 1978. *Orientalism*. New York: Pantheon.

Sallis, Eva. 1999. *Sheherazade through the Looking Glass: The Metamorphosis of the Thousand and One Nights*. Richmond, Surrey: Curzon.

Sanders, Julie. 2006. *Adaptation and Appropriation*. London: Routledge.

Sanga, Glauco. 2010. "Sull'origine della fiaba." In *Pulsione e destini*, edited by Francesco Benozzo, Mattia Cavagna, and Matteo Mesciari, 175–219. Modena: Anemone Vernalis Edizioni.

Schacker, Jennifer. 2003. *National Dreams: The Remaking of Fairy Tales in Nineteenth-Century England*. Philadelphia: University of Pennsylvania Press.

Schlumpf, Erin. 2011. "Intermediality, Translation, Comparative Literature, and World Literature." *CLCWeb: Comparative Literature and Culture* 13 (3). http://docs.lib.purdue.edu/clcweb/vol13/iss3/5. Accessed April 2, 2012.

Seifert, Lewis C. 2001. "The Marvelous in Context: The Place of the *Contes de fées* in Late Seventeenth-Century France." In *The Great Fairy Tale Tradition: From Straparola and Basile to the Brothers Grimm*, edited by Jack Zipes, 902–33. New York: Norton.

———. 2002. "Orality, History, and 'Creoleness' in Patrick Chamoiseau's *Creole Folktales*." *Marvels & Tales: Journal of Fairy-Tale Studies* 16 (2): 214–30.

Sellers, Susan. 2001. *Myth and Fairytale in Contemporary Women's Fiction*. New York: Palgrave MacMillan.

Sexton, Anne. 1971. *Transformations*. Boston: Houghton Mifflin.

Shaheen, Jack G. 2003. "Reel Bad Arabs: How Hollywood Vilifies a People." *Islam: Enduring Myths and Changing Realities*. Special issue of *Annals of the American Academy of Political and Social Science* 588 (July): 171–93.

Shankar, S. 2012. "The 'Problem' of Translation." In *Flesh and Fish Blood: Post-Colonialism, Translation, and the Vernacular*, 103–42. Berkeley: University of California Press.

Sherman, Sharon R., and Mikel J. Koven, eds. 2007. *Folklore/Cinema: Popular Film as Vernacular Culture*. Logan: Utah State University Press.

Shojaei Kawan, Christine. 2011. "Fairy Tale Typology and the 'New' Genealogical Method: A Reply to Willem de Blécourt." *Fabula* 52 (3/4): 297–301.

Sinavaiana, Caroline. Forthcoming 2013. "Amerika Samoa: Writing Home." *The Oxford Handbook of Indigenous American Literature*, edited by Daniel Heath Justice and James H. Cox. London: Oxford University Press.

Smith, Eric D. 2009. " 'The Only Way Out Is Through': Space, Narrative, and Utopia in Nalo Hopkinson's *Midnight Robber*." *Genre* 42 (Spring/Summer): 135–63.

Smith, Kevin Paul. 2007. *The Postmodern Fairy Tale*. New York: Palgrave MacMillan.

Smith, Linda. 2005. Foreword to *AlterNative: An International Journal of Indigenous Peoples* 1 (1): 1.

Smith, Linda Tuhiwai. 1999. *Decolonizing Methodologies*. London: Zed Books.

Smith, Paul Julian. 2007. *"Pan's Labyrinth (El Laberinto del fauno)*. Review of *Pan's Labyrinth*. Dir. Guillermo del Toro. *Film Quarterly* 60 (4): 4–9.

Snow White. 1974. Retold by Paul Heins. Illustrated by Trina Schart Hyman. Boston: Little, Brown.

Sommerfeld, Walter. 2003. "Museen-Plünderungen in Bagdad—'Go in Ali Baba! It's All Yours.'" *Süddeutsche Zeitung*, May 10. www.embargos.de/irak/irakkrieg2/berichte/museen_pluenderungen_sommerfeld.htm. Translated by George Paxinos. "Plundering the Museums of Baghdad" available on counterpunch.org. Both accessed on November 18, 2012.

Soyka, David. 2002. Review of *Skin Folk*. SF Site. www.sfsite.com.08a/sk133.htm.

Spivak, Gayatri Chakravorty. 1993. "The Politics of Translation." In *Outside in the Teaching Machine*, 179–200. New York: Routledge.

———. 2003. *Death of a Discipline*. New York: Columbia University Press.

———. 2005. "Translating into English." In *Nation, Language, and the Ethics of Translation*, edited by Sandra Bermann and Michael Wood, 93–110. Princeton, NJ: Princeton University Press.

———. 2006. "World Systems and the Creole." *Narrative* 14 (1): 102–12.

———. 2010. "Translating in a World of Languages." *PMLA: The Profession*: 35–43.

St-Pierre, Paul. 2000. "Translating (into) the Language of the Colonizer." In *Changing the Terms: Translating in the Postcolonial Era*, edited by Sherry Simon and Paul St-Pierre, 261–88. Ottawa: University of Ottawa Press.

Staiger, Janet. 2000. *Perverse Spectators: The Practices of Film Reception*. New York: New York University Press.

Stam, Robert. 2000. "Beyond Fidelity: The Dialogics of Adaptation." In *Film Adaptation*, edited by James Naremore, 54–76. New Brunswick, NJ: Rutgers University Press.

———. 2005. "The Theory and Practice of Adaptation." In *Literature and Film: A Guide to the Theory and Practice of Adaptation*, edited by Robert Stam and Alessandra Raengo, 1–52. Malden, MA: Blackwell.

Stephens, John, and Robyn McCallum. 2002. "Utopia, Dystopia, and Cultural Controversy in *Ever After* and *The Grimm Brothers' Snow White*." *Marvels & Tales: Journal of Fairy-Tale Studies* 16 (2): 201–13.

Sternberg, Hannah. 2011. "Pro-Israel Heroes Come to DC Comics." NewsReal-Blog. January 26 and www.newsrealblog.com/2011/01/26/pro-israel-heroes-come-to-dc-comics/. Accessed March 31, 2012.

Stolzoff, Norman. 2000. *Wake the Town and Tell the People: Dancehall Culture in Jamaica*. Durham, NC: Duke University Press.

Stone, Kay. 2008. *Some Day Your Witch Will Come*. Detroit: Wayne State University Press.

Sugita, Hideaki. 2006. "The Arabian Nights in Modern Japan: A Brief Historical Sketch." In *The Arabian Nights and Orientalism: Perspectives from East and West*, edited by Yuriko Yamanaka and Tetsuo Nishio, 116–53. New York: I. B. Taurus, 2006.

Sullivan, Robert. 2003. Poetry reading. Korean Studies Center, University of Hawai'i at Mānoa. January 30.

Szumsky, Brian E. 1999. "The House That Jack Built: Empire and Ideology in Nineteenth-Century British Versions of 'Jack and the Beanstalk.'" *Marvels & Tales: Journal of Fairy-Tale Studies* 13 (1): 11–30.

Tatar, Maria. 2004. *Secrets beyond the Door: The Story of Bluebeard and His Wives*. Princeton, NJ: Princeton University Press.

Tatar, Maria, ed. 1999. *The Classic Fairy Tales: A Norton Critical Edition*. New York: Norton.

Tatar, Maria, ed. and trans. 2010. *The Grimm Reader: The Classic Tales of the Brothers Grimm*. New York: Norton.

Teaiwa, Teresia. 2010. "What Remains to Be Seen: Reclaiming the Visual Roots of Pacific Literature." *PMLA* 125 (3): 730–36.

Teverson, Andrew. 2008. "Migrant Fictions: Salman Rushdie and the Fairy Tale." In *Contemporary Fiction and the Fairy Tale*, edited by Stephen Benson, 47–73. Detroit: Wayne State University Press.

———. 2010. "'Giants Have Trampled the Earth': Colonialism and the English Tale in Samuel Selvon's *Turn Again Tiger*." *Marvels & Tales: Journal of Fairy-Tale Studies* 24 (2): 199–218.

Tiffin, Jessica. 2009. *Marvelous Geometry: Narrative and Metafiction in Modern Fairy Tale*. Detroit: Wayne State University Press.

Todorov, Tzvetan. 2006. "Narrative-Men" (1971). In *The Arabian Nights Reader*, edited by Ulrich Marzolph, 226–38. Detroit: Wayne State University Press.

Tosenberger, Catherine. 2008. "Homosexuality at the Online Hogwarts: Harry Potter Slash Fanfiction." *Children's Literature* 36: 185–207.

Turner, Kay, and Pauline Greenhill, eds. 2012. *Transgressive Tales: Queering the Grimms*. Detroit: Wayne State University Press.

Tymoczko, Maria. 2010. "Translation, Resistance, Activism: An Overview." In *Translation, Resistance, Activism*, edited by Maria Tymoczko, 1–22. Boston: University of Massachusetts Press.

Uther, Hans-Jörg, ed. 2004. *The Types of International Folktales, a Classification and Bibliography*. Based on the system of Antti Aarne and Stith Thompson. FF Communications No. 284. Helsinki: Academia Scientiarum Fennica.

Valente, Catherynne M. 2011. *The Girl Who Circumnavigated Fairyland in a Ship of Her Own Making*. New York: Feiwel and Friends.

Vandermeersche, Geert, and Ronald Soetaert. 2011. "Intermediality as Cultural Literacy and Teaching the Graphic Novel." *CLCWeb: Comparative Literature and Culture* 13 (3). http://docs.lib.purdue.edu/clcweb/vol13/iss3/20. Accessed on April 2, 2012.

Vaz da Silva, Francisco. 2012. "Hansel and Gretel across Media: A Transcultural Perspective." Paper presented at the "Fairy Tale Vanguard Conference," Ghent, Belgium, August 20–22.

Velez, Diva. 2008. Review of *Year of the Fish*. TheDivaReview.com. August 28. www.thedivareview.com/Year_of_the_Fish_Movie_Review.html. Accessed March 2, 2012.

Venuti, Lawrence. 1995. *The Translator's Invisibility: A History of Translation*. New York: Routledge.

———. 1998. *The Scandals of Translation: Towards an Ethics of Difference*. London: Routledge.

———. 2000. "Translation, Community, Utopia." In *The Translation Studies Reader*, edited by Lawrence Venuti, 468–88. London: Routledge.

Verdier, Yvonne. 1978. "Grand-mères, si vous saviez . . . Le petit chaperon rouge dans la tradition orale." *Cahiers de Littérature orale* 4: 17–55.

Verevis, Constantine. 2006. *Film Remakes*. Edinburgh: Edinburgh University Press.

Waldron, David. 2008. *The Sign of the Witch: Modernity and the Pagan Revival*. Durham, NC: Carolina Academic Press.

Warner, Marina. 1994. *From the Beast to the Blonde: On Fairy Tales and Their Tellers*. New York: Farrar, Straus and Giroux.

———. 1998. *No Go the Bogeyman: Scaring, Lulling, and Making Mock*. New York: Farrar, Straus and Giroux.

———. 2001. "Ballerina: The Belled Girl Sends a Tape to an Impresario." In *Angela Carter and the Literary Fairy Tale*, edited by Danielle Roemer and Cristina Bacchilega, 250–56. Detroit: Wayne State University Press.

———. 2006. *Phantasmagoria: Spirit Visions, Metaphors, and Media into the Twenty-First Century*. Oxford: Oxford University Press.

———. 2012. *Stranger Magic: Charmed States and* The Arabian Nights. Cambridge, MA: Belknap Press of Harvard University Press.

Warner, Marina, ed. 2004. *Wonder Tales: Six French Stories of Enchantment*. 1994; New York: Oxford University Press.

Wat, John. 2012. E-mail message to author. April 30.

Wendt, Albert. 2009. "Tatauing the Postcolonial Body" (1996). Reprint in *SPAN* 62: 83–103.

Wendt, Albert, Reina Whaitiri, and Robert Sullivan, eds. 2010. *Mauri Ola: Contemporary Polynesian Poems in English*. Auckland, NZ: Auckland University Press; and Honolulu: University of Hawai'i Press.

White, Bill. 2008. "*Year of the Fish*: This Cinderella Is Not for Children." Review of *Year of the Fish*. Dir. David Kaplan. *Seattle Post-Intelligencer*, September 25.

Williams, Christy. 2010. "The Shoe Still Fits: *Ever After* and the Pursuit of a Feminist Cinderella." In Greenhill and Matrix, *Fairy Tale Films: Visions of Ambiguity*, 99–115.

Willingham, Bill. 2002. *Fables: Legends in Exile*. Vol. 1. New York: Vertigo DC Comics.

———. 2006a. *Fables: 1001 Nights of Snowfall*. New York: Vertigo DC Comics.

———. 2006b. *Fables: Arabian Nights (and Days)*. Vol. 7. New York: Vertigo DC Comics.

———. 2006c. *Fables: Wolves*. Vol. 8. New York: Vertigo DC Comics.

———. 2008a. "The Fables Road: An Afterword by Bill Willingham." In *Fables: War and Pieces*. Vol. 11. New York: Vertigo DC Comics.

———. 2008b. *Fables: War and Pieces*. Vol. 11. New York: Vertigo DC Comics.

Willingham, Bill, and Tasha Robinson (interviewer). 2007. "Interview." A.V. Club. August 6, 2007. www.avclub.com/articles/bill-willingham,14134/. Accessed March 10, 2012.

Willingham, Bill, and Dan DiDio (interviewer). N.d. "Interview." *Comic Book Resources*. http://video.comicbookresources.com/cbrtv/2011/cbr-tv-cci-bill-willingham-on-fables-fairest-more/. Accessed on March 9, 2012.

Willingham, Bill, and John Hogan (interviewer). N.d. "The Power of Fables: An Interview with Bill Willingham. Part 2." Graphic Novel Reporter. http://graphicnovelreporter.com/content/power-fables-interview-bill-willingham-part-2-interview. Accessed on March 10, 2012.

Wingfield, Marvin, and Bushra Karaman. 1995. "Arab Stereotypes and American Educators." *Social Studies and the Young Learner* 7 (4): 7–10. Also in *ADC: American-Arab Anti-Discrimination Committee* in a post September 11, 2001, version. www.adc.org/index.php?id=283&no_cache=1&sword_list%5B%5D=stereotype. Accessed on April 8, 2012.

Wolf, Werner. 2005. "Intermediality." In *The Routledge Encyclopedia of Narrative Theory*, edited by David Herman, Manfred Jahn, Marie-Laure Ryan, 252–56. London: Routledge.

————. 2008. "The Relevance of 'Mediality' and 'Intermediality' to Academic Studies of English Literature." In *Mediality/Intermediality*, edited by M. Heusser et al., 15–43. Göttingen: Gunter Narr.

————. 2011. "(Inter)mediality and the Study of Literature." *CLCWeb: Comparative Literature and Culture* 13 (3). http://docs.lib.purdue.edu/clcweb/vol13/iss3/2. Accessed on April 18, 2012.

Wohlwend, Karen E. 2009. "Damsels in Discourse: Girls Consuming and Producing Identity Texts through Disney Princess Play." *Reading Research Quarterly* 44 (1): 57–83.

Wood, Houston. 2008. *Native Features: Indigenous Films around the World*. New York: Continuum.

Yamashiro, Aiko. 2011. "The Year of the Fish." Review of *Year of the Fish*. Dir. David Kaplan. *Marvels & Tales: Journal of Fairy-Tale Studies* 25 (1): 178–81.

Yeh Shen: A Cinderella Story from China. 1982. Retold by Ai-Ling Louie. Illustrated by Ed Young. New York: Philomel Books.

Young, Katharine. 1987. *Taleworlds and Storyrealms: The Phenomenology of Narrative*. Dordrecht: Martinus Nijhoff.

Zhang, Juwen. 2005. "Filmic Folklore and Chinese Cultural Identity." *Western Folklore* 64 (3–4): 263–80.

Zimmerman, Mary. 2005a. *The Arabian Nights*. Evanston, IL: Northwestern University Press.

————. 2005b. *The Arabian Nights*. Dir. John H. Y. Wat. Mid-Pacific Institute School of the Arts. Performed by Jason Ellinwood, Gilani Moiseff, Shoshana Cohen. May 6–15.

————. 2005c. "The Archaeology of Performance." *Theatre Topics* 15 (1): 25–35.

————. 2009. "Empathy through Storytelling with Mary Zimmerman." Uploaded on YouTube on May 20, 2009. http://lookingglasstheatre.org/content/node/1627. Accessed on April 11, 2012.

Zimmerman, Mary, and Joel Markowitz (interviewer). 2011. "An Interview with Director Mary Zimmerman." DC Theatre Scene. February 15. http://dctheatrescene.com/2011/02/15/an-interview-with-director-mary-zimmerman/. Accessed on April 12, 2012.

Ziolkowski, Jan M. 2006. *Fairy Tales from before Fairy Tales: The Medieval Latin Past of Wonderful Lies*. Ann Arbor: University of Michigan Press.

Zipes, Jack. 1979. *Breaking the Magic Spell: Radical Theories of Folk and Fairy Tales*. Austin: University of Texas Press.

————. 1999. "Breaking the Disney Spell" (1995). Reprinted in *The Classic Fairy Tales: A Norton Critical Edition*, edited by Maria Tatar, 332–52. New York: Norton.

———. 2001. "Cross-Cultural Connections and the Contamination of the Classic Fairy Tale." In *The Great Fairy Tale Tradition: From Straparola and Basile to the Brothers Grimm*, edited by Jack Zipes, 845–69. New York: Norton.

———. 2006a. *Fairy Tales and the Art of Subversion: The Classical Genre for Children and the Process of Civilization*. 2nd ed. London: Routledge.

———. 2006b. *Why Fairy Tales Stick: The Evolution and Relevance of a Genre*. New York: Routledge.

———. 2008. "*Pan's Labyrinth (El laberinto del fauno)*." Review of *Pan's Labyrinth*. Dir. Guillermo del Toro. *Journal of American Folklore* 121 (480): 236–40.

———. 2009a. "The Indomitable Giuseppe Pitrè." In *The Collected Sicilian Folk Tales of Guiseppe Pitrè*, edited and translated by Jack Zipes and Joseph Russo, vol. 1, 1–20.

———. 2009b. *Relentless Progress: The Reconfiguration of Children's Literature, Fairy Tales, and Storytelling*. New York: Routledge.

———. 2011. *The Enchanted Screen: The Unknown History of Fairy-Tale Films*. New York: Routledge.

———. 2012. *The Irresistible Fairy Tale: The Cultural and Social History of a Genre*. Princeton, NJ: Princeton University Press.

Zipes, Jack, ed. 1993. *The Trials and Tribulations of Little Red Riding Hood*. 2nd ed. New York: Routledge.

———. 2012. *German Popular Stories by the Brothers Grimm Adapted by Edgar Taylor*. Maidstone, Kent: Crescent Moon.

Zipes, Jack, trans. 1987. *The Complete Fairy Tales of the Brothers Grimm*. New York: Bantam.

Zipes, Jack, and Joseph Russo, eds. and trans. 2009. *The Collected Sicilian Folk Tales of Guiseppe Pitrè*. 2 vols. New York: Routledge.

Žižek, Slavoj. 1989. *The Sublime Object of Ideology*. New York: Verso.

Zolkover, Adam. 2008. "Corporealizing Fairy Tales: The Body, the Bawdy, and the Carnivalesque in the Comic Book *Fables*." *Marvels & Tales: Journal of Fairy-Tale Studies* 22 (1): 38–51.

Zuern, John. 2010. "Mind Your Own Business: Cisco Systems in the Power/Knowledge Network." In *Cultural Critique and the Global Corporation*, edited by Purnima Bose and Laura E. Lyons, 182–214. Bloomington: Indiana University Press.

FILMOGRAPHY

Die Abenteuer des Prinzen Achmed. The Adventures of Prince Achmed. Dir. Lotte Reiniger. Germany: Comenius-Film GmbH, 1926.

Aladdin. Dir. Ron Clements and John Musker. USA: Walt Disney Pictures, 1992.

Aladdin and the Wonderful Lamp. Dir. George Albert Smith. UK: George Albert Smith Films, 1899.

Ali Baba et les Quarante Voleurs. Dir. Ferdinand Zecca. France: Pathé Frères, 1902.

Amarcord. Dir. Federico Fellini. Italy: F.C. Produzioni, 1973.

Ashpet. Dir. Tom Davenport. USA: Davenport Productions, 1990. DVD 2005.

La Barbe bleue. Bluebeard. Dir. Catherine Breillat. France: Flach Films, 2009.

Beastly. Dir. Daniel Barnz. USA: CBS Films, 2011.

La belle et la bête. Beauty and the Beast. Dir. Jean Cocteau. France: DisCina, 1946.

La belle endormie. The Sleeping Beauty. Dir. Catherine Breillat. France: Flach Films, 2010.

Cendrillon. Cinderella. Dir. Georges Méliès. France: Star-Film, 1899.

The Company of Wolves. Dir. Neil Jordan. Writers Neil Jordan and Angela Carter. UK: Incorporated Television Company, 1984. DVD 2002.

Dancehall Queen. Dirs. Rick Elgood and Don Letts. Jamaica: Hawk's Nest Productions, 1997. DVD Palm, 2004.

El laberinto del fauno. Pan's Labyrinth. Dir. Guillermo del Toro. Spain/Mexico/USA: Tequila Gang, 2006.

Enchanted. Dir. Kevin Lima. USA: Walt Disney Pictures, 2007.

Ever After. Dir. Andy Tennant. USA: Twentieth Century Fox, 1998.

La fée. The Fairy. Dir. Dominique Abel, Fiona Gordon, Bruno Romy. France/Belgium: MK2 Productions, 2011.

Freeway. Dir. Matthew Bright. USA: Kushner-Locke Company, 1996.

The Frog King. Dir. David Kaplan. USA: 1994. DVD 2007.

"The Fruit of the Poisonous Tree." Episode in Television Series. *Once Upon a Time*. USA: ABC, January 29, 2012.

The Golden Compass. Dir. Chris Weitz. USA/UK: New Line Cinema, 2007.

Grimm. Television Series. Executive Producers and Writers David Greenwalt and Jim Kouf. USA: NBC, 2011–12.

Hansel and Gretel. 헨젤과 그레텔. Dir. Pil-Sung Yim. South Korea: Barunson Film, 2007.

Hansel and Gretel: An Appalachian Version. Dir. Tom Davenport. USA: Davenport Productions, 1977. DVD 2005.

Hansel and Gretel: Witch Hunters. Dir. Tommy Wirkola. Germany/USA: Paramount and Metro-Goldwyn-Mayer, 2013.

Hard Candy. Dir. David Slade. USA: Vulcan Productions, 2005.

Harry Potter and the Sorcerer's Stone/Harry Potter and the Philosopher's Stone. Dir. Chris Columbus. Cowriter J. K. Rowling. UK: 1492 Pictures, 2001.

Harry Potter and the Chamber of Secrets. Dir. Chris Columbus. Cowriter J. K. Rowling. USA/UK/Germany: 1492 Pictures, 2002.

Harry Potter and the Prisoner of Azkaban. Dir. Alfonso Cuarón. Cowriter J. K. Rowling. UK/USA: Warner Bros. Pictures, 2004.

Harry Potter and the Goblet of Fire. Dir. Mike Newell. Cowriter J. K. Rowling. UK/USA: Warner Bros. Pictures, 2005.

Harry Potter and the Order of the Phoenix. Dir. David Yates. Cowriter J. K. Rowling. UK/USA: Warner Bros. Pictures, 2007.

Harry Potter and the Half-Blood Prince. Dir. David Yates. Cowriter J. K. Rowling. UK/USA: Warner Bros. Pictures, 2009.

Jack the Giant Slayer. Dir. Bryan Singer. USA: New Line Cinema, 2013.

King Kong. Dir. Merian C. Cooper and Ernest B. Schoedsack. USA: RKO Radio Pictures, 1933.

Little Red Riding Hood. Dir. Catherine Hardwicke. USA/Canada: Warner Bros. Pictures, 2011.

Little Red Riding Hood. Dir. David Kaplan. USA: Little Red Movie Productions, 1997. DVD 2007.

MirrorMask. Dir. Dave McKean. UK/USA: Jim Henson Productions, 2005.

Mirror Mirror. Dir. Tarsem Singh. USA: Relativity Media, 2012.

Once Upon a Time. Television Series. Creators Adam Horowitz, Edward Kitsis. USA: ABC Studios, 2011–12.

Le Palais des mille et une nuits. The Palace of the One Thousand and One Nights. Dir. Georges Méliès. France: Star-Film, 1905.

Le petit poucet. Hop-o'-My Thumb. Dir. Marina de Van. France: Flach Films, 2011.

The Princess and the Frog. Dir. Ron Clements and John Musker. USA: Walt Disney Animation Studios, 2009.

The Princess Bride. Dir. Rob Reiner. USA: Act III Communications, 1987.

Puss in Boots. Dir. Chris Miller. USA: DreamWorks Animation, 2011.

Red Hot Riding Hood. Dir. Tex Avery. USA: Metro-Goldwyn-Mayer, 1943.

Scheherazade, Tell Me a Story. Dir. Yousry Nasrallah. Egypt: Misr Cinema Company, 2009.

Sex and the City. Dir. Michael Patrick King. USA: New Line Cinema, 2008.

Shrek. Dir. Andrew Adamson and Vicky Jenson. USA: DreamWorks Animation, 2001.

Shrek 2. Dir. Andrew Adamson, Kelly Asbury and Conrad Vernon. USA: DreamWorks SKG, 2004.

Shrek the Third. Dir. Chris Miller and Raman Hui. USA: DreamWorks Animation, 2007.

Sinalela. Dir. and writer Dan Taulapapa McMullin. Samoa/USA: 2001.

Sleeping Beauty. Dir. Clyde Geronimi. USA: Walt Disney Pictures, 1959.

Sleeping Beauty. Dir. Julia Leigh. Australia: Screen Australia and Magic Films, 2011.

Snow White and the Huntsman. Dir. Rupert Sanders. USA: Universal Studios, 2012.

Snow White and the Seven Dwarves. Dir. David Hand. USA: Walt Disney Pictures, 1937.

Sydney White. Dir. Joe Nussbaum. USA: Morgan Creek, 2007.

Tangled. Dir. Nathan Greno and Byron Howard. USA: Walt Disney Pictures, 2010.

The Thief of Bagdad. Dir. Raoul Walsh. USA: Douglas Fairbanks Pictures, 1924.

The Thief of Bagdad. Dir. Ludwig Berger, Michael Powell, Tim Whelan. UK: London Film Productions, 1940.

Witchslayer Gretl. Dir. Mario Azzopardi. Canada/USA: Chesler Perlmutter and SyFy, TV 2012.

The Wizard of Oz. Dir. Victor Fleming. USA: Metro-Goldwyn-Mayer, 1939.

Year of the Fish. Dir. David Kaplan. USA: Funny Cry Happy, 2007. DVD Gigantic Pictures, 2007

INDEX

coloniality, 22–23, 207–8n32; and colonialism, 16, 17; constitutive of Euro-centric modernity, 22, 198, 208n30; countering it and colonialism, 47, 71, 194, 200–202. *See also* orality

comics and graphic novels: hybrid media, 235–36n30

convergence culture, 9, 73–76; transmedia storytelling in, 73–74

Cooper, Carolyn, 136, 230n27

Coover, Robert, 8, 16; "The Door: A Prologue of Sorts," 41

Coppola, Maria Micaela, 50

Cornfeld, Li, 203n2

creoleness, creolization, 29, 42, 212n19; Caribbean Creoles, 44, 47–48, 212n20, 213n22, 228n14; creolizing the folk and fairy tale, 37, 71, 113, 131–34, 136

Crowley, Karlyn and John Pennington, 50, 216n40

dancehall culture, 131–36, 229n20, 229–30n27, 230n29

Daniel, Noel, 193

Datlow, Ellen, and Terri Windling, 26, 41

d'Aulnoy, Marie-Catherine, 9, 58, 194, 211n14,

D'Costa, Jean, 40, 213n23

De Caro, Frank, and Rosan Augusta Jordan, 208n34

decolonizing fairy-tale studies, 23–24, 140, 196, 202; call to provincialize the Euro-American literary fairy tale, ix, 21–23, 45–47, 65, 72, 196–201; denaturalizing appropriation, 139–40, 144; power

relations to other wonder genres, 6, 30, 38, 47, 71, 195, 201; reorientation to fairy-tale genre, 36, 37, 40, 71, 72, 142. *See also* fairy-tale genre; folktales and fairy tales; orality; relocation

Dégh, Linda, 5, 102

Delarue, Paul, 209

del Toro, Guillermo, 107–8, 194, 226n5, 227n11; *Pan's Labyrinth*, 77–78, 81–86, 98, 99, 119–21, 220n5, 220n6, 221n10, 222n17

De Souza, Pascale, 213n22

Dillon, Grace, 38, 47, 214n30

disidentification, 90–91, 93, 98, 223n24

Disney Corporation, 15, 74, 116, 119, 207n27; commodification of fairy tales, 5, 55, 80, 115–16; Disney princesses, 3, 78, 80–81, 115, 221n9

Disney fairy-tale films, 12, 74, 111, 221n7; *Aladdin*, 146, 152, 153, 232n5; *Alice in Wonderland*, 84; *Beauty and the Beast*, 79, 83, 111; *Cinderella*, 78, 79; *Lilo and Stitch*, 196; *Pinocchio*, 79; *Sleeping Beauty*, 115; *Snow White and the Seven Dwarves*, 52, 55, 78, 148, 169, 220–21n6, 228n19. *See also* Lima, Kevin, *Enchanted*

Disney fairy-tale films: book and movie formulaic opening, 78–80, 83, 99, 107; fairy-tale characters transported to New York City, 37, 114; gender construction in, 7, 110; parodies of Disney fairy-tale tropes, 11, 12, 79, 116–18, 206n22, 206n23; in popular cultural

Makdisi, Saree, 207n30
Makinen, Merja, 109
Mardrus, Joseph Charles Victor, 180,
238–39n44
Martin, Ann, 50, 54, 59, 216n44
Marzolph, Ulrich, 23, 150, 154–55,
207, 233–34; and Aboubakr
Chraïbi, 233; and Richard van
Leeuwen, 165, 231, 237, 238
Mathers, E. Powys, 144
Mayer, Sophie, 68, 69, 218n51
McAra, Catriona, and David Calvin, 3
McCarthy, Bill, 207n30
McCloud, Scott, 235
McMullin, Dan Taulapapa, interme-
dial *Sinalela* narratives, 37–38,
65–70, 71, 217–18, 219
Meder, Theo, 9
Méliès, Georges, 134, 152, 194
Mignolo, Walter, 15, 26, 71, 131, 200,
207–8; and Madina Tlostanova, 22
Miyazaki Hayao, 15, 151
moʻolelo, 139
Moyle, Richard, 217n47
music: in *Bluebeard*, 96, 224n31; in
Dancehall Queen, 124; in *Hansel
and Gretel*, 100, 225n40; in *Year of
the Fish*, 124

Naithani, Sadhana, 23–24, 139–40,
200–201
Nasrallah, Yousry, *Scheherazade, Tell
Me a Story*, 195
network society, 14
Ngũgĩ wa Thiong'o, 200
Nurse, Paul McMichael, 150, 152
Nussbaum, Felicity, 207n30
Nussbaum, Joe, *Sydney White*, 109

Oishi, Robyn, 217n47, 218n49
Once Upon a Time, television series,
121; "Fruit of the Poisonous Tree"
episode, 146–49; and book, 74
oral traditions and orature: 45,
200; coloniality and orality, 22,
207–8n32; counterhegemonic
perspectives on/revaluing of orality, x, 23–24, 48, 51, 59, 69–70,
72, 200–201; illiteracy as mark of
the premodern, 19, 22–23, 198;
participating in intertextual web,
19–24, 33, 48, 138, 196, 197–202,
208–9n5, 213n23, 213n24,
226n4, 239n48, 242n9; staged
orality, 38, 49; women's, 19, 70.
See also translation; and individual discussions of fairy-tale
adaptations
Orenstein, Catherine, 121
Orientalism, modernity, and the
fairy tale, 21–23; Edward Said,
150, 153, 231n32; translations
of *Arabian Nights* 153, 231n3;
unlearning, 24, 151. *See also
Arabian Nights*, adaptations of;
Bae Chan-Hyo
Orme, Jennifer, "Narrative Desire
and Disobedience," 82, 227n10;
"Queer Desires," 28, 50, 52, 58,
59, 60–61, 63, 216; "Re-Framing
Scheherezade," 152; Review of
Marvelous Geometry, 231n31

Payne, John, 144
Perrault, Charles, 9, 11, 12, 20, 21, 27,
32, 33, 58, 65, 72, 76, 78, 197, 199,
211n14, 213n23

Straparola, Giovan Francesco, 20, 58, 197, 199, 226n5, 242n7
Sugita Hideaki, 151, 231n3
Supple, Tom, *The Thousand and One Nights*, 188
Švankmajer, Jan, 76

tale of magic. *See* fairy tale
Tarnowska, Wafa', 195
Tatar, Maria, 4, 10, 75, 76, 190, 206n21, 223n26, 228n15
Taylor, Edgar, 220n2
Teaiwa, Teresia, 201, 218n50
Tennant, Andy, *Ever After*, 109–11, 116, 134, 206n24, 226n3, 227n8
Teverson, Andrew, 20, 23, 204n10
Tlatli, Moufida, 195
Todorov, Tzvetan, 33, 59
Tong, Kevin, 74
traditional referentiality, 19, 213n4
transformation. See adaptation; fairy tale and individual/social transformation; fairy tales, twenty-first-century North-American field of cultural production
translation, 145, 155; and adaptation, 32–33, 144, 145, 155; appropriative translation of oral narratives and non-European wonder genres, 3, 22–24, 139, 152–53; culture of, 144–45, 180, 200; domesticating, 232n9; introducing Shahrazad in English-language translations, 144; in ongoing process of global production and reception of fairy tales, 3, 16, 24, 144, 231n1; Orientalizing and de-Orientalizing practices of, 29; retranslation to counter prejudice, 180, 184–87; translation-adaptation,

151, 220n2. *See also Arabian Nights/ The Thousand and One Nights*, translations of
translation across media, 35, 137
translation as transporting and displacing characters, 145, 146–49, 156–78
tricksters: Anansi tales and Hopkinson's *Skin Folk*, 44, 46, 47, 212n18, 212n19, 213n23, 214n27; and *Arabian Nights*, 187; in *Fables*, 165–68, 174; and *Dancehall Queen*, 131–33, 136; rabbit figure in Korean tales, 105–6
Turner, Kay, 203n3; and Pauline Greenhill, 52, 65, 219–20n57
Tymoczko, Maria, 145, 155, 232n9
Tzang Merwyn Tong, *A Wicked Tale*, 121

Valente, Catherynne M., 12–13, 206–7n25
Vandergrift, Kay E., 9
Vaz da Silva, Francisco, 106, 225n41, 241n6
Venuti, Lawrence, 144, 145, 232n9
Verdier, Yvonne, 41
Verevis, Constantine, 209n7, 210n9
Vess, Charles, 156; and Michael William Kaluta, 169

Waldron, David, 217n46
Wallerstein, Immanuel, 207n32
Warner, Marina, "Ballerina" 41; *From the Beast to the Blonde*, 4, 5, 8, 56, 185, 204n6, 211n16, 216n41, 228n15, 239n48; *No Go the Bogeyman*, 88, 107, 225n39; *Stranger Magic*, 20, 24, 40, 150, 155, 165, 211n14, 235n25; *Wonder Tales*, 5, 189

ACKNOWLEDGMENTS

The stories, writings, and people from whom I have been learning made this book possible, and I am grateful for the inspiration, challenges, and questions they have afforded me. All errors are mine alone.

I am especially indebted to Chan-Hyo Bae, Sunkyung Cho, Steven Gin, Dina Goldstein, Nalo Hopkinson, the LookingglassTheatre Company, Dan Taulapapa McMullin, and John Wat for their generous permission to reproduce their work.

Working with Wayne State University Press has been a joy. In particular, I want to thank Annie Martin, Kristin Harpster, Jamie Jones, Sarah Murphy, Emily Nowak, Kristina E. Stonehill, and Maya Whelan for the splendid teamwork, attention to detail, and womanly smarts. It was also a pleasure to work with copyeditor Dawn Hall, whose professionalism and grace I greatly appreciate.

Ongoing conversations with Donald Haase, Donatella Izzo, Ulrich Marzolph, Sadhana Naithani, Jennifer Orme, Cathy Lynn Preston, John Rieder, and Jack Zipes sustained me, intellectually and personally, and were particularly significant over the years to my shaping this book. I am deeply grateful to Esther Figueroa, Cynthia G. Franklin, Candace Fujikane, Lee Haring, Laura E. Lyons, Ulrich Marzolph, Ravi Palat, John Rieder, and Jack Zipes for feedback on this project, strong support toward its completion, and/or overall encouragement. Stephen Benson's and Vanessa Joosen's publications as well as the conferences they organized, respectively in 2009 and 2012, have been inspiring. Tim Chung, Anne E. Duggan, Pauline Greenhill, Karin Kukkonen, Sabina Magliocco, Stefano Rosso, Laurence Talairach-Vielmas, Christy Williams, and Ida Yoshinaga helped me with specifics in a timely and generous fashion. The two anonymous readers for the press offered generous comments and helpful recommendations to improve the manuscript that I hope to have put to good use. Warm thanks go to Sahoa Fukushima whose collaboration and steady support made a tremendous difference to me as I was readying the manuscript for production.

I was fortunate over the years to have probing and imaginative interlocutors at the University of Hawai'i at Mānoa in courses such as English 780F Folklore and Literature ("Fairy Tales Transformed?" in 2007, "Translation, Adaptation, and Genre" in 2008, and "Questions of Translation and Adaptation" in 2010); English 480 Studies in Folklore and Literature ("Twenty-First-Century Fairy-Tale Fiction" in 2009); English 385 Fairy Tales and Their Adaptations (2010); and English 491 Senior Honors Tutorial ("Twenty-First-Century Fairy-Tale Fiction and Film" in 2011). The 2007 graduate seminar marked a turning point in my thinking about fairy tales, and I have since then benefited from discussions about intertextuality, fairy tales, folklore and indigenous studies, translation, and retellings with Alohalani Brown, Steven Gin, Bryan Kamaoli Kuwada, Carmen Nolte, Jennifer Orme, Nicole Sawa, Aiko Yamashiro, Ida Yoshinaga, and Christy Williams. Working with Sarah Medeiros, John McClain, Robyn Oishi, and Chelsea Sassone, now graduates of the Honors Program, was also rewarding.

The homework, reading, and exchanges that went into *Legendary Hawai'i and the Politics of Place: Tradition, Translation, and Tourism* (2007/2013) profoundly impacted *Fairy Tales Transformed?*, and I especially thank Noelani Arista, kumu Coline Aiu, Lynn Davis, Candace Fujikane, Noelani Goodyear-Ka'ōpua, Monica Ghosh, ku'ualoha ho'omanawanui, Craig Howes, Lalepa Koga, Bryan Kamaoli Kuwada, Paul Lyons, Brandy Nālani McDougall, Puakea Nogelmeier, Jonathan Kamakawiwo'ole Osorio, Haunani-Kay Trask, Reina Whaitiri, and John Zuern for teachings, writings, and questions that have, in recent years, challenged me to deepen my commitments to and understandings of stories, histories, and activism.

Other significant conversations have grown out of conferences I traveled to as well as UHM symposia. I started working on this book in 2006, and presenting at these large and small gatherings advanced my ideas and writing: the American Folklore Society conference every year in the 2006–2012 period; the International Conference on the Fantastic in the Arts in Orlando, Florida (ICFA 2010, 2012, and 2013); "Contes, Fairy Tales, Fiabe et Genres Apparentés" at the University of Lausanne, Switzerland (May 2006); "Les réécritures du conte de fées" at the University of Nanterre, France (June 2008); "Happy Endings" at the University of Caen, France (January 2009); the "Fairy Tales and Nature" symposium at the University of Toulouse, France (February 2009); "The Fairy Tale after Angela Carter" at the University of East Anglia, United Kingdom (April 2009); the International Society for Folk-Narrative Research meeting in

Athens, Greece (June 2009); the Folklore Studies Association of Canada Meeting in Montreal, Canada (May 2010); and "Fairy Tale Films" at the University of Winnipeg, Canada (August 2011). Meetings that invigorated me in 2012, the bicentenary of the publication of the first volume of the *Kinder- und Hausmärchen* (Children's and Household Tales) by Jacob and Wilhelm Grimm, include "Placing Texts: Folk Narrative and Spatial Construction" at the University of Tartu, Estonia; "The Grimm Brothers Today *Kinder- und Hausmärchen* and Its Legacy, 200 Years After" in Lisbon, Portugal; "Folk Narrative Studies Today" at the University of Göttingen, Germany; and "Fairy Tale Vanguard" at the University of Ghent, Belgium. I thank all organizers, Francisco Vas da Silva in particular, for their contributions to expanding and reinforcing international networks of folknarrative and fairy-tale scholars. Engaging with other women scholars at the American Folklore Society, ICFA, and other meetings has been especially nourishing; I want to acknowledge, in addition to colleagues and friends I have already mentioned, the intellectual sparks that conversations about folk and fairy tales with Shuli Barzilai, Diana Bianchi, Regina Bendix, JoAnn Conrad, Luisa Del Giudice, Grace Dillon, Martine Hennard Dutheil de la Rochère, Ute Heidmann, Nadia Inserra, Jeana Jorgensen, Anna Kérchy, Kim Lau, Kristin McAndrews, Margaret Mills, Catia Nannoni, Dorrie Noyes, Marilena Papachristophorou, Armelle Parey, Helen Pilinovsky, Jennifer Schacker, Veronica Schanoes, Delia Sherman, Kay Turner, and Peggy Yocom have ignited for me.

At the University of Hawai'i at Mānoa, I had the good fortune of coorganizing events that in different ways transformed my thinking about literature: the 2004 "Moving Islands" Festival of Writers that featured writers from the Pacific (Albert Wendt, Rodney Morales, Jully Makini, Witi Ihimaera) and the Caribbean (Michelle Cliff, George Lamming, Nalo Hopkinson); the 2007 "Translation: Theory, Practice, Trope" with Gayatri Chakravorty Spivak, Hosam Aboul-Ela, Noelani Arista, Yunte Huang, and Donatella Izzo as guest speakers, and S. Shankar, Susan Schultz, Arindam Chakraborty, Joel Cohn, Puakea Nogelmeier, Reina Whaitiri, and John Zuern from UHM; the 2008 "Folktales and Fairy Tales: Translation, Colonialism, and Cinema" with Donald Haase, Vilsoni Hereniko, Sadhana Naithani, Noenoe Silva, Wazíyatawin, Steven E. Winduo, and Jack Zipes as well as Leilani Basham, Heather Diamond, Wimal Dissanayake, ku'ualoha ho'omanawanui, Maria Kaliambou, S. Shankar, Caroline Sinavaiana, Robert Sullivan, Houston Wood, and John Zuern; and in February 2013, with S. Shankar, Vilsoni Hereniko, ku'ualoha ho'omanawanui, Jon Osorio, Anjoli Roy, Tino Ramirez, "Words in the World: Oratures, Literatures, and New Meeting Grounds," an event that brought together speakers Hosam Aboul-Ela, Daniel Justice, Pualani Kanaka'ole Kanahele, Kimo Keaulana, Francesca

Orsini, Chantal Spitz, Ngũgĩ wa Thiong'o, Albert Wendt; panelists Yung-Hee Kim, Bryan Kuwada, Ruth Mabanglo, Kara Miller, Craig Santos Perez, Alice Te Punga Somerville; and poets Donovan Kuhio Colleps, Keali'i MacKenzie, Brandy Nālani McDougall, Craig Santos Perez, No'u Revilla, and Lyz Soto.

The joys and challenges of being in the Department of English at UHM have fostered my work. Travel grants from the university and departmental course releases helped me develop and complete the book. I am also happy to acknowledge the support of the 2011–2015 "Fairy-Tale Films: Exploring Ethnographic Perspectives" Standard Research Grant from the Social Sciences and Humanities Research Council of Canada (SSHRC), for which Pauline Greenhill is the principal investigator and I am a collaborator.

Finally, my thanks to Bruna Louise Bacchilega Rieder for the joy she brings to my life and for her love and encouragement, and to Tim Chung for the good conversations we have had about film, stories, and food, and for the joy he gives Bruna.

www.ingramcontent.com/pod-product-compliance
Lightning Source LLC
Chambersburg PA
CBHW051102030726
47504CB00006B/1742